Dear Thing

Dear Thing

Julie Cohen

St. Martin's Griffin
New York

This is a work of fiction. All of the characters, organizations, and events portrayed in this novel are either products of the author's imagination or are used fictitiously.

www.stmartins.com

The Library of Congress Cataloging-in-Publication Data is available upon request.

ISBN 978-1-250-08150-6 (trade paperback)
ISBN 978-1-4668-9350-4 (e-book)

Our books may be purchased in bulk for promotional, educational, or business use. Please contact your local bookseller or the Macmillan Corporate and Premium Sales Department at (800) 221-7945, extension 5442, or by e-mail at MacmillanSpecialMarkets@macmillan.com.

First published in Great Britain by Bantam Press, an imprint of Transworld Publishers, a Random House Group company

First U.S. Edition: March 2016

10 9 8 7 6 5 4 3 2 1

To Anna, Ian and Kieran

Dear Thing

Dear Thing,

I want to tell you a story.

Once upon a time, when we still believed in wishes, there lived a prince and a princess. The prince was handsome and clever, and the princess was beautiful and good, and they were deeply in love.

That's something you might ask about one day, when you're older. **What is love?** Some people think it's magic. Some people think it's biology. In this case, the prince and his princess seemed meant for each other. It's difficult to explain why; he liked football and she liked concerts. She liked old things, and he liked new. Their life together was a series of compromises. Maybe that's what a 'happily ever after' really is.

The prince asked the princess to marry him. Their wedding was a wonderful day, full of silver and gold and flowers and joy. The prince danced to 'Boogie Wonderland' and nearly knocked over the top table. I wish you'd been there to see it. In a way, you were there; the princess and the prince had certainly thought of you. They already wanted you. A perfect child, who would make their love complete.

But the years went by, and went by . . . and you never appeared.

It's not much of a fairy tale, is it?

1

1

A Little Secret

The day before she was supposed to have the test, Claire escaped the music block so she could look again. Her suede boots spotted with wet as she walked across the grass past the pet shed. Two lower-school boys were checking on their guinea pigs, their breath rising in clouds. She raised a hand to them in greeting and headed for the small path leading into the wood that surrounded the school.

On the field a group of girls were playing hockey. As soon as she entered the wood, their cries of encouragement faded. She tightened her right hand around the objects in her pocket and quickened her steps. She skirted rhododendron bushes, pine needles releasing scent beneath her feet, until she reached the rusted iron gates tucked in a corner near the school boundaries. She pushed open the gate and walked into the cemetery.

The St Dominick's students rarely came here. The one time she'd brought half a dozen A-level students, thinking it might give them some inspiration, they'd shuddered and told her that they'd been whispering scary stories about the nuns' graveyard for years. There was a rumour about a crying lady, and another about a swirling mist. But in the light of day, the graveyard wasn't frightening: sunshine streamed through the towering pines above and pooled around the grey stones. They were all different shapes and sizes, some very old, some recent. Although St Dominick's School hadn't housed nuns for many years now, Sisters of the Order who had moved elsewhere were occasionally buried here, where they'd started their lives of service. The newer graves towards the outside were low granite blocks. One or two had plastic flowers in baskets next to them.

Claire moved into the centre of the graveyard. The engraving on the stones here was nearly illegible. In the trees above, a magpie clattered.

She wore a woollen jacket. The left pocket held her phone. The right held two objects carefully wrapped in toilet paper. Claire looked around before she took them out, though she knew that she was alone. Not even a ghostly nun watched her unwrap the pregnancy tests.

She'd seen the blue lines already; they'd appeared almost immediately when she'd taken the tests, but that had been in the staff toilet, where the light wasn't good. She couldn't have been sure it wasn't wishful thinking. Now, she held up the first test and squinted at the lines.

Positive. A clear, dark positive. Same with the second one. She hadn't made a mistake.

She sank onto the grass, ignoring the cold and damp, staring at the tests on her lap.

She should ring Ben. And her mum. She wasn't supposed to take a test yet. She and Ben had both agreed that it would be wisest to wait until she had the proper test, tomorrow morning at the fertility clinic.

But she couldn't wait. All through the school day, through

the mild rebukes to Year Seven to pay attention, please, through the rehearsals for the Easter term concert and the department meetings, she'd been thinking about one thing: her tiny embryo, hers and Ben's, the single one inside her, the only one that was good enough.

Please take, she'd been thinking. Exactly as she'd been thinking for every minute of the past ten days since it had been introduced into her womb.

Please take. Driving to school. Brushing her teeth. Washing the glasses in the sink. *Please take.* Sharing dinner with Ben. The first thought, waking up and going to sleep.

Hold on and live. I want to meet you.

She left her phone in her pocket. Right now, after everything, she wanted to be alone with her secret. To convince herself it was true.

Claire gently laid both of her hands on her stomach. 'Hello,' she said softly.

She lifted her face and let the winter sunshine warm her skin.

'Only one?' Romily frowned, glancing across the playground at the little girl and her mother who stood there by the gate, waiting. 'I thought you were going to ask more.'

'I decided I only wanted to ask one friend,' said Posie serenely.

'What happened to all the invitations you took into school? With the printed-out maps in them? Didn't you give them out?'

Posie opened her book bag for Romily. Creased pink envelopes lined the bottom.

'You didn't give out any of them? Posie, they took ages to do.'

'I gave out one.' Posie nodded to the girl.

'I thought Amber was coming.'

'No.'

'You told me last week that she was your best friend.'

Posie started humming. Her heavy blonde fringe was too long; Romily couldn't quite see her eyes. She could see the girl's mother checking her watch, however, so she put her arm round Posie's shoulders and went over. Posie took her friend's hand and the two of them skipped off.

'Hi,' Romily said to the woman, holding out her hand. 'I'm Romily. Thank you so much for letting your little girl come for Posie's birthday.'

'It was a bit of a surprise,' said the other woman. 'She only let me know about it yesterday.'

'Sorry,' said Romily. 'Posie tells me your daughter is the only one coming, so I can take her in my car if you like and bring her back after tea. We're going to her godparents' house, just outside Sonning. It's bigger.'

Romily could actually see the mother weighing it up: having a couple of hours to herself, versus the perils of letting her daughter go off with a relative stranger. She could try pulling out her ID; people tended to be a little more trusting once they saw the 'Dr' before her name. At least until they found out that her doctorate was in entomology, and that she spent her working life among dead bugs.

'Mum,' said the little girl, skipping back, 'it's starting to rain.'

'All right,' her mother said. Hurriedly, she and Romily exchanged phone numbers, addresses, all the usual responsible-adult ritual, and then she rushed off to her car to get the extra seat for Romily. Another look of doubt crossed her face when she saw Romily's Golf.

'I'm a careful driver,' Romily assured her. 'I just haven't washed it for a very long time.'

'I'll see you at seven,' the mother said, giving her daughter a kiss on the cheek and handing her a plastic bag with a wrapped present in it. 'Be a good girl.'

Waiting in the after-school traffic, Romily checked out the girls in the back seat in her rear-view mirror. Posie's friend was smaller than she was, with her hair in neat bunches done up with pink ribbons. She sat with her hands clutched together, looking out of the window while Posie sang softly. Her uniform was pressed, her shoes shiny. Romily couldn't remember ever having seen her before in her life.

Then the heavens opened and Romily had to concentrate on driving around the clogged one-way system and out of town. The landscape opened up as she left Brickham, though the fields were no more than green smears through the car windows. Her best friend Ben and his wife Claire lived on the outskirts of Sonning, a pretty little village on the Thames full of thatched houses and London commuters. She negotiated the tricky right-hand turn into the narrow lane with the ease of long practice, and pulled up on the gravel drive next to Claire's Audi.

'Aw, Ben's car isn't here,' Posie said.

'He'll be here,' said Romily, who had noticed already. 'He sent me a text this morning.'

'Come on!' Posie was out of the car before Romily could unbuckle herself, and running up to the front door of the stone house as if trying to dodge raindrops. She opened the door without knocking and went inside. Her friend followed her, skirting puddles that Posie had run through. Rain soaked through the shoulders of Romily's jumper as she went after them, carrying the box full of party supplies.

Inside, they breathed the aroma of baking and fresh flowers. The air was warm. 'Wow, this is a nice house,' said Posie's friend, gazing at the exposed beams, the living area with its squashy ivory sofas and baby grand piano. Pink and purple balloons hung from the doorways and light fixtures.

'You can put your present here,' Posie instructed her, pointing to an occasional table. 'We can play wherever we want to in the house, but we have to take our shoes off first. Romily, could you please get the animals out of the car?'

'There are animals in the car?' Romily had put down the box and her boots were half off already; her hair was dripping down her neck.

'Yes, I put them in the back seat this morning because they wanted to come to the party. They're in that bag.'

'That bag,' repeated Romily, trying to remember if she'd seen one or not. She didn't feel like going back to the car for an imaginary bag of leopards. She'd fallen for that one before. 'What kind of animals are they?'

'Rita and Lorna and Joe. You know.'

'Ah, yes. Posie, are you sure that nobody else is coming?'

'That's why I brought the *animals*.'

'Hello, beautiful Birthday Girl!' Claire appeared in the doorway to the kitchen and crossed the living area to hold out her arms to Posie. 'Remind me, how old are you today?'

Posie hugged her hard around the waist and kissed her cheek. 'Seven.'

'Oh dear, how could I have forgotten? Hello,' she said to Posie's friend, who smiled shyly. 'What's your name?'

'Amelia,' said the girl.

'Come on!' Posie bolted up the stairs, her friend following. Claire watched them go. She was wearing slim-fitting trousers and a silk blouse. Her diamond ring sparkled as she smoothed her honey-blonde hair back and turned her attention to Romily.

'Hi, Romily.'

'Hi,' said Romily, conscious of her own damp and uncombed hair, her jeans with the ragged cuffs that had soaked up the groundwater. She hopped on one foot as she pulled on a boot. 'Thanks for having them, Claire. And for the balloons and everything. I told Posie it was a school day for you too, but she insisted, and Ben said—'

'It's my pleasure. How many of them are coming?'

'That's it.'

'I thought she wanted a big party.'

'So did I. Is . . .' Romily hesitated.

'Ben had to be in London for a meeting today but he said he'd be home before the cake.'

'Oh – I was just going to ask if you minded if I used one of your umbrellas.' She shoved her foot the rest of the way into her boot and vaguely indicated the antique umbrella-stand near the door. 'Posie forgot something in the car.'

'Of course, help yourself. I'll put the kettle on.'

It had started blowing as well as pouring outside, and Romily chose what was probably the only broken umbrella in the bunch. She struggled to keep it upright as she went back to her Golf and retrieved Posie's bag of cuddly toy animals. As she shut the door she thought she heard tyres crunching on gravel, but when she looked up, Ben's car still wasn't there. Nor had any other parents turned up with more kids. A gust of wind caught the umbrella, tearing it from her hand, and she had to chase it across the flawless lawn, the bag of animals flapping against her legs. By the time she got back to the house she was muddy, wet and even more dishevelled.

Romily took her time removing her boots and

8

straightening her clothes and hair. She took the toy animals out of the bag and posed them by the door, where Posie would see them when she came downstairs. Distantly, she could hear the girls laughing. If she'd known Ben wasn't going to be here until later, she'd have taken a little bit more time at the school. Or maybe thought up some topics of conversation beforehand.

The most awkward thing about being alone with Claire, she thought, arranging Joe the giraffe, was that Claire didn't seem to find it awkward at all. Which meant that all the awkward-feeling fell on Romily.

Romily picked up the damp cardboard box from the flag-stone floor. In her stripy socks, she walked across the living area, past the gleaming piano and the antiques tastefully mixed with modern pieces, and into the sugar-perfumed kitchen. 'That cake smells gorgeous,' she said heartily as she entered.

'Thanks!' Claire was putting a knitted cosy on the teapot. 'I actually made the cake last night but I've got some biscuits in.'

'I have no idea how you do all of this.' Romily put the box on the hand-distressed kitchen table. 'Weren't you working today?'

'Oh, I had the cookie dough in the freezer. I made it last week because I knew I wouldn't have time today.' Claire twirled her finger round her head in a self-deprecating way probably meant to denote mild craziness.

Romily opened the box. 'I've got frozen pizza and oven chips here for their tea – way too much for only two girls. And some sweets and some bottles of lemonade.'

'Lovely.'

Not compared to homemade biscuits and cake, thought

Romily. Claire, though, accepted the packaged offerings with apparent enthusiasm before she poured Romily a cup of tea and added two sugars, exactly as she liked it. She then arranged the food on baking trays on top of the Aga, ready to go in, and pulled out the chair across from Romily's, placing her mug on a coaster. 'Only the one friend could come, in the end?'

'I thought she'd invited more. That was the whole point of having the party here instead of at our flat, so there would be more room. I gave her twenty invitations. I thought it was strange that I hadn't had any replies from parents, but I've been too busy to chase it up. I'm rubbish, I know.'

'Of course not.'

Romily sighed. 'Oh well, less washing up, I suppose.'

'Do you have some party games planned?'

'Er, no. I was thinking they could just, you know, play for a while. Then give them their tea, have some cake, a bit of singing, go home. Open presents at some point. I picked up a piñata.' She retrieved the papier-mâché horse full of party treats and her book-shaped gift for Posie from the bottom of the box. They were both rumpled and slightly damp, from either the rain or thawing oven chips.

'I put out some dressing-up clothes upstairs,' Claire said. 'And I thought maybe they'd like to do their nails?'

'That could get a bit messy,' Romily said doubtfully, looking at the pristine kitchen.

'I don't mind. I didn't really want to prepare any activities in case you'd got it all planned out.'

Romily tried to think of recent parties she'd been to with Posie. She couldn't think of one offhand, not since the big one in that church hall with the bouncy castle and everyone shouting. Posie had spent most of the time under the table pretending the other children were ogres. Romily had tried to coax Posie out, but she hadn't tried too hard because actually she thought that was a pretty accurate assessment.

'I think we'll just take it as it comes,' she said.

Claire nodded, and they fell silent.

Romily racked her brain for something to say, something that wasn't *that question*. Because if Claire was going to say something about *that*, she surely would have said it right away, wouldn't she?

And was Romily even supposed to know about *that*? Did Claire know that Ben had told her?

It wasn't as if Romily spent hours discussing personal problems with Ben or anything – they had other things to talk about – but Ben and Claire had been going through IVF for so long, it tended to creep into conversation. And he was so excited about this embryo.

'So . . .' she came up with at last, 'how are you? School okay?'

'I'm fine, thanks,' said Claire. 'School is going well.'

'That's good.'

Claire had a little smile on her face, as if she had some sort of secret. Possibly she was amused at Romily's ineptness. Maybe she did know that Romily knew about the baby stuff. But Romily couldn't ask that, either.

Romily traced circles on the wooden tabletop. 'Um. So . . . been to any good concerts?'

Posie stuck her head into the kitchen. 'Auntie Claire, can we have a tea party for the animals? Can we use your tea set?'

'Of course. I'll put some squash in the teapot for you. Do you want to take the blanket from the sofa and spread it out on the floor? It'll be like a picnic then.'

'Ambrosial!' She disappeared, and Claire gave a clear, lovely

11

laugh that was so happy that Romily looked at her more carefully. She did look good. Maybe even better than usual. Sort of glowy. Romily heard that happened.

'"Ambrosial",' repeated Claire. 'Her vocabulary is getting better every day. I don't know if my eleven-year-old students even know that word.'

'She reads a lot,' said Romily, though Claire already knew that. Posie was their main topic of conversation.

'I'll get the tea set out for the girls. Do you mind putting the candles on the cake?' Claire gestured to the cake, sitting on a high stand on the worktop. It was an incredible thing, towering with pink icing and scattered with delicate pink flakes.

'What kind is it?'

'An angel cake with rose-flavoured icing.'

Romily picked one of the flakes off the icing and tasted it. 'Sugared rose petals? You didn't make these, did you?'

'We had a lot of roses last year.' Claire was deftly tipping warm biscuits onto a plate.

'I hope you checked for aphids.' Romily extracted a candle from the packet and put it haphazardly near the centre. 'It was a good year for them. That said, they're probably quite tasty. They make honeydew.'

'I'll remember that. You can have aphid-flavoured cake for your birthday.' Claire went out of the kitchen, leaving Romily wondering whether that was an affectionate joke or some kind of dig.

It wasn't as if Claire and Romily were a mystery to each other. They'd known each other for years. They'd been at university together and spent quite a bit of time hanging out in a big group. Over the years their group of university friends had coupled up and all got on with their adult lives.

In the normal order of things, Romily would have kept in loose touch with Claire the same way she kept in touch with other people she'd been with at uni: status updates on Facebook and maybe a brief reunion at weddings. She would have asked about her news and nodded politely and moved on to talking to someone else.

Except for the fact that Claire was married to Ben.

She put the candles on the cake, probably more crookedly than Claire had meant her to. Through the French windows to the garden, she could see that it had stopped raining and the clouds had parted to let some sun through. She wandered out to the living area. The girls sat on a blanket on the floor with the stuffed animals arranged around them; Claire was pouring pink squash into flowered porcelain cups. Posie's friend sat tidily between the toy giraffe and the toy lemur, wearing a silk scarf around her shoulders. Romily noticed that her school uniform fitted her quite well, unlike Posie's, whose jumper was too small in the sleeves and kept riding up to show her shirt-tails. Posie had acquired a large hole in one knee of her tights, and also a broad-rimmed beribboned straw hat which was wider than her body.

'Lorna is an actress,' she was telling her friend, pointing to the cuddly bear in a tutu. 'She's in a big play in London. And Joe is an astronaut, and Rita is a dinner lady but she also trains elephants. What do you want to be?'

'Um. A princess?'

'A princess is *boring*. You can be a – an archduke. And I'll be your wife, the archduchess. Okay, would you like a biscuit, archduke?'

The front door opened and three heads lifted in happy expectation. Posie jumped up. 'Ben!' she cried, running to him.

He wore a dark suit, but he'd loosened his tie and he carried a large box wrapped in silver paper, tall enough to come up to nearly his chest. Fresh air and sunlight streamed through the door behind him, and the scent of the newly fallen rain. His brown hair had gone curly with the damp.

'Hey, Birthday Girl,' he called. 'I brought you a present.'

'A big present!' said Posie joyfully. 'Wow.' She hugged him and he ruffled her hair.

'Bigger than you, peanut. Hey, Rom.' Ben waved to Romily, greeted Posie's friend, and then crossed to Claire and kissed her. 'I couldn't resist a trip to Hamley's. Had a hell of a time getting that on the tube, though.'

Claire gave him an extra kiss back. 'Softy.'

Posie began tugging the box across the carpet to where the tea party was set up. 'What is it, what is it?'

'Not telling.'

'Whatever it is,' said Romily, 'it's never going to fit in our—'

'Can I open it now?' said Posie. 'Please?'

'Let me help you with it.' Ben picked up the box effortlessly and carried it to the centre of the room. 'Go ahead and open it. It's yours.'

'Fantastical!' Posie began ripping at the silver paper, making no effort to preserve the pretty paper as she usually did. Her friend joined her, peering curiously. 'Oh, it's a castle!'

'You bought her a castle,' Romily said quietly, as Ben helped Posie dismantle the cardboard box to reveal the doll's house beneath. Turrets and everything, with climbing roses on the painted grey stonework.

'It's got a dungeon and a secret passage,' he told Posie, who squealed and stuck her head inside the rooms.

'This is epic,' she said, her voice muffled.

'Glad you like it, peanut.'

'I love it!' Posie flew out of the castle, kissed him and hugged him, hard, and then kissed and hugged Claire. Then she immediately went back to her new toy.

'Job well done,' said Ben. 'I think it's beer o'clock for grown-ups, don't you?' He went into the kitchen, removing his suit jacket as he went, and Claire and Romily followed him.

'I mean, thanks and all,' said Romily, 'but that's never going to fit into our flat. It's practically the *size* of our flat.'

'She can keep it here.' Ben opened the fridge and took out a couple of bottles of lager. He passed one to Romily. 'We don't mind, do we, Claire?'

'Of course not.'

'And then when she comes here, she can play with it. It's probably better that way anyway. Kids get tired of toys they see all the time.'

Somehow Romily doubted that Posie was going to get tired of this particular toy very quickly, but she drank her beer. What was she going to do? Make Ben take it back? He liked to spoil his god-daughter.

'How do you feel?' Ben asked Claire. 'Do you feel good? Do you feel pregnant?'

Claire looked from Ben to Romily, and back to Ben. 'Do you think that maybe—'

'Oh, Romily knows all about it. I couldn't keep it to myself.' He took Claire's hand. 'I can't wait for tomorrow when we know for certain. This afternoon I called a client Mrs Embryonic Transfer.'

'Ben!'

'Okay, I didn't. But I was severely distracted all the same.' Ben ran his hand up her arm, and then cradled her face. 'Are

15

you sure we shouldn't take a test now? Just to put ourselves out of our misery? Fifteen hours can't make much difference, can it?'

'Actually, I took a test this morning.'

Ben stared at her.

'And you didn't tell me? Is it bad news? Is it good? Did it take?' He put his bottle down and dropped to his knees in front of Claire. 'Tell me!'

'Sorry, Romily,' said Claire over Ben's head. 'He's a little bit dramatic.'

'Tell me something I don't know,' said Romily.

'Claire,' said Ben from the floor, and his voice was serious.

'It's not conclusive,' Claire said. 'You can still get false results from residual hormones. We should wait till we have the official results from the clinic.'

'Okay. We should. But you didn't. What did the test say?'

'Positive.'

Ben yelled a triumphant whoop and jumped up.

'A really strong positive, Ben,' said Claire, and her face was radiant. 'I took two this morning at school, and then another one this afternoon. They were all the same.'

'We're going to have a baby!' Ben picked her up and whirled her around in his arms. Claire laughed, her feet flying out behind her and narrowly missing the Aga.

'Plenty of things can still go wrong,' she told him, but he bent her back and kissed her, passionately, like a hero in a black-and-white film.

Romily felt a burning in her eyes. She didn't have to watch them, together in the sunshine streaming through the French windows. She'd seen it a million times. But she did watch them.

'How are you feeling?' he murmured.

16

'Wonderful.'

'You look amazing,' Romily said. 'You've got a sort of bloom to you. I was thinking it earlier.'

They both looked at her at the same time, as if they'd forgotten she was there. Well, why wouldn't they? 'Congratulations,' she added.

Ben set Claire back on her feet and turned to Romily. 'I'm going to be a daddy!'

She beamed back at him. 'Congratulations, Daddy.'

'We've still got a long way to go,' said Claire. 'Nine months. And the official test tomorrow. Which might say otherwise.'

'It won't. This time we know it's a good, healthy embryo. A baby.' Ben held out his arms, wide enough to embrace the whole kitchen, the whole world. If Romily had thought Claire's happiness was beautiful, his was nearly blinding. 'Forget the beer. I'm going to find some champagne. You can have some, can't you, Claire? A little bit?'

'Better not.'

'Romily and I will drink it, then.'

'I need to drive home.'

'Stay the night!'

'I've got to take— er, Posie's little friend home.'

'Amelia,' supplied Claire.

'That's it.'

'Then I'll drink the sweet taste of my wife's lips,' declared Ben, and he took Claire in his arms again.

This time, Romily didn't watch them kissing. 'I'll just tell the girls to wash their hands and get ready for pizza,' she said. She didn't think Ben and Claire heard her, and when she went into the other room, the girls had their heads together inside the castle and didn't look up, either. She made a detour to the bathroom, where she discovered that her dark cropped

17

hair was stuck up all on one side, and probably had been since she'd been caught in the rain.

She tidied it as best she could, taking her time, and then washed her hands and tried a bit of Claire's hand moisturizer and, for good measure, counted how many blue tiles there were around the sink (thirty-eight) before she went back to her daughter.

Quietly, she sneaked on sock-clad feet, her hands outstretched to surprise Posie with some birthday tickles.

'So why do you go to Crossmead if you live all the way out here?' Amelia was asking.

'Oh, I told my mum that I wanted to go to school there.' Posie's voice was offhand. 'But I definitely live here.'

Romily stopped.

'Who was the lady who picked us up from school, then?' Amelia asked.

'That's Romily.'

'Isn't she your mum? My mum thought she was your mum.'

'No, my parents are Claire and Ben. They're the best parents in the world.'

Romily coughed loudly, and Posie pulled her head out of the doll's house.

'Pizza's ready,' Romily told them. 'Go and wash your hands, please.'

'Okay!' Posie trotted to the bathroom. Amelia followed, looking even more bemused than she'd been since Romily had first met her.

Romily stood near the doll's house for what felt like quite a long time before she joined the party in the kitchen.

Afterwards, after the oven chips and the singing, after Posie closed her eyes and made a wish that Romily thought she could probably guess, after she'd unwrapped the anticlimax of a jigsaw puzzle and an illustrated edition of *Alice Through the Looking Glass*, after they'd dropped off Amelia, sticky and still bemused, at her house, Romily glanced back at her daughter in the rear-view mirror of her car and asked, 'Posie? Why did you tell your friend that I wasn't your real mother?'

'Oh,' said Posie, 'we were just playing.' She closed her eyes and settled back in her seat, as if she were going to sleep.

Romily drove on, through the artificial light and the traffic. She switched on the radio to keep her company.

2

Sweet Things

Claire awoke at twenty-five minutes past six, reached over to turn off the alarm before it sounded, and then tucked her arm back into the warmth beneath the duvet. She lay in the hollow of Ben's embrace, his knees fitting into the bend of hers. His breath stirred the hair on the top of her head.

She could tell when he woke up a few moments later, because his hand crept to her belly. His fingers spread out over her nightgown, seeping warmth down to where their baby slept. 'Morning,' he whispered. 'Both of you.'

Claire smiled and settled back against his chest. Her body felt so alive. 'What've you got today?' she asked.

'I've got lunch with the Kahns and then I'm taking them for a walk-through of the site. Then, as it's Valentine's Day, I might take my wife out to dinner, if she's willing.'

'I'm willing. I have to go into school this morning to do some marking.'

'During half-term? You should be lazing around in bed. Only time in your life you've got a good excuse.'

'Then I've got a shower this afternoon for Lacey.'

He tightened his arms around her. 'It'll be yours next.'

'My mother doesn't approve of them. She says they're an American habit.'

'Your mother will never know.' He nuzzled her neck. 'I love you. I think you're amazing.'

'I love you too.' She turned around in his arms and ran both her hands up his chest. Even after years of marriage she marvelled at his size, the strength of him. How he could make her feel safe and cherished. He pulled her closer.

'Seems like we should do something so it doesn't feel like this baby was conceived in a test tube,' he murmured. He kissed her, and then drew back. 'Claire?'

'I don't want to hurt the baby.'

'Dr Wilson said it was all right, as long as we were careful.'

'I don't think I would be able to relax.'

He didn't frown or turn away, he didn't do anything but keep on holding her, but Claire said, quickly, 'I know it's been a long time since we've been able to have a normal sex life, to make love whenever we want to. I miss it, too. But just a little bit longer, Ben.'

'Yes. It's better to be safe.' He kissed her forehead, then got up from the bed and pulled on his dressing-gown. 'Let's ask the doctor again when we see her next time.'

'I'm sure it will be fine, very soon.'

'Ah well, you know what they say about anticipation heightening the appetite. Stay there, I'll get you a hot water with lemon.'

'Thanks,' said Claire. He left the bedroom and Claire settled back onto the pillows.

'Do you have children?'

Claire shifted slightly on Lacey's sofa to face the woman who was talking to her. She didn't know most of the women

21

in the room. Two of them were from school – Lacey had just started teaching geography last year, ironically to cover another teacher's maternity leave – but the others were Lacey's friends or family. All of the guests had been seated around the room according to birth sign; it was supposed to help break the ice and help them get to know each other.

'No,' she answered, doing her best to put on a gracious smile, as she always did when asked this question by someone who didn't know. Today, it was a lot easier.

'No wonder your skin is so gorgeous! All that sleep.' The woman leaned forward. She had straightened hair and blue circles under her eyes. 'Tell me – do you get to go to restaurants?'

'Sometimes.'

The woman let out a long stream of a sigh. 'Oh, I dream of restaurants. Ones that have proper cutlery. And menus that aren't designed for children to colour in.'

'I get excited about a bowl of chips at the soft play centre,' added the woman on the other side of Claire.

'Tell me about it,' said the first one. 'Do you know how Paul and I celebrated our wedding anniversary? Tub of Häagen-Dazs at the cinema during a Disney film.'

'I forgot about ours,' called another woman from across the room. 'Harry and Abby both had chickenpox. I remembered two days later and it hardly seemed worth it.'

'Does your husband give you flowers?' the first woman asked Claire.

'Er . . . sometimes.' There had been a bouquet on the table when she came downstairs this morning.

'I got flowers for Valentine's Day last year!' said the second woman. 'Ellie ate them. We had to go to A&E. I didn't get flowers this year.'

'Were they poisonous?'

'We were mostly worried about the cellophane wrapper. She didn't do a poo for three days. I was terrified.'

'Once, Alfie didn't do a poo for *two weeks*. I shovelled enough puréed prunes into him to choke a horse.'

'You have all this to come,' said the first woman to Lacey. Lacey sat in a flowered armchair in the sunny, cramped front room of her flat, her hands folded over her protruding stomach. She smiled as if the idea of shovelling puréed prunes into a baby's mouth was just about the best thing in the entire world.

Claire thought that probably wasn't too far from wrong.

'Wine?' Lacey's mother, who was a sweet lady with very red hair, was circulating the room with a bottle of Pinot Grigio. Claire shook her head and held up her glass, already full of mineral water. 'That's a beautiful cake you've made,' Lacey's mother said. 'And so delicious. Aren't you having any?'

'Thank you. And no, I don't really eat cake.'

'Are you gluten-free?' asked the first woman. 'No wonder you're so slim. I just look at a piece of bread and I gain half a stone.'

'I just try to eat healthily,' said Claire. 'But I love making cakes.'

'What's the baby going to be called?' someone asked Lacey.

'We're calling him Billy.'

There was a collective sigh of appreciation.

'I like the simple names,' said the first woman. 'There are too many trendy names around. There's a girl at Alfie's nursery called Fairybelle.'

The women launched into a discussion of their children's names: what they were almost called, what they were glad they weren't called, what they would have been called if they had been born the opposite sex. The woman whose daughter had eaten the cellophane off her flowers got up to use the loo and Georgette, the other St Dominick's teacher, slipped into the place next to Claire.

'I'm sorry,' she murmured. 'It's all baby talk.'

'It's okay. I'm used to it. Besides, it's Lacey's day. She looks wonderful, doesn't she?'

They both looked at Lacey. She was generally the sort of person who didn't call much attention to herself: a hiker, a camper, a good teacher.

She looked wonderful.

'Still,' said Georgette, 'I think that people could be a little bit more sensitive. Not everyone wants to talk about babies all the time.'

Georgette had two children. Claire remembered when the youngest had been born; it was about the time Claire herself had gone through her third and final IVF treatment that had been allowed on the NHS, before they'd gone private. Claire had been given an invitation to the christening, but there was a little handwritten note in it: *I'll understand if you don't want to be around babies.*

She hadn't gone to the christening, not to avoid the babies but to avoid the understanding.

The women in this room were complaining about their lives, but underneath they were happy. Claire could almost smell it, with the nose of an outsider. They exuded warm yeasty contentment. It was the same way, she noticed, whenever women with young children got together. The conversation revolved around little sacrifices or disasters, about mishaps and made-up worries, but its function wasn't to communicate information: it was to establish relationship. To mark out common ground.

24

We are mothers. We do battle with nappies and Calpol. Look upon our offspring, ye mighty, and despair.

The truth was, she would give up anything to be like the women in this room. She was tired of feeling the sharp stab of pain every time she passed a playground. That raw ache of yearning at Christmas. She was tired of feeling like a failure, once a month, like clockwork.

But that didn't mean she wanted to talk about it. Or to be pitied.

And now she didn't have to be.

'Actually,' she said, 'it's fine. I'm really happy.'

Georgette widened her eyes. 'Oh my God, has something happened? Are you . . .?'

'I think Lacey's going to open her gifts,' Claire said, and Georgette transferred her attention to the main business of the afternoon.

Claire thought back to the warm moments in bed with Ben this morning before he'd woken up, imagining a little one cuddled up with them. She could picture Ben's expression as he watched her feeding their child from her body. Warm and sweet. That would make up for any blip in their sex life. Or the several blips over the years as they'd adjusted from thinking of sex as something fun, to thinking of it as something that was supposed to make babies but didn't.

They'd talked about names a long time ago, when they thought it would be easy to have children. Back when they'd been actively trying not to have children – she'd gone on the pill before they'd started having sex, and at first she'd made him wear a condom as well. Ben called it 'double bagging'. They'd lain in bed together in his single bed at university, or still later, in their first real double bed as a married couple,

25

and planned their family. A boy first, named Oliver. A girl called Sophie. Or perhaps a girl called Olivia and a boy named Sid. The names had seemed so new and yet traditional, then; now, with the passing of years, they were too popular.

They hadn't talked about names for a while now. It seemed such an innocent thing to do, but it was too much like tempting fate. They'd have to talk about it again soon. She liked her father's name, Mark, if it were a boy. Or Lucille, if it were a girl, after Ben's grandmother. Old-fashioned names, with a connection to family.

Or maybe they could go for something totally left field, like Fairybelle. Thumbelina. Bathsheba. Excalibur, for a boy. Excalibur Hercules Lawrence.

Claire smiled. Maybe it was even safe to joke about it.

'Oh, lovely!' cried Lacey, opening a box of Babygros. Her mother cooed and passed around a plate of biscuits. Claire felt a twinge in her abdomen, down near her bladder. Too much mineral water.

'What did you give her?' whispered Georgette.

'A photograph album. Excuse me.' She got up and slipped out.

The bathroom was through the bedroom. There was already a Moses basket set up on a stand next to the bed, lined with fluffy blue blankets. A mobile made of orange fish hung from the ceiling, low, where the baby would be able to see it. It swayed gently with the breeze of her entering the room.

The twinge became a drag, and then a pain. She put her hand low down on her stomach, where the pain was. She'd been told not to panic if she felt the odd twinge or pang. There was a lot going on inside her body, but everything was in the right place. Her baby was nestled safely within her, fed by her blood, swimming in fluid. Claire breathed deeply, breathed smoothly, as she'd learned in her Yoga for Fertility class, and watched the toy fish dancing.

The pain twisted and sharpened. It sank its grip deeper, into her lower back. A moan escaped Claire, mid-breath, and she put both of her hands on her belly now.

She only just got to the bathroom as the bleeding started.

Claire sat, staring at the pink shower curtain, but not for too long. Not so long that the others would notice. Then she moved with brisk efficiency. She found Lacey's store of sanitary towels under the sink and took two; she didn't think Lacey would mind. She wore one on top of the other. Then she flushed the toilet twice, washed her hands and touched her temples with her wet fingers. Not more than that, or she'd ruin her make-up. She kept her gaze averted from the Moses basket and the mobile as she exited through the bedroom. She picked up her handbag from the floor in the hallway, where she'd left it, and then hesitated before going into the kitchen. Lacey's mother was alone in there, opening another bottle of wine.

'I'm really sorry, but I've got to go,' said Claire. Her voice sounded too loud to her, too rehearsed. 'I don't want to disturb Lacey while she's opening gifts; can you say goodbye for me afterwards?'

Lacey's mother looked at her with quick concern. 'Are you all right, dear?'

'Oh yes, fine. Ben's just called me. He's lost his car keys so he needs me to drive over and pick him up.'

'Oh, what a nuisance. I'm sure Lacey will be sorry you've had to leave early. Do you want some of this food to take home with you?'

'No, no thank you.' From the living room, she could hear all of the women cooing over the latest baby item to be unwrapped. Tiny clothes, tiny toys. Everything soft and pure.

'Are you sure you're all right? You're looking quite pale. Georgette tells me you're expecting.'

'Georgette must have got the wrong end of the stick, somehow.' Claire forced a laugh. 'No, I'm just sorry I have to leave the party. Thanks for giving Lacey my apologies.'

She escaped to her car. The fresh air stung her eyes. Other than that, she didn't feel anything.

Claire drove straight to the M4. She turned off the radio and listened to the sound of the car. She didn't seem able to think, but the site was programmed into her satnav and her body seemed to take over the driving by itself. It was good for that, at least. She got off at the correct junction and followed the B roads between hedges and around curves, obeying directions from the calm, impersonal electric voice.

The Kahns' site was over the county line in Oxfordshire. She turned down the unfinished lane, the car lurching over the ruts and bumps, wondering where the nearest chemist was. She was going to need more towels.

The house was a skeleton of metal beams. Ben was in a Hi-Vis jacket and a hard hat, showing something on his iPad to Mr and Mrs Kahn and their eldest son, also in protective gear. They were smiling, looking pleased about the new home Ben had designed for them. In the next field over, she could see their other three children playing football.

He spotted her car and, after apologizing to the Kahns, came over. He opened the door and his smile melted away.

'What's wrong?'

'I think I'll need you to drive home.' Her voice caught.

'Claire? What's going on? Why didn't you ring?'

'I needed to see you.'

Now that she'd stopped, she didn't feel as if she could get out of the car. It was safer in here. She slid somehow from the driver's seat to the passenger seat, over the gear lever and her handbag. She heard distant laughter in the field.

Ben got in and put his cool hand on her forehead.

'You're white as a sheet.'

'I'm sorry,' she whispered. She closed her eyes and curled up in the seat like a child.

She felt Ben drop off to sleep sometime around three o'clock in the morning. She lay there for a while, thinking, until the pain in her lower back wouldn't let her be still, and then she slipped out from his arms, got up and took some painkillers. There was no point in being careful any more.

Downstairs, she made herself a cup of strong tea with milk and sugar. She found her laptop and powered it up on the kitchen table. It was better to keep busy, or at least to keep her hands busy.

That was where she was, squinting at the screen, when Ben came downstairs just after six, rubbing his face. His eyes were puffy, the T-shirt and pyjama bottoms he'd slept in wrinkled. 'How are you?' he asked.

'I'm doped up on Ibuprofen.' She put the cursor in a new cell in the spreadsheet and carefully typed in *chocolate fondant*.

'I'm glad you took some. You have a little bit more colour.' He put his arms around her from behind as she sat. 'Shall I make us some breakfast? You didn't eat anything yesterday after we got back from hospital.'

'Okay.'

He looked more closely over the top of her head. 'What are you doing? You're not marking, are you?'

'I'm not marking.' She typed *vanilla*, and then checked the calendar, deleted it, and typed *Victoria* instead. She was careful not to look at him, not at his slept-in clothes nor the grief in his face. She couldn't afford to change her mind.

'What are you doing, then?'

'I've made a spreadsheet of cakes,' she said.

'What?'

'Do you know how many cakes I've made over the past six years? Take a guess. Don't look.' She covered the screen with one hand.

'I've no idea.'

'Just a rough estimate. I've made a cake for all of our birthdays, for Posie's, for your dad's, Christmas cakes. Cakes for bake sales at St Dom's and for my tutor group. Village fêtes. Then there were all those coffee mornings for the Fertility Support group. And the ones I've brought round to dinners and lunches. Guess how many.'

'Sweetheart, I know you need a distraction. But you should be resting.'

'I've counted eighty-six cakes. That's counting a batch of cupcakes as one cake, though I'm not sure that's precisely accurate. And I'd usually make four lemon drizzles at once and freeze some, because the fertility ladies kept on asking for them. I've counted that as one cake too.'

'Okay,' said Ben. 'You've been very prolific in the cake-baking area. You're very good at it.'

'Do you know how many I've eaten? Not the whole cake, obviously. I mean a slice.'

'I don't know.'

'None.' She put her finger on one spreadsheet entry. 'Remember that coffee-walnut cake with the espresso ganache I made for your birthday? I really would've fancied that.'

'You can't have baked eighty-six cakes and not eaten any of them.'

'I didn't even lick the spoon.'

Ben paused at that.

'But,' said Claire, 'I don't have to worry about that now. I've decided, Ben. I'm through.'

'Through with what?' She couldn't see his face as he stood behind her. But she knew him. She could feel his expression in his hands.

'With this,' she said. 'With all of this. The dieting to stay at the optimum BMI for fertility, the hormones, the injections. The down-regulating and the stimulations. Peeing on sticks. Having my eggs taken out of me and fertilized in a test tube and put back into me.'

'You don't mean that,' said Ben. 'You're upset because it didn't work this time. But it'll work the next time, Claire.'

'I do mean it.' She closed her laptop with a snap.

Ben took his arms from around her. He pulled out a chair and sat beside her, closely, eye to eye. She gathered her courage and looked him in the face.

'You haven't had to do what I've had to do,' she said. 'All you had to do was come in a cup.'

'I've been through it too,' he said quietly.

'You're not bleeding our child out right now,' said Claire. Ben flinched.

'That's not fair,' he said.

'I'm not feeling very fair. None of this is fair. I was at a baby shower yesterday when I started miscarrying.' She shook her head. 'I'm not going to any more showers, either. Why should I torture myself?'

'Well, I can understand that. But we mustn't give up. We still have lots of chances left, and we shouldn't rush into any big decisions when we're in an emotional state.' He took her hand. 'Maybe we need a holiday.'

'We can't fix this with holidays. We can't afford one, anyway. We're already in debt enough with the IVF.'

'Let me worry about that.'

'I'm a failure. That's not going to change.'

He squeezed her hand. 'You're not a failure, Claire.'

'It's my fault we can't have children.'

'It's not your fault.'

'It's my eggs. None of them is any good. You've heard the doctors as much as I have. We've tried IVF ten times now.' She held up both her hands, fingers splayed. 'And this was the only time out of ten that we've had a positive result. I was born with those eggs. I didn't make them faulty. They just are. I've been faulty all my life.'

'You're not faulty,' said Ben. 'You're perfect.'

'I've lost weight. Then I lost too much weight, so I had to gain weight and then I gained too much so I had to lose it again. I've taken vitamins and done meditation and read a library full of books. Every single thought I've had for the past six years has been about fertility. I'm tired of it, Ben. I can't do it any more. If we're not meant to have children, we're not meant to. We might as well accept it.'

She got up and put the kettle on again.

'I haven't suffered as much as you have,' said Ben. 'But this isn't unusual. IVF only has about a thirty per cent success rate. We've known that from the start.'

'That's not good enough for me. Not any more.'

Ben stood. 'I know you're hurting. But if we give up, we've been through all of this for nothing.'

'Don't you think it's time to cut our losses?'

'Let's have a break, and think about it some more.'

'I shouldn't have let myself love it,' she said. 'I knew there was a good chance it wouldn't make it, that it wouldn't become our child. I knew it was only a bundle of cells. But I could feel it in there, inside me. I thought it was growing. I kept on touching my belly – it was like a little secret. I loved it. I couldn't help myself.'

He tried to take her in his arms, but she stepped away.

'It's okay, Ben. I don't need to think about it any more. I'm not going to change my mind. I decided this morning while you were asleep, and as soon as I decided that I was stopping, I felt so much better. I'm sad that this didn't work out, but there's a huge freedom to it, too. I feel as if an enormous weight has been lifted off me.'

'But . . . all our plans?'

'Our plans are hurting me. I've thought constantly about having a baby for so long. And that's not the worst thing; the worst thing is having hope. Every cycle, I'd get to hoping this was the one, this time it was going to happen. And then . . . nothing.'

'I feel that way too.'

'Then you'll respect my decision.'

'We were so *close*.'

'And that makes it worse.' She knelt and found the caster sugar in the cabinet. She could feel him standing behind her: his surprise, his dismay.

He didn't say anything for several moments. 'Claire,' he said at last. His voice was full of anguish. 'Please.'

Still on her knees, she closed her eyes. She couldn't look at him, or go to him. Not now. It would make her weaker, make her complicit in her own failure.

'I know I'm letting you down,' she said. 'But it's better to

33

decide now than to keep on disappointing you. And it's my body, Ben. I'm sorry.' She took out the sugar.

'Why won't you look at me?' he said. 'What are you doing?'

'I'm making a coffee-walnut cake with espresso ganache.'

He left the room, and Claire stood. She began to measure out the sugar, gram by gram.

3
The Answer

The Rose and Thistle was busy tonight for the quiz to benefit the Berkshire Air Ambulance; Romily waved at some of the regulars and dumped her corduroy jacket at their usual table by the low-beamed fireplace before she went up to the bar.

'He's usually here before you,' said Liz, the landlady. Romily suspected she had a bit of a crush. This was Ben's local – low-ceilinged and thatched, and decorated with horse-brasses and dried hops. If Romily wanted to have a drink and not drive, it was a bus ride and half a mile's walk.

'I'll get his pint, anyway,' Liz went on. She began pulling two pints of Tanglefoot.

'You can be on our team,' said one of the regulars, Glenn, joining Romily at the bar. He wore a Barbour jacket and corduroys, a weekend country squire.

'Thanks, but if he doesn't turn up I'll try it solo.'

'You'll never get the current events round.'

'How do you know I haven't been watching the news? Like, constantly?'

Glenn smiled and shook his head. 'I've watched you do these quizzes. I know your weaknesses.'

'You're scaring me now.'

'Who's Prime Minister?'

'That's easy. Barack Obama.'

'You're going down, love.'

'Want to lay some money on it?'

Glenn hesitated.

'Didn't think so,' said Romily.

Liz slid over the two pints and Romily took them to the usual table. She watched the door. Ben hadn't replied to her texts for over a week. He'd missed football last Saturday. He and Claire might have gone away, but you'd think he'd have mentioned something, especially since they'd agreed to do the quiz ages ago. It was a total waste to get a babysitter just so she could hang around the Rose and Thistle by herself. If she'd known, she could have traded tonight for another night during the week, and gone out and done something else. Something like . . .

Well, she couldn't think of anything at the moment. But she could have done something. Gone to a movie; she hadn't been to a movie in ages. Popped up to London for a lecture.

Though of course she could do those things in the evening any time she wanted to, really, because Ben and Claire would always babysit if she asked. It wasn't the wasted babysitter that she minded. It was Ben not getting in touch. She understood. He had a real life. He had a marriage and a wife, now pregnant.

She noticed, to her surprise, that she'd drunk more than half of her pint. She glowered at the door and worked on the rest of it. At the end of the bar, Muz, the long tall hippy who ran the quiz, was getting his papers ready. He turned on the microphone and it let out a long screech of feedback, just as it always did. She squinted and endured it. Competition in these village pub quizzes was fierce; according to Ben, people talked strategy for months beforehand. Every other team was made up of six people, which was the maximum allowed. She and Ben were usually the only twosome, though that hadn't stopped them winning the last three years in a row. The other teams were already conferring in low voices, as if the Rose and Thistle were some sort of hop-strewn battle zone.

'On your own?' Muz asked as he distributed the answer sheets.

'Looks like it.'

'I saw him driving out of town with his missus last night.'

She bit her lip and looked over the picture round. Damn. Glenn was right. She knew none of these people. 'When are you going to do a picture round about insects?'

'You'd have an unfair advantage.'

'I always have an unfair advantage,' she muttered, 'but tonight he's with his wife.'

'Then his twin just walked in,' said Muz, and Romily looked up, smiling.

Ben's face was like thunder. He glanced at Romily and the single full pint in front of her, and went straight to the bar.

'There may be trouble ahead,' Muz commented. 'What have you done?'

'It wasn't me,' she said. 'Probably work.'

Liz gave him a big greeting. Romily couldn't hear what either of them said, and Ben had his back to her so she couldn't see his face either, but from the way Liz's grin melted away, he hadn't reciprocated her good cheer. Romily busied herself with the picture round again.

Another pint appeared on the table and Ben plopped

down across from her in his usual chair. 'Give that here,' he said, and Romily passed the sheet of paper over. She watched as he picked up the pencil Muz had left on the table and rapidly filled in answers, raising his drink to his mouth with his left hand. By now, the two of them would normally be trading banter with the other teams, but Ben was radiating 'don't talk to me' vibes. The regulars kept well clear.

Ben was hardly ever in a bad mood. She had the good sense not to ask him what was wrong. She steadily made her way through her second pint, the one that had been meant for Ben. When he had filled in half the picture round she said lazily, 'Team name?'

'Don't care. You do it.'

She scrawled *Lumbricus terrestris* on the top of the sheets – upside down on the one Ben was working on.

'What's that?' he asked.

'Earthworm. Keeping our heads down.'

He grunted and finished his bitter. 'It's your round since you didn't get one for me.'

'I—' She shut her mouth. No point. She got the beers from a much less ebullient Liz and brought them back to the table.

They got through another pint, the general knowledge round and part of the current events round without exchanging any unnecessary words, and Romily began to feel, along with the bitter sloshing around in her stomach, a taint of dread. The last time she'd seen Ben he was so happy. There was one possible explanation for such a huge shift in mood . . . but that wouldn't make him angry, would it?

Maybe he wasn't angry.

She looked more closely at him. It was in the corners of his eyes. She could hardly believe she'd missed it.

'Is Claire all right?' she asked quietly. Kicking herself for not seeing it before.

He finished writing down *John Ratzenberger* and gripped the pencil in a fist. 'We lost the baby.'

Muz asked another question. Romily didn't hear it. 'Oh Ben, I'm so sorry,' she said.

She wanted to get up, go to his side of the table, and take him in her arms. But they didn't do that sort of thing, she and Ben. She moved her fingertips towards his hand, the one that gripped the pencil, and let her own hand rest there, a fraction of an inch from his white knuckles.

'I'm sorry,' she said again. 'When – when was it?'

'Last Thursday afternoon. I was on site. I wasn't even there when it started.'

'I thought she was doing so well.'

'We all did.'

She bit her lip for a while, watching him. The tension had left his face and his skin was slack. He looked into his beer, seemingly examining the froth on the side of the glass.

'It will work better the next time,' she said.

He swallowed. 'That's the thing,' he said. 'She says she won't try any more.'

'What? Really?'

'Yes. She wants to give up.'

'Well . . . she's discouraged. It makes sense. She needs some time to recover.'

'That's what I thought.'

'There you are.' She drank her beer, hoping the conversation was over.

'But she says she won't change her mind.'

'It's early days.'

'I've never seen her like this. I can't seem to reach her. She won't listen to me.'

'Oh.'

'I know it's been horrible for her. Worse than for me. I know that. But how can she give up? That makes it all for nothing.'

'Um.' Romily took her hands back and curled one around her pint, looking around the room. Everyone was absorbed in the quiz.

'It was always the plan. We'd finish university, we'd get married. She'd get her PGCE and teach while I worked my way up in a firm. We'd move to the countryside and we'd start a family and she'd stop work and I'd set up on my own.'

'Yes.'

'And okay, it was taking longer than we'd expected, but these things happen. We were working through it, step by step. Now she's given up.'

Someone cleared their throat nearby. Romily looked up to see Muz hovering, holding out his hand. 'Er . . . current events sheet?'

Ben handed it over. Muz raised his eyebrows at the half-empty paper, but put down the film round sheet in its place and went to the next table.

'She won't talk to me,' Ben said. 'She says I'll try to convince her. I just want to discuss it.' He put his head in his hands.

Romily heard the quiz questions going by. She didn't know what to say.

'You . . . have you talked about adoption?' she ventured.

'We wanted our own child. Claire looked into it, of course. Do you know how long it takes? Or how unlikely it is to get

40

a baby?' He drained his pint. 'I don't know. Maybe we have to talk about that now. But I'm not ready to give up the dream, Romily. I can't believe she is.'

She stood. 'Want another?'

'Yes.'

She went up to the bar. She was a pint ahead of him, but she didn't feel drunk. She was trembling.

She'd never seen Ben like this. Her sunny, optimistic, energetic Ben. Ben who was a force of nature and who always knew all the answers.

'Is he all right?' Liz asked.

'He's fine,' Romily said. 'Just having an off night.' She glanced over at their table, though, and she knew it was more than an off night. He looked lost. As if his entire world had been ripped out from underneath him.

'I'll have a couple of tequilas as well,' Romily said.

She brought all the drinks back to the table. 'Here. Drink this.'

Ben screwed up his eyes, but he drank the tequila. 'It's bad for your sperm count,' he said. 'Not that it matters any more, I suppose.'

She downed her shot. It seemed to take effect immediately.

'It's not *fair*,' she said. 'There are millions of women who don't even want children and get pregnant anyway. All the women who drink and smoke and do drugs and stuff.' She drank her beer to take away the taste of the tequila. 'I think it would be so much easier sometimes if we did what ants or honeybees do. Collective parenting. Everyone related. It's an elegant solution.'

'If we're going to talk bugs, I'm going to need another tequila,' said Ben. He went to the bar and came back within a few minutes.

41

'Posie wants you two to be her parents anyway,' Romily said after they'd drunk their second shots.

'No, she doesn't.'

'She really does. And I can't blame her. You know, the thing is, if I didn't—' She stopped. Tequila was dangerous; there was a reason she never drank it around Ben. She started again. 'If you weren't my friend, I would hate you. You're brilliant, you're talented, you're successful. You married the love of your life. Everybody who meets you falls in love with you.'

'Don't be silly.'

'I'm serious. Look at Liz up there.'

They both looked. The landlady was watching them, her brow furrowed. When she realized she'd been spotted, she smiled slightly and waved before pretending to wipe down the bar.

'She's just being nice,' said Ben.

'And look at me,' Romily continued, and then corrected herself again. Damn tequila. 'I mean, look at my life compared to yours. I live in a poky flat in a rubbish town, I've never got any money, I love my job, yeah, but it's not exactly the sort of thing you can talk about at cocktail parties, even if I got invited to cocktail parties, which I never am. I haven't been on a date in . . . well, a long time.'

'You've got one thing that I haven't,' Ben said quietly. 'You've got Posie.'

'Yeah. But that's not fair either. Here you are, you've been planning for years to have children, and me, I use a dodgy condom one night and bam!'

'Posie's wonderful.'

'She is, and I love her, but she wasn't exactly intentional. As you remember.'

'I remember. But it was the right decision, true?'

'Of course. I mean . . . yes. I think she's amazing, I wouldn't trade her for the world. She surprises me all the time. But you wouldn't say I'm a natural motherly type. You get the soft-focus part of parenthood on the telly. All those toilet-paper adverts with the cute kids and the dogs. There are so many things that you don't really sign up for. Colic, or carsickness, or nappy rash. There's a lot of laundry. And all the board games, over and over and over again round and round that little circle till you want to scream. And when they're hurt, it's like a chunk of you has been ripped out, you just completely revert to primitive mode. As for the mothers in the playground . . .'

If she'd meant to comfort Ben, it wasn't working. He looked as if she'd kicked him in the stomach.

'Right.' She cleared her throat. 'Anyway. Enough of that. What we need to do is think up an action plan.'

'I don't know, Romily. Maybe Claire is right. Maybe it's not meant to be.'

'Nonsense. Have you ever let me give up? Even when I wanted to?'

Ben considered his pint. 'No.'

'Well then.' She took the abandoned film round sheet, turned it over, and picked up the pencil. GET BEN AND CLAIRE A BABY, she wrote at the top. Then she decided that looked too much as if they were going to pick one up at the local supermarket, so she erased it and wrote HOW BEN AND CLAIRE CAN HAVE A BABY.

'*One*,' she said, writing it down. '*Adopt*.'

'I don't know.'

'*Two*. Um . . .' She scratched her forehead with the pencil and drank some more of her beer. '*Get pregnant naturally by mistake*.'

'That's not going to happen, short of a miracle.'

'Well, miracles happen. Biology is not an exact science. Anyway, this is brainstorming absolutely every possibility. We'll see if anything sticks. Three. *Try fertility treatment again.*'

'But that's exactly what Claire swears up and down she won't do. I wish I could do it instead of her. I wish I could go through it.'

The expression on his face made her feel sick, but she put some cheerfulness in her voice. She'd always been able to make him laugh, at least. 'Let's try another tack. *Four. An incredible scientific breakthrough that hasn't happened yet e.g. men giving birth.*'

'Romily, this is ridiculous. You should never be given tequila.'

'*Five. Aliens.*'

He was smiling now, at least a little, and that was worth something. She pressed on. '*Six. Borrow someone else's ovaries.*'

'What?'

'Yeah. It's Claire's eggs that are the problem, right? Use donated eggs and your own sperm. Then the child will be yours.'

'It won't be Claire's.'

'Will that be a problem for her?'

'I . . . don't know.' He thought about it for a little while.

'It's still more treatment, anyway,' Romily said. 'More embryo transfers. So maybe not a good idea.'

'The doctor said she might have trouble keeping a pregnancy, even if we do get an embryo. We have to do more tests.' Ben rubbed his forehead. 'She says that the hope is the worst.'

Romily sighed and studied the list. Her writing was quite wobbly, due to the tequila no doubt. Still, there was something in it that was niggling at her. An idea, maybe, that was trying to make its way to the surface.

'Hey,' said a voice next to their table. They looked up to see Glenn holding two more glasses of tequila. 'I just brought these over to thank you for failing to do the quiz. We won for the first time.'

'Should've taken the bet,' Romily told him, and accepted the tequila.

'If you could arrange to do the same next time, we'd appreciate it.'

'Don't count on it.'

Glenn saluted them and went back to his team, who exchanged high-fives with him.

Ben leaned his elbows on the table and propped his chin on his hands. 'I know you're trying to help, Romily, but this is – I feel terrible. I feel sick. I've never argued with Claire. We've had little disagreements, but nothing like this. She won't touch me or even really look at me. And I can see that she's hurting, but I can't do anything to comfort her because it always leads to the same thing. I still want a baby. And she's given up.' He knocked back his shot, and so did Romily.

And then it came to Romily, in a big blinding revelation that felt like a firecracker popping in her head.

'Ben!' she cried. 'I've got it! I can get pregnant for you!'

'Shut up, Romily.'

'No! I mean it. I can carry the baby, and give birth and everything, and then you and Claire would have a baby.'

'Shut *up*, Romily.'

'We can use your sperm and my eggs – not, I mean – not that we would have to have sex, of course. We could use,' her hands seemed suddenly quite sweaty, 'a turkey-baster or something and then I'd be the pregnant one, and Claire

45

wouldn't have to go through any more treatments at all, but it would be your baby. And I've already had a baby, so I know that I can do pregnancy and birth. The physical part was quite easy for me. And I have no desire whatsoever to have any more children, so it wouldn't be a problem to hand over the baby when it was born.'

'Romily,' said Ben, 'this is one of those so-called brilliant strokes of genius you get when you're drunk and forget about the next day.'

'No! I mean yes, I am drunk, but in this case, this really is a brilliant stroke of genius. Being pregnant wouldn't be any trouble to me at all.'

'You didn't enjoy being pregnant with Posie.'

'No, but I was worried the whole time. How I was going to support her, how I was going to carry on my research and writing up a PhD with a baby, whether I'd like her or not. And the whole – you know, her father. But this time, I wouldn't have those worries. I'd know the baby was going to a good home – the best home in the world, in my opinion.'

'I'm . . .' She watched him think about it. 'No, it's too much to ask.'

'No, it's not! Look.' She grabbed the pencil again and wrote, in letters big enough to fill up the rest of the page: SEVEN: *Romily* WILL HAVE THE BABY FOR YOU!!! She held up the paper in front of Ben's face. He gently pushed it down.

'This is a big thing, Romily.'

'But Ben, seriously. You and Claire deserve a baby. And if I can help you, I will. I owe you so much. All those times you've looked after Posie . . .'

'We wanted to do that. We love Posie. You don't have to pay us back.'

'And Posie wouldn't even be here if it weren't for you,

Ben.' She held his gaze with hers. 'Remember that night.'

'I remember it.'

'You're just about the most important person in my life,' she said, her heart beating hard. 'Let me do this for you.'

'Do you mean it?' Ben asked her quietly.

'It's nine months. What's nine months, compared with what Posie and I owe you? I'll do it.'

She watched him thinking. She could see the exact moment when hope came back into his eyes.

'You would have a baby for us?' he said. As if he couldn't quite believe it.

'I would do anything for you. Anything.'

He didn't say a word. He reached across the pub table and took her face in his hands and he kissed her, suddenly and hard. Then he wrapped his arms around her and hugged her.

'Thank you,' he whispered into her hair. 'Thank you. Thank you.'

Romily clung to him, her head spinning, her breath gone, her cheek pressed against his chest, tasting beer and tequila and her best friend on her lips.

4

Pear Tree

'Good morning!'

Claire patted the soil down around the bulbs, making sure they were snug in their new home, before she looked up. Ben was coming across the lawn, carrying two steaming mugs. He wore a T-shirt and pyjama bottoms, and seemed not to care that his bare feet and the hems of his pyjamas were getting soaked.

'Looks like you've been hard at work already,' he said, handing her one of the mugs and squatting beside her.

'I found these bulbs in the garage and thought I'd take advantage of the sunshine.'

'It's a good day for growing things.' Ben smiled up at the sky.

'You slept in the spare room last night.'

'I'd had a few to drink and I didn't want to disturb you,' he said. 'Besides, I had a lot to think about.' He sat on the grass. 'I'm sorry, Claire. I haven't been seeing things from your point of view. I've been so focused on the idea of us having a baby together that I haven't truly understood how hard it's been for you. I thought that we were both going through it together, but you're right: it's your body. It's worse for you.'

'Okay,' said Claire quietly.

'It was insensitive of me to try to persuade you to try more IVF. I can understand how you feel that it just sets you up for more failure.'

'Okay.'

'I've been too single-minded. It's the way I always am. I decide I want something, and then I go for it with all I've got. But I should listen to you.'

'I'm sorry too,' she said. 'I know how badly you want this. I want it too. If I could, I would.'

He drew her over to sit on his lap, on the ground. 'You've got dirt on your forehead,' he said, brushing it off.

'I'm not happy about it either,' she said. 'I've always assumed I'd have children, ever since I was a little girl. I always assumed I'd have them with you. Every time I've come out to this garden I've thought about how great it would be for the children to play in. I've seen the football pitch on the lawn and the swing in the pear tree. I've seen them so strongly in my imagination that I haven't taken the time to see what's already here.'

'We have a good life. Yes.'

'It's a future that's completely different from what I imagined. But it doesn't have to be a bad future. If we love each other, we can be happy, can't we?'

He kissed her cheek and hugged her tight to him. 'I'm already very happy,' he said.

She let herself relax into his arms, closing her eyes, hearing the blackbird singing in the pear tree. The real pear tree, that was there right now, that blossomed sweet every spring and gave them gifts of fruit every autumn. The pear tree that was fine by itself, without a swing on it.

'What time is it?' she asked.

'Don't know. About half eight? It's a miracle I'm not hungover, considering the amount of tequila we got through last night.'

'How much did you win the quiz by?'

'We didn't win. I'm afraid I unburdened myself on Romily.'

'Hmm.' Claire knew, of course, that Ben talked with Romily; they could only spend so long answering quiz questions and arguing about football. After a drink or two, Ben was bound to mention one or two things about his private life.

Her mother had often expressed horror that Ben had a female friend, but Claire wasn't the sort to interfere with her husband's friendships. Marriage was based on trust, after all. But she wasn't entirely happy that he would discuss all the ins and outs of their private lives in the pub. Then again, it might not be a coincidence that he'd apologized this morning.

'Did Romily help you see the female point of view?' she asked.

'In a way.'

'Well, then I suppose I should thank her.' She ruffled his hair. 'Let's go inside. You must be getting a wet bottom.'

'What's that you say? You want a wet bottom?' He tipped her off and dumped her on the grass.

'Ben!'

He launched himself on top of her, wrapped his arms round her, and rolled with her over and over down the lawn, her squealing, him laughing, his body heavy and warm over and under hers, both of them damp and muddy and breathless when they stopped at the trunk of the pear tree, lying side by side.

'You're crazy,' she giggled.

'I told you, I'm happy.' He kissed her mouth once, and again.

'We should go in.'

'Let's just lie here for a minute.'

They gazed upward into the complicated branches of the pear tree. The blackbird, which had stopped singing at their approach, resumed its song.

Be here now. That was what Hannah, her Yoga for Fertility instructor, always said. Let go and relax and feel the moment. Claire had never been very good at that. One time Ben had bought her a spa weekend that included a session in a flotation tank: an entire hour of lying on her back in warm, extremely salty water, gazing up at false stars made of fairy lights, listening to flighty New Age music. You were supposed to relax and feel the moment. Be part of the water, be part of the music. Some people dropped off to sleep, the therapist said.

Claire had clenched her fists, closed her eyes to keep out the salt water. She'd felt like a board, a corpse, every small movement sending her spinning and rippling towards the sides of the tank. She kept on bumping her head and feet on cold tiles.

Maybe the whole problem had been that she was too focused on the past and the future to let go. Maybe she needed to do more things like this: a few spontaneous moments with her husband, lying on the grass.

She took his hand and his fingers curled tight around hers. She felt her muscles letting go, relaxing into the earth.

5

The Hangover

Romily scraped open one eye and then immediately shut it. From her brief glimpse, the room appeared to be wobbling.

Tequila. Ugh. How did Mexicans survive that stuff?

Slowly, she pushed herself up to a sitting position, propping herself up against the headboard of her bed, and took a few sustaining breaths before she attempted opening her eyes again. A needle of pain stabbed her temple, but the room more or less stayed still, so she reckoned she was ahead. She looked around in case she'd miraculously remembered to put a fresh glass of water on her bedside table, but all that was there was a teetering stack of books and, half-hidden beneath a slightly used tissue, her comb.

So that's where her comb was. She looked at her watch, still on her wrist: half past ten. 'Posie?' she called, and winced.

No answer. Romily swung her legs out of bed and stood up. She was wearing her jeans and T-shirt from the night before, but she had managed to remove her shoes. They lay beside the bed, upside down. She stepped over them and went next door to Posie's room.

Posie had made a tent out of her duvet with one of Romily's long-handled nets as a pole and lay inside it, reading a book by torchlight. She glanced up when Romily peered in.

'It's Sunday,' she said. 'I don't have to go to school.'

'I know,' said Romily, though she was relieved to hear it. She didn't feel quite able to stand for any length of time, so she sat on the floor next to Posie's bed, running her dry tongue around her dry mouth. 'How was Mrs Spencer?'

'She was fine. I beat her at charades and she let me stay up till ten.'

'What are you reading?'

Posie showed her the cover, which featured men in armour with big helmets. 'Romans.'

'I don't feel all that well today, Pose.'

'That's okay.' She pointed to a stack of books beside her in the tent. 'I've got loads. Did you and Ben win the quiz?'

'I don't think so. No, actually I can say with authority that we didn't. We'd never have drunk so much if we'd won. When you're older, I advise you to stay the heck away from tequila.'

'The Romans drank aquavit.'

'And look what happened to them. It's probably a good idea to steer clear of that too.'

'All right.'

Romily closed her eyes again and leaned her forehead on the side of Posie's bed. It was quite restful in here, with the blinds drawn and only the sound of Posie turning pages.

They hadn't won the quiz last night. Because she'd been too busy offering to have a baby for Ben.

Romily's eyes flew open and she sat up straight. She hardly noticed the spike of headache.

Ben. That list. The last sentence all in capitals. They'd had more drinks and he'd put her in a taxi but she had the list folded up in her back pocket. She reached down and touched the corner of it, still there and real.

'Romily? Why are you staring at me like that?'

She'd talked about a turkey baster. She'd said she'd do anything for him.

Her mind whirred backwards, trying to remember everything she'd said, in two strands: one about having a baby for him, and one about what she'd said otherwise, about how she felt. What had he heard? What had he understood?

He'd thanked her. He'd kissed her.

'I'm trying to read,' Posie said.

Romily jumped to her feet. 'Toast. I'm making toast. Want some?'

'Can I have it in my tent?'

'Sure.' Romily beat a retreat out of the bedroom and through the darkened lounge to the kitchenette, a cramped den of a space that Romily always thought looked as if it had been tacked on as an afterthought. She unplugged the kettle, plugged in the toaster, and put in the last two slices of bread, leaving the end because Posie didn't like it. She poured herself a large glass of water and stood, not drinking it, chewing on her lip.

'Shit,' she said out loud to the cereal boxes, the dried-out basil plant, the unwashed mug in the sink. 'I am a fucking idiot.'

Maybe Ben had been really drunk, too. Maybe this morning he wouldn't even remember their conversation.

Who was she kidding? He'd remember every word. Ben never forgot anything, and he'd certainly never forget something like this. She took the paper from her back pocket and there it was, in black and white, in her own, more than slightly wobbly handwriting: SEVEN: ROMILY WILL HAVE THE BABY FOR YOU!!!

She crumpled it up into a tiny ball and chucked it into the bin. On second thoughts she didn't want it in landfill for ever; she took it out and stuffed it into the compost pot, beneath tea bags and a banana peel. It would go out into the garden and the slugs would eat it into lacy holes, wasps would chew it up to make nests.

At least she didn't feel hungover any more. Amazing what a whole-body panic-driven adrenaline surge could do for you. It was an entirely different type of sickness that was coursing through her body. She washed her hands and splashed her face in the kitchen sink, but it didn't help. When the toast popped up, she smeared margarine and honey on it and brought it on a plate to Posie's room.

'Thanks, Centurion,' said Posie without looking up from her book. Romily didn't quite trust her voice not to give something away, even as absorbed as Posie was with the Romans, so she made a random sound and went into the bathroom to switch on the hot water.

In the mirror she looked as rough as she'd expected to, with the added benefit of a wild, hunted look in her eyes. It was the expression of a person who'd inadvertently given away the most important secret of their life and was waiting for the axe to fall.

Eleven years of keeping her mouth shut, of looking away, of smiling and going along and pretending. And then a shot or two of tequila was all it took, in the end.

'Stupid,' she muttered. 'Stupid stupid stupid. He knows. Or if he doesn't yet, he will.'

Because why on earth would you offer to have a baby for a man, to give up nine months of your life and etch

55

stretchmarks into your belly and commit yourself to endless blood tests and pelvic-floor exercises, unless you were completely and utterly in love with him?

And always had been, since the moment you'd first seen him?

6

An Assignation

Meet me in the bar of the George Hotel in half an hour. Don't tell anyone. B

Romily stared down at her phone. So this was how her friendship ended, on a Monday lunchtime: with a text and a meeting in secret to spare the feelings of the people they loved.

She was in Brickham Museum's staff kitchen, ignoring the persistent dripping of the tap and the rattle of the fridge, trying to self-medicate with caffeine and sugar. Yesterday's hangover still hadn't disappeared. Or maybe it was pure, naked fear that was making her head ache and her stomach lurch.

On Saturday night, Ben had been too preoccupied with thinking about having a baby to realize the true meaning of Romily's offer. But he'd had time now, to think it through. And now he was meeting her to talk about it. From today, their friendship would be over. Or worse, it would be stilted. Every time they were together, she'd be wondering if he was thinking, *She's in love with me.* Ben was decent; he'd be concerned. He'd be dismayed. He'd feel sorry for her. She'd watch him being cautious with his words, with his gestures, so as not to lead her on. All of their easy comradeship, the way they could take the piss out of each other, the way they didn't have to talk but could talk if they wanted to . . . it would be gone. He would be being kind, rather than being her friend.

She wouldn't be able to bear it.

Maybe it was best not to go. If it was over, it was over; why talk about it? They could make a clean break. Never talk again. It would hurt, but she could move on. It would be better than drawing out the torture for years.

But she couldn't do that to Posie.

Romily gulped down the rest of her extra-strong, extra-sweet instant coffee. It had gone cold. She checked the clock on the kitchen wall, which told her she had twenty minutes to get across the centre of town to the George.

'Damn it,' she said, and went to find her coat.

It was raining, an icy February rain that trickled down the back of her scarfless neck. She shoved her hands in her coat pockets and tried not to think about the conversation that was awaiting her.

The thing is, he would say, *I'm so flattered, Romily.*

The thing is, I love Claire.

The thing is, I've never thought of you like that.

He would say it kindly. He might touch her hand.

The George was a functional red-brick slab on the west side of town. It housed business travellers and conferences and was unlikely to attract anyone she or Ben knew. Romily looked for Ben's car outside, but either he hadn't turned up yet or he'd parked it somewhere out of sight. She took a deep breath and pushed through the revolving door to the lobby.

Inside, the hotel was entirely anonymous, modern in a way

that was clean and inoffensive. There were a few people at the desk and sitting in the scattered armchairs drinking coffee or reading their mobile phones, but none of them took any notice of Romily as she crossed the polished floor towards the bar. It was, she realized, the perfect place for a secret meeting. No one cared what anyone else was doing; everyone was quiet and discreet. It was just the sort of hotel you'd choose if you were carrying on an affair.

On Saturday night he'd reached across the table, taken her head in his hands, and kissed her. Romily could still feel Ben's lips on hers, the hard pressure, the heat of his skin.

No. Surely not?

She wiped her palms on her jeans and went into the bar. Here, the windows had been slightly tinted and the lights were turned low, presumably to give lunchtime drinkers the illusion of being in a sophisticated night spot. Ben was at a table in the far corner. He jumped up when he saw her enter and rushed over to her.

'Rom. Thanks so much for coming. I wasn't sure you would be able to get away at such short notice, but I didn't know if I could find another spare hour during the day.'

'Oh well, you know. Those insects have been dead for a long time; half an hour isn't going to make much difference.'

He laughed, but his face was worried. 'How are you?' he asked her. 'Are you okay?'

'Yes, fine.'

He touched her lightly on her shoulder to guide her to the table. 'I've ordered you a coffee, but maybe you'd prefer a pint?'

'Coffee is good.'

He'd already drunk half of his and as he sat across from her he seemed jumpy, as if he'd had too much caffeine. She stalled by selecting brown and white sugar lumps from the bowl on the table and dropping them one by one into her drink. They made small ripples. He was watching her in a way he didn't usually watch her. Almost as if he was seeing her for the first time.

'So,' she said, her heart pounding, trying to keep the spoon from rattling against her cup. 'A secret meeting, Mr Bond?'

'I haven't been able to stop thinking about Saturday night.'

She made a noncommittal sound and carefully poured in the milk.

'I've been turning it and turning it around in my head. Looking at it from every angle. I haven't said anything to Claire, not yet. I needed to see you first.'

'Okay.'

He was rubbing his thumb across his palm, first with one hand and then the other, as if he were trying to find the right words to say. She didn't trust herself to say anything. He'd been arguing with Claire. He'd kissed Romily at the quiz.

No. Wishful thinking. But how could she think about anything else, with him looking at her like that?

'Can you—' he began, and then shook his head. 'We drank an awful lot that night. I wouldn't be surprised if you didn't remember what you said.'

'I remember.'

'It was – I mean, it could change everything. So I have to be certain that you absolutely meant it.'

She couldn't bear it any longer. 'Meant what, exactly?'

'About having the baby for us.'

It swept over her like a wave of cold water. 'That's it?' she said. 'That's all? That's what you've been looking at from every angle.'

'Well, yes. It's a big step.'

Of course. Ben wanted a baby. He didn't care about why she'd offered to do it. To understand why she'd offered, he'd have to love her back.

Interesting how the end of hope felt much the same as the end of despair.

'What else would there be?' he said.

'Nothing.' She was blushing, but she raised her cup to her lips to cover up. 'It's just a big step, as you say.'

A big step that she'd been successfully pushing out of her mind because she'd been too worried about losing her friendship with Ben.

'You're regretting it,' he said immediately. 'I can see you're uncomfortable. That's fine, Romily. That's why I wanted to meet up. I wouldn't want to put any pressure on you. It's amazing that you even offered.'

'Do you . . .' She stalled for time. 'Do you think that Claire would go for it?'

'I don't know. I had to ask you first. It all depends on you.'

He was still watching her that way, as if his entire life depended on her. Which it did, because he wanted her to have his baby.

Now was her chance. The moment to say she'd been drunk, that she'd been too impulsive. She could say that she needed some more time to think about it, that she wasn't sure if it would work out with her job or with Posie. She could say she was too afraid of getting attached to the baby and being unable to give it up.

The thing was, all of those would be lies. She'd been drunk, yeah, and she was always impulsive. But she'd meant it when she'd offered: because Ben wanted a family so much, because she had a womb going spare. And there was no real, logical reason not to mean it still. She'd been pregnant before, and she knew she could do it again. She could do her work just fine while incubating a foetus, and schedule time off for the delivery in advance. Posie might find it a little strange, but she'd adjust. And Romily really did have no desire for another child.

There wasn't a single good reason *not* to have a baby for Ben and Claire. And here he was in front of her. It would make him so happy, and all she had to do was use a turkey-baster and spend nine months making herself eat healthily and drink milk. It would give him everything he wanted, and for Romily, nothing would really change.

And she'd been telling the truth on Saturday night. Even knowing now that he could never love her, even having always known, she would do anything for Ben.

She met his eyes for a moment, and then had to look away, at the sugar bowl. All that sweetness jumbled together.

'Okay,' she said. 'I'll do it.'

7

A Known Quantity

'Romily said *what?*'
'Romily has offered to have the baby for us,' Ben repeated. 'She's offered to be a surrogate.'

Claire turned off the programme they'd both been watching. Or pretending to watch; Ben had been jumpy all evening, all through dinner, as if he had something he really wanted to say. Claire had never imagined it would be this.

'She says she's happy to use her eggs,' he continued, 'and we can use my sperm for artificial insemination. She knows she can conceive and carry a baby to term, because of Posie. She doesn't want any more children. I'd be listed on the birth certificate as the father so I'd have legal rights anyway, and we could formalize adoption to give you rights within weeks of the baby's being born. We have one or two things to be cautious of, but there should be no real issue with a private adoption with all parties consenting. I've been researching the legal ins and outs.'

'When did Romily say this?'
'On Saturday, in the pub.'

Claire crossed her arms. 'You were deciding our reproductive future in the *pub*?'

'Not deciding, no. Just talking about it. But isn't it an amazing idea, Claire? Don't you think we should consider it? It would be my baby, genetically. And yours by adoption. You wouldn't have to go through a single moment of treatment. And we'd have a child. A child all our own, from the moment it's born. It could come straight home with us from hospital. What do you think?'

'I think you've made up your mind about all of this without thinking of me at all.'

'I *am* thinking about you. It's a way that we can have a family without you having any more treatment.'

'Because Romily would be having my baby.' She shook her head. 'No way.'

'Don't you think we should even consider it? Maybe not now, but in a little while, after we've had some time to get over the miscarriage?'

As if she could forget all about the life that, so briefly, had lain inside her. The thought seemed so empty and cruel.

'For one thing, it's none of Romily's business. For another thing, I can't believe that you discussed it with her. And for a third, how could she have a child and give it up?'

'She wouldn't be giving it up,' Ben said. 'It would never be hers in the first place. Genetically, yes, and legally until the adoption papers go through. But in all the ways that matter, the baby would be ours. She doesn't want any more children. She's giving us a chance to have our baby, Claire.'

'You mean, I couldn't make children for you so now you want to use another woman.'

'That's not it at all.' Ben reached for her, but Claire stood up.

'That's it exactly. You went behind my back and came up with this crazy idea, just when you knew I was finally getting some peace.' Something occurred to her. 'Is this why you were so happy yesterday morning? Because you'd come up with this?'

'I didn't want to say anything to you about it until I was sure that Romily really meant it. I didn't want to get your hopes up.'

'My *hopes up*?' She threw her hands in the air. 'I'd decided the hoping was finished, Ben. You haven't heard *anything* I've said.'

She turned to leave the room. Behind her, she heard Ben say, 'We could still have the swing on the pear tree.'

Claire perched on a chrome stool in her sister Helen's newly redecorated kitchen. The sleek breakfast bar was covered with a wipe-clean tablecloth.

'The thing is,' said Helen, 'it's not such a bad idea, in the abstract. Josh, give that back to your sister.'

'I had it first!'

'I don't care. You're older than her, give it back.'

Claire watched her nephew stomp across the slate floor out of the kitchen. 'You can't seriously think it's a good idea that my husband wants another woman to have his baby.'

'On the other hand, you'd have a baby at the end of it.' Helen offered Claire another biscuit. 'And people pay a lot of money to have a surrogate. Presumably she'd do it for free.'

'This isn't about money.'

'But it never hurts to consider it.' A wail came from the other room. 'Josh! Give it back to your sister!'

'But why would Romily even want to do it?'

'You've been friends since university, haven't you?'

'She was friends with Ben before I ever met him, so that's how I knew her. We haven't really spent much time together, just the two of us. We don't have much in common.'

'Aren't you godmother to her daughter?'

'That's because she asked Ben to be godfather and I was part of the package.' Claire nibbled at a biscuit. 'It makes sense to have a godmother and godfather who are married. I'd do the same thing, if we ... Anyway, she's Ben's friend mostly.'

'Do you think there's something going on between them?'

'Hels!'

'Well, I have to ask. It's the obvious question.'

This was what Helen was like: if she thought something, she said it. Claire had to admit that this was one reason why she'd come to visit her sister this afternoon. And the same reason why, quite often, she stayed away.

'It's not like that,' Claire said. 'They talk football most of the time. They go to the Rose and Thistle, which is always full of men. He treats her like one of the blokes.'

'As long as you're sure, then— Sarah! Stop teasing him! Sorry, Claire, I need to sort this out.'

While Helen was out of the kitchen, Claire pictured Romily. Gangly, awkward, with her thick, cropped dark hair with the cowlick at the back that never lay down properly. Her frayed-hem jeans, her battered tennis shoes and her bitten nails; the freckles on her nose like a child's, the way she sat on a chair always with one leg folded beneath her. Romily didn't look old enough to be a mother, or to have a PhD. From the back she looked like a teenage boy, the type who would have beetles and snails in jars on bedroom shelves, frogs in her pockets. She melted into corners, lapsed into day-dreams or abstract mental classification. She'd always tagged along, turned up at odd hours according to her own chaotic schedule.

She'd been a fact of Ben's life when Claire had met him. If she'd ever been hostile to Claire, that would have set Claire's back up, but she'd never been anything but friendly in an off-hand way. Ben said she was shy.

Posie was more vivid in Claire's mind; she'd spent more time with Posie than with her own nephews and niece, because Romily had needed help with childcare in the early years. Posie was a bright smear of warm limbs and blonde hair, dreamy blue eyes. She had a sweet smell of her own, like apples in a bowl. Claire's arms knew by themselves how it felt to hold her small body. The little girl was hungry for mothering, for cuddles and exchanges of girly confidences. She looked nothing like Romily, who treated her with absent affection. As if Posie were a favourite specimen that she was fond of but not quite sure what to do with.

There were secret moments, when Posie was asleep in the bedroom they called hers, curled under the quilt that Claire's grandmother had made. Or when she greeted Claire with a big hug and a kiss. Or when Claire handed her a tissue, or when Posie's hand crept by itself into Claire's. In those secret, private moments, Claire sometimes pretended that Posie was hers.

It didn't do anyone any harm. In reality, Claire knew she couldn't let herself love Posie too much. It wouldn't be wise to love her as much as she'd love her own child – not with her full heart. Not when in the morning, after sleeping under Claire's grandmother's quilt, Posie was going home with Romily.

Claire knew Posie. She loved Posie. And yet Posie had come from Romily's body. And now Romily was offering her body to Claire and Ben, as if it were a bicycle to be borrowed for a little while and then returned.

'I don't get why she'd want to do it,' she said again, when Helen returned from sorting out the squabble. 'It's a big commitment.'

'I wish I'd thought of it,' said Helen. 'I couldn't do it, not after all the problems I had with Sarah. But I wish I'd thought of it. I wish I'd offered.'

She looked sad, and Claire hugged her. 'Don't be silly. That's lovely of you to say, but you couldn't possibly.'

'It would've solved a lot of problems.' Helen shrugged. 'Oh well, no use thinking of it now. But if this Romily is healthy and she's willing, maybe you should give it a shot. At least she's a known quantity, right? You know she's got good genes – she's clever, isn't she? You know she can give birth. You like her daughter. You know she's not going anywhere.' Sarah toddled into the kitchen, and Helen broke a biscuit in half and gave it to her. 'You know a lot more about her than you would an anonymous egg donor, or another surrogate. Or the parents of a child you'd adopted.'

'But it's the way that Ben went about it, without even telling me.'

'He's desperate. You both are, aren't you?'

Does it show so much? She looked around at her sister's modern kitchen, which was saved from being minimalist by the plastic tablecloth, the children's drawings on the refrigerator. She'd hardly been here at all in the past four years since Josh had been born.

'What would Mum say?' she said instead.

Her sister smiled. 'Ah, well, there's another thing. Sarah, don't eat that, you've just dropped it on the floor!'

68

8
Building Blocks

Months ago, they'd promised to take Posie and Romily to Legoland in Windsor in the first week of the Easter holiday. The night before, Claire lay in bed with her head on Ben's chest.

'What if she's changed her mind?' she asked.

'She won't. Once Romily makes up her mind, she doesn't change it.'

'Unlike me.'

He stroked her hair. 'I went about it the wrong way. I shouldn't have sprung it on you like that.'

'No more deciding my life in the pub, all right?'

'Agreed. But you do want this to happen, don't you, Claire?'

She'd thought of little else for weeks. All of the calm she'd felt that day under the pear tree had fled. She'd been able to feel calm because she'd been at the end of hope, and now there was this new possibility. Her mind gnawed away at it: pros, cons, legal issues. She'd been on internet surrogacy forums to read the stories. There were happy ones and some sad ones. There were a lot of couples who were looking for a surrogate and hadn't yet found one. She recognized the desperation lying under their typed words.

'For six years,' she said, 'every month that's gone by has felt like another month that's been stolen from us. Another chance gone. If this is another chance, I can't pass it up.'

'So we'll ask her?'

'Yes.' She wished she could feel that calm again. She wished she could know that this was right. But how would they know without trying?

'Yes,' she repeated.

Romily twisted her hands in the pockets of her jeans and watched Posie skipping ahead of them down the path towards a robotic dinosaur made out of Lego. The sun was too bright, the park too crowded, and the colours and canned music more or less obscene. She didn't quite dare to look at Ben or Claire.

Ben hadn't mentioned their conversation again, not since their secret meeting in February. Aside from texted arrangements about today, they'd barely been in contact. Meanwhile she knew that he and Claire were talking about it. Talking about her.

She glanced over at Claire, walking beside her down the stepped path. She looked breezy and cheerful in white trousers, spotless white pumps and a primrose-yellow top. Romily, as usual, had forgotten to do laundry and was wearing her last pair of black jeans and a green T-shirt with a hole in one sleeve. Claire's face held no clue to her thoughts.

Wouldn't she be wondering why Romily had volunteered? What if she had worked it out and told Ben, and now they were going on this outing, which Ben had insisted on paying for, to pretend that everything was all right

70

because they felt so sorry for her and her unrequited love?

The two of them. A united front. 'Poor Romily,' she pictured them saying this morning, in their sun-drenched kitchen, over fresh-brewed coffee and home-baked croissants. 'Poor, deluded Romily. It's a good idea to do something nice for her to show her there's no hard feelings. Let's include Posie so she'll remember that she's not all alone in the world. Even though Posie would just as soon have us for parents, and who can blame her?'

Ouch.

She hurried to catch up with Posie, but Ben slipped in front of her and swung the girl up onto his shoulders. They strode ahead, Posie giggling madly, leaving her with Claire.

'Er . . .' she said. 'How's your holiday going so far?'

'Lovely,' said Claire. 'Yours?'

'Not too bad.'

'Nice day, isn't it?'

'Yes. Very nice.'

There was no snarling, no spitting, no 'stay away from my man' vibe. Maybe all Claire was thinking about was her baby. Maybe she'd already refused the idea. She'd probably be worried that any baby genetically Romily's would have an unhealthy interest in aphids.

By the time they got to Pirates' Landing, Romily was ready to scream. Ben hadn't spoken a single word to her; he was entirely engaged with Posie, laughing, joking around, going on the rides with her and leaving Claire and Romily to stand there together, watching. Claire kept the conversation light and general, marvelling at the Lego reproductions of London and Paris.

Finally, finally, Posie ran off to play on the pirate ship-shaped playground. Romily took her chance to escape and buy them all cups of tea, and when she got back to the bench where they'd been sitting, she saw Ben exchange a look with Claire. They were holding hands, sitting close together.

'We've got a few minutes now to talk,' he said. 'About the baby.'

Relief. Yes, it was about that after all.

'Great,' said Romily. 'So I suppose the question is, do you want me to have this baby for you or not?' She gave them their paper cups, which were already starting to become mushy at the seams.

'It's an incredibly generous offer,' said Claire.

'It's the single most amazing thing anyone has ever offered to do for us,' said Ben.

'Oh, well, it's only nine months, right? What's nine months in the scale of things?'

'Do you really want to do it?' asked Claire. 'I know you told Ben you did, but I want to make completely certain that you're willing. It's a huge ask.'

Romily looked from one to the other of them. They were so hopeful. They'd be brilliant parents.

'Sure. Why not?'

Both of them relaxed noticeably, as if they'd been holding the same breath together.

'Thank you,' said Claire.

'No problem.' Romily kicked her feet, trying to be casual. Posie was still safely occupied in the play park. 'So how do we go about it, do you think?'

'Well,' said Claire. She was suddenly efficient. Much more like the Claire Romily knew. 'If we're doing this, we'll do it properly. We'll get you started on pre-natal vitamins right away, for a start.'

'We can make an appointment to see Dr Wilson at the clinic,' said Ben.

'Why do I need to see a doctor?' asked Romily.

'To make sure you're healthy,' said Ben. 'That your eggs are in good shape and there's no reason for you not to get pregnant.'

'A check-up. Right. I can see my own doctor for that, surely?'

'Dr Wilson can talk you through everything, though,' said Claire.

'What's there to talk about? I've had a baby. I know what it's like.'

'But this is a complicated procedure. They stimulate egg production, then they extract the eggs, and then they fertilize them and re-implant the embryo. And maybe you'd prefer that we found an egg donor, so you're not . . . er, genetically related to the baby?'

'That would be a delay, wouldn't it?'

'Months,' said Ben.

'I can see how it might come to it,' said Romily, 'but it seems unnecessarily complicated to medicalize it. To bother with the whole test-tube thing.' She faced Claire. 'I don't know how you went through all that. And all the drugs, all the tests.'

'I – well, we always thought that in the end, it would be worth it.'

'Does it hurt?'

Claire stiffened. 'It's uncomfortable. I wouldn't say it hurt. Not physically.'

'Far be it from me to criticize science,' said Romily, 'but it seems as if there's an easier way to do this. We could use a turkey-baster or something for artificial insemination. Then if

73

it doesn't work the first time, we can just try again. No doctors, no expensive equipment, no big deal.'

'No big deal?' said Claire.

'Well, you know what I mean.'

'I'll do some research,' said Claire. 'There has to be an ideal way of going about it.'

'Romily is a biologist,' Ben reminded her.

'But she's never actually *tried* to get pregnant,' Claire said, and then she put her hand to her mouth, as if she'd not meant to reveal that she knew that. 'I mean—'

'And to be honest, I do know a lot more about the mating habits of Japanese stag beetles than human reproduction,' Romily said. 'It can't be that complicated, though, can it? Hello, Sperm. Hello, Egg. Let's get together and make a . . . thing.'

'A thing,' Ben repeated. 'Are you sure that PhD isn't mail-order?'

'There is quite a lot you can do to maximize your chances of conceiving,' Claire said. 'Basal temperature charts, ovulation kits. I have a lot of it already. We can monitor your cycle, enhance your diet, start you on half an aspirin a day.'

'Right,' said Romily. 'Okay. It's all new to me, but it's your baby.'

'This is really going to happen,' said Ben. 'I can hardly believe it.' He gazed around him, at the children playing. 'I feel we should be drinking champagne or something.'

'And what's wrong with tea?' Romily asked.

'Nothing. Absolutely nothing.' He grinned at her and at Claire, and raised his paper cup. 'A toast. To our thing.'

'To our thing,' said Claire, tapping her cup against his.

Romily raised her own. 'To your thing.'

74

9

Smiley Face

Claire was heading down to the staff room for a break-time cup of tea, students chattering around her, when she saw Georgette stepping out of her classroom into the corridor ahead. There was no mistaking the narrow shoulders and hips, the brown hair twisted up into a ballet-dancer's bun. Georgette spotted Claire as she closed the door and her eyes widened with curiosity. Claire stopped as if she'd just remembered something and made a gesture with her hands, half-frustrated, half-apologetic. Then she turned round and headed back the way she had come.

'Aren't you coffeeing?' asked Lindsay, passing her in the doorway of the music block. Claire shook her head.

'I didn't do enough marking over the holiday,' she said.

'I'll bring you one. And a biscuit.'

'Thanks.'

Lindsay was lovely, in her early twenties, just starting out at St Dom's. She was in charge of the choral teaching. Claire wondered if she'd talk with Georgette in the staff room during break. If she did, she might be bringing back questions as well as a cuppa and a custard cream.

With everything that had happened, Claire had forgotten about Georgette, and how she knew about Claire's sudden departure from the baby shower. The Latin teacher was part-time, and Claire's path hadn't crossed with hers. Georgette had evidently forgotten too, but now she would be talking at break time. There were going to be curious glances in the staff room, and discreet enquiries about how she was doing. Claire needed to be prepared.

But what was she going to say? *Yes, I was upset because we lost the pregnancy, but it's all hunky-dory now because Ben's friend has offered to have a baby for us?*

St Dominick's was a lovely school. That was exactly what everyone called it: lovely. The grounds were lovely, the boarding houses were lovely, the students were lovely, the staff were lovely, the parents were lovely. Although it had stopped being a Catholic school some years ago, the prospectus still emphasized the caring atmosphere, the ethos of compassion. In Claire's experience, that compassion was often founded on quick-spreading gossip.

It had been the same, she supposed, when she'd been at school herself. She dimly remembered whispered bulletins, secretive notes. The difference was, they'd been children then, and none of the gossip had been about *her*.

One of her Year Nine students sat in the corner of the classroom, his spiky-haired head bent over a sheet of composition paper. It was the same pose he'd held through the entire last lesson. He looked up as Claire entered and headed for the desk where she'd left her laptop. 'Aren't you taking a break, Max?' she asked, falling into her default pleasant tone. As much as she might complain to herself about how everyone in the school was in each other's pockets, she loved the music and she loved the students. It was a good job. It was *lovely*.

'I wanted to keep working on this,' Max said.

'That's fine, though I'd have thought you'd want to see your friends after the holiday?'

He shrugged and scribbled on the paper.

'Did you have a good Easter?'

Max shrugged again. 'Boring,' he said, addressing the table rather than her. She could see he was writing musical notes on the staves – he'd already written half a sheet full – but he was too hunched over for her to be able to read it. His class-work, thus far, had been rather desultory, so she was pleased he was making an effort on this assignment. Composition was something that most children found very difficult.

'Do you mind if I use the computer in here while you're working?'

He grunted. His body language was the classic adolescent 'stay away', so she settled herself in front of her laptop and logged in, tilting the screen away from Max's line of vision.

There was so much information, so many support groups, so many discussion forums. From the internet, you'd never guess that most people managed to have children without any help whatsoever. She found her ovulation charts, and sent a blank one to the printer to make several copies for Romily.

The look of surprise on Romily's face when Claire had mentioned kits and tests. As if she hardly believed that such things existed. The two of them lived in different worlds.

If they went through with this, the baby would be genetically half Romily's. It might look just like her, though theoretically that wouldn't lead to too many questions; Ben had dark hair too, and dark eyes. Romily was intelligent and healthy. Posie, her child, was intelligent and healthy. What more could Claire possibly ask for?

It seemed, though, with every attempt to have a child, she

and Ben became more and more removed from the natural, normal way to have children. Making love hadn't worked, so they'd tried the charts, the temperature-taking, the ovulation kits. Then the clomiphene to stimulate egg production. Then the IVF, with her body at the mercy of drugs and instruments. And now they were involving a whole other person.

'Everyone asks the same thing,' Max said.

She stopped on her way to the printer. 'Pardon?'

'How are you? How was your holiday? They don't want a real answer. They just want to tell you about the amazing things *they* did.'

'Let's have an agreement,' said Claire. 'I won't tell you about my holiday if you won't tell me about yours.'

He didn't smile, but he stopped frowning a little. 'Yeah. I can live with that.'

'Do we need to stop off at the chemist?' Ben asked her. 'Or do you have some ovulation kits left?'

'I think I might have one.' She knew she did; she could picture it on her side of the bathroom cabinet. 'I printed off the charts at work.'

'We don't have to drop the stuff off today,' Ben said. 'We can take a little longer to think. There's no hurry.'

But he was so excited. Since they'd talked it over with Romily at Legoland, he'd been like a boy waiting for Christmas. So optimistic, so happy that they were giving it another go.

'No, we can go today if she's expecting us. Besides, it's bound to take ages before anything happens.'

By the time they finished at the chemist's rush hour was in full swing and it was difficult finding a place to park in the centre of town; however, Ben managed to squeeze in between two vans on the next road over from Romily's flat.

He took the box and the plastic bag and Claire walked with him around the block, though his footsteps were so rapid that she had to hurry to keep up. He went down the steps to the basement flat in front of her in the same characteristic way he went down the stairs in their house: quickly, almost skipping every other step, making a syncopated rhythm. He didn't have to knock before Romily opened the door.

'Hey,' she greeted Ben, and then she saw Claire behind him and her smile froze a little. 'Hi!'

'We've brought round the tests and charts,' Claire said – unnecessarily, because of course Ben had already arranged this with Romily, but she felt, somehow, as if she needed an explanation to be here. She'd never been inside the flat before. When she and Ben picked Posie up, Claire tended to wait in the car, with its engine running.

She followed Ben inside. She'd assumed, more or less, that Romily's flat would be chaotic and jumbled, like Romily herself. The door opened straight into the front room. A sofa and armchair were squeezed into the limited space, and books lined the walls, stacked in piles along the skirting boards. The walls were painted apple green, probably in an attempt to brighten up the flat, and although they were mostly bare, two framed canvases smeared with blue and orange hung over the sofa. Claire recognized Posie's work. Ben immediately put the box and bag on the coffee table and sat, with the ease of familiarity, in the armchair.

'This is nice,' Claire said, trying to hide the implication that she hadn't expected it to be.

'Ah. Thanks.' Claire followed Romily's gaze as it settled on the worn carpet and then glanced over two dying potted plants on the windowsill. 'Well, it does all right for me and Pose. Cup of tea?'

'That would be lovely.'

Romily scooped up Posie's crumpled school uniform from the sofa and kicked a pair of stray trainers aside on her way to the kitchenette, which was fitted into an alcove in the front room. Posie appeared in the doorway and ran to Ben to give him a hug, and then Claire.

'I didn't know you were coming over,' she said happily. 'Come to my room, I need to show you my base camp.'

Claire stroked the thick yellow fringe back from Posie's eyes. 'All right.'

'I'll come, peanut,' said Ben. 'Claire needs to have a cup of tea, she just finished work.'

' 'Kay. I'm in Peru today.' The child paused in tugging Ben's hand towards her room. 'Romily, can I have a honey sandwich?'

'Don't you think it's best not to tempt the killer bees?' said Romily.

'Peanut butter, then.'

'Two seconds.'

Posie scampered off, pulling Ben along with her. 'She's eaten every meal possible in that tent,' Romily said, switching on the kettle. 'God knows what the sheets look like by now.'

Claire settled onto the sofa, dislodging a pile of unopened post which had been perching on the arm. She stacked it onto the coffee table, neatly, beside the box they'd brought. It had not escaped her notice that Ben was leaving her alone with Romily whenever he got the chance. It was because she'd mentioned that she didn't know Romily very well.

'How do you take your tea?' Romily asked.

'White, no sugar.'

Romily opened a cupboard. 'I think I have some biscuits –

no, Posie must have eaten them. Would you like a peanut-butter sandwich as well? I do have honey if you prefer.'

'That's okay.'

'Do you mind if I do? I forgot to have lunch today.'

'Not at all.'

'Ben, want a sandwich?' Romily called. The 'no' came back muffled, as if he was already in the tent.

Claire watched as Romily smeared peanut butter on four pieces of white bread and stuck them together on two plates. She couldn't remember the last time she'd bought shop-made sliced white bread, let alone eaten it.

Romily cut each sandwich in half with the same knife she'd used to spread the peanut butter, squishing the filling out of the sides. 'Pose!' she called, starting on the tea. She looked carefully into two mugs and rejected them before settling on two mismatched flowered ones. Posie flitted into the room, collected her sandwich, and disappeared again.

'Won't it spoil her dinner?' Claire asked.

'Oh God no. Nothing spoils her dinner. It's like having a wild animal in the house, sometimes. As long as you keep it well-fed, it doesn't show its claws.'

Whenever Claire had Posie to stay, she carefully avoided giving snacks too close to mealtimes, which she made sure were balanced and healthy, full of different colours and textures. The little girl loved Claire's food and fell on it with an eagerness that always made Claire feel warm inside. From the looks of the kitchenette, Posie didn't get home cooking very often.

Romily put the mugs and the sandwich on the coffee table. The sandwich plate went on top of the pile of post. 'Your kid will probably have an all-organic, all-homemade diet,' she said, licking peanut butter off the side of her hand.

This was so close to what Claire had been thinking that she immediately shook her head. 'I might start out that way but I'm sure I won't keep it up.'

'You will. If anyone can, you can.'

Claire took a sip of her tea. It was too strong, made more the way Romily liked it than the way she did. She put the mug back down.

'They say you should steer clear of peanut butter while you're pregnant,' she said. 'If you've got a history of allergies.'

'Which I don't,' said Romily, taking a big bite of her sandwich. 'Has Ben?'

'He hasn't.'

Romily went on eating. Claire folded her hands on her lap. She could hear Ben and Posie playing in the bedroom. 'When do you think we should tell Posie about what we're trying to do?' she said.

Romily finished chewing before she replied. 'I'll find the right time,' she said and Claire heard the emphasis on the *I*.

Suddenly, for the first time since she had met Ben's friend, she had a sense of Romily's world, a whole world in which Claire herself played very little part, maybe even less than Romily played in Claire's. The green-painted walls, all these books and the people who sent the unopened letters. Claire saw Posie fairly often, but Romily woke up with the little girl, put her to bed, was responsible for her every minute of every day. Knew about her allergies or not, knew, down deep, that her daughter belonged to *her*.

'Of course,' Claire said quickly. 'I'm sorry. You will. I didn't mean to imply—'

'Let's take it one thing at a time. I have to get pregnant first,' said Romily, with her normal heartiness, and Claire was left wondering if she'd imagined the emphasis, the setting of boundaries. 'What's all this stuff you've brought?'

Claire opened the bag. 'I've got pre-natal vitamins – several kinds because I found one brand gave me indigestion. Some supplementary folic acid. I've got you a digital thermometer so you can do basal temperature readings, and some ovulation testing kits.'

'Basal temperature readings.'

'Your body temperature goes up slightly when you're ovulating. If you take your temperature every morning before you get up, and you do a chart and plot your results on it, you can establish your normal temperature, and it should be quite clear when it spikes. You're most fertile on the day or two beforehand. Here are some charts I did, for example.' She found them in her folder and showed them to Romily.

'Right.'

'Of course, if your cycle is regular, you can predict better when you'll ovulate, because it's about halfway through.'

'Okay.'

Claire paused. Could she ask if Romily's cycle was regular, or not? Normally it would be too intrusive, but in their position . . . ?

'You can also tell by the consistency of your cervical mucus,' she said instead. 'It's slippery when you're ovulating. There are some pictures here.'

'Right.' Romily wiped her hands on her jeans and took the photographs Claire had printed out.

'Of course sperm live for some time, so you're fertile before you ovulate as well. Experts say that the best thing to do is to have sex every few days. But that's not exactly possible in our situation.' Claire laughed, and then stopped because she sounded silly.

'I don't want to spend more time with the Big Bird Baster than necessary.'

'Well. You don't have to use that, obviously. I bought some syringes.'

Romily poked in the bag and found them, as well as the specimen cups. 'You've really thought of everything. Have you got pregnancy tests in here too?'

'I didn't— I don't usually plan ahead that far. Not at this stage.'

Romily stopped chewing. 'Oh. Okay. Of course not. I'm sorry.'

Claire looked at her for a moment. She was wearing jeans with holes in the knees, and a white button-up shirt that looked as if it had originally belonged to a man. She looked more like a twelve-year-old boy than a grown woman, and yet she was entirely certain of her own fertility. She made no sense to Claire at all.

The words burst out of her. 'Romily, I appreciate what you're doing so much but I think I need to ask, why are you doing this? Is it something you've just decided to do? It's – I just ask because I need to know because I . . .' She trailed off.

'What did Ben tell you?'

'He said it was because you cared about us. And because we helped you look after Posie when she was a baby.'

It sounded so unconvincing; not enough reason to offer to carry a baby for someone else and then give it up.

Romily's gaze darted in the direction of Posie's bedroom. She bit her lip, and appeared to come to a decision.

'Has he ever told you why I've got Posie?' she asked quietly.

Again, Claire wondered how much she was allowed to say. Ben and she had discussed Posie's estranged father, though

84

Claire had never met him. Ben talked about how irresponsible he was and how Posie and Romily were lucky to be shot of him. 'I don't think I know all the details.'

'I didn't mean to get pregnant. It was a total mistake. Her – father and I had pretty much split up before I even found out that I'd fallen pregnant; he was going away to work for the foreseeable future and we'd decided there wasn't any point staying together. And then I missed a period. I'd just started my PhD, I had hardly any money except for my grant and a bit that my dad left me. I'd never pictured myself as a mother. I told him and we both decided it was best if we got rid of it.'

Claire opened her mouth, and then closed it.

'I'm aware of the irony when compared to your situation,' Romily said.

'I . . . didn't know that.'

'Ben convinced me to have her. The day before the appointment, I . . . I asked him to go with me. I didn't have anyone else. We stayed up all night talking.'

'Where was I?' She'd remember if Ben had been out all night, even eight years ago.

'I think you were at your mother's.' Romily's cheeks were tinged pink; she didn't quite meet Claire's eye. 'He told me how precious life was. How the love between a mother and child was the most amazing thing ever, and he knew because he'd lost his mum. He . . . he knew that my mum died when I was a kid, too. So I cancelled the appointment.'

Claire didn't know how to react to this: the insight about her husband, or Romily, or their friendship. Not only did Romily have a life that was entirely separate from hers, she and Ben had history that Claire knew nothing about.

'He's very convincing,' Claire said.

85

'So you see,' said Romily, 'it all fits together. I've got Posie because of Ben. So you and Ben will have a child because of me. It's fair. That's why I'm doing it.'

She finished her sandwich, and wiped her mouth with her hand. Then she drained her tea and stood.

'You said that ovulation happens about halfway through my cycle?'

Claire pulled herself back to the present. 'About. It's different, obviously, for different women.'

Romily pursed her lips slightly, thinking. 'That's just about today. Let's see.' She grabbed one of the ovulation tests from the bag. 'What do you do, pee on the stick?'

'It's best at about two o'clock in the afternoon.'

'Well, if we never try, we never know, right? No point wasting time. I'll be right back.'

Claire sank into the sofa cushions as Romily left the room. This life-changing discussion between her husband and his friend had happened while she was visiting her parents, and she'd never heard anything about it. Why not? Because Ben was protecting Romily? Because Romily had asked him not to say?

Though the story was new to her, she wasn't surprised that Ben would advise Romily to keep her baby. He loved children. Eight years ago, they'd still been planning to have a big family. And he still missed his own mother, to this day.

It made sense, but still, she was staggered by the simplicity of the other woman's thought processes: *I had a baby because of Ben, so I'll have a baby for Ben.*

As if it were that easy.

Something poked into her back. Claire investigated behind the cushion and found an umbrella, slightly damp. And also a sock.

'Come and see my camp,' said Posie, who'd appeared next to the sofa. Claire put the umbrella and the sock on the floor and followed Posie down a short dark corridor to her room. It was tiny, a box room really; all of the surfaces that weren't taken up by the bed were covered with stacks of books and discarded clothes. There were several crumb-strewn plates scattered around. The flowered duvet was held up, tent-like, with some sort of pole. On closer scrutiny, it looked like a butterfly net.

Ben was in the tent already, lying full-length on his stomach and perusing a colouring book. He grinned at Claire. 'Quite a set-up, isn't it?'

'Where are you exploring?' Claire asked.

'I told you,' said Posie, 'it's Darkest Peru.'

'Oh. Yes, sorry, I forgot.'

Posie clambered into the tent, sitting cross-legged beside Ben. 'Come in! There's plenty of room and the crocodiles won't get you.'

The sheets were indeed smeared with peanut butter, though at least it looked fresh.

'Maybe we should help your mum change your sheets before I go.'

'That would ruin my tent.' Posie's hand darted out and clutched Claire's leg. 'Argh! Look! It's a Giant Hissing Cockroach!'

Claire jumped and looked around for an actual cockroach before she realized that Posie was playing.

'They only live in Madagascar.' Romily's voice came from the doorway. 'I thought you were in Peru.'

'It's a village in Madagascar *called* Peru,' replied Posie.

'Can't argue with that logic.'

'Plus, you had one once as a pet.'

'That was only a temporary housing solution for the cockroach,' Romily told Claire. 'It's long gone, don't worry. Anyway, I just did the test. Does a smiley face mean what I think it means?'

'Cockroaches don't have smiley faces,' said Posie.

'You got a smiley face?' asked Claire. 'On the test?'

'Very smiley.'

Ben scrambled out of the tent. Claire stared at Romily, who had her hands in her pockets and was looking pleased.

'With any luck we can make that thing tonight,' she said.

'What thing?' asked Posie crossly.

But it's too soon. It's too quick. It's too simple.

'Does this mean what I think it means?' asked Ben. He grabbed Romily's shoulders and she smiled up at him. 'You're ovulating *now*?'

'What are you all talking about?' Posie poked her head out. 'And the crocodiles have eaten your legs, by the way.'

Claire caught Romily's eye. Romily shook her head, slightly.

'It's a grown-up thing,' Romily said. 'It's boring. We'll tell you later, if it happens.'

'I said, they've eaten your legs!'

'Ouch!' yelled Ben, immediately falling to the floor and clutching his knees.

'We don't need to rush,' said Claire. 'Next month will be fine.'

'Well, I am sort of busy today with the crocodiles and all. Will I still be on the boil tomorrow, do you think?'

'I'd think so.'

'Tomorrow,' said Ben from the floor. 'We'll try tomorrow.'

Posie sat on his stomach. 'We need to go to Antarctica first,' she said.

10
Bombs Away

One of Claire's websites had advised choosing relaxing music to aid conception. Naturally, Romily had chosen *London Calling* by The Clash. She sat on the edge of the bed in Ben and Claire's guest room, holding the slim syringe in her hand.

They were waiting for her downstairs, though they didn't expect her for another half an hour. She was supposed to lie on the bed with her legs in the air for that long afterwards. With all these rules, it was a wonder that any children were ever born.

She'd made up her mind: she was ready. Thanks to her conversation yesterday with Claire, Claire wouldn't suspect she was doing this because of the way she felt about Ben. She could help her friends and keep her secret safe, too.

But when it came down to it, now that Ben's sperm was actually here in this syringe, warm in her hand, fresh from his body . . .

Romily glanced at the door to the ensuite bathroom. It wasn't too late to change her mind. She could squirt the syringe down the sink, wash it down with water, wait half an hour and go downstairs with her mission supposedly accomplished. No one would be very surprised if she didn't fall pregnant the first time. Or the time after. And by then, Ben and Claire might have found another option.

But they wouldn't have.

Romily exhaled and fell backwards onto the bed. She'd thought she'd be fine about it. But this was so intimate, this little syringe from Ben. It was even more intimate, theoretically, than if they had somehow got drunk and slept together by mistake. This was intentional. She was trying to have his baby.

Eleven years ago, Benjamin Lawrence had lived in the same university hall of residence as Romily. She was on the first floor and he was in the room directly above hers on the second. He was studying architecture, she was studying zoology. She first saw him when she was going in and he was going out, and her heart, used to being lonely, thumped in her chest so hard it nearly hurt. He was tall and sparkle-eyed, curly-haired and perfect. It had taken her three more weeks before she got up the courage to speak to him.

And a year later, before she'd got up the courage to tell him how she really felt about him, he'd met Claire.

She was being silly. This wasn't an intimacy; it was a favour. It was a biological transaction, an act to ensure the propagation of the species. It was an experiment, albeit one that she had to do with her trousers off.

Claire and Ben were waiting downstairs for their new life to begin.

Romily arranged herself on the bed. On the CD, Joe Strummer sang in his broken-glass voice. His baby was getting a brand-new Cadillac.

Dear Thing,

When I was a little girl, I had a book called How Babies Are
Made. It was beautifully illustrated with photographs of
paper cut-outs of the womb, the fallopian tubes, the sperm.
The illustrations were so exquisite and careful that the sperm
even had shadows. The book started with a hen and a cock-
erel, and in the following pages the egg was laid and the
chick was hatched. Then it showed two dogs mating, and
some puppies being born. Finally, it showed a man and a
woman lying in bed together under a flowery blanket. They
were smiling and holding each other.

   You weren't conceived that way.

   At some point, all of us want to know where we came from.
But I've come to realize that when we ask about our origins,
we're not really asking about the egg and the sperm, the cut-
outs and the shadows. We're asking about the stories. How
our mother and father met. Why they loved. Stories count
more than cells and DNA.

   So it might interest you to know that you came into being
during one spring afternoon in a theme park inspired by
children's building blocks. They're quite interesting, these
blocks. They're manufactured in plastic with interlocking
parts, and each of them can be combined with any others in

91

an infinite number of ways. You could start with a single block, add another and another and some more, and end up with an elephant. Or a spaceship. A castle, a nuclear missile, a garden of flowers.

In that one block lies an entire universe of possibility. Nothing about it is pre-determined or inevitable. The final form that block will take depends on the combinations that are made the fortunate mistakes, the leaps of imagination, the environment and chance. It will become something more than itself.

You were conceived when three people came together and agreed to try to make you. We didn't know what we were letting ourselves in for. But I think it's important for you to know that it was a beautiful day, and that everything we did, we did because of love.

All the other things were just technicalities.

11
Testing

As usual, Romily didn't hear her alarm; she only woke up when it stopped.

'Shit,' she muttered, reaching over and picking up the clock. Ten past nine. And the battery was dead, again, so it might be later.

She launched herself out of bed, yelling, 'Posie! Get up!' Pulling on her clothes from yesterday, she went to Posie's bedroom. Her daughter was a lump under the covers; Romily shook her shoulder. 'Wake up, Pose. We're late.'

Posie grunted, turned over and went back to sleep. Romily paused while gathering Posie's school uniform and shook her again. 'Wake *up*. You're going to be late for school.'

She had to pull the duvet off before Posie was roused enough to sit up. 'What?' she said, brushing her fringe from her eyes.

'Late.'

'Romily. Again? I'm going to get detention.'

'Well, maybe you should listen to your alarm clock when it goes off.'

'What about yours?'

In the lounge, Romily's phone was ringing. 'Get dressed,' she said, throwing Posie's uniform on the bed. 'I need to answer that.'

'I don't believe I'm going to have to stay in at lunch because of you,' muttered Posie as she pulled off her night-gown. Romily ignored her – not because Posie wasn't right, but because arguing wasn't going to make them any earlier – and went to the other room to dig out her phone. As soon as she found it in her jacket pocket it stopped. One missed call: Ben.

Rain streaked down the windows to the street. Where were Posie's wellies? Romily got down on her knees and looked under the sofa. There was one . . . what about the other?

'You're going to have to have school dinner today,' she called, checking under the armchair.

'It's fish.' Posie's voice, from the other room, dripped with disgust. 'It stinks.'

'Well, you don't eat fish. What's the vegetarian option?'

'Fake fish.'

There. Right back, near the wall. Romily stretched, reached, and snagged the welly with the tips of her fingers. When she pulled it out, dust bunnies dangled from both the welly and her arm.

'I'm sorry, Pose, but I don't have time to pack you a lunch today. Just hold your nose or something.' She blew off the dust and set about looking for her own boots. By the time she'd assembled them, her phone had beeped with Ben's message.

Posie came in, pulling on her cardigan, her face sour. 'Can we take the car?' she asked. 'I hate today already, and I just got out of bed.'

'We'd be even later with the traffic. We'll have to walk. Where's your homework?'

'It was spellings. I have a test. You were supposed to go through them with me last night.'

'Why didn't you remind me?'

'You never mentioned it.'

'It's *your* homework, Posie. *You're* supposed to remember.'

'Jesus Christ, Romily, I'm only seven.'

Romily closed her eyes, tried to count to ten, only got to four because they were really late. 'Have you washed your face?'

Posie turned around without a word. Romily picked up her phone again and opened Ben's text message. *So have you taken the test yet?*

For a confused moment Romily wondered how Ben knew about Posie's spelling test, and then she remembered. It was two weeks later already.

She hurried to her bedroom and reached in the top drawer, where she'd stowed all the things that Claire had brought round. She took out a narrow box, realized it was an ovulation test, and tried again until she found a pregnancy one. *99% ACCURATE FROM THE FIRST DAY YOUR PERIOD IS DUE*, it screamed on the side of the box. It was some sort of comment on the state of her life, when her male friend knew her menstrual cycle better than she did. The test was too small to conceal in her hand, so she shoved it up her jumper.

Posie was in the bathroom, frowning at herself in the mirror and brushing her teeth at the slowest rate known to humankind, and the church bells down the street were chiming the half-hour, so Romily didn't have time to pee on a stick right now. 'Come on, come on,' she said to Posie in passing, and hid the test in her handbag before her daughter

95

could stomp out into the living room. She bundled Posie into wellies and a mac, threw on her own boots and jacket, and got them each a cereal bar and a banana from the bowl before they rushed out of the door.

'This one is all brown and spotty,' said Posie. Romily exchanged it for hers, which was slightly less ripe. Posie wrinkled her nose and began to eat it as they walked.

'We've got to hurry.' Romily peeled her own banana and remembered she'd forgotten to take her pre-natal vitamin. She'd dumped some outdated vitamins that she'd bought and never taken, and decanted the pre-natal ones into the bottle in her medicine cabinet. Posie might not know what the word 'pre-natal' meant, but she did know how to use a dictionary. And besides, the picture of the gurning baby on the bottle sort of gave it away.

She'd take it later. In her handbag, her phone beeped again. Ben would be at work already, anxious for news.

'Come *on*, Posie.'

'I can't eat and run at the same time.'

'That doesn't mean you have to go at a snail's pace.' She took Posie's hand and tugged her along the pavement. Not for the first time she wished she'd chosen to rent a flat a little bit closer to Posie's school. Like, ideally, across the street. But when Posie was a baby the most important thing had been to find something affordable with two bedrooms, close enough to the museum and university so that she didn't have to waste money on petrol or buses; she hadn't thought ahead to the school run. And besides, today they were so late that nothing short of a Tardis was going to get them to school on time.

'Romily, you're pulling my arm off.'

'Walk faster, then.'

'I can't. My feet hurt. My shoes are too tight.'

'They are? Since when?' Romily ditched the banana peels into a bin and rushed Posie across the street in a momentary gap in traffic.

'I don't know. I think I need new ones.'

'Oh, Posie, why didn't you tell me?'

'I did. Just like I told you about the spelling test.'

'You didn't.'

Posie set her face into a scowl and it stayed there all the way to school. Romily had to buzz at the gate to be let into the empty playground. She hauled Posie up the steps into the school office.

'I'm really sorry we're late,' she said to the school secretary, who regarded her with unfriendly eyes. 'The battery went dead on the alarm clock.'

'Again?'

'I'll get a new one.'

'Mrs Summer—'

'Doctor.'

'Dr Summer, Mariposa's teacher is worried that her tardiness is affecting her education.'

'I'll get a new battery and a new clock. Tonight. Promise. While I'm here, I've got to pay for Posie's school dinner.' She dug in her jacket pocket and pulled out the only coins she found: one pound and two ten-pence pieces. 'Er . . . can I pay you the extra tomorrow?'

The secretary took the coins and went back to her typing as if she were washing her hands of this entire mess.

Romily knelt down and pushed Posie's damp fringe back. 'I'm sorry about your shoes, Pose, but you'll have to put up with them for today. We'll go shopping for new ones after school.'

Posie turned away and headed for the door to her classroom.

'Good luck on the test,' Romily called after her. She didn't reply. Romily watched her, the narrow shoulders in her mac, the tights sagging at the knees, the hair that hadn't been combed properly. So small and young, the kid with only one parent. Could've been herself at that age.

Romily straightened up and sighed. Then she took off out of the door at a run for work, pulling her hood up over her head to shield her from the rain.

Her way took her down the towpath along the Thames, passing ducks and moor hens on the water and mothers with pushchairs and bicyclists on the path. She swerved to avoid goose droppings, ran past council blocks and expensive towers of flats. The rubber soles of her boots slapped on the pavement and made echoes in the underpass. The Brickham Museum was in the centre of town, in the former Town Hall – a Victorian gothic building of red and grey brick. From the front, it had swooping arched windows, pointed towers, a cathedral-like entrance with modern glass automatic doors. She slipped through them, returning the hello from the volunteer who was already standing with her clipboard, ready to greet visitors. Downstairs, the museum charted the history of Brickham, from medieval abbey to Victorian industry to modern shopping. Romily made her way through the box room, with its rolling shelves of school lending boxes, and signed out the key for the entomology collection. She went straight up the narrow back staircase, past the offices where she waved at the women already hard at work, to the third floor and the inner study, a crowded room with three desks, three computers, shelves and shelves of things waiting to be put away, and a small window up high in the north wall.

No one else was here yet. She breathed a sigh of relief, hung up her wet coat in the corner and put her bag on the only desk which had a view of the window. On a Tuesday, she had to battle for the desks with a volunteer working to catalogue the biscuit tin collection and an art student doing a PhD on equestrian statuary. Not that she minded either of them – Sheila and Layla were nice enough, and she'd been a PhD student and a volunteer herself in her time – but she'd been working here longer than either of them and she liked being able to see a little daylight.

But this wasn't the place where her work really lay. That was up another flight of stairs, a small and even narrower one that ended in a single door covered with yellow warning stickers. She went up, unlocked the door and stepped in.

The mothball scent of naphthalene, the noise of the fans constantly whirring. Some cabinets were modern green-military metal, others mahogany. She knew the contents of all of them, but hers was the big rosewood one at the back of the room under the sloping rafters. The one with the glass door and the narrow shelves, each one with a brass knob. There was a small brass plaque on the top of the cabinet: *Collected by Amity Blake, 1847–1907.*

She opened the glass door and carefully slid out drawer No. 70. Watching her feet on the steps, she brought the glass-topped drawer downstairs and put it on the desk. It contained dozens of insects, each secured with a pin, each labelled in a tiny script with a reference number to a catalogue which had long ago been lost.

Amity Blake had been the only daughter and heir of brick manufacturer Absolom Blake. Very little of her history was known, except for the fact that when she was twenty-eight and a spinster her father had died, leaving her his entire fortune, and instead of using it as a dowry to attract a man, Miss Amity Blake had gone travelling around the world collecting insects. Miss Blake wasn't unusual – Romily had the impression that every Victorian with time to spare spent it larking about in fields with a net and a killing jar – except that she was a single woman.

The collection had been donated to the museum not long after Amity's death, and some of it had been displayed, though two world wars and ever-decreasing financial backing meant that the collection had never been catalogued properly.

Romily had first discovered Amity's rosewood box of wonders when she was a newly minted PhD student. One look and she'd fallen in love. Working in the time she probably should have spent writing up her own research, especially with a toddler at home, Romily had identified species from Africa, India, Malaysia and the Philippines, all places supposedly off-limits to a Victorian spinster. Romily had convinced one of the museum's local history volunteers to look for a surviving photograph of Amity, but they hadn't found one. It didn't matter to Romily. She could picture Amity perfectly: an upright, unhandsome woman, with a netted hat and sensitive fingers and a pair of pince-nez for delicate work. She'd have hacked through miles of bush wearing near enough a full-length gown.

She was Romily's hero.

After she'd finished her PhD she'd stayed on as a volunteer, balancing unpaid work on the collection with a bit of teaching and a bit more work waiting tables in a local café, writing grant applications after Posie went to sleep. Nineteenth-century female scientists were trendy, and there was local interest besides, and Romily had been given funding to further catalogue the collection.

100

Drawer No. 70 was full of dun-brown moths. Amity tended to collect a variety of different species rather than many individuals of the same species, and she liked to arrange them by colour rather than by species or where they were collected, which made Romily's job that bit more challenging and exciting. A Cabbage White butterfly from Berkshire might be nearly rubbing wings with an *Appias phaola* from the Congo. She reached into her handbag for her glasses case and found the pregnancy test.

Oh yes. That was the first thing. She pulled out her phone as well. There were five messages and three missed calls, all from Ben. Of course, he was going crazy waiting to hear whether he was about to have a baby or not.

So not only was she a rubbish mother, she was a rubbish friend. Decisively, she hid the test back in her handbag and, carrying it, left her domain for the staff toilets. On her way, she stuck her head into the staff kitchen where Hal, the museum manager, was gloomily stirring his cup of tea.

'Hal, can you log into the computer on desk one for me, please?'

'Dr Summer.'

She stopped. 'Yes, Hal?'

'Dr Summer. You are an educated woman. Can you explain to me why, in a country that is no longer a global superpower, we do not celebrate the great legacy of knowledge that is the only thing that remains to us?'

'It's a recession, Hal. The council puts museum services at the bottom of the list. Did you have a budget meeting yesterday, by any chance?'

'We need to be sexier,' he muttered. 'Provide a more relevant experience to the community. Science for its own

101

sake is dead. Mark my words, we'll have Simon Cowell doing educational voiceovers next.'

He drank deep of his tea, as if pronouncing the doom of the world had made him thirsty.

Her phone beeped again, reminding her that she had other matters to attend to. Swearing under her breath, she resumed her original path to the staff toilets.

It was the second plastic stick she'd peed on in just over two weeks. She pulled up her jeans and waited in the cramped toilet cubicle. The result came up almost instantaneously, in plain, clear text.

Pregnant, 1–2 weeks.

Some emotion rose up in a rush from her stomach, clenched her heart, closed her throat. Her surroundings wobbled. *It's his baby*, she thought, and she leaned against the wall of the cubicle.

I'm going to have his baby.

She didn't know whether that thing lodged in her throat was a laugh or a scream. She closed her eyes and forced in a breath, and then another. What should it be? Which one did she want? Which was safer?

She hadn't thought it would really happen. Not so fast. Not the first go. She'd thought she'd have time to reconsider.

But she had reconsidered, before they'd done the bit with the syringe. And she'd decided she would do this.

And now it was done. Their cells had met and merged. They were dividing inside her to make a brand-new person, and it was way too late to turn back.

She listened to the cistern running, the ventilation fan with the missing blade, and thought about how weird it was that so pivotal a moment in so many people's lives should be taking place in a lavatory. And not a very pleasant lavatory at that.

For the next nine months she was going to be the vessel for someone else's child. And though she'd downplayed it, nine months was, in fact, quite a *big* chunk of time. Posie would be nearly eight by the time this baby – *this baby!* – was born. Anything could happen in that time.

So what did she want to do right now? Did she want to laugh, or did she want to scream?

'Don't tell anyone,' Claire said into the phone. She was standing with her back against the music staff-room door, so that nobody would come in by mistake.

'What?' said Ben, forty miles away in his office in London. 'This is big news. We're going to have a baby!'

'But we might not.' She couldn't breathe. The terror, again, of having something to lose.

'Claire, Romily's not going to change her mind. You don't know her like I do. Once she's decided something, she sticks with it one hundred per cent.'

'That's not what I meant.'

'Oh. I know, sweetheart. It's frightening. But Romily's healthy, she's had a baby before. There's no reason to think that anything will go wrong this time.'

This time. Because Romily, unlike Claire, was able to carry babies.

That wasn't what he meant. She swallowed. 'I just think it would be prudent to keep it to ourselves until the end of the first trimester, that's all.'

'But don't you want to talk about it with your friends? Helen?'

'Not until it's certain. And Ben, what if she does change her mind?'

'She won't.'

Claire thought about Romily's untidy flat, her spontaneous meals, the laundry filed in the sofa cushions. 'I don't know if she's as single-minded and determined as you think she is.'

'This is the person who got a PhD whilst looking after a colicky baby.'

'Well, to be honest, we did a lot of the looking after too.'

'I think we should celebrate, just us. It's a big step. I told Romily I'd leave early and take everyone to the Swan for dinner.'

'Including Posie? Because I don't think Romily has told her anything about this yet.'

'Including Posie. She deserves to celebrate too. She's going to be a . . . what is it? Godsister?'

'Half-sister,' whispered Claire.

'Godsister. I think Romily should be godmother, don't you?'

'You're getting way ahead of yourself, Ben. Just like you always do.'

He laughed. 'You're right. I'm excited, that's all. I'll pick you up at home at five.'

'Okay. But don't tell anyone. Please.'

He paused.

'Oh no, Ben. You haven't, have you?'

'Only Justin. And Elaine. But they've got children, they know how it works.'

'Having children doesn't mean you know how it works when you can't have children.'

'Claire, it will be fine.' His voice was soothing. 'It's all going to work out. I promise you.'

She twisted the hem of her skirt around her finger. 'I don't have a good feeling about it. It's happened too quickly and too easily.'

'Maybe it's happening quickly and easily because this child was meant to happen.'

'And our babies, the ones that you and I were trying to make, weren't?'

'No, I don't mean that, of course I don't. It's just – this feels good. Doesn't it?'

'It felt good the last time, too.'

He paused again. 'Sweetheart, I thought you were happy about this. I thought you agreed it was the best thing to do.'

'I agreed that it was the *only* thing to do. There's a difference.'

'Why can't you just be happy?'

'Because she's pregnant with your baby and I'm not.'

'This is *our* baby.'

'I have to go. The bell just went.'

She pressed the 'end call' button, her heart pounding in her ears. She breathed deeply, for two full minutes. She hadn't known she'd feel jealous until she said it.

She hadn't known that she would suddenly, wholeheartedly hate the woman who was carrying her baby instead of her.

Max was in her classroom, bent over a guitar. He'd taken to hanging out there at lunchtimes, practising whatever songs he liked, shifting from one to the other. Claire didn't see the harm, and the music was pleasant.

He glanced up when she entered the room. 'Are you all right, Mrs Lawrence?'

'What? Oh yes, Max. Thank you. Fine. You?'

He strummed a chord and then another.

'I'm fine too,' he said.

'I think I'll have the mushroom stroganoff,' Romily said to the waitress and folded up her menu.

'I'll have sausages and mash,' said Posie.

'They're real meat sausages, Pose.'

'That's okay. I've had them before. It's Ben's favourite.' Posie beamed across the table at Ben, who beamed back. Though to be fair, Ben hadn't stopped beaming from the moment he'd picked them up at the flat.

'How about I give you a taste of mine,' he suggested.

'No, I want a whole sausages and mash for myself. Romily says she doesn't mind if I have meat if I want to have it because it's my choice but she's not cooking it.' Her voice sounded exactly like Romily's when she said it.

'I'll have the mushroom stroganoff too,' Ben told the waitress. 'That way, if Posie doesn't like the sausages we can swap.'

'I'll like it.' Posie sucked milk through her bendy straw.

Romily, who happened to know that Ben was not keen on mushrooms, mouthed *Thanks*.

She'd been beaming too. She'd decided, after giving Ben the news, that the best feeling for her to have was unalloyed joy. Uncomplicated, straightforward, and happy. Why choose to feel any other way?

'I'll have a salad,' said Claire.

'That's not much,' Ben said. 'You're not planning on stealing my mushrooms too, are you?'

'I'm not very hungry.'

Claire hadn't said a lot, just played with her mineral-water glass. Romily wondered if, now that they'd started for real on this baby thing, she was getting cold feet. If she'd decided she didn't want to do this, it was going to be pretty crappy for Romily and Ben. And the baby, of course, whatever it was.

Ben seemed cheerful enough. 'Want to go outside and see the ducks, peanut?'

'Yeah.' Posie hopped off her chair and they went out of the door of the pub, down to the Thames which flowed at the end of the beer garden.

Romily was left with Claire. She seemed to be being left alone with Claire a lot, lately. She cleared her throat.

'So,' she said. 'It's good news, eh? I didn't expect it to happen so fast. But that's good, anyway. You two have been waiting long enough.'

Claire appeared to come back from whatever distant cloud she'd been floating on since they'd entered the pub. 'Yes. We've been waiting a long time.'

'Well, hopefully only nine months now. Posie was two weeks late, so maybe we'll have to wait a little bit longer for this one too.'

'Do you feel any different?'

'No, not really. I wouldn't have known if I didn't do the test.'

'You don't even feel pregnant?'

Romily shrugged. 'But I didn't feel pregnant with Posie, either. I didn't quite believe it until my belly started to grow.'

Claire was watching her with an expression that was calm, unemotional. No wonder Romily could never figure out what she thought.

'Do you intend to stay vegetarian throughout your pregnancy?' Claire asked.

'Um. Well, yes.'

'We'll have to look into additional supplements to make sure the baby gets everything it needs.'

Romily opened her mouth to say that Posie had grown pretty well on Pot Noodles and veggie burgers, but Ben and

Posie came back then, so instead she said, 'Excuse me, I'm going to nip to the loo before our food shows up.'

Ben helped her by pulling back her chair for her, and when Romily stood up she caught a glimpse of Claire's face. And this time, she could read the expression. It was un-disguised dislike.

Then it was gone.

12
What to Expect

Ben turned up at Romily's flat on a Sunday with two enormous cardboard boxes.

'Is it a present for me?' Posie wanted to know immediately.

'No, but I do have this.' He took a notebook covered with multicoloured birds out of his pocket, and a matching pen out of the other pocket. 'I thought maybe you could write me a story in it.'

Romily, who had already glimpsed *What to Expect When You're Expecting* beneath the flap of one of the boxes, added, 'In your room.'

'Fortuitous!' Posie took the notebook and pen and disappeared.

'Are you sure you really want a kid?' Romily asked Ben. 'She's been up since five thirty this morning. We've already gone around the park four times on her bicycle and she's still not worn out. And then she cost me six quid in cake and hot chocolate, and asked me what the difference was between Jesus and Mohammed.'

Ben chuckled. 'Clever girl.'

'Children are expensive and they never let you sleep.'

Romily sank onto the sofa. 'You are heading for eighteen years of being torn between wanting them to go away and leave you alone for a minute, and being petrified when they wander out of your sight.'

'I'll take her out this afternoon if you want to have a nap.'

'I wouldn't mind, to be honest. She was go go go yesterday, too.' Romily winced, and crossed her arms in front of her chest. 'And my boobs are killing me.'

'That's good news.'

'You wouldn't think so if they were attached to your chest.' Romily poked open the first box. 'Has Claire been shopping?'

'Spent all day yesterday at it. I have no idea what's in there.'

'One, two, three, four pregnancy books.' Romily lifted them out and peered inside. 'More vitamins. Cocoa butter. It's a bit early to worry about stretchmarks, don't you think?'

'She's very thoughtful.' Ben went to Romily's little fridge and took out a Coke. He leaned against the kitchenette arch, crossing his legs at the ankles, completely at home, and cracked the can open. She realized this was the first time she'd been alone with him, even for a minute, since confirming that she'd carry his baby. Those few moments alone with a syringe of his sperm didn't really count. She delved back into the box.

'Lavender essential oil. A Chopin CD? Am I supposed to be playing this to your embryo to make it more intelligent or something?'

'I have no idea. Maybe Claire thinks it will help you relax.'

'Because Posie is the cleverest little kid I know and she mostly listened to Green Day.'

'Claire's done a lot of research. She's very good at this sort of thing.'

Romily pulled out a cloth-covered notebook, embellished with embroidered flowers and suns and clouds. '*My Pregnancy Journal*,' she read. 'You have got to be kidding me. What am I supposed to write in there? *Five weeks: my tits hurt. Three months: getting fat. Six months: really fat now. Nine months: oh look – a baby.*'

'I think she had some ideas about that. There's a printout or something.'

Romily unfolded a piece of paper that had been slipped between the pages. '*Children who have unconventional beginnings – those conceived via surrogacy, or those who are adopted or fostered from birth – can often benefit from being reassured that they were wanted before they were even born. Write letters to your unborn child, describing your emotions. Explain why he or she is so important in your life. This can be a good idea for the adoptive parents as well as the surrogate or biological parents, and will give a rich resource for your child when he or she is curious about his or her origins.*' She put down the paper. 'So she wants me to write letters as well as keeping a diary? This is feeling more like a homework assignment than incubating a kid, Ben.'

'It's only a suggestion.'

'Letters describing my emotions. What the hell is *that* all about? Why would a kid I'm not keeping care how I feel while it's using my womb-space for nine months? Even if I did want to spill whatever non-existent emotions I had onto a page for posterity, which I do not, I can't think of anything worse – and where am I going to find the time anyway, when I'm popping vitamins every five minutes?'

Ben held up his hand. 'Okay, okay, it's not compulsory. Claire likes sharing emotions. Talking things through.'

'I don't.'

'I know.'

'The whole thing makes me feel like I'm going to come out in hives. Claire can write the letters if she thinks it's important. The best thing for this baby is for me to just fade into the background. It's not mine, it's yours.'

'Well, we did hope you'd be his or her godmother.'

'You did? Or Claire did?'

He grimaced slightly, and Romily could see she'd hit a sore point.

'She doesn't even like me much,' Romily said, putting the diary and the printout back in the box. 'I mean, not to make things difficult for you, Ben, but you have to admit we hardly have anything in common these days except for you. Which is fine, because I don't have to have anything in common with her. As long as she wants this baby, that's good with me. But I don't think she trusts me.'

'Of course she trusts you.'

'Then why has she sent half a tonne of vitamins and a Chopin CD?'

Ben sighed. He came and sat down next to Romily on the sofa.

'You have to understand Claire,' he said. 'So much of what has happened with us for the past few years has been completely beyond her control. She didn't choose to have faulty eggs, nor to lose the pregnancy. You can't blame her for wanting to be part of the process.'

'She *is* part of the process. She's getting the baby at the end of it, isn't she?'

'Yes, Romily. But I think she's going to want more input.'

'For example, giving me homework to do?'

'Well, I thought she'd want to come to the midwife appointments, maybe. And it's natural that she wants to look after you while you're carrying a baby for us. We both do.'

'That's fair enough. It's your baby. But it's my body.'

Ben frowned. 'Are you having second thoughts about this now?'

'Oh, no,' she said quickly. 'No no no no. Of course not. It's just . . . all of this is a bit much. All this stuff. I have to keep it hidden until we tell Posie, for one thing. And I don't need it, not really.'

'But if you do need something, anything, you'll let us know, won't you? I've been looking into all the legal ins and outs and I've made an appointment with a solicitor. The most important thing seems to be that we can't give you anything that could be construed as payment, because that's illegal in the UK. But we can cover your expenses, and your maternity clothes, and whatever pay you might lose for time off work, so you're not out of pocket.'

'Don't be ridiculous,' Romily said, uncomfortable. 'If I have trouble accepting a Chopin CD, I'm not about to ask you for a new wardrobe. Anyway, this isn't the issue. The issue is that I can't be pregnant and be a mum and be working and jump through hoops, too, to fulfil what Claire thinks a perfect pregnancy would be like. I don't have time for everything.'

Ben took Romily's hand. 'She's never had it,' he said softly. 'Never once, what's easy for you. And preparing for every eventuality is how she copes with uncertainty. Let her be a little part of it, Romily.'

His palm and fingers were warm around hers. Almost guiltily, she withdrew her hand.

Claire doesn't know what she does have, she thought. *Nor that I want him, too.*

'All right,' she said.

★

'No,' said Claire.

Ben had been waiting for her when she got in from her walk. There was a large bouquet of flowers beside him on the table, in a vase that was too small for them. She ignored them.

'You don't have to take any time off work,' he said. 'She's made the first appointment for five o'clock. You'll have plenty of time to get there.'

'I'm not going to a midwife appointment.'

'Claire, this is our baby. I thought you'd want to be involved. More involved than sending boxes of supplies for me to deliver. Don't you think you'll regret it later, if you aren't?'

'This isn't about regret. This is about self-preservation. I know what I can and cannot do, Ben. I can buy vitamins, I can buy supplies from the internet. I can research what's best for a developing pregnancy. But I cannot go and sit in a midwife's reception room next to a woman who's having a baby for me.'

'Why not, darling? I'd be there too.'

'It will be full of pregnant women. I'll feel like a failure.'

'You're not a failure. We're going about things a different way, that's all.'

Claire went past him to the tap and got herself a glass of water. 'Let's stop talking about this. We're just going round in circles. I'm not attending the midwife appointment, not this one. I can't.'

'No one in the waiting room is going to know that you've tried to get pregnant,' Ben said. 'They'll think you're Romily's sister, or her friend, or her lesbian lover. And who cares what they think, anyway? This is about us.'

'But I'll know. I always know.'

He sighed. 'And I'm in the middle here with Romily. You

haven't seen her since the day she took the positive test. She's worried that you don't like her.'

'Right at this moment, I don't.'

'So you can't go to the midwife with her, fair enough. But what if you did something else together, just the two of you relaxing and having a good time? I could get you a spa day—'

Claire laughed, once, humourlessly. 'A pregnant woman can't do a spa day. You're not allowed any of the treatments.'

'Okay, something else then. Lunch, or the cinema. A gallery.'

'Ben, she's pregnant with your baby and I'm not. A visit to a gallery isn't going to change that.'

Ben got up. He put his hand on her neck, and stroked his thumb down her nape. Claire didn't respond.

'She's not my wife,' he said. 'You are.'

'Don't ask it of me, Ben. Please.'

'She's doing the most incredible thing for us. For *us*, Claire.'

'She told me it was for you. Because you convinced her to have Posie.'

'Whatever she does for me, she does for you too. She knows that.'

Claire put down her glass of water and braced both her hands against the sink. It was a salvaged farmhouse sink of heavy white porcelain, cold and smooth under her hands. 'I've been trying to sort it all out in my head, Ben. I know it's an incredible thing. I know I should be happy that we're going to have a family. But it's all been too fast. I haven't had time to assimilate it. You have to let me come to terms with it in my own time.'

'Maybe you should write a diary, or letters. Like you asked

115

Romily to do. It could help you sort out your emotions.'

'I'm not sure the baby would want to read what's going through my head right now.'

'I hate to break it to you, Claire, but I don't think the baby's going to come out reading.'

She managed a shaky laugh.

'I love you,' he told her. 'I'll accept that maybe I can't understand how you feel, not exactly. But I think it's important that you try.'

'Maybe . . . maybe later. After the first trimester, when it's safer.'

'I know you're worried about losing the baby. But there's no reason to think it'll happen this time.'

And don't you think your certainty hurts me? she thought, but she didn't say it. Instead, she turned and went into his arms.

'I don't have that innocence any more,' she said, her cheek against his chest. 'I can't afford to hope.'

He kissed the top of her head. 'I'll have to hope for both of us, then.'

13

Rupert or Guinevere

'Romily,' said Posie, 'why have we got a big box of vegetables outside our front door?'

Romily, who had been trying to tighten her bra straps as she walked so that her boobs didn't move quite so much, and had just about given it up and decided she needed to buy some new, proper bras, preferably ones involving some sort of hydraulic lift system, stopped and looked where Posie was pointing. Sure enough, there was a big box of vegetables outside their front door. *Stonyfield Organic Farm*, it said on the side.

'I think we've been visited by the veg fairy,' said Romily, though of course she knew who'd arranged it. Lady Bountiful, sending gifts from a distance. She'd be sending a cleaner next; Romily hadn't missed the way she'd looked around the flat the one time she'd been there. Because God knew that healthy babies were never born in a house that had a few dust bunnies. 'Help me take it in.'

It looked like a huge pile of healthiness in their otherwise barren kitchen. Cabbage, onions, leeks, courgettes. Great. All stuff she had to cook, and which created smells too. Smells were a problem just now; everything made her want to retch. Romily peeled a carrot, gave it to Posie and then lay down on the sofa, putting her feet up on the arm. All by themselves, her eyelids drifted shut.

The morning sickness was new. She'd never been so much as nauseated when pregnant with Posie. But this was nearly constant, dragging her down, stopping her from thinking properly. For the last three mornings, she'd had to get up at 5 a.m. to run to the toilet and vomit. At the museum, she couldn't even get close to anything remotely smelling of naphthalene; she'd been stuck working on the database. Eating supposedly helped, but she wasn't ever hungry.

She hadn't mentioned it to Ben, knowing if she did, a big box of organic, safe nausea remedies would turn up at her door.

Crunch.

She opened her eyes. Posie was standing over her, chewing on her carrot.

'Nice rabbit impression, Pose.' She closed her eyes again. 'I'm really tired, love. I'll make tea in a minute, I just need to rest first. Why don't you look up cabbage recipes on the internet?'

'I know what's wrong with you.'

Her blue eyes were serious under her blonde fringe. Romily sat up.

'There's nothing wrong with me. I'm absolutely fine, Pose.'

'No, you're not. You're tired all the time. You keep on taking those pills when you think I'm not looking. You keep on sending me out of the room when you talk to Ben and Claire. And now you're trying to get us to eat more healthy food.'

Romily made a mental note to no longer underestimate

118

Posie's powers of observation. 'None of that means anything is wrong, Posie. I'm just trying to get healthier.'

'Even I know that you get healthier by exercising, not by lying on the sofa every day after school. And I've heard you throwing up.' Posie sat down next to Romily and took her hand, a gesture that was so un-Posie-like that Romily sat up even straighter. 'You've got cancer, haven't you?'

'What? *No*, I haven't got cancer.'

'It's okay, I've looked it all up so I understand. I can help look after you. It's your breasts, isn't it? Mrs Corrigan is starting up a Knitting Club at school so I can join that even though I don't like clubs, because you'll probably want some hats for when your hair falls out.'

'Posie. I do not have cancer.'

'You're just saying that to make me feel better. But I'm old enough. I can know the truth. I want to know the truth.'

A tear ran down Posie's cheek. Romily took her by both shoulders and looked her in the face.

'Mariposa J. Summer. Listen to me. I am telling you the truth. I do not have cancer. How long have you been thinking this?'

'I don't know. A while. Since you've started having all these private conversations with Ben and Claire.'

Weeks, then. And Romily knew how Posie built things up in her imagination. Every detail, every dramatic possibility there could be.

'Oh, Posie,' she said, taking her daughter in her arms. Posie buried her face in Romily's neck and sobbed loudly. Romily stroked her hands down her back, patting and whispering that it was okay.

How long had it been since she'd held Posie as she cried? She'd held Posie all the time when she was very little, after falls or bumps or disappointments. When her best friend hadn't liked her any more or when she'd lost her favourite teddy. And before that, when she'd been tiny, and her cry meant anything and everything.

It had been some time since.

She held her daughter and breathed in the smell that was only hers, felt the tears falling hot on her skin. Posie was really upset. Just because she was clever, just because she lived in a world of her own, didn't mean that she wasn't affected by what was happening. This was what came of hiding things from her and planning things that didn't include her. This precious child, hurting.

'I'm so sorry, little girl,' she murmured, as the sobs quietened and Posie began to draw in long, hitching breaths. 'You must have been very worried.'

Posie sat up. She rubbed the tear trails from her face with a hand. 'I wasn't worried about myself. I knew that if you got very sick or died I'd go to live with Claire and Ben.'

Of course she did. Romily remembered the birthday party, and nearly shook her head. It wouldn't be such a bad result for Posie, in the long run. Oh well, at least Posie had been worried about her.

'If you died,' Posie said, 'would I be an orphan?'

Romily bit her lip. 'Uh. Well, technically maybe not, since both of your parents have to be dead for you to be an orphan.'

'And you don't know where my father is.'

'That's right.'

'Could he maybe be dead?'

'It's statistically unlikely.'

Posie thought about this, wiping her nose on the sleeve of her jumper.

'Not on your sleeve, please, Pose.'

'So what is wrong, if you're not sick? Is something wrong with Claire or Ben?' She looked panicked.

'No. No no no, nothing is wrong with Claire or Ben. The thing is, Posie . . .' Romily took a deep breath, feeling her breasts aching and her body exhausted. 'The thing is, that I'm pregnant.'

Posie's eyes grew very large. Tears had clumped her normally pale eyelashes together, making them dark. 'You're going to have a baby? I'm going to have a brother or a sister?'

'Well, no, not that either.' She took another breath. 'You know how Claire and Ben don't have children?'

'They have me.'

'I mean children of their own, who live with them all the time in their house. They've wanted to have children very, very much, but they haven't been able to.'

'Don't they know how?'

'No, they – they know how, but something is wrong that means that they can't conceive a baby by themselves. Claire's been seeing lots of doctors and they've been trying to help, but nothing has worked.'

'She isn't sick, is she?'

'Not sick sick, but she has problems. You remember how human babies are made, right?'

This had been the subject of many earnest and detailed discussions about a year ago, but Posie hadn't brought it up for a while.

The child recited: 'A man's sperm meets with a woman's egg when they have sex and they both use half their chromo-somes to make a whole baby, but it happens inside the woman's body and she doesn't lay the eggs like insects do.'

'Some insects,' Romily corrected automatically. 'Well,

121

Claire's eggs are apparently not very good for making babies. So I offered to let them use mine. I said I would get pregnant for them, and when the baby was born, I would give it to them and it would be theirs.'

'Whose sperm did you use?'

'Ben's.'

Posie screwed up her face. 'You had sex with him? Ugh.'

'No, we used artificial insemination.'

'That's when you breathe into someone's mouth.'

'That's artificial respiration. For this, Ben put some of his sperm in a little container. We didn't have to touch each other.'

'And you put the sperm in your vagina so it would meet your egg.'

'Yes.'

'And now you're pregnant.'

'Yes. And that's why I have sore boobs and why I'm tired and why Claire is sending us all kinds of vegetables to eat so that the baby grows up nice and healthy.'

'Are you allowed to have a baby for someone else?'

'Of course you are. It's called being a surrogate.'

Posie thought about this for some time. 'Well,' she said at last, 'that's not such a big deal.'

'I'm glad you think so.'

Posie settled herself more comfortably on the sofa, her legs draping over Romily's stomach. Romily adjusted them slightly so they weren't pressing down on her bladder.

'Where will the baby live?'

'At Ben and Claire's house, with them.'

'It won't have my room, will it?'

'I really don't know which room they'll choose for the

nursery. But there'll always be space for you at their house, I'm sure.'

'If it's a girl I'll let her play with my castle doll's house.' Posie said it with the air of someone conferring a great favour.

'Hey, don't gender stereotype the kid before it's even been born. A boy might like to play with a doll's house too.'

'It'll be my little brother or sister.'

'Except that it'll have different parents.'

Posie jumped up. Romily winced as a sharp elbow grazed her chest. 'This is so exciting! I'm going to go and make a card for the baby to say congratulations for being made.'

'I think the baby would like that very much.'

'If it's a boy, he should be called Rupert. And if it's a girl, she should be called Rapunzel. No, Guinevere. Guinevere Mariposa, after me. And I'll help look after her and I can push her around in the pram and everyone will know that we're sisters.'

'Well, biologically you'd be half-sisters, but in fact—'

'Can I use your phone? I'm going to ring Claire and tell her about my ideas for names.' All traces of tears were gone.

'I don't know if Claire's around this afternoon,' Romily said carefully. 'Maybe you should text Ben instead. That way he'll get it as soon as he finishes work.'

She dug in her pocket and handed Posie her mobile, which she scampered off with towards her room. At the door, she paused and looked back.

'I'm glad you don't have cancer,' she said.

14

The Mother Theme

Everyone in the clinic thought they were a couple.

In the Rose and Thistle, all of the regulars were locals and they always asked about Claire, who came in with Ben sometimes for a meal. At the football, Romily and Ben were obviously mates in supporters' tops. Through the years she'd been his little female sidekick, his buddy, an honorary man.

In an ultrasound clinic waiting for the dating scan, holding her pregnancy notes in a plastic folder, she couldn't be taken for an honorary man. Of course, Ben was wearing a wedding ring and she wasn't, but she could have taken hers off for any number of reasons. Or lost it. She probably looked like someone who would lose her wedding ring.

Stop it, she thought.

Ben looked up from his sheaf of papers and smiled at her. 'I'm sorry I'm not much of a conversationalist today,' he said. 'I need to go through all of this before tomorrow.'

'It's okay. I'm glad you could take the time off to be here.' *Besides, it's easier to construct elaborate fantasies if you're not talking.*

'I wouldn't miss it for the world. The first chance to see our child.'

She knew who the 'our' was that he was talking about, and immediately said, out of guilt, 'It's too bad Claire couldn't make it.'

'It's hard for her to get time off during the term,' said Ben, though it didn't sound entirely convincing. As Romily had not set eyes on Claire for nearly two months, she suspected it was more than that. But Ben hadn't said a word about Claire having second thoughts, or about the obvious fact that Claire couldn't stand her and didn't trust her. He was adamant that everything was fine. Probably because he wanted to spare her feelings.

And the sad truth was that it was easier for Romily if Claire wasn't around. Except for these errant thoughts, which were probably the result of hormones, and which she really should get under control.

'Romily Summer?' The ultrasound technician poked her head outside of the scan room, a file in her hand. Romily got up. The technician had short greying hair; she could be the same technician who had scanned Romily when she'd been pregnant with Posie. She thought it was probably the same room, though she didn't remember it all that well. All scan rooms no doubt looked just about the same.

'Lie down, please, Romily. Is this Daddy here with you?'

'Yes,' said Ben, and Romily could see his chest puffing out a bit with pride. In Romily's opinion, it was a little bit creepy to call the man 'Daddy', as if the baby could hear or as if he were Romily's own father – but she knew it was the first time Ben had been called 'Daddy'.

'You can sit by the side there. Now I'm going to need your top up, please, Romily.'

'He's not my husband,' Romily told the technician. She wasn't exactly sure why she was saying this, after basking in

125

mistaken impressions in the waiting room, but it seemed important now. For the record.

'We have all kinds of families here,' the technician said. 'Top up, please?'

Reluctantly, Romily pulled up her T-shirt. Ben had never seen her bare belly before. 'It was artificial insemination,' she said. 'I'm a surrogate. I'm not keeping the baby.'

The technician seemed entirely unfazed. 'Do you want me to turn the monitor away so you can't see it?'

'Why?'

'Sometimes women who are giving up their babies for adoption say they don't want to see the scans so they won't bond with the baby.'

'At ten weeks, a human foetus looks like a cross between ET and a tadpole,' Romily said. 'I don't think I'll be bonding with it.'

'I will,' said Ben.

The technician squirted the warmed gel on Romily's stomach. That was something that had changed, at least; she remembered the gel as being freezing cold. 'So this is your dating scan, so we'll know when your baby is likely to be born.' She applied the scanner to Romily's belly and started rolling it around.

Ben watched the screen. Romily watched Ben. She could see the exact moment when the baby appeared because his eyes got wider, his face softened in wonder.

'Is that it?'

'Yes. Here's the head, here's the spine. You can see the heartbeat is good and strong.'

He leaned closer to the screen. Romily could feel the warmth from his body. 'Hello, little thing,' he said.

Romily followed his gaze. The baby was a white shape, a

little body in a sea of black and grey. 'It looks like you,' she said.

'Can I have a printout? I'd like to share with my wife.'

'Of course. Do you want one too, Romily?'

'No, thanks.'

'It's so tiny,' Ben said, and she was drawn to him again instead of the screen. She had never seen him looking so rapt. So in love.

Right now, right at this very moment, Ben was looking at their baby. He was looking inside Romily's body and seeing his child taking shape.

In the empty classroom, Claire removed student work from the bulletin boards and replaced the fading coloured backing paper with a fresh sheet from the roll. It was busy work; the display wasn't that old and didn't strictly need to be replaced yet. However, it kept her hands occupied.

She'd had ultrasounds before. Lots and lots of them, to see what was inside her. To see what was wrong.

In the diagrams of a woman's reproductive system, everything was clear and neat: ovaries, fallopian tubes in a pair, uterus in a delicate curve, nestled inside the body. In her ultrasounds she looked as if she was made up of a maelstrom of clouds. Chaotic and imperfect. She hadn't been able to identify any of her parts, but nodded as the consultant had pointed them out.

She stapled the paper to the board, neatly, every three inches. One dull thunk after another.

'Hey Mrs Lawrence, do you mind if I come in and practise?' Max lingered at the door, holding his guitar.

'Max? Of course, you're welcome.' He came into the classroom and headed for a stool in the corner. 'Weren't any of the practice rooms free?'

'I didn't feel like being on my own so I thought I'd see if you were here.'

'As long as you don't mind the sound of my stapler.'

He shook his head and bent over his guitar. Claire watched him for a moment as he strummed a few preparatory chords, his slender fingers holding the instrument as if it were part of him. But she got the feeling that while he wanted company, he didn't want to be watched, so she turned back to her display board.

She'd been that way with music, once. She took every opportunity to play, to lose herself, following the notes without even thinking of her fingers or the score or who else was around. Her father used to tease her, tell her she'd never find a husband if she spent all her time practising the piano.

'I don't need a husband,' she'd told him. He'd laughed as if he knew better.

Her mother talked about her becoming a concert pianist, travelling the world, but she didn't care about that, either. It was the music that mattered. Not boys, not money, not the world.

And then she'd met Ben.

She glanced at Max, utterly absorbed in what he was doing. He'd segued into a soft, slow progression of chords, lilting like a lullaby. It was a teenage thing, that absorption. You couldn't afford it once you were grown up. No matter how beautiful the music was, there was still the mortgage and the credit cards. The laundry and the garden. The reports to be written, the lessons to be planned, the dozens of little tasks and annoyances that weighed down your hands.

The other woman who was carrying your husband's baby.

She finished with the backing paper and began cutting lengths of scalloped edging to finish off the sides. She had some photographs she'd printed out of the autumn concert to put up; maybe she'd include some of Year Seven's drawings, too – the ones they'd made whilst listening to Mendelssohn. Some of them were quite exquisite, whimsical like the music. Claire went to the filing cabinet to find them. Leafing through them, she found that she was humming: a soft, slow progression of notes.

She looked at Max at the same time he looked up at her, and a small smile touched his face. He'd heard her.

'Did you write that yourself?' she asked him. 'It's beautiful.'

'Just something I've been working on.' He dropped his gaze back to his guitar, and then looked up at her again.

'It sounds like a lullaby. Safe and warm.'

'It's the mother theme.'

He blushed as soon as he said it, as if he hadn't meant to, and Claire put the drawings down and came to lean on a chair across from him. 'What do you mean?' she asked. 'A theme, not a song? Is it part of a bigger composition?'

Max nodded. 'I've – I've got it in my head. Different people, with a different bit of music each. You put them all together, weave them through.'

'It's very ambitious. Is that what you've been working on writing down?'

'Yeah.'

'How much of it have you worked out?'

'A few bits.'

'Can I hear another?'

He played a hard and fast riff, bluesy and dirty. She'd heard it before, tacked on to the end of another song he'd been playing, and assumed it was in the charts at the moment.

'That's Alan,' Max said. 'The bloke at the newsagent's at home who ogles all the young girls.'

Claire laughed. The sound surprised her a little. 'Have you done anyone I know?'

'Mrs Greasley,' he said, and blushing again, played a few bars of a sweet tune to the beat of a militant march that suited the headmistress exactly. Iron fist in velvet glove, that was Veronica Greasley. Claire clapped her hand to her mouth and he smiled at her, shy and proud.

'That's incredible, Max.'

'It's just something I'm doing.'

'Well, I'm very impressed.'

'It's nothing, really.'

'It's more than nothing. Have you played the mother theme to your mother yet? I think she'd be very touched.'

Max scowled. He gripped his guitar. 'She's my stepmother. She's too busy. And she doesn't like music anyway.'

Claire paused. She was a music teacher, and that was all. At St Dom's, the division was quite clear: the teachers taught, and the students' emotional well-being was looked after by the pastoral staff – the heads of house, and the deputy head in charge of boarding. When a student told you something personal, an issue that might affect their happiness or their education, as academic staff it was your duty to pass it on to the appropriate member of the pastoral team and bow gently out of the conversation.

If Max said anything else to her, anything that indicated there might be trouble at home, she'd have to advise him to talk to his head of house about it.

But that's not how relationships worked, not in real life. People weren't purely teachers or purely pastoral staff. They weren't either pupils or children.

She wasn't really staying late at school to put up a bulletin board. She was here because she was too afraid to be anywhere else.

'Well,' she said at last, 'you're always welcome to come here and play it for me. I'd love to hear more and help you if I can.'

He didn't say anything, and she took the drawings back to the bulletin board and began to pin them up. Behind her he picked out a melody, hit a wrong note. She tactfully ignored his mumbled swearing and waited for him to try it again. The clock said half past five. Ben was probably finished by now. He was probably on his way to his car, a photograph of the scan in his pocket, or more likely in his hand because he was poring over it, taking in every detail.

'They don't even fucking care about me,' said Max suddenly, and there was so much anger and hurt in his voice that Claire forgot about his head of house and about her husband holding the photograph of his baby. She went to Max and sat down across from him.

'Who doesn't?' she asked gently.

'Dad and Jemima. Dad's always at work, or up in his constituency running surgeries or whatever, and Jemima has the gym and her clubs and her charities and her hair. They send me away to school so they don't have to deal with me. I even learned how to play this thing at a fucking holiday club when they went to South Africa.' He looked down at the guitar with loathing.

'But you're good at it. You're very good at it.'

'I might as well be playing a bin lid as far as they care.'

'Jemima's your stepmum?'

Max grunted. 'Half my dad's age. It's disgusting.'

'What about your real mother?'

'She's on her third marriage. I don't see much of her, either.'

'So the mother theme—'

'It's in my head. I made it up.' He played it, quickly and

131

harshly, crashing the chords together. 'Listen, don't think I'm crazy or anything. I don't like sit around pining for the perfect parents I never had, despite that song. It's just, it would be nice to be noticed once in a while. And I keep thinking about what would happen if Jemima got up the duff.'

'You'd have an ally,' said Claire. 'My brother and sister were good friends to me growing up.'

Max shook his head. 'It would go one of two ways. Either Jemima would throw herself into it, like a new cause or a new fashion, and the thing would be spoiled rotten, or she'd ignore that one too, and it would have a miserable life. Either way, I hope it never happens.'

'Your dad must care about you, if he fought for custody of you.'

'I don't think he had to fight very hard. Plus, it looks good that he has me. Politically.' He played four notes, upbeat like an advertising jingle. 'That's my dad's theme. Always on message.'

Claire bit her lip. 'Have you talked to your head of hou—'

'I'm not going to talk to Mr Doughty. He and Dad are like this.' He pressed his fingers together.

'What about—'

Max played his militant march again.

'I see.'

'I don't want to talk about it anyway,' he said. 'I just want to play music. Okay?'

Claire stood up. Briefly, she touched Max's shoulder.

'Play all you like. As long as you don't mind my listening.'

Dear Thing,

Grown-ups are complicated. They hardly ever say what they mean. You have to look under the surface of their words and try to figure out what's really going on. Some grown-ups, maybe even most grown-ups, carry secret feelings around, hoarded and shielded inside them within layers and layers of protection. Sometimes they don't even know themselves that those feelings are there until they burst out, fully formed.

It doesn't make any sense, does it?

Babies, on the other hand, are simple. They need food and warmth and changing and love. They might like a toy or two and they like watching sunlight as it filters through cool green leaves.

You don't know how lucky you are, Thing. Hold on to it for as long as you can.

15

Hormonal Madness

I can do this whole pregnancy thing, no problem. I'll sail through it. I'll hardly notice.

And pigs might fly.

Romily was working in the conference room: just her and a council laptop, no specimens, no window. Drawer 70 remained in Amity's cabinet. The merest whiff of naphthalene made Romily want to throw up. She couldn't work in the study room either; Layla, one of the women who volunteered on Tuesdays, used a particularly sweet honeysuckle perfume.

It wasn't just scents that made her queasy. Posie had a loose tooth, and every time she wiggled it with her tongue, Romily had to cover her eyes. Even the thought of that loose tooth was enough to set her off. Along with the particular shade of brown river water on her way to work in the morning. Or warm, humid weather. Or the fuzzy side of Velcro. Or the concept of earrings.

Basically, Romily thought, sipping her glass of water that was about to tip over the edge from refreshingly cold to nauseatingly tepid, she was a big pathetic ball of hormonal madness and she had no idea what to do about it.

And meanwhile Amity's collection sat untended upstairs.

'Romily?' Layla stuck her head into the room, and Romily instinctively held her breath. 'You've got a visitor waiting in the lobby.'

Ben? Romily jumped up, grabbed her bag and skipped down the stairs and through the ground floor of the museum to the white-painted, high-windowed lobby, a smile on her face.

Ben wasn't there. The only person in the lobby was a blond man with his back to her. At the sound of her trainers on the red-tiled floor he turned around. But she knew who it was already.

'Hi, Romily,' he said.

Romily clapped her hand to her mouth. She bolted for the door behind him at the far end of the lobby. The man, startled, lifted his own hands as if to fend her off or embrace her, but she pushed past him and raced through the door into the ladies' toilet. She only just made it in time before she vomited her breakfast into the bowl in a violent and noisy gush. She retched again, and again.

Her hands were shaking, her eyes watering and dimmed.

What was he doing here?

She heard the door opening. *Please no*, she thought, but she couldn't move from the toilet. Not yet.

'Are you okay?'

The voice made her heave again. Over the noises she was making, she heard the door open further and booted feet come in.

'Is it the flu, or is it me?' he asked.

'Mmph,' she said, and realized she hadn't shut the cubicle door. She tried to do it with her foot, without moving her head or upper body, but she couldn't find it. Apparently

135

he had opened that too. She didn't dare look around.

'Can I get you anything?'

She shook her head, and then had to retch again. There was nothing left of her breakfast, but her stomach didn't seem to care. A hand appeared next to her head, holding a wad of toilet paper. The fingers were tanned and wholly familiar. She took the paper and wiped her mouth.

'I think those are the same trainers you were wearing when I last saw you,' he said. 'Nice to know some things never change.'

The sickness was abating a little bit, so she flushed the toilet and sat on the floor, leaning against the wall. His hand appeared again, holding a bottle of water. She shook her head.

'Water will make you feel better.'

'I'm okay.' Her throat was raw. 'Go away.'

'It's a new bottle. I haven't drunk out of it.'

She took it, his hand retreated, and the cubicle door swung shut again. She could see his well-worn boots and the bottoms of his trousers beyond the door, but the rest of him was out of sight. Romily took a long drink and pulled herself together enough to stand up. She still felt nauseated, but it was a dull sinking rather than a panic, and she wasn't sure if it was caused by morning sickness or by seeing Jarvis again.

Trust him to follow her into the cloakroom, so she couldn't have a moment's peace to be sick by herself.

She rubbed her face, hard, with her hands and came out. He stood by the sink, and aside from the tan he looked the same. Tall, rangy and a little bit too skinny, still with his unruly thick hair. There were some lines around his eyes, but she wasn't sure if they were new or if they were more noticeable because of his tan, which also brought out the blue of his eyes.

136

She forgot, sometimes, how much Posie looked like him.

'So,' he said. 'It's been a while.'

'We're in a toilet, Jarvis. I wouldn't mind some privacy.' He didn't immediately leave, so she suggested, 'If you're determined to have a conversation, I'll meet you in the museum café in ten minutes.'

'Right.' With an abruptness that she remembered as typical, he went out and she was left alone, staring at the space where he'd been.

'Shit,' she said. She stood there for a minute or two, and then looked at herself in the mirror. She looked bloody awful: wide-eyed, slack-mouthed, and distinctly green. She splashed her face with water, brushed her teeth with her finger, and ran her hands through her hair. Nausea still throbbed dully in her stomach, but it was controllable. For now.

She found some mints in her bag and was seriously tempted to bolt. But where? And what good would it do? If he knew she worked here, he'd find her again sooner or later. If he wanted to.

And for some unknown reason, it seemed that he did want to.

Romily crunched two mints at once and went to find Jarvis in the café near the museum entrance. It would be okay, she told herself. It was bound to be a flying visit. Popped in to say hello. A quick cheeky how-are-you after eight years of no contact. Just the sort of thing that Jarvis would do, now that she thought of it.

She had to try not to puke any more, and not to talk too much, and she would be fine.

He was sitting at a table next to one of the big floor-to-ceiling windows, stirring sugar into his coffee, and she had a

137

split second to look at him unobserved. He wore loose-fitting khaki trousers, battered hiking boots, and a light blue cotton shirt with the sleeves rolled up over his forearms. It wasn't tucked in and it looked as if it had never seen an iron. Though probably in the places where he'd been, ironing wasn't a priority. Nor haircuts. He didn't have any bags or cases with him, which probably meant he was staying somewhere locally rather than passing through. But with Jarvis, who knew? He could have left his luggage at the airport; it could have been lost in the Andes. Or wherever.

He glanced up and saw her, and Romily had another urge to run away. She mastered it and went to sit across from him. There was a cup and a small teapot in front of her place – mint tea, from the smell.

'Are you finished vomiting?' he asked.

'I think so. It wasn't intentional.'

'That's good to know.' For the first time, he smiled. It was only a half-smile, with the corners of his mouth turning down rather than up. She remembered that too. 'The tea will help.'

She poured it out from the pot and breathed in the steam. It felt cleansing.

'Um,' she said. 'How are you?'

'I'm fine, thanks.'

'How did you know where I was?'

'I saw Anil at the Natural History Museum. He told me you were cataloguing the never-ending Victorian spinster collection. It's a bit of a legend in those parts, apparently. How long have you been at it?'

'I started not long after you left.'

'I half-expected to run into you in the field.' He finished stirring his coffee and took a long drink, looking at her over the rim of it.

'The collection is keeping me busy here.'

'PhD finished?'

'Yes.'

'Congratulations, Dr Summer. It's what you always wanted.'

'Thanks.' She blew into her tea, then took a sip. 'Where — where have you been?'

'Mostly South America for the past couple of years.'

'I saw your work on Discovery.' Late one night, flicking through the channels, she'd glimpsed his name on rolling credits. Her heart had thumped, her stomach turned round. She'd stayed away from nature documentaries after that, not trusting herself to analyse every shot to try to guess who was behind the camera. Not that she knew enough about film, or about him, to recognize his style.

Who was she kidding? She'd know his style anywhere.

'Mm,' he agreed.

'Are you . . . back in England for long?' She concentrated on the table.

'I'm staying in London for a while. Catching up.'

'Oh.'

Silence fell. On the next table, an elderly woman was telling her companion about the queue in the Post Office.

Jarvis cleared his throat. 'Is the tea helping?'

'Yes. I think so. Thanks.'

She glanced up, and he was looking at her, so she looked back down.

Over the years, Jarvis had evolved in her mind into more of an idea than a person. A set of genes, a name on a television screen that was never referred to. It was by far the easiest way to think of him. Now, she could smell his coffee and if she lifted her gaze slightly she could see one of his hands resting on the table. There was a bit of twine loosely tied round his wrist, and a half-healed cut on his index finger. He'd collected that string and knotted it one-handed, or someone had tied it around his wrist for him. It had significance, or it did not. He'd bled when he'd cut his finger. Probably sworn, put his finger in his mouth. She could feel his eyes on her. The silence stretched out again.

She wished he'd go away.

'You haven't got the flu, have you?' he said. 'You're pregnant.'

That startled her enough so that she looked up, full into his face. 'You can tell?'

'It was a wild guess.'

'I'm fatter, aren't I?'

'Not exactly.'

He'd withdrawn his hands from the table, and had them on the arms of his chair, as if he were bracing himself.

'Happy?' he asked.

'Yes. Yes, it's all going well, so far. Aside from the throwing up, which was supposed to have stopped by now.'

'Is it—' He cleared his throat again, and continued in his offhand tone. 'Is it Ben's?'

'Yes.'

'Great. Great. Well, as I said. Nice to know some things never change. That you got what you wanted in the end.' He stood up. 'I'll be getting back to London. I'll give your regards to Anil.'

'I . . . okay.'

'Bye, Romily.' Jarvis turned and headed for the café exit.

Without him looking at her, she was free to stare as he left. His hands in the pockets of his trousers, the loose tails of his shirt. The way the hair at the crown of his head fell in an untidy and entirely familiar whorl.

'Shit,' she said to herself, and then she was up, hurrying after him, digging in her bag. 'Jarvis. Wait.'

He stopped near a display of brochures. 'It's all right. I wasn't expecting a welcome committee.'

'I have something I need to show you.' She found her purse, opened it and pulled out the photo. It was a school photo from last September and the corners were worn. Posie's jumper was clean and her fringe was freshly cut, but her hair was beginning to unravel from her plaits. Her smile turned down slightly at the corners, as if she were making an ironic comment on the process of school photographs.

Romily gave it to him. Her fingers, she noticed, were shaking. Jarvis took it.

'Who's this?' he asked.

'It's my daughter Posie,' said Romily. 'Short for Mariposa. It's Spanish for—'

'Butterfly.'

'She was seven in February.'

He turned it over to look at the blank back. There was no explanation there. He turned it over again and looked at it while Romily gnawed at her bottom lip.

'Seven years old,' he said.

'Yes.'

'She doesn't,' he said slowly, carefully, 'look like Ben.'

'Ben isn't her father.'

The photograph fluttered to the floor. Jarvis grabbed her by both shoulders.

'Romily, what have you done?' he shouted.

16
Discovery

The entire café – the entire museum – went silent. Jarvis, so laconic until now, towered over her, his face furious. Romily tried to back away, but she couldn't escape his grip.

'Not here,' she said. 'Let's not do this here.'

'You were the one who shoved that photograph into my hand. What are you playing at, Romily? Is she mine? Am I her *father*?'

'Outside, please. Please, Jarvis.' She was suffocating. She was going to throw up. She was going to faint. 'Please,' she said again.

He abruptly let her go, stooped to retrieve the photo, and strode out through the lobby, his boots making crisp and angry bangs. She followed him out through the sliding glass doors into the warmth of summer. Without looking at her, he struck off in a random direction, still walking fast. She trotted to keep up with him, gulping air.

'Am I her father?'

'Yes.'

'Fucking hell!' He yelled it. A pedestrian stepped quickly to the side.

'I don't blame you for being surprised,' she said.

'Surprised? That's a bloody understatement. "Hello Jarvis, nice to see you, it's been a while – oh, and by the way, here's a photo of your kid"!'

A flock of pigeons took flight. He kept on walking, the photograph in his fist.

'I wasn't sure how to tell you,' she said.

'About seven years ago would have been good!'

'You knew when I got pregnant – when we, you know, when we talked.'

'When we agreed that it had been a mistake, you mean – that you didn't want a baby, and that you weren't going to have it?'

'You didn't want one either. You were going away.'

'We neither of us wanted one. And then you, apparently, changed your mind.' He stopped and turned to her. 'Is that what happened? Or were you lying to me and you planned to keep her all along?'

'No! I wasn't lying. I changed my mind.'

'After I left, or before?'

'After. I . . .' She didn't think that mentioning Ben would help at this point. 'After.'

'When were you going to tell me? Not ever?'

'I didn't think you'd be interested.'

'You didn't think I'd be interested? In the fact that I'm a parent?' He started walking again. 'Fucking hell!'

She tagged along beside him. 'But then you showed up today and I couldn't not tell you.'

'Meaning that if I hadn't shown up today, I'd have never known?'

'I didn't know where you were.'

'It wouldn't have been that hard to find out.'

'When you left, you said it was better if we— we decided not to keep in touch.'

'I didn't know that you were going to keep my child!'

'You were going to the back of nowhere for two years. You left your phone behind.'

'There are messages, Romily. Emails. I could pick those up.'

'I didn't have your address.'

'I have a family! Parents, brothers, sisters. You knew they were in London, or Dorset! You knew who I was working for! You saw my footage on the Discovery channel, for fuck's sake! I wasn't in outer space, you could have got in touch if you wanted to.'

'We were finished. We never really started. You said it yourself.' Though if you'd asked her two days ago, Romily wouldn't have been able to quote exactly what he'd said.

'A baby changes things,' he said.

'A baby doesn't change anything. Neither one of us wanted to be tied down, and you were going on this huge exciting assignment. It was the chance of a lifetime. You said you didn't want a child. You were very definite about it.'

'Even if you didn't believe I wanted to know, don't you think I should have been given the choice?'

He stopped and looked directly at her when he asked that, and the guilt that she'd been so strenuously denying hit her. It was worse than the nausea.

'I'm sorry,' she said. 'I didn't think.'

'No, you didn't.' He dug the heels of his hands into his eyes. 'She looks just like my sister Sally at that age.'

'She's a good kid.'

'Fuck.'

None of this was what Romily had expected. Though, she realized, she hadn't been expecting anything. She hadn't even thought about it. Not today, not over the past seven years. Somehow, she'd just assumed it would never happen. Jarvis didn't want a baby, they'd split up never to see each other again, that was the end of it.

Except it seemed it wasn't. It seemed she might have made a huge, catastrophic mistake, not only with her life, but with Posie's.

'What . . . do you want to do?' she asked.

'I want,' said Jarvis, his hands still covering his eyes, 'to walk into the nearest pub. And then I want to order a large drink, and drink it, and then I want to order another. I do not want you to come with me,' he added. 'I'm too angry with you to look at you.'

'Okay.'

'And then I want to go back to London and not speak with anyone for a few days. I want to get this through my head. And then, I will call you.'

'You don't have my number.'

'I have it.'

Before she could ask how, he was walking away, with long strides that told her how much he wanted to get away from her. Romily leaned against the wall of the nearest shop, breathing hard, trying to suck enough air into her lungs.

Why did she tell him? She and Posie had been fine without him. Hadn't they? And Jarvis may have conveniently forgotten, but Romily knew with all the certainty she was capable of that eight years ago, back when they were lovers about to split up, back when he was about to embark on the assignment that was going to make a name for him as a wildlife cameraman, he definitely did not want a baby. She hadn't wanted a baby, either. Until after Jarvis had gone, until she'd spoken with Ben.

145

And even then, for thirty-four weeks after that, Romily didn't know if she'd be able to do it, if she'd be able to be a mother. Not until the midwife handed her the hot little squirmy body, still smelling of amniotic fluid, with her slick of pale hair and her screwed-up eyes, the perfect limbs and the stub of the cord sticking out of her belly. Then she knew that she'd fight and fight for this child, no matter what. That she would keep her safe.

Which included keeping her safe from people who didn't want her.

All at once she was angry at Jarvis, no longer on the defensive. Posie was his daughter. It was a shock to find out about her, but surely the appropriate, the grown-up response to finding out you had a child was not to yell and swear in the street and then go in search of the largest drink you could find?

She shouldn't have told him. It was only that he looked so much like Posie; she'd had some wild feeling of guilt, some mad idea that they would bond.

And now she was in exactly the position she'd avoided all these years: with Posie having a father who didn't want her, but who could get in touch and disrupt all their lives at any moment.

Romily felt dizzy and sick. Carefully, she made her way back to the museum. But her refuge had been invaded now. She'd tell them she was unwell, go back to the flat and crawl into bed until she had to pick Posie up. No point telling her anything about it, not now. Maybe Jarvis wouldn't even bother to get in touch. If he had her phone number, he could have rung any time in the past eight years anyway. Probably he would decide to leave the country as soon as possible, go back to South America where he didn't have any pesky responsibilities.

It was only when she was climbing the steps to the front entrance, trying to concentrate on keeping down the few sips of mint tea that were the only thing in her stomach, that she realized that Jarvis had taken Posie's photograph with him.

He didn't call until two weeks later.

17
Wanted

The dinner had not been a success. In the passenger seat of the car afterwards, with Ben driving home, Claire switched on Radio 3 to fill the silence.

She'd had a bit too much wine. Mike had kept on filling her glass, for one thing, circulating with the bottle every time an awkward pause fell. Or – to be more generous – he'd probably seen that she was on edge, and he was trying to help her relax.

Priya had been a bridesmaid at Claire's wedding; they'd known each other from school. When Priya married Mike, years later, Claire had been one of her bridesmaids, too. By the time Priya started getting treatment for infertility, Claire had been through it already and she was always there on the end of a phone line or for coffee. She told Priya the best websites to visit, the best clinic to contact, what to expect at each appointment.

They hadn't seen Mike and Priya for nearly a year now. Their twins, conceived following their first cycle of IVF, lay asleep upstairs. Their snuffling came through the baby monitor perched near the dining-room table. Everything else, all of the bottles and nappies and toys, had been cleared out of sight.

Before coming out tonight, Claire had made Ben promise not to mention their surrogacy arrangement. She waited for Mike to ask him why he was so obviously happy; she waited for Ben to respond to Priya's looks of sympathy.

He hadn't said anything, though at one point he'd disappeared into the back garden with Mike to look at the turf he'd laid, and Claire hadn't been able to stay in the dining room with Priya making conversation about people they both used to know and trying not to talk about babies. She'd been certain that Ben was going to blurt out their secret, so she'd brought his glass out to him. They'd been talking about building a shed. Ben made their excuses soon after.

She'd apologized, but it didn't help her feel better, or restore Ben's good mood. She'd been the one to ruin the evening, the one who'd made Mike and Priya feel bad for being happy, the one who hadn't trusted her own husband.

What is wrong with me? she asked herself now, gazing out of the window at the passing lights, not listening to Mahler, not talking with her husband. *Why can't I let him have his joy? Why can't I share it?*

Ben's phone rang and though she hated it when he did that, he automatically took it out of his pocket to glance at it whilst he was driving. 'Sorry, I've got to take this.' He pulled the car over into a layby. 'Ed. What can I do for you?'

Claire judged it safe to look at him. He was frowning in the lights from the dashboard, the phone to his ear. She turned down the radio.

'Uh huh. I understand. Yes, a full ground survey might have picked it up, but you decided against it.' He rubbed the steering wheel with his free hand. 'I know that delay is frustrating,

149

but it will require a redesign, and that, of course, has implications for the budget. Yes. Yes, I understand but . . . Monday morning. Yes. I'll see you then.' He hung up and sighed. 'They found a well on the old site. The Vaughans want to move the building.'

Claire put her hand on his leg. Down deep, she felt mostly relief that his disappointment with her had transferred to frustration with work. 'Can you do it?'

'Within budget? Not a chance. I've got a furious client and I'm going to have to cancel everything on Monday. This will take at least all day. Oh no!'

'What?'

'I'm supposed to be meeting with Romily on Monday.'

She stiffened slightly, and pulled her hand away from his thigh. 'A midwife appointment?' Though she knew it wasn't; she had all the routine ones imprinted in her memory. Unless this was an emergency. 'Is something wrong?'

'It's not a midwife appointment. We're meeting for coffee.'

She was irritated with herself for her momentary stab of panic. 'Well, you can reschedule that, surely?'

'Not so much. She's not answering her phone.'

'What? Something is wrong?'

'She says everything's fine with the baby. She's answering texts, but she won't pick up a call, which isn't like her. She just lets it go to voicemail and then responds by text. So I pinned her down to meet me on Monday to find out what's going on. Can you go instead?'

'What? Why me? She won't want to see me.'

'Claire,' said Ben. He took her hand. The dashlights made his face slightly blue. 'It's going to be all right. Romily is fourteen weeks pregnant now. She's beyond the first trimester danger zone. This baby is going to be okay. You can stop being afraid.'

'But you just said something was wrong.'

'I just said there was nothing wrong with the baby. I'm worried about Romily.' He leaned his head back on the seat. 'I'm worried about you as well. I know you're afraid, but there's this huge change going on in our lives and you won't let us discuss it with anyone. I feel as if I'm living in a minefield. Have you even looked at the scan picture on the fridge, or have you been closing your eyes every time you've got out the milk?'

'I've looked at it,' she said quietly.

'I keep waiting for you to give us permission to be happy.'

'I want to be happy. I just . . . it's hard.'

'Maybe you and Romily don't see eye to eye about everything. And I can understand why you'd resent her a little bit. But in the end it's about our child. You do want this baby, don't you?'

For some reason her student Max flashed into her mind. What he'd said about his stepmother getting pregnant. What he'd said about himself.

She'd been keeping herself from wanting this baby too much, out of self-defence. But when did that cross the line into wilful indifference?

'I want the baby,' she said. 'I do.'

'Then go and see Romily. Please. Help her with whatever's going on. She needs us both, and we need her.'

A car passed them, and its headlights lit up the interior of their car. The space between them.

'All right,' said Claire.

Claire was there early. Ben had arranged to meet Romily in Starbucks, a place Claire never normally went into because if she was going to treat herself, she preferred the

151

independently owned coffee shop down the road. She ordered a cappuccino and a lemon muffin and chose a table by the window.

She was determined to be rational, sensible, generous. Not necessarily for Romily's sake, but for Ben's. And for the baby's.

Romily appeared ten minutes late and though Claire waved, she stood in the doorway for a few moments before she spotted her. Romily looked awful. She wore a man's jumper rolled up at the sleeves and her face looked puffy and pale; her hair had grown out of its crop and was shaggy and unkempt. Claire stood up as Romily approached.

'Where's Ben?' asked Romily. Up close, she looked even worse. Her complexion was so pale it bordered on green, and she had dark shadows under her eyes. Her lips were chapped and her nose was pink. There was near-panic in her eyes. Obviously Ben hadn't told her that he couldn't make it.

'He had a problem with a client,' Claire told her. 'So I came instead. What would you like to drink?'

'I'll get it.'

'No, I insist.'

'No, I will.' Romily turned and went to the counter. Every step was weary.

Well. This was going swimmingly. Claire sat back down and took a sip of her coffee. Eventually, Romily came back with a large frozen pink drink.

'That looks interesting,' Claire said pleasantly.

'It's okay, it's got fruit in. Theoretically.' Romily scraped back the chair and sat heavily in it. Under the roomy jumper, there might have been a bit of a roundness to her belly, but she was so slender it was hard to tell.

'How are you feeling?'

152

'I know, I look awful.'

'I . . . didn't mean to imply—'

Romily waved her hand. 'You don't have to imply anything. I own a mirror. And besides, I feel awful.' She put her drink down on the table without tasting it.

'Is everything okay? With the baby?'

'Your baby is fine. It's the damn hormones that are doing me in.'

'Ben said you had a bit of morning sickness.'

'It started out as a bit. For the past week I've been sick every two hours on the dot. It's got to the point where I don't bother to eat anything that looks substantially different coming out than it did going in. Weetabix is the easiest. No offence to all that food you sent or anything.'

'That's awful. I'm sorry.'

'It's not your fault. Well, it is, sort of.' She laughed, but not as if she found it funny.

'I thought morning sickness wasn't supposed to last past the first trimester,' Claire said.

'In theory, not for most women. I never even had it last time. I'm just getting unlucky this go round.' She poked her cup with a finger. 'How are you, anyway?'

'Fine, thank you. We saw some friends on the weekend. Priya and Mike. You might remember them from the wedding.'

'Oh yeah.'

'How's everything else? How's Posie?'

'Posie is fine. She misses you.'

Claire bit her lip. 'Yes, I can imagine. Sorry.'

'I'll tell her you said hi.' Romily sat back in her chair and crossed her arms. 'So Ben couldn't make it so you came to check up on me?'

'He was a bit . . . worried. He said you weren't answering his phone calls.'

'He shouldn't be offended. I haven't been answering anybody's.'

Possibilities zipped through Claire's mind. Romily had changed her mind. She had antenatal depression. She'd told her work and they'd sacked her. Posie had taken the news badly.

'Don't look so terrified,' Romily said. 'Your baby is fine, I told you, though I haven't had much energy to cook those amazing vegetables or write those heartfelt letters you thought were such a good idea.'

Her tone was so sarcastic that Claire snapped, 'Actually I wasn't thinking about the baby or the letters. I was thinking of you.'

'Worried about whether I'm following all the instructions you gave me?'

'No, I—'

'Because there were a lot of them. Books and printouts and pamphlets. Everything in incredible detail. If Ben hadn't repeatedly assured me otherwise, I'd have thought you didn't trust me to get it right.'

'That's not—'

'Because I have actually done this before, you know. And Posie hasn't turned out so badly. I'm not completely hopeless when it comes to incubating a baby. I don't need every self-help manual on the planet.'

Romily's eyes were fierce in her tired face. She looked rumpled, almost feral. Claire sat taller in her chair, trying to keep her voice calm, to be the rational one.

'Ben keeps on saying that I should get involved,' she said. 'I don't think it's fair that I should be attacked for it.'

'*Ben* told you to be Lady Bountiful?'

'I was only sending you things to help. I had no idea it was offending you so much. I shall certainly stop if you want me to.'

'Oh, that's right, it's all my fault. You've always been the helpful one, the generous one, with Posie and now with this. Don't you ever think that it might make me feel like I'm not good enough?'

People were watching them. Claire lifted her finger to her lips. 'Shh.'

'Don't shush me! I'm hormonal and I feel like shit and I don't need someone telling me how to live every minute of my life, what to eat and how to act! I can make decisions by myself, about my own body. Posie's all right, isn't she?'

Claire had had enough. She pushed her chair back and said, clearly and loudly, every word enunciated, 'Don't you think I would do anything to feel just like you do right now?'

Romily stared at her. Silence hung between them.

Then Romily put her head down on the table and burst into tears.

Claire reached out to touch her, then took her hand back. Then, seeing how weary, how defeated the other woman looked, she did touch her on the shoulder. 'Romily, please don't cry.'

'Sorry,' said Romily, to the table. 'Sorry. I'm so sorry. It's the hormones, and the sickness, and the lack of sleep and . . . everything.'

'It's okay.' Claire gave her a napkin.

'It's not. I shouldn't complain. Not to you.' Romily took the napkin, wiped her nose, and sat up. 'Let's get out of here. The smell of coffee is making me want to puke.'

Claire got up and she and Romily went to the door

together. Claire grabbed a few extra napkins on the way out and handed them to Romily.

'Thanks. Oh God, I'm a mess.' Romily laughed shakily as they stepped outside.

'You're not feeling well. Shall we walk to the park?'

'Okay. I think the fresh air will help.'

They didn't say anything as they made their way to the park near the centre of town, with its Victorian borders and mossy fountain. A crowd of teenagers sat on the lawn below a CCTV camera post, defiantly passing around fags and a bottle of vodka. The women found a bench facing the bandstand, away from the scent of smoke, and sat down.

'I didn't mean to have a go,' Romily said. 'Some of the things you've sent have been really nice. I like the cocoa butter cream.'

'But not everything.'

'Well . . . let's say it's not all to my taste. But I shouldn't have yelled at you about it.'

'Point taken,' Claire said. 'I honestly never expected you to interpret my gifts as criticism.'

'No, of course you didn't. I can see that now. You've never—'

'Been pregnant,' Claire finished for her. Romily smiled.

'I was going to say, "felt like an incompetent fool". But maybe they're not so different.'

'Oh, trust me. I've felt that way.'

Romily shot her a look that said she clearly didn't believe her. 'Actually, this fresh air is helping.'

'Would you like a mint?'

'You can stop taking care of me, Claire.'

'I'm just—' Claire began, but Romily was half-smiling. Some colour had come back to her face. Claire took a deep breath. 'I don't know what else to do. This is all new to me.'

'Me too. Not the pregnancy, but having a baby for someone else. I'm used to being on my own, I suppose.' Romily dug in her bag and found a plastic container with grapes in it. 'Have a grape.'

Claire took one and so did Romily.

'We haven't spent much time together without Ben,' Claire ventured. 'Since we left university.'

'We haven't spent any time together without Ben.' A ladybird landed on the arm of the bench next to Romily, and she watched it.

Claire wondered what to say next. Romily had asked her to stop helping her. But Ben was right; she did need to be more involved, and that couldn't just be sending supplies any more. She couldn't sit by, feeling powerless and unhappy.

'Have you . . .' She swallowed. 'Have you felt the baby moving yet?'

'No. It's pretty early for that, still.'

'The books say about fifteen weeks.'

'They also say I should have stopped throwing up by now.'

'Do you think there's something wrong?'

'No, I'm sure it's fine. I'll ask the midwife when I see her next week, but I think it's just one of those things. Every pregnancy is different. Apparently the babies don't read the books first.'

'I only know from books.'

'Yeah.' Romily ate a grape. 'I am sorry about that, Claire. I know it's been hard for you.'

'Thanks,' she said automatically, though she didn't want Romily's sympathy. But this conversation seemed necessary, somehow. And Ben had asked her to find out if there was a problem. 'You haven't been answering your phone,' she ventured.

'No. I've felt pretty wretched. And there was a . . . a phone call I didn't really want to receive. So I had the ringer turned off. But even when I knew it was Ben, I didn't want to answer because he'd know there was something wrong and want to rush over.'

'That's Ben. Mr Fix-It.'

Romily laughed. It was throaty and deep and genuine.

'But then you decided you did want to see him,' Claire prompted.

'I needed to talk to someone. It's been going round and round in my head and I can't talk to Posie about it, or anyone at work. Although they've asked a few questions after what happened in the café.'

Claire didn't say anything, didn't offer help. She waited.

'The thing is,' Romily said, 'I can't really blame you for thinking I'm not much good at this mothering thing, because I'm not. Posie's turning out okay, but that's not because of me. I'm just bumbling along, not knowing what I'm doing.'

'Is Posie all right?'

'Yes. No. I don't know. She seems all right, but what if she's missing out on something big? She must be, I think, or else she wouldn't want to spend so much time at your house. She wants a father and a mother who are normal, who love each other, with a nice house and a nice garden and nice things. She doesn't want a mother who's a flake and a father who's never even known about her.'

Claire blushed. She couldn't deny that she'd thought something very like this herself.

'It's not like this baby I'm carrying for you. You and Ben have wanted this for ages. It's going to be the most wanted

158

baby in the history of the world. But Posie . . . I didn't want her. Jarvis didn't want her.'

'She doesn't know that.'

'She'll find out sooner or later. And how is that going to make her feel?' There was real anguish in Romily's voice.

'But you do want her now,' said Claire.

'I had to be convinced to keep her. And I never told her dad.'

'From what Ben said, he wasn't much interested.'

'But what if he might have been? What if I'd told him ages ago and he'd decided to stay and be a real dad to her? Would he have been any good? Or would he hate us for taking him away from what he really wanted to do?'

'Romily, you can't operate on "what ifs". And you can't beat yourself up about something that happened in the past, about what you did and didn't want.'

Like me, she thought. *Like me not wanting to know about this baby here, right now, in the belly of the woman sitting next to me. My baby. Because I'm so hung up on the fact that I should have been able to conceive it myself.*

'Nothing about being a mother is easy,' Romily said. 'None of it. You have to make these decisions that will affect your child's entire life. Everything you say and do has the potential to change them in some way for the better or the worse. And there's nobody else who can do it. You have to do it all yourself.'

'Unless there's a father,' Claire managed to say.

'Unless there's a father like Ben, you mean. Because the wrong father can fuck it up just as much as the wrong mother.'

The wrong mother who couldn't even think about her baby when it was growing in the womb because she was too frightened to look beyond her own failure.

Claire swallowed, hard. She gazed at Romily's stomach. Underneath that jumper, inside Romily, was her baby. Hers.

I'm so sorry, little thing.

'I think you just have to make up for it,' she said. 'You have to make sure they know that they are wanted now, even if you didn't want them to begin with.'

'I don't know,' Romily said passionately. 'That's the problem. I don't know if he wants her really, or if he's just curious or acting out of duty. I haven't seen him for so long. He might see her and get her all excited to have a daddy, and then go away again and never get in touch. How am I supposed to know what's best for Posie?'

Claire looked up from Romily's stomach to her face. It was flushed. She was nearly crying again.

'Wait,' she said. 'Is that what you're upset about? Has Posie's father got in touch?'

'He wants to see her. He rang a couple of days ago. I don't know what to do. But I suppose you're right. She needs to know about her father.'

Oh my God, thought Claire. Had she said that?

'I didn't – I couldn't possibly give you advice, Romily. I don't know anything about it.'

Romily was already in the act of reaching in her bag for her phone. 'You're right, anyway. I have to stop being afraid and just face the truth. Posie is his child and parents should know their children.'

'Yes,' said Claire. 'Yes, they should.'

18

A United Front

At home, Claire took the scan photograph off the refrigerator door. She made herself look at it full on, memorizing every curve, every shape. She imagined the baby floating inside its borrowed womb, still small enough to nestle in her hand.

The doorbell rang and she shoved the photograph into her pocket like a guilty secret. When she opened the door, she was surprised to see her mum and dad standing on the step.

'Hello, darling!' trilled her mother, embracing her. Her soft cheek pressed against Claire's, smelling of her familiar Chanel.

Claire's father reached round and hugged her, too. 'We're on our way to Helen's for a few days. Thought we'd stop by and see how you were getting on. A few miles extra on the M4 never hurt anybody.'

Maisie, the latest of her parents' Golden Retrievers, nosed between them and sniffed Claire's hand with her greying muzzle, leaving a bit of slobber on her sleeve. Then she lumbered off to the front lawn to relieve herself. Claire remembered riding on the back of Maisie's mother

Moo-Moo, clutching handfuls of her yellow fur, pretending she was on a pony. Moo-Moo was buried in her parents' back garden now, under an Amber Queen rose.

'Come in,' Claire said, her mind rushing forward to the contents of her refrigerator and freezer. 'You'll stay for supper?'

'But we'll have to be going right away afterwards,' her mother said. 'Mark, would you get the boxes from the boot? I had so much extra bedding, I thought you could use some in that south-west corner? Annuals, but they'll be pretty in September. Not the marigolds, Mark, those are for Helen. The other ones. I've got some jars of marmalade and some elderflower cordial you forgot to take with you last time. I've got a sourdough starter for you as well.' She bustled in, set her canvas bag down with a clink, and surveyed her daughter. 'You've gained weight, haven't you?'

'Maybe a little.'

'About half a stone, I'd say. Good. You've been dieting too much, but you know this yo-yo-ing isn't good for you either.'

'I'm fine,' said Claire automatically.

Her father paused at the door with a boxful of plants. 'Straight to the back? Ben's still at work?'

Claire heard the crunch of tyres on gravel through the open door. 'That's him now. Go ahead and put the kettle on, Mum. We'll be right there.' She hurried outside to meet Ben's car.

He looked exhausted. He'd left early in the morning before Claire was up, moving quietly. Lying still in bed, she'd watched him getting dressed. When he'd dropped a soft kiss on her head she'd closed her eyes so he would think that she was asleep. She wished now that she'd kissed him back.

'Did it go all right?' she asked him as he got out.

He gazed at the Jaguar saloon. 'What are your parents doing here?'

162

'They're on their way to Helen's. They're only staying for supper. Is it all sorted out, the redesign?'

'It's been non-stop all day. It's going to set everything back months, and the Vaughans are not pleased.'

'Oh Ben, I'm sorry.'

'Can't be helped. You saw Romily?'

'Yes. She's fine.'

Maisie came up, wagging her tail, looking for a stroke. Ben ruffled her ears and she followed them up to the house. He took a deep breath before stepping through the door. Claire's dad had come in through the back and was hanging up his Barbour in the cupboard under the stairs. 'Hello, Mark,' Ben said, all traces of his exhaustion hidden. 'What a pleasant surprise.'

They shook hands. Ben and her father got on well; they listened to cricket together and shared appreciation of her father's home-brewed ale, though Helen's husband Andrew was clearly the favourite, mostly because he asked his father-in-law for investment advice. When Claire had suggested that Ben might do the same, even if he ignored it, just to make her father feel good, Ben had said he had enough advice from his own father, thank you, and he'd rather eat fried unskinned hedgehogs than ask for any more. But he'd said it *cheerfully*.

In the kitchen, her mother had already set out the teapot and cups and was slicing a loaf cake which had also come from her canvas bag. When it came to tea, the Hardy family never wasted any time. She embraced Ben.

'Is that your marmalade I see, Louisa?' he said. 'You must be a mind-reader. I just finished the last jar this morning.'

He looked drained and had clearly had a difficult day. He hadn't texted or rung to ask her how her meeting with Romily had gone; Claire had been worried about that, but seeing him now, she could see it was because he'd not had a moment. He probably wanted nothing more than to take a long hot shower and collapse in front of the television with a cold bottle of lager. But he was going to have tea and make conversation with her family instead, because he knew it was important to her.

Love swelled in Claire's heart for her husband. She took his hand and squeezed it, and he gave her a tired smile. She was so lucky to have him.

She wanted a baby with him, but the reason she wanted to be a mother at all was because of her parents. She'd had the perfect childhood, full of comfort and laughter and love. She wanted to give the same thing to her own child.

'Mum, Dad, I'm glad you're here,' she said. 'We have something wonderful to tell you.'

Her mother clapped her hands. 'You're pregnant, aren't you? I knew you'd gained weight.'

'How'd it happen?' asked her father. 'Your mother said you'd given up treatment.'

Ben's fingers tightened on hers. She held on to him, hard.

'We're using a surrogate,' she said.

'What's that?' asked her father. 'Some new technology?'

'My God,' said her mother. 'You're doing what?'

'A surrogate is when another woman has the baby for you,' Claire said to her dad.

'You're letting *another woman* have your baby?'

'Mum, lots of people do it. It's not so strange.'

'It's unnatural, is what it is.'

'There are precedents in nature,' said Ben. 'For example, ants and bees have queens who produce all the offspring, and the other insects look after them.'

'With all due respect, we are people, Benjamin. Not ants.'

'Mum,' said Claire. 'This is our choice. We're happy about it.'

'How are you going to find a woman to volunteer to do such a thing?'

'We've found her already.'

Her mother pulled out a chair and sat down. 'This is all so unexpected. Aren't you worried she'll keep it?'

'No,' said Ben.

'We're not,' said Claire. 'She's already got a daughter and she doesn't want any more children.'

'That's what she might say now, but she won't feel that way when she sees the baby. You can't carry a child in your womb for nine months and not fall in love with it. It's unnatural.'

'Mum—'

'I've had three children, Claire. I do know what I'm talking about.'

'And I've done a lot of research on surrogacy. People automatically assume that the surrogate mother is going to want to keep the baby because there have been some high-profile cases where that's happened. But hundreds of people do this all over the world every year and most of the time, it goes perfectly well. There are associations to help people, support groups, everything.'

'You're doing it through an association?'

'No. She's a friend. We arranged it ourselves.'

Claire's mother paused, to let this sink in.

'So do you have any legal recourse if it goes wrong?' asked her father. 'Our solicitor Fredericks is very—'

'It won't go wrong,' said Ben.

'What about adoption?' said Claire's mother. 'Wouldn't it be easier to have a child when its parents have already decided they don't want it?'

'We want *our* baby,' said Ben.

Louisa passed the tea around and they took a sip in silence.

'So let me get this straight,' said Claire's dad. 'You're making a baby through IVF—'

'An embryo,' corrected Claire's mum. Claire had given her a book.

'And putting it into this other woman? So it's your baby, but it's in her body?'

'That's gestational surrogacy,' said Claire. 'That wouldn't work for us. My eggs are no good. We've been through years of IVF and hardly harvested any. We're using traditional surrogacy, with her eggs and Ben's sperm.'

'So it won't even be your baby?'

'It is my baby,' Claire said. 'In every way that counts, it's my baby. Look. Here it is.' She took out the photograph from her pocket and gave it to her mother.

'You've done it *already*?' she said. 'I thought you were just talking about it.'

'The baby is due in January.'

Her mother looked close to tears. 'I don't understand. Why didn't you tell us before?'

'It happened so quickly. Romily offered, we made the decision, and she was ovulating right then so we went ahead.'

'We knew it was right,' said Ben. 'So there was no point in waiting.'

This wasn't quite accurate, but another thing Claire had learned about being married: you presented a united front in front of your parents. Once, when they'd first been married, Claire had made an off-hand remark about how Ben always had to be reminded to do the washing-up. She didn't mind that, really; he always did it when she asked, but at the time she'd been a bit annoyed. Her mother had taken it as a personal crusade to educate Ben in the desirability of helping your wife in the kitchen, pointing out how helpful Mark was, how he did everything without being asked. Which he did. Claire had never seen her father fail to do the washing-up, or fail to hang up his wet towels, or fail to remember a birthday or anniversary. He took her mother out to dinner and they went to ballroom dancing classes together and they never, ever argued.

As a child and a teenager, she'd told her mother everything. It was only since becoming an adult, since marrying Ben, since realizing that she herself wasn't perfect, that she'd begun the soft process of concealment, of gently obscuring parts of her private life. It wasn't an untruth she offered her mother: it was an edit.

From the expression on her mother's face right now, she'd been unaware of the editing.

'If it was so right,' Louisa said, 'why didn't you tell us?'

Claire went to her mother, who was still holding the scan photo, and hugged her. One part of her was thinking this was another person she'd let down with her worry, with her detachment. But another part, a bigger part, was wondering, for the first time, if one day her own grown-up child would edit its own life. She was almost excited at the idea of being kept in the dark, because that meant there would be some-one to do it.

'I'm sorry, Mum,' she said. 'We were going to tell you. We just wanted to make certain that nothing was going to go wrong this time. Before you got your hopes up.'

'But it seems such a risky proposition anyway.'

'I couldn't believe it myself,' said Claire. 'I've been worried that the baby didn't exist, that it was a figment of my imagination. Especially as I'm not pregnant myself and I can't feel the physical changes. But we've got the scan here, Mum. It's going to be born, and it's going to be ours.'

'Well, if you're going through with it, then of course you must do what you think best. I just don't want you to be hurt, darling. I don't want you to be hurt.'

She held her mother tighter. 'I won't be. I promise.'

'What should we tell everyone?' asked her father.

'Tell them the truth,' said Ben. 'That we're having a baby in January, and a surrogate is carrying it for us, and that we're incredibly happy and we'll take the baby to visit everyone once it's born.'

Her father went round to stand behind Claire and Louisa, looking down at the photograph she held. A gentle, mischievous smile touched his face, and he put his hand on his wife's shoulder. 'I know what I'll say. I'll tell them you're doing an Elton John. That'll shut them up.'

'You,' said Ben, after a very late supper and when they were alone at last, in their bedroom, 'were amazing.'

'I was truthful,' she said. 'That's all. And you were right to make me go and see Romily. I've been too afraid, and it's wrong.'

'So we can shout out about our baby from the rooftops?'

'Well, maybe start with friends and family first. Before the rooftop shouting.'

He took her in his arms. 'I love you.'

Claire nestled her head into his shoulder. She kissed the side of his neck. 'How tired are you?'

'Not too tired at all.' He slid his hand downwards and pulled her closer.

Her sister Helen rang first thing the next morning, before Claire left for school. 'So you went through with it after all,' she said. 'You kept that under wraps.'

'Sorry, Helen. We didn't want to say anything until we knew it was all right.'

'Mum is going round in circles and Dad has been muttering about talking to Mr Fredericks.'

'And what do you think?'

'I think it's great.'

'You do?'

'Even Mum had to admit that you looked happy. And once you've got a baby we'll see more of you. That's good enough for me.'

Claire spent most of Saturday afternoon composing an email and sending it to her various groups, friends, relatives and colleagues. Ben said it was so good that she might as well send it to his contact list too. She printed off every single response and tucked them into a scrapbook so that the baby could see them when he or she was older. Every email, every card that came through the letter slot, made her feel that this was really going to happen.

Or almost as if it was really going to happen. She could pretend the rest.

19
The Right Thing

It wasn't raining yet at least, which was good. And Posie hadn't suspected anything. Romily wasn't sure whether that was good or not. The little girl sprinted ahead of her across the park to the playground and immediately swarmed up the cone-shaped rope climbing-frame. Romily followed through the gate, went to the nearest bench and sat down. She checked her phone, but he hadn't texted her to cancel.

'See, Romily, I can do this one too!' called Posie to her, hanging off the pinnacle and waving. Romily waved back.

She'd chosen this park because it was across town from the one they normally went to. They'd been here before, so it was comfortable, but not too often, so it had some novelty for Posie. It was also far enough away from their flat so that if this all went terribly wrong, they would never have to come here again. The heavy grey skies meant that the play park was empty of other children, although some hardy souls were playing football in the adjoining field. Romily craned her neck, looking out for Jarvis.

'You're not watching!'

'Sorry, Pose.' She forced her attention back to her

daughter, who was now trying to balance on one foot on the slender rope, the toes of her other foot pointed like a ballerina's. 'Be careful there.'

'Don't worry, I can fly!'

But you can't, Romily thought, halfway off the bench, poised to run and catch her if she fell.

She had looked into some of the baby books Claire had sent her last night when she couldn't sleep, searching for a chapter on what to do when your child met their father for the first time in their lives. Unsurprisingly, there wasn't much advice in there. The closest she got was a paragraph suggesting that she express breast milk so that Daddy could give the night feed and let Mummy get some extra sleep.

Romily remembered the night feeds alone in her old one-bedroom flat. How she went to bed with Posie beside her so the baby could latch on in the night without either one of them really waking. How some nights when Posie wouldn't settle she'd pace the flat, from bedroom to front room to bathroom to bedroom again, patting Posie on her bottom, murmuring lullabies of Latin names she'd memorized long ago. *Ephemeroptera. Embiidina.*

Those were the most alone times: four in the morning when the rest of the world was asleep, and four in the afternoon when the rest of the world was at work. The times when you willed the hours to pass so you could pick up a phone and talk to someone who understood language. The times when you knew there must be something wrong with you for wanting this to be over because everyone knew that mothers and babies made a world of two, made perfect happiness together. Because even carrion beetles could nurture and protect their young without feeling bored and desperate and alone.

171

Posie put both her feet on the rope and Romily sat on the bench, sighing in relief. Out of the corner of her eye she saw a blond man in a dull green jacket.

'Watch this!' called Posie again and Romily said, 'Okay,' but she didn't stop watching Jarvis, who stood outside the barrier watching his daughter. He had one hand on the gate but he didn't open it. She couldn't read the expression on his face, whether he was going to step inside or turn away.

'Look, no hands! Whoops!'

Instinctively Romily was off the bench again, but Posie managed to catch herself. Romily felt rather than saw Jarvis sit on the bench beside her.

'How do you handle the terror?' he asked her in a low voice.

'Badly.'

On the climbing-frame, Posie was pushing her feet one way on the rope and her hands the other way on the central pole, making the cone spin on its axis. Her entire attention was on going as fast as possible. Her hair tumbled around her face and her jacket was half-open.

'She's bigger than in the picture,' said Jarvis.

'That happens.'

'When was her birthday?'

'February the seventh.'

He grunted. They both watched Posie, who, deciding that the frame was spinning as fast as it would go, scrambled down and jumped off. She landed with a happy whoosh, sure on both feet, and ran to the swings.

'She's brave,' said Jarvis.

'That's quite new. She started walking early, but she was physically timid up until she started school. She's mostly a reader. She has an amazing imagination.'

'Bright girl.'

'Frighteningly so, sometimes.'

'What have you told her all these years?'

'That I didn't know where her father was.'

'Nothing else about me?'

'Not much.'

'Kind of you.' There was a frown between his eyebrows.

'I didn't want her to be expecting you to turn up. I didn't want her to be disappointed if you didn't.'

'That's rich.'

'We're doing fine on our own.'

'I have a life, you know, Romily. I wasn't expecting to be hit over the head with this. If I haven't been around for eight years, that's your fault. Not mine.'

She set her jaw. He crossed his arms.

'What did you tell her about today?' he asked.

'Nothing. I wasn't sure you'd come, to be honest.'

He shot her a look at this. 'You haven't a very high opinion of me, have you?'

'I have no opinion at all. You don't have to be involved if you don't want to be. The less I think about it, the less I worry I've made a horrible mistake.'

'What's your horrible mistake, in your opinion? Telling me now, or not telling me before?'

'Take your pick.'

'Oh, believe me, I know which one was the horrible mistake.'

She took a deep breath. 'Okay, here's the deal. Someone said to me that it was important that a child should know they are wanted. If you plan to be part of her life, then you can tell her who you are. If you don't, then don't. Either way is fine. Today, you've got a free go. But if you want to see her

173

again after this, we'll have to tell her who you are and she'll need to know she matters to you. I'm not going to have my daughter mucked around.'

'I'm her father.'

'You produced the sperm, yes. Whether you're going to do anything else is up to you.'

'No,' said Jarvis. 'Up till two weeks ago, it was up to *you*.'

'Like it or not, those are the rules.'

'I don't think you have much right to be setting rules. Not after you robbed me of the chance to make up my own mind.'

'Romily!' Posie came running up from the swings, panting. 'Do you have my bottle of water?'

Romily produced it. Posie took a long drink, oblivious of the man sitting beside her mother. She handed the bottle and the cap back to Romily separately. 'Come and push me,' she said, and ran back to the swings.

Romily and Jarvis considered each other for a long moment. Then Jarvis got up and went to the swings.

Romily pulled her legs up on the bench, wrapped her arms around them and rested her chin on one of her knees. *My* daughter, she thought. *Mine.*

But she stayed where she was.

Not far off nine years ago, when she'd recently started her PhD and Ben and Claire had started planning their wedding, she had met Jarvis on a blind date set up by some of her Museum of Natural History buddies. They'd met at the Queen's Arms in South Kensington; Romily got to the pub very early and had been sitting there for two and a half hours, drinking pints of London Pride and rereading *The Man Who*

Mistook His Wife For a Hat. He'd turned up carrying a large parcel which he put down on the table.

'You've started without me,' he said. He was wearing a T-shirt and combat trousers. He was thinner than Ben, untidier than Ben, fairer than Ben. When he ran his hand through his hair, slightly damp from sweat, his T-shirt rode up enough so she could see a hint of skin.

You'll do, she thought.

'You're late,' she said. 'What's in the parcel?'

'It's my cousin's birthday gift. I missed the Post Office.'

'I'm on London Pride.'

'Excellent.'

He'd returned with a pint for each of them and a shot of Jack Daniel's for himself. 'I need to catch up,' he said.

Four hours later, they were in his bed in his studio flat in Hackney. The walls were papered with his photographs of woodpeckers. He'd won an award.

'I'm not looking for love,' she told him, her head on his hard shoulder, running her hand up and down his chest to see how it felt.

'Now that's a relief,' he said. 'I'm off round the world anyway. Someday.'

'So am I.'

He bent his head to kiss her and pull her closer so they could make love again.

As Romily recalled, most of their dates went like that.

On the swings, he pushed Posie higher and longer than Romily would have pushed her, and then he spun her on the roundabout so fast that she couldn't stop laughing. When the ice-cream van passed the park, Posie got her usual hopeful look and Jarvis loped over to the van, his hand in his pocket.

175

Romily opened her mouth to protest but then she shut it. He had not bought her an ice cream in seven years. Typical that Posie didn't ask her permission, though. And she noticed that Jarvis bought two cornets, ignoring Romily.

The two of them sat side by side on the swings to eat their ice creams and Romily watched them from her bench. They were talking about something but she couldn't hear what. She itched to go over and join them. She would go over if Posie seemed at all uncomfortable, or Jarvis seemed at all angry. But they just chatted.

Jarvis didn't stop her from wiping her mouth on her sleeve.

Posie jumped up and ran to the climbing-frame again. 'Watch!' Romily heard her call. Jarvis watched for a little while, then he picked up her discarded ice-cream wrapper and brought it over to the bin near Romily's bench.

'I don't think that went too badly,' he said.

'She gets on with most grown-ups. It comes with being an only child. What did you talk about?'

'I didn't tell her I was her father, if that's what you're asking.'

It was, but Romily shrugged. 'We're fine,' she said. 'She hasn't got a big hole in her life or anything like that.'

'I like her.' His voice caught.

Romily hugged her knees and concentrated on watching Posie, who climbed on, oblivious.

Jarvis cleared his throat. 'I want to see her again.'

'That means you're going to tell her.'

'It's my right.'

'I'm not thinking of what's best for you, Jarvis.'

'I'm staying at my brother-in-law's flat in London. He'll let me stay as long as I like.'

'And when do you go off again?'

'I don't know. I haven't decided yet.'

She stood up. 'You can't muck her around, Jarvis. I warned you.'

'Because you have always, one hundred per cent, made decisions for her that were the right ones. Correct?'

'You don't know what it's like to be a parent.'

'Funny, that,' he said, and his voice was dangerously low.

'Romily! Jarvis! Watch!'

Posie hung upside down from the climbing-frame. She waved at them, clambered upright, and hung upside down again from another rung.

'Good work, Pose,' called Romily.

'I'm off now, Posie,' called Jarvis. 'Nice to meet you.' He turned to Romily. 'I'll ring you next week.'

Romily watched him go. She wondered whether they were doing the right thing.

20

Inner Calm

'You've booked us into pregnancy yoga,' said Romily. Her voice sounded less than enthusiastic.

'I think it'll be fun,' Claire said, tucking her gym membership card back into her purse. 'It'll be good for the three of us to do something together for the baby. Also, studies have shown that it can reduce morning sickness.'

'Well, that would be worth getting a babysitter for.'

'Yoga helps you live in the moment,' Claire added. 'Which is something I could do with.'

'And I get to see the women in their tight leggings,' said Ben. 'So it's win-win all round.' He was grinning. It was so easy to make him happy, Claire thought, and when he was happy it was catching. And things seemed easier between her and Romily this time. As if their argument in Starbucks had cleared the air.

Ben opened the yoga studio door for Claire and Romily, but Romily paused on the threshold, taking in the mirrors and the wooden floors, the New Age music playing, the serene-looking women sitting on blue mats, their hands folded over their swollen bellies. For a moment,

Claire expected her to turn around and leave.

'Why isn't there pregnancy football, is what I'd like to know,' Romily muttered, and went in. She was wearing loose drawstring jogging bottoms and a mismatched T-shirt. At seventeen weeks, in clothes that weren't too big for her, she was definitely beginning to show; there was a roundness to her stomach and it looked as if she'd gone up a bra size or two. Ben, still grinning, fetched mats for all of them and they settled in a row on the floor with him in the middle. Claire automatically assumed the lotus position, closed her eyes and breathed in and out, seeking to empty her mind of the thought that yet again she was in a room full of other women who were going to have babies.

She was going to have a baby too. It was all right. Everything would be all right. As soon as this baby was in her arms, it wouldn't matter whose womb it had grown in.

'Welcome,' said a musical voice, and Claire opened her eyes. The instructor squatted in front of them. It wasn't one Claire had seen before; there must be a different one for the antenatal and fertility groups. She was wearing purple leggings and top, and smiling directly at Ben. 'How lovely to see a father here as well.'

He was the only man in the room — possibly, from the way the instructor was looking at him, the only man in the world. 'It's a pleasure to be here,' said Ben.

'It's so important for the father to be involved every step of the way,' said the instructor. 'Yoga can help you find an inner calm that bonds the parents together. Of course, the baby can feel that togetherness in the womb.'

'Of course.'

'Some fathers even experience pregnancy symptoms along with their partners. Are you?'

Claire heard Romily's soft snort of amusement. Ben smiled wider. 'I have had a strong craving for pickled onions,' he said.

Claire nudged him, and for the first time the instructor turned her attention to her. 'And you're Mummy?'

'I . . .' she began, as beside her Ben gestured to Romily. Claire flushed, conscious of her lack of pregnancy, even more obvious in her workout clothes.

'We're both Mummy,' said Romily.

'Oh,' said the instructor. 'You're sisters? Or friends?'

'We're both Mummy,' repeated Romily. 'And Ben is Daddy.'

'To . . . for both of you?' The woman's gaze travelled between Claire, Romily and Ben.

Claire opened her mouth to explain the surrogacy situation, but before she could do so, Romily said, 'Yes. We're both having Ben's baby.' She smiled brightly at the instructor.

'Oh. Oh well, that is very . . . interesting.'

'We're extremely excited about it.'

'Whilst at the same time having a deep inner calm,' added Ben.

'And togetherness,' said Romily. 'Lots and lots of togetherness.' She caught Claire's eye and winked.

The entire room was watching them now. Ben was revelling in it, his chest practically puffed out at having been revealed as a super-stud.

Claire bit her lip to stop from smiling.

'We're quite keen to work on our flexibility,' she said, and heard Romily stifle another laugh.

'Right. Well, that's . . .' The instructor stood. 'Are there any injuries I should know about? Any problems?'

'I'm throwing up regularly,' said Romily.

'I'm having a little trouble being in the now,' said Claire.

'I don't have any problems at all,' said Ben.

The instructor glanced between the three of them again, but Claire kept her face straight, through long practice of being in front of a classroom with a poker face. Ben and Romily smiled innocently.

'Right,' she said. 'Okay. I think we'll start with a Sun Salutation, everyone . . .'

'Thanks to the two of you, I now need to switch gyms.' They'd come back to Claire and Ben's house still in their workout gear, not having fancied the scrutiny of fellow pregnancy yoga practitioners in the changing room, and were now having tea in the kitchen. Claire put slices of banana cake on plates. 'If I go back there again they'll probably give my name to *The Jeremy Kyle Show*.'

'It's not so bad,' said Ben. 'I quite enjoyed it, actually.'

'Of course *you* did.'

'We only told them the truth. We *are* all having a baby together. If she wanted to have a dirty mind, that was her own fault.'

'You might have helped her along a little.'

'All that Mummy and Daddy stuff,' said Romily. 'It's sickly. Just because you're having a baby, it doesn't mean that your identity is erased. And just because you're not the actual pregnant one, it doesn't mean that you don't exist.'

'Thanks,' said Claire quietly.

'Well, it's true.' Romily accepted her cake and dug in straight away.

'I'm sorry I dragged you both along. It was a disaster. Every time she said "Downward Dog", you laughed,' Claire said to Ben.

'The mental image was too strong.'

'I think it might have helped with the sickness,' said Romily. 'I'm certainly hungry enough. This is good. Can I have another piece after this?'

'You're looking better,' said Claire, cutting it for her.

'I actually slept last night. And I've started this fun game at work, where I'm counting how many times Hal stares at my stomach before he'll get up the nerve to ask if I'm pregnant.'

'They don't know yet?' asked Ben.

'It's none of their business. And besides, I like playing with their heads.'

'But you'll want to take maternity leave.'

'No such thing. My funding deadline runs out at the same time, regardless. And besides, I'm giving the baby to you as soon as it's born. A couple of days, and I'll be back with the bugs.' She took a huge bite of cake, and turned to Claire. 'Have you asked for maternity leave yet?'

'I sorted it out before the summer holidays: six months from next Christmas. But I doubt I'll go back. We always planned for me to leave work when we had a baby.'

'Don't,' said Romily. 'You might want that job to go back to. Something that's your own, something to prove that you have a brain and aren't just a nappy-changing automaton.'

'I can't imagine wanting anything else.'

'Well, maybe you won't. I did – I was desperate for it, to be honest. But you and I are pretty different.'

'We are,' said Claire, but today that didn't seem like such a big problem. Maybe Ben had been right. All she'd needed to do was to spend time with Romily. 'How'd it go with Posie's father, by the way?'

'Posie's *father*?' Ben said.

Romily blanched, her cake halfway to her mouth. 'Er.'

'Posie's father has got in touch? He knows he's got a daughter?'

'He . . . er, turned up a few weeks ago.'

'Is that why you weren't answering your phone?'

'Yeah. I didn't feel like talking about it.'

'But you talked about it to Claire?'

'Claire gave me some good advice, actually.'

'You gave Romily advice? And you didn't tell me?'

'I . . . thought it would be best coming from Romily,' said Claire. And she'd been too focused on her own relationship with Ben, with the unborn baby, with her own feelings. With counting the congratulations cards that came through the post and wondering if it meant something that they hadn't received more.

'So what did you advise her to do?' Ben asked. 'Tell him to get lost?'

'I said . . . I said that a child should know that she was wanted.'

'Jarvis did not want Posie.' He turned to Romily. 'You told him to bugger off, right?'

'No.'

'What? He's been away for nearly eight years with no interest in his child whatsoever. The man clearly has no sense of responsibility at all.'

'He didn't know he had a child,' Romily said.

'He didn't deserve to have a child. You told him you were pregnant and he immediately left to go to the other side of the world.'

'Well, to be fair, we had agreed for me to have an abortion first.'

183

'He didn't even hang around to make sure you were all right. He left that to me. How'd he find out about her, anyway?'

'I told him.'

'*You told him?*'

'Ben,' said Claire, putting her hand on Ben's arm.

'What, you gave him a ring? Suddenly, now?'

'No, he turned up at work. I'm not exactly sure why, to tell you the truth. And he looked so much like Posie, that I . . .' Romily shrugged. 'I couldn't help it.'

Ben got up from the table. 'I cannot believe you want that toerag in Posie's life.'

'It's not that I want it so much as I owe it to him. I think Posie deserves to know her father.'

'It doesn't make a big happy family, Romily. It can tear everything apart. You don't know anything about Jarvis, you haven't seen him or heard from him in years. Does he have a steady job? A home in this country? Does he have any other children?'

'I don't know. He's quite angry with me. We haven't really discussed everything yet.'

Ben raked his hands through his hair. 'Okay. This is what we have to do. You have to see a solicitor and agree contact rules. You and Posie need to be protected.'

'No,' said Romily. Claire marvelled at her calmness, much more pronounced now than when they had been meditating earlier. 'I don't want it formalized. I just think Posie should maybe get to know her father, even if it's only for a little while.'

'She doesn't need Jarvis. She has me.'

'But you're not her actual father,' said Claire. 'And we're about to have a baby of our own. That's going to change things.'

Ben turned to her. 'Whose side are you on?'

'I wasn't aware that there were sides. Children need people to love them. It's obvious.'

'It's not as simple as that.'

'But it sort of is,' said Romily. 'I think.'

'I'm going to have a shower.' Ben left the room. Claire and Romily exchanged a look.

'Sorry for dropping you in it,' Claire said.

Romily was rather pale. 'I think that's the first time Ben and I have had an argument.' She took a long breath, and Claire could see she was genuinely shaken. The calmness must have been an act. 'Though I suspected this was how he'd react, which was why I didn't tell him.'

'If you'd met up with him instead of me last week, do you think you would have made a different decision?'

Romily frowned. 'I don't know. It's done, anyway.'

'How did Posie take it?'

'She doesn't know yet. I thought . . . I thought they should meet each other first.' She stood up. 'It's getting late.'

'For what it's worth, I think you've made the right decision. Ben will come round. He always does.'

Romily bit the inside of her lip, but she didn't answer.

21
Family

'Why are we going to that same park again?' asked Posie from the back of the car.

'We're meeting someone there.'

'Oh.' Posie's voice lost its petulance. 'Who is it? Is it Ben?'

'No. It's Jarvis.' Romily glanced in the rear-view mirror.

'Oh. Oh, okay.'

'Do you like Jarvis?'

Posie considered. 'Yeah, he's all right. He's been to Guatemala.' She pronounced the word carefully. 'Did you know that?'

'I didn't, no.'

'Well, he has. And he bought me an ice cream.'

'Is that to say that you would like anyone who bought you an ice cream?'

'I don't know. No, I don't think so. I wouldn't like Dennis Farmer if he bought me an ice cream.'

'Who's Dennis Farmer?'

'He's a boy at school. He picks his nose.'

'Posie, everyone picks their nose at some time or other. You should probably give him a chance.'

186

'Not everyone wipes it on your maths paper when you're not looking.'

Romily had to concede that point. 'So you do like Jarvis. Regardless of the ice cream.'

'He's a wildlife photographer. So that's pretty cool. I could maybe do that. It would go with all the exploring.'

'It certainly would.'

Posie went quiet, and when Romily glanced back again, she could see that her daughter was thinking. Romily smothered the urge to say anything more, just as she'd been smothering the urge not to come to the park this morning. She'd been half-expecting a phone call from Ben, either to apologize or to tell her off some more, but he hadn't been in touch. Claire, on the other hand, had texted *Good luck!*

She didn't like having argued with Ben. While it was happening, she'd felt oddly in control, even though she was saying things that she wasn't certain that she meant. But then afterwards, the impact had hit her. He'd never disapproved of her before. They'd always worked on the assumption that they thought the same way about most things.

'I know what's going on,' said Posie from the back seat. Romily pulled herself out of her thoughts.

'Is this another one of your theories?' she asked.

'You're meeting up with Jarvis again and asking me what I think of him because he's your new boyfriend.'

Romily laughed aloud. 'Oh. Oh dear – no, Pose. That's not true.'

'I don't mind if he is.'

'He's not my boyfriend.'

'Why don't you have a boyfriend, then?'

'Because I've got more important things in my life. Like

you, for one. Here we are.' Romily parked the car with mingled dread and relief. It was sunny today, and the park was busy. From here, she could see across the field to the play park, where a now-familiar figure was already waiting on the bench.

Posie ran on ahead; Romily tried to keep up, noticing, as she had for the past week or so, that she was beginning to move with the pregnant woman's waddle. Jarvis was watching them approach.

'Hey,' he said, standing up, his hands in the pockets of his trousers.

'Hi,' said Posie. 'Do you pick your nose?'

'Posie!'

'I'm going to refuse to answer that question,' Jarvis said. But he was smiling now, in that way he had with the corners of his mouth turned down.

'Romily says that everyone does.'

'I'll bow to Romily's expert opinion.'

'*I* don't.' Posie plopped herself down in the middle of the bench. Jarvis sat beside her, leaving space at the other end for Romily.

'Don't believe her for a second,' Romily told Jarvis. She was struck again by the resemblance between them: the colour of their eyes, the thickness of their hair. The freckles across their noses. Nervousness rose up in her like nausea, and she opened her bag to look for a mint, even though she hadn't been sick for days now. It was as if the yoga had flicked some sort of nausea switch to off. Or maybe it was just time for her to stop being sick.

'Are you going to push me on the swings in a minute?' Posie asked him.

'If you want me to.'

'Yeah. First though, Romily won't tell me why we're meeting you at this park again.'

Romily gave up her search for a mint. She met Jarvis's gaze over Posie's head. He'd lost his half-ironic smile now. He looked, quite frankly, terrified.

'Er,' he said. 'And you want to know.'

'Don't you have a car to get to our house? The bus goes right by it.'

'I . . . think your mother wanted to meet here because it was neutral. Do you know what that means?'

'Yes. I have the best vocabulary in my class.'

'I'm not surprised.' Jarvis took a deep breath.

Romily hadn't expected him to be scared. *Good*, she thought. *You should be terrified. This is terrifying.*

'The thing is, Posie, that . . .' He met Romily's gaze again.

'We have something to tell you,' Romily said.

'What?'

You or me? The meaning in his face was clear. *Which is better?* Romily shrugged. As if she had any idea.

'What is it?' Posie asked Jarvis, which seemed to settle it – for him, anyway.

'It's that I'm your father.' Jarvis swallowed, took another deep breath, and sat up straighter. 'I'm your father.'

Posie's brow furrowed, in the way it did when she was thinking.

'Really?'

'Yes,' said Romily. 'He is.'

Posie looked from Jarvis to Romily. 'Were you two married or something?'

'No, we were never married,' said Romily.

'But did you actually have sex?'

'Um,' said Jarvis.

189

'Yes,' said Romily. 'We did.'

'So where have you been since I was born?' Posie asked Jarvis. 'Guatemala?'

'Er. Partly. I didn't know about you, you see.'

'But you had sex with Romily. So you knew there would be a baby.'

Jarvis had a spot of colour on each of his cheekbones. Romily came to his rescue. 'There isn't a baby every time that people have sex, Posie. Sometimes people have sex for fun.'

'Okay. That's weird.' Posie turned to Jarvis again. 'So you and Romily made me but you didn't know about it, you thought it was just for fun, and you went off to Guatemala.'

'Something like that,' said Jarvis. 'If I'd known about you, I don't think I would have stayed away for so long.'

'But now you know, so you're going to stay in England.'

'I—'

'He wants to get to know you better, Posie,' said Romily, before Jarvis was pressed into more commitment than he'd planned on. 'So that's why we've met up, and why he's told you that he's your father.'

'I thought we could do some things together,' said Jarvis. 'I'd like to spend some time with you.'

'I think that would be all right,' said Posie. 'What should I call you? "Dad"?'

'Since you call your mother by her name, why don't we try "Jarvis"?'

'Okay.' Posie jumped off the bench. 'Come and push me on the swings, Jarvis.'

'Be right there.'

As soon as she was occupied elsewhere, Jarvis slumped back onto the bench and rubbed his hand over his forehead. He'd been sweating.

'It went okay,' Romily told him.

'I've never been so embarrassed in my life.'

'She's the queen of awkward questions, that one.'

'She . . . seems very knowledgeable about sex. For seven.'

'She's curious. I'm a biologist.' Romily resumed her search for her mints, found a packet, and passed him one. 'You'd thought about what she should call you beforehand, hadn't you?'

'Yes. Why does she call you Romily, anyway?'

'It seemed to suit me more than "Mum". Do you – you don't have kids? I mean, any other kids?'

'No. I have nieces and nephews, but this is all new to me.' Posie beckoned to him from the swings, where she'd nabbed a free one. 'Is she just going to accept me, like that?' he asked.

'It comes out later sometimes, in unexpected ways,' Romily said. 'She's had quite a bit to think about lately.'

Jarvis glanced down at her stomach. His face tightened, and he got up to join Posie. Within a few minutes, her shrieks of joy reached Romily.

She put her hands on her stomach. This little thing growing inside her wasn't going to have these issues. Right from the start, there would be no doubt about who its parents were. Posie might get over-excited and try to claim it as a brother or sister, but that wouldn't be a problem. It wasn't possible for a baby to have too many people loving it.

Romily's own father, William, had died ten years ago of heart failure. He was an accountant. She wished Posie could have met him. Romily remembered long weekends fishing with him, listening to cricket on the radio, examining the ecology of the riverbank. An amateur biologist, he had a little notebook wrapped in oilskin in which he wrote down the scientific names of the creatures they spotted, the measurements of the fish that they caught and released. Romily still had it somewhere. One year, they had caught the same brown trout seven times.

She tilted her head back and closed her eyes, letting the sun warm her face and the sounds of children pass around her. She saw her father in Posie: the concentration and abstraction, the quick turn of her head sometimes, the throw-away facility in calculation. Her mother had died when Romily was young, and was nothing more than a warm memory and photographs, but Romily knew she was there in Posie's sharp chin, the same as Romily's.

Jarvis must be finding these similarities too. He'd said Posie looked like his sister Sally. Strange that Romily's own daughter could resemble someone whom Romily didn't know, that this little girl who was wholly familiar to her, whose body she had borne and bathed and tended, still contained some secrets.

Maybe this baby she was carrying would look like Ben. Or maybe it would look like Romily's own lost family.

Under her hand and inside her, the baby shifted. A stretching, an adjustment.

Romily opened her eyes. She looked down at her belly. 'Do it again, Thing,' she whispered.

For a minute, two minutes, nothing happened, while the sun shone and the children laughed and Romily's daughter ascended and descended the arc of a swing. Romily heard and saw none of it. She pulled the material tight against her stomach and concentrated on this being inside her, half of her and half of Ben, who was alive.

It somersaulted. Fleetingly she saw a ripple moving near her hand.

A bubble of joy burst inside Romily and she laughed.

It was four days later when she was dragging a complaining Posie around the supermarket that it came out.

Romily couldn't find the tofu. This happened on a regular basis, as the supermarket seemed constantly to reclassify tofu as a ready meal, or a salad, or a meat substitute, or a sandwich ingredient, or a World Food, or a type of pasta, and moved it around the store accordingly. She had a theory that every time a frustrated vegetarian turned to bacon, the supermarket got a kickback from the meat industry.

'I want to ride inside the trolley,' said Posie for the eighteenth time.

'You're too big to ride in the trolley and besides, it's full of food. Let's look over here with the chilled food.'

'It's cold over here.' Posie rubbed her bare arms in her sundress.

'It's only for a few minutes, Pose, just calm down.' The smell of the rotisserie chickens reached her from across the shop floor. The tofu wasn't here, either. 'Maybe I should just get more eggs. Will you eat eggs for dinner?' She tried to do a mental inventory of her refrigerator. There was about a tonne of organic beetroot and something called kohlrabi which she hadn't figured out what to do with yet. From Claire's organic box scheme, of course.

'Eggs make the house smell funny. I want pasta. Can I have jelly?'

'If they have the right kind. And we've already had pasta three times this week.' Romily put yoghurts in her trolley, although she had a sneaking suspicion that they hadn't eaten the last ones yet and that they were merely hidden behind the kohlrabi. Did they need margarine? What about toilet paper?

Exactly when had her life become made up of these burning questions?

'I think that we should all live in Sonning,' said Posie.

'What?' asked Romily, reaching for the milk.

'At Ben and Claire's. It's big enough. Jarvis doesn't have anywhere to live in England, so he could live there. He could have the spare bedroom. And you could have the other bedroom, and Thing could share with me. I wouldn't mind the crying. I could cuddle it.'

Romily put the milk in her trolley. Then she squatted so she was face-to-face with Posie, who was still rubbing goosebumps on her arms.

'That's not going to happen, Posie. I know you would like it, but this baby in my tummy is going to belong to Ben and Claire. Not to us. And they don't know Jarvis well enough for him to live with them.' Let alone that Ben would probably try to knock Jarvis into next week if he saw him. 'And besides, we have our own flat, you and me.'

'But it's not big enough for Jarvis to stay there if the two of you get together.'

'Why,' said Romily, 'do you think that Jarvis and I are going to get together?'

'It makes sense. You must have cared about each other once, right, or you wouldn't have made me. Because you only have sex with people you care about. That's what Claire told me.'

'When did Claire tell you this?'

'Oh, ages ago.' Posie waved her hand. 'Anyway, I know you haven't seen him for a long time, but now that he's back you probably will fall in love again.'

'Posie,' said Romily.

'And then we can be a family.'

194

Romily dropped her head into her hands. She tried to sort this out, to understand the right thing to say, something that would let her daughter down gently, that would crush her dreams without crushing her. But they were in a supermarket, and a part of her brain was still dwelling on toilet paper.

'It's not as easy as that,' she said, finally.

'Yes, it is.' Posie smiled at her, serene. Then she pointed over Romily's shoulder. 'And look, there's the tofu.'

22

B Flat Major

Summer days were too long.

Claire had made an orange chiffon cake for the village fête, and several lemon drizzle cakes while she was at it, for the freezer. She left one out for the IVF support group. She hadn't been for months now, not since she'd miscarried and decided to give up on treatment, but she was thinking she might go on Thursday. She was just about ready to face the group in person, rather than via email, and she knew that they would all be happy for her. Or at least they'd act as if they were happy for her. The ones who had succeeded with IVF would probably feel sorry for her, and the ones who were still trying would thank God that they weren't that desperate just yet.

On second thoughts, she put the extra cake into the freezer with the others.

She did her yoga, and she washed the curtains in the spare bedroom and hung them out on the line to dry in the sunshine. She wrote a letter on proper paper, and put it aside for later. She made herself a salad for lunch. She weeded the garden and sprayed soapy water on her roses, which had

196

shown signs of a few aphids. She squinted at the little green insects and tried to see the honeydew Romily had said they made, but she couldn't see anything and she wasn't going to taste to find out. She thought about ringing Ben, but they'd already chatted this morning and besides, he was busy. Helen and Andrew were on holiday with the kids. She rang her mother, who wasn't home. She picked up the novel that her book club was reading, a complicated story about several generations. She hadn't been to book club in months, either; after a few glasses of wine, they spent too much time talking about their children. She put the novel down and went for a walk instead, on her usual route through the fields south of the village to the Thames. She watched the ducks squabbling and the swans not deigning to notice anything.

By the time she got back, it was only quarter past two.

She shook out her hands to loosen them, fluttered her fingers and sat down at the piano. The piece on the music-stand was a Bach fugue with melody and counterpoint twisting in mathematical perfection, and she hadn't practised enough. She never had time to practise, although she had all the time in the world.

Once, the hours had slipped away while she was at the piano. Other children had to be forced to practise; her own parents had had to force her outside to play, to get some fresh air, and even then, the music would spin through her. She would jump rope to its time, run to its cadence.

The melody tripped along. Her fingers didn't feel light or deft enough. Claire closed her eyes and tried to let the music guide her hands. Fugue in G Minor, BMV 861. She told her students how this music had been written for clavichord, but how when you played it on a modern piano, it gave the piece its own haunting beauty and subtle warmth. Today, however,

197

her fingers couldn't convey it. She struggled for technical accuracy, tangled her notes together and stopped with her eyes still closed. This fugue ended in a B flat major chord. Uncertainty leading to resolution, solemnity to happiness.

By themselves, her fingers formed a tune from her memory. Soft, lilting, familiar, also in G Minor. For a moment she tried to place it — it was modern, something she'd heard on the radio? — and then she remembered. It was Max's tune. The one he called the mother theme.

Poor Max. She wondered what sort of summer holiday he was having, and she played the tune again.

Abruptly, she stood up and shut the piano. She went up the stairs.

When they'd first moved into this house — her cottage in the country, close enough for Ben to commute to the city — they'd called the small, sunny south-facing room at the back of the house 'the nursery' and they expected it to be filled soon. They didn't call it that any more. The other bedrooms were their bedroom, Posie's bedroom, the guest bedroom. This room, with its single bed with the white duvet cover scattered with daisies, with its flowered wallpaper that they'd never bothered to change and its rag rug on the floor, was where her sister had set up her travel cot for her own children, where her brother's son slept when they visited. No one ever said its true name.

Claire stood in it now. It smelled faintly musty, as rooms in old houses do when they're not aired and used. She opened the window and looked out at the garden, at the pear tree that was waiting for its swing.

Birdsong would come through the open window. Even in winter, the light would shine in and make patterns on the wall. From their room next door, she and Ben would be able to hear the faintest snuffle, the most sleepy cry.

'Yellow,' she said aloud. Light sunshine yellow, the colour of delight. They would choose a cot in pale wood and hang a mobile from the ceiling. A single wooden chair stood against the wall; she climbed on it, stretched up her arm and took hold of a corner of the old flowered wallpaper where it had become unstuck from the wall. She tore it off in a great, satisfying strip and dropped it curling onto the floor. And a CD player on the chest of drawers, to play music. This baby should have sunshine and music all of its life.

She peeled off another strip, and another.

23

Quickening

Posie was already in bed and Romily was flicking through the television channels and not finding anything when she heard the knock at the door. She recognized the sound right away as being Ben's knock, but she paused to tie up her dressing-gown over her pyjamas before she opened the door.

He wore a still-crisp white shirt, with his tie loosened slightly. It had been ten days, with July moving into August, since they'd argued. The relief at seeing him was incredible. She nearly stumbled back with the force of it.

'Hello stranger,' she said, to cover up.

'I came from work. Are you going to let me in, or am I too big an ass?'

She stepped back and let him in. As always, he filled the little room with his presence, carrying the faint scent of aftershave and of the outside summer air.

'I'm sorry,' he said. 'Posie is your daughter. It's not my decision to make.'

'You're right.' She pointed to the fridge. 'I think there's a bottle of lager somewhere in the back if you want it.'

'Do you want something?'

'Apple juice.'

He opened the bottle and poured her juice, everything looking smaller in his hands, and joined her on the sofa. 'What you watching?'

'I can't find anything but reality shows.'

'*A Question of Sport* is on in a minute.'

She flipped it over. He settled beside her, stretching his long legs out as if he were there for the duration. 'Isn't Claire expecting you home?' she couldn't help but ask.

'She knows I'm working late. She's pretty busy with all her little projects. She's started decorating the nursery.'

'She texted me a photo.'

Ben shot her a wry smile. 'The two of you are pretty tight these days, aren't you? Ganging up on the poor bloke.'

'We didn't gang up on you, and besides, you were wrong.'

'Let's not argue,' he said. 'I get enough of it all day at work. You're my relaxing person, Romily. I don't want to have to examine every word before I say it. It's what I've always liked about you. You're not complicated.'

'No.'

Nothing complicated at all about how she breathed him in like a woman saved from drowning. How she was aware of the exact distance between his hand and her leg on the sofa cushion. How every time he raised his bottle of lager to his lips, she remembered that time, that one time, his lips had touched her own.

Inside her, a poke and a twist. 'Oh,' she said.

'What?'

'The baby just moved.'

Delight broke on Ben's face, like the sun. 'Really? What's it doing?'

'It sort of flips itself around. I've felt it more and more the past few days, especially when I've been sitting still.'

'Is it doing it now? Can I feel?'

A pause, but maybe not long enough for him to notice. 'Of course, you're its father.'

She untied her dressing-gown and parted it, leaning back in the sofa to expose her belly. Her pyjamas were nothing special, a vest and loose cotton trousers, but they were a bit too small for her in the chest and the belly now. The vest had crept up a little, seeking the path of least stretching, and when Ben put his hand on her stomach his palm lay directly on her skin.

He was warm, warmer than the August night. She had to close her eyes for a moment because his touch was so intimate, so overwhelming, but opened them almost immediately, aware of her mistake. He wasn't looking at her face. He hadn't seen.

'I can't feel anything.'

Oh dear Lord, of course he couldn't have seen. He had his hand on his friend's stomach because he wanted to feel his child move. He had no idea he was touching Romily's deepest desire.

'It . . . might take a while before it does it again.'

'Do you think it might help if I talked to it? They say babies can hear.'

'I don't know.'

Ben leaned over so his face was inches from her stomach. His hand stayed where it was. 'Hello, little dear Thing,' he said. 'It's your daddy speaking.'

His words made caresses of warm air on her skin. She had stretchmarks from Posie there, silvery-white, waiting to blossom again. She didn't know what was worse: watching him with his mouth so close to her, or closing her eyes and merely feeling. She wished she'd pulled down her top. She wished she were a million miles away, up a tree somewhere, in a jungle – anywhere so she wouldn't have to feel the thing she wanted most to feel in the world.

In the beginning, she used to dream about it. Ben would touch her, by mistake maybe, and the two of them would fall together, heedless, starving for each other. The dreams, during waking hours and during sleep, were so vivid that in reality, once he was Claire's, she kept half a foot's distance from him at all times. Six inches of clear air. No handshakes, no air-kisses, no embraces when their football team scored a goal.

Through years the dreams had faded. She had been able to be less strict about avoiding casual touches. She had felt safer, protected by the knowledge that he had no idea of what she really wanted.

They had still never touched like this. All alone, in her flat, with Posie asleep.

'I can't wait to meet you,' Ben told the baby inside her. 'I can't wait to hold you and kiss you.' He glanced up at Romily's face, and she did her best to smile. 'It's funny, isn't it, to think that it's already a little person. But until we see the baby we won't know who it is.'

'Funny,' agreed Romily. Her throat was dry, but she couldn't make herself move enough to pick up her glass. She wondered if Ben could hear her heart beating.

'There it is!' His head shot up, his eyes wide with surprise and awe. 'The baby moved!'

She hadn't felt it. 'The talking must have worked.'

'Either that or it's very interested in *A Question of Sport*.' He addressed her belly. 'That's my kid.'

The baby distinctly kicked. Ben laughed.

'That's amazing,' he said. 'Will it do it any more?'

'I don't know.'

He straightened up. 'I'm not taking my hand off it, then. I don't want to miss a single bit.' He arranged himself on the sofa beside Romily, so his arm lay alongside her and his hand stayed spread on her stomach. 'Is that okay with you?'

Yes. No. 'It's your baby.' She wondered if she should pull down her top, but then that would call attention to the fact that it had been up. That she'd noticed he was touching her naked skin. 'I'm a little cold though.'

'Here, then.' He pulled a flap of her dressing-gown over her stomach and his hand. Which was worse, because now it felt as if he was touching her in secret. Romily swallowed.

'You're not going to be sick, are you?'

If she said yes, he would stop. She should say yes and end the torture. 'No. No, I don't think so. I seem to be done with the morning sickness now.'

'Good. I'll watch this with you and then I'll go. The baby moved!' He laughed again and held up his lager. 'That's worth a toast.'

She groped for her glass and clinked it with his. 'To a kicking baby.'

'I can't wait to tell Claire.'

Romily took a long, long drink. She tried to focus on the television.

24
Amity

S he'd reached the next to last drawer.

Romily stood in the little slope-ceilinged room with its noisy fan and its mothball smell and contemplated the rose-wood cabinet. It wasn't just Amity's collection that was nearing its end; her funding wasn't going to last much longer, either. She'd have to look for a new job in the New Year. It might mean commuting to London, maybe, with all the juggling of childcare and school runs that that entailed. It might mean moving herself and Posie away.

Once upon a time she'd pictured herself as an explorer, just like Posie wanted to be. She saw herself tramping through jungles. Discovering a species no one had seen before. Amity had had the same dream, and for years Romily had been living it vicariously through her.

When the project finished she'd have to say goodbye to Amity and go back to real life. Maybe there weren't any jobs out there, not for single mothers with a PhD in invasive lady-birds who had to work their hours around their childcare. Maybe her future lay in making lattes in Starbucks.

Then again, maybe a move to Brazil would be a good

option. Posie would certainly love it, and it might be best for Romily's own peace of mind to be far away from Ben.

Romily sighed. Delaying work on drawer No. 71 wasn't going to solve anything. And to be honest, she was excited about it. She slid the drawer out. It was full of wasps, each one pinned to a tiny label in Amity's faded handwriting, referring to a catalogue that no longer existed. Faintly she heard the phone in the study room ringing so she brought the drawer downstairs and answered it.

'You've got a visitor,' Hal told her. 'I'm taking her to the staff kitchen.'

'Who is—' she started to say, but Hal had rung off. She made her way down to the staff kitchen. Hal was outside it.

'I think she has cake,' he said. He followed her into the kitchen, where Claire was standing holding a flowered tin.

'Hi,' Romily said, more than a little surprised.

'What's in the tin?' Hal asked, eyeing it and not going away.

'I made some cupcakes.' Claire was looking around the kitchen. She seemed nervous, though she was covering it with a smile.

'Don't worry,' said Hal. 'We don't let her bring her horrible dead bugs down here.'

'Shut up, Hal. Claire, this is my supportive and knowledgeable colleague, Hal Watson, the museum manager. I suspect he wants to get his greasy mitts on your cupcakes.'

'I like cupcakes.' He edged closer.

'Are you fond of bugs too?' Claire asked him.

'Give me the creeps. My degree's in geology.'

'He prefers dirt,' said Romily. 'What brings you here with cupcakes?'

'Oh, it's the summer holidays and I have some free time. I

thought you might like these.' She put the tin on the cleared table and opened it.

It was full of beetles. Hal actually jumped back. Romily leaned forward.

There were a dozen cupcakes, each iced white, each with a beetle on it. Romily picked one up. The Stag Beetle was beautifully executed in icing and liquorice. Its mandibles jutted out and there was even a faint green sheen on its elytra.

'This is incredible. You made these?'

'Yes. I . . . had some spare time, as I said. I found the pictures on the internet. I'm sorry if they're not very accurate.'

'For something that's edible, it's remarkably correct.' Romily looked at it from all angles. It smelled delicious, like sugar and vanilla. 'I thought you hated insects.'

'It was a good challenge to make them out of icing.'

Hal reached into the tin and took a cupcake with a Tiger Beetle on it. He checked it carefully to make sure it was just decoration before he shoved it into his mouth. 'Good,' he said through crumbs and icing.

'Of course, Hal,' said Romily, 'you may have one of the cakes that Claire made especially for me. Thank you,' she added to Claire, genuinely touched. 'That's a really nice thing for you to do.'

'Oh,' said Claire, and she smiled and shrugged. 'I love making cakes.'

Romily bit into her cupcake. Hal was right; it was good. 'Are you going to have one?'

'Oh no, not right before lunch. Besides, they're for you.'

'Hear that?' Romily said to Hal, and put the lid on the cupcakes and moved them away from Hal's hand before he snatched another one. 'Actually, do you want to have lunch with me? My treat, to thank you for the cupcakes. The café here has decent sandwiches and homemade soup.'

'That would be nice.'

'I'll look after the cakes,' said Hal. 'Lock them away in my drawer. Otherwise these jackals around here will scoff them all.' He took the tin and bore it away with him.

'Ben says he felt the baby move,' Claire said as they went down the twisting stairs.

Romily ducked her head. 'Er. Yes. It's a squirmy little thing sometimes.'

'It's so exciting. I can't imagine it.'

'If it starts up I'll let you know so you can feel. Before long it'll be keeping me up at night. I remember Posie used to get the hiccups as soon as I went to bed.'

'That must feel strange.'

They came out onto the museum floor just as three kids ran past, trailing paper Roman helmets and swords made out of cardboard tubes. There was a reason Romily usually had her lunch at her desk. Still, she didn't think that Claire would want to share her cheese and pickle sandwich and broken Ryvitas.

'You must love the summer holidays, as a teacher,' Romily said. 'All that spare time.'

'Yes, well, there's a bit too much of it sometimes.' Claire laughed lightly. 'Ben's got a lot of work on, so he's off early and home late. Of course, that's understandable, and he'd prefer to take the time off while I'm off, but it doesn't always happen. So I've got the house to myself.'

Imagine having time like that. Endless time to sleep if you wanted, or read, or just do nothing. Not having to worry about what to feed a child or how to keep it entertained or about doing the laundry at the last minute because nobody had any pants or socks clean. And all that big house to wander around in, bright and beautifully decorated, knowing that when you were asleep, your husband would slip into bed beside you.

'Wait till you have the baby,' Romily said. 'You won't even have enough time to use the toilet.'

'I can't imagine,' Claire said again. They reached the café. During term time it was filled with the staid murmur of pensioners but today it was pandemonium. The kids with helmets and swords massed around the big tables in the corner, their parents shouting at each other over the noise. Three tables under the window were taken up by a gang of mothers and babies. Prams barricaded them in, along with a litter of bottles and baby-wipes and small plastic containers of baby-approved snacks.

There was a single table in the middle that was free except for two empty cups. 'Shall we—' began Romily, pointing at it, but then she saw Claire's face.

She'd gone pale; her blue eyes had tight lines around them and she was gnawing, worrying at her lower lip. Her hands clutched the strap of her bag. Romily followed her gaze to a woman inside the pram barricade who had draped her baby over her shoulder and was rubbing its back. The baby's face was visible: milk-drunk eyes, pouted mouth, peg of a chin.

'On second thoughts,' Romily said, 'it's too noisy to hear ourselves think in here. Let's go somewhere else.'

'Yes,' said Claire. She sounded grateful. 'Let's.'

Only when they reached the pavement outside did Claire release her death grip on her handbag.

'You must hate me,' said Romily.

'Sorry? No, of course not. Why would I hate you?'

'Because you want to be pregnant like me. You want to have a baby of your own. And you tried so hard for so many years and then I push the plunger on a syringe of sperm – and whoops! There I am, knocked up. And then you send me all this lovely food and gifts to help me feel better, to show there's no hard feelings, and I take it as a criticism and throw it in your face.'

'I'm grateful to you,' said Claire.

'Then you're a better person than I am. Does it . . . is it hard every time you see a baby?'

Claire was silent and Romily was afraid she'd offended her. 'It won't always be this way,' Claire said at last. 'It'll be much easier once this baby is born and I can hold it.'

'I think you're very brave.'

'No. Not brave. It's just coping. Haven't you ever wanted something and not been able to have it?'

'I . . . oh look, here's a pub.' They went inside. The scent of beer wasn't too bad; they stood at the bar and took menus. 'I wanted to travel the world,' said Romily. 'But I had a baby instead.'

'You can do it when she's grown.'

'At this point, it looks like Posie's going to do it for me. It isn't as difficult for Ben to see babies, is it?'

'It's not his failure.' Claire gazed down at her menu, and Romily thought the topic was finished. But then she said, 'I did hate you.'

Romily put down her menu.

'That was why I didn't come and see you at first,' said Claire. 'I was jealous. I'm not proud of it.'

'You shouldn't be jealous of me. My life is a mess.'

'I don't think you can truly be jealous of someone you understand,' said Claire. 'And I can see that you've been

210

struggling too. Posie's father, and all those big decisions. Your life hasn't turned out exactly how you'd planned it either. But that's okay.' She took a deep breath. 'Anyway, the cupcakes were to say all that. I'm sorry I hated you. You didn't deserve it.'

Romily felt her cheeks flushing. 'It's all right. I don't blame you.'

'In the end,' said Claire, 'I think we want the same things.'

That night, alone in her bed, with the baby quiet inside her and her daughter asleep next door, Romily took out her green notebook. She opened to a blank page.

DON'T LOVE BEN LAWRENCE, she wrote. Again and again, down the entire page, as if writing it could make it come true.

DON'T LOVE BEN LAWRENCE.

25
A Window In

Claire could hardly believe that this picture here on the screen in front of her was of her baby. Snub nose, delicate, intricate spine, legs curled up to fit into the womb.

'The baby seems so big,' she whispered. Ben took her hand in the darkened room and they gazed at this window into Romily's body.

'It looks like a little person already, doesn't it?' he said.

'At twenty weeks, Baby's about the size of a banana,' said the technician cheerfully. 'The measurements look good. Everything looks good. Would you like to know what the sex is?'

Claire squinted at the screen. With the legs curled up like that, she couldn't tell. 'Do we want to know?' she asked Ben.

'Don't you think it's better if it's a surprise?'

Romily looked up from her book. She had it propped just above her belly. 'You don't want to give little Thing a name?'

The technician laughed. 'You call it Thing?'

'It's sort of a nickname,' explained Claire quickly, in case the technician thought they were strange for giving a baby such a detached name. Though the technician had been very kind, not registering any surprise at all when Romily explained that she was the surrogate and that Claire and Ben were the real parents. 'Romily's daughter started using it and it stuck.'

'I like it,' said the technician, typing something into her computer. 'It's better than some of the names I've heard, believe me. Last week I had a couple who'd named their baby James Tiberius Kirk. After the *Star Trek* captain?'

'That's a lot to live up to when you're not out of the womb yet,' said Romily. 'Kid might not even like space travel.'

'Well,' said the technician, 'Thing appears to be perfectly healthy and a good size. Do you want to keep a photograph? One copy or two?'

'One will be fine,' said Romily. She went back to her book.

Claire took the photograph out to the waiting room while Romily got herself dressed again. She and Ben stood, their heads close together, staring at it. At their future.

'I can hardly believe the baby's grown so much,' she said.

'All that organic food is paying off.' Ben kissed her cheek. 'Does it feel real to you now?'

She traced the baby's outline with her fingertip. 'You know, it does.' She grinned at Ben. 'It really does.'

She held it against her body, close against, as if Thing were growing inside her.

26
Shifting Sands

It was Jarvis's idea: a day on the coast near the end of the summer holidays, to get to know each other better. He borrowed a Mercedes saloon from a friend even though Romily told him she had a perfectly good Golf, and packed a picnic even though Romily told him she really did know how to make sandwiches, and picked them up outside her flat in the morning. He waited in the car for them, motor idling, while they gathered together the metric tonne of stuff that was necessary for a day on the beach. Posie insisted that she should ride in the front seat, so Romily sat in the back by herself and closed her eyes and listened to the rock music on the radio and the breeze blowing in through the open windows and the steady stream of conversation between her daughter and her father. They seemed to have a lot to talk about. Posie, of course, could talk to anyone when she had a mind to, but Jarvis had a treasure of anecdotes from his travels around the world with a camera, and he held Posie rapt.

The stories weren't told for her benefit, but Romily couldn't help but listen. He'd ridden an elephant in India and been spat at by llamas in Peru; had his tent ransacked by baboons in Botswana and lain in wait for seven days for a Bird of Paradise in New Guinea. He'd had malaria despite the tablets and lost two stone. He'd broken his wrist falling from a tree in Bolivia and he'd climbed back up anyway to carry on shooting the macaws because it was two days' trek to the nearest hospital and he reckoned he might as well get the footage before he was forced to take a week off in La Paz in a sling.

Romily had dreamed of a life like that, once upon a time. Not the broken wrist, obviously, nor the malaria. Jarvis clearly had no regrets that he'd left England; he'd been having all sorts of adventures while she'd been in a small flat changing nappies and classifying someone else's insect collection at work.

Her mind drifted away off to sleep and she didn't wake until they were on the chain ferry to Sandbanks. The tang of sea air came through the windows and she sat up straight, taking in the sky that seemed much bluer down here, the noise of the ferry, the seagulls wheeling overhead. Posie was nearly jumping up and down in her seat. Jarvis drove them to a car park and Posie was out of the car almost before it stopped.

'Be careful!' Romily called to Posie, who was hurtling over the dunes. Jarvis, carrying the picnic basket and a blanket and Romily's hold-all filled with clothes and buckets and spades and sun cream and hats, loped ahead and casually took Posie by the hand. Romily followed, carrying the towels, placing her feet carefully in the sloping sand. Her centre of gravity had changed. By the time she got to the beach proper, Jarvis had already dumped the equipment and he and Posie were running towards the surf, whooping.

215

Posie was wearing her swimming costume under her clothes, but she hadn't bothered to take them off of course, so they were going to get soaked. Romily considered going after her and divesting her of her shorts and shirt, but they were having such a good time already and she had spare clothes. So she spread out the blanket a nice distance from the closest family and sat on it, kicking off her sandals and burying her feet in the warm sand.

It was a beautiful day: sunny, with a breeze coming off the sea. The beach was busy, but not crowded, full of the happy screams of children and the rhythm of the surf. Across the water she could see the Isle of Wight. She breathed in the unfettered air. From the looks of it, she needn't have come along, as far as Posie was concerned, anyway. She was perfectly happy with her new exciting playmate. But the nap in the car had been wonderful. She wasn't sleeping enough. And it was good to get away for a day, even if it was nowhere more exotic than the Dorset seaside.

Jarvis wore a T-shirt and a pair of battered knee-length shorts, and he and Posie were chasing the waves up and down the beach. Posie's hair flew loose and Jarvis was laughing. No one watching them would take them for anything else but father and daughter.

How long would he stay in the country? One thing he hadn't mentioned in his stories was a wife or a girlfriend. But there had to be someone after all this time, even with his travelling. There had to be a reason he'd come back to England in the first place. Romily knew that Posie's notions of everyone living together in Ben and Claire's house as a big happy family would never happen, but how were they going to rearrange their lives, the three of them?

'Romily!' Posie was running up the beach towards her, her

feet slipping in the sand. She was, predictably, soaked to the skin. 'Come and play!'

'You're having a good time with Jarvis,' Romily said. 'You don't need me.'

'We want you!' Posie grabbed her hand with her cold, sea-wet fingers and tugged. 'It's fun.'

Romily got to her feet and went along with Posie. Jarvis was waiting for them, ankle-deep in shifting water, his hair ruffled by the wind. He grinned at her, the sort of grin she hadn't seen from him for eight years, and rare enough even back then. It made him look younger.

'Your daughter reckons she can command the sea by the force of her will,' he said.

'I wouldn't put it past her.'

'Let's do it together.' Posie reached out and took Jarvis's hand with her other one. 'One, two, three, run!'

They launched together into the surf, chasing the wave down the slope. It foamed away from them and the sand hissed under their feet. 'And stay there!' yelled Posie, and then she screamed as the water came rushing back, backpedalling up the beach with Romily and Jarvis on either side.

'There's this thing called the tide,' began Romily, but then they were running back towards the sea as it retreated, and up the beach again as it advanced. Breathless, laughing, with salt on their lips and in their hair, grasping slippery fingers and swinging Posie between them.

On a downward run, just as the sea was about to turn and rush back, Posie let go of their hands and sprawled headfirst into the water. Instinctively Romily grabbed for her, but Jarvis got there first and Romily collided with him. He steadied her with one arm, pulling Posie up with the other.

'Again!' spluttered Posie, her hair in wet rat's-tails,

217

laughing. She squirmed free of Jarvis and rolled in the froth. For a split second Romily was held against Jarvis's side. She could feel his ribs against his wet shirt, the lithe strength of his chest and arm, his quick breath.

Then he let her go and backed away a step or two.

'I think the idea is to play in the sea, Pose, not to drink half of it,' said Romily, wringing water out of her top.

'Lemonade,' said Jarvis, reaching down and hauling a giggling Posie out of the water again. 'And then shell-hunting. Come on, explorers, let's go.'

'I don't want to wear a hat,' said Posie, scrambling up the beach to where they'd left their stuff.

'You will,' said Romily and Jarvis at the same time. 'Young lady,' added Jarvis. Romily covered her mouth with her hand.

She twisted off a strawberry stem and handed the berry to Posie before popping another one in her mouth. 'You,' she said to Jarvis, 'really do know how to pack a picnic.'

The blanket was littered with sandwich crusts, empty crisp packets, crumbs of cake. Posie had commandeered a corner of it for her treasures and she rearranged her shells and sea-weed in a circle, with the one fossil they'd found in the centre: a curve of ammonite. A drop of strawberry juice ran down her chin and she absently wiped it away on her bare arm.

'We used to come here every summer,' Jarvis said. 'We had picnics just like this one, only I remember vast quantities of potted meat.'

'Ew,' said Posie.

'Don't knock it. It's hard to be a vegetarian when you're a world explorer.'

'I might eat snake, maybe.'

'Snake is delicious.' He poured the last of a tube of crisps into his hand and tipped them into his mouth. 'I never found a fossil on this beach, though. I've got a boxful of fossils that I found further along the coast.'

'Bet I can find more.'

'I'll take you up on that. In a minute.' He leaned back on his elbows, his legs stretched out in front of him. Romily found herself looking at his feet. They were dusted with sand, long, lean and familiar, as familiar as his body had felt an hour ago in the surf.

In a different world they might have been here as a family. She would have heard about his childhood picnics already. She would probably be sick of hearing about his childhood picnics.

'You've got a big family, haven't you?' she asked, memory tickling. 'Still in London?'

'Spread out all over the South of England. You can't throw a stone without hitting one. They'd like to meet you, Posie.'

'You've told them about her?'

'Yes.' He raised his eyebrows as if he expected her to object, but she didn't. She was too relaxed, and besides, he had a right.

'They probably all hate me for not telling you sooner.'

'No. That is, my mother does. But my sisters say I am a feckless gadabout and that they'd think twice about telling me, too.'

'They say that?'

'Not in those words exactly. But I know them well.'

'I'm going to have a brother or sister soon,' volunteered Posie. 'We call it Thing.'

'Posie.'

'Yes,' said Jarvis. 'How . . . when is the baby due?'

'At the beginning of January.'

'You and Ben must be pleased.' He pulled his leg up, away from her.

'And Claire's pleased too,' said Posie. 'Claire has decorated the nursery already. I saw it, it's yellow like sunshine. I don't mind sharing it. They have a spare room for you, if you want it, Jarvis, because I know you don't have a house in England.'

'Posie, leave it.'

Jarvis frowned. 'Claire decorated the nursery?'

'Yes, Claire doesn't have good eggs so Romily is having the baby for her. She and Ben used artificial respiration.'

'Insemination, Posie, and that's enough. Why don't you build a sandcastle.' Romily pushed buckets and spades in her direction. She felt Jarvis's stare.

'Okay,' said Posie, and went a little way off to start digging sand.

'Ben is still married to Claire?' Jarvis said, in a low furious tone. 'You're acting as their surrogate?'

'Yes. It's no big deal, Jarvis. I volunteered.'

'What are you, fucking stupid?'

'Pardon me?'

'I take that back. You're clearly not stupid, but you must be insane.'

'Jarvis, this is none of your business.'

'You're carrying Ben's baby. It's yours and Ben's.'

'Genetically it's ours, but legally—'

'Legally! As if that matters. You've been in love with Ben for years.'

It was like a punch in the chest. 'How—'

'I've got eyes, Romily. You might call him your best friend, but I was never fooled by that. He's some sort of god to you – who knows why.'

'You don't know anything.' The two of them were both on their knees now, face to face, talking in a cross between shouts and whispers. Two metres away, Posie dug in the sand, humming quietly to herself.

'Your capacity for self-delusion hasn't changed at all,' said Jarvis. 'Do you really think you're going to be able to give this baby away?'

'Yes. Yes, of course I will. Ben and Claire want this baby. It's theirs.'

'You couldn't give up Posie, and you didn't even love me.'

Romily put both her hands on her stomach. 'It's different.'

'The difference is, this one is Ben's. Or maybe you're using this baby as leverage to finally get Ben for yourself.'

'Like I used Posie as leverage to get you to stay? Oh no, wait – I didn't do that, did I? You said you wanted freedom and I let you have it.' Romily scrambled to her feet and grabbed her sandals. 'I'm not having this conversation with you. I'm going for a walk. Look after Posie for me.'

Jarvis said something else, but she didn't hear it. She was walking rapidly across the soft sand towards the dunes. A path led her through them between tufts of spiky grass.

How did he know? She'd never told him. She'd never told anyone, except for the pages of that notebook. She'd been hiding it for years with everything she said and did. She'd even chosen Jarvis initially because he was the opposite physical type to Ben.

Except she'd built her entire life around being near Ben, and now she was having his baby.

Romily left the path and climbed over a dune, brushing through grass. Jarvis was full of shit. This was Ben and Claire's baby, and she wasn't going to have any trouble giving it up, because it was theirs. Theirs, together. Not hers. Not to be used as leverage, or emotional blackmail, or something to torture herself with. She was an incubator for their child, pure and simple, and if she happened to have deeper feelings for its father than she let on, well then, that was nobody's business but her own. Certainly not Jarvis's.

You couldn't give up Posie, and you didn't even love me.

Posie was hers, though. She'd been Romily's, and nobody else's, right from the beginning. Although Romily never could have guessed how complex and hurtful and wonderful and exhausting that belonging could be.

A seagull hovered above her, riding the air currents, using minuscule movements to hang still in the air. Back there on the beach, her daughter and her daughter's father dug in the sand together and laughed and forged a relationship. Whatever Romily did affected Posie, and Jarvis did have a say about that. Whether she liked it or not, Posie was not only hers any more.

And Jarvis had seen how she really felt about Ben. He was the only one in the world to see it.

What if he was right? What if she had volunteered to have Ben's baby because somewhere, down deep, she thought it would make him love her?

The wind and sun made her squint. From here she couldn't see the beach; the dunes were too tall. She turned to climb back over the dune towards the sea, and when she'd reached the top, a bird exploded out of the grass to her left at the same time as her foot slipped in the sand. She put out her hands but there wasn't anything to grab hold of, only waving grass, enough to unbalance her further, and her foot caught on something, a root or a stone or a hole, and momentum pitched her forward onto her face. She slid down the dune, a high bird-cry in her ears, catching at nothing.

She came to a stop and lay there, sand in her mouth and eyes, trying to work out whether she was hurt. She could feel scratches on her face and knees, but her ankle throbbed and she felt as if she'd been punched in the belly. *My baby*, she thought, and rolled over and put both her hands on her stomach, too late to protect it.

'Mummy!'

'Romily!' Jarvis came running up to her, Posie behind him. 'Are you okay?' He put his hands on her arms gently, his eyes probing her face.

'Guess I can't fly after all,' Romily said, and tried to smile.

'Can you sit up? Have you hurt yourself?'

'I think I'm all right.' She sat up, ignoring a pull of pain, spat out sand, and reached out to Posie. 'I'm okay, Pose. Don't worry, sweetheart.'

Posie threw herself into Romily's arms. Romily winced, but held her.

'What happened?' Jarvis was kneeling next to them. 'Did you slip?'

'I caught my foot in a hole or something. It's okay. I think I twisted it.'

'We need to get you to a doctor.'

Romily saw the fear in Posie's face. 'No, no, I'm fine.'

They had attracted a small crowd of fellow beach-goers. One of them handed Jarvis a water bottle, which he gave to her so she could rinse out her mouth. The adrenaline had caught up with her, making her feel dizzy and sick. She bent her head and put it between her knees.

She hadn't broken anything, by the feel of it. She'd fallen harder because of being front-heavy, and she'd have some bruises and scrapes. She might have struck a rock or a root, or something hard. But as long as the baby was fine . . .

Through the pain and the dizziness and the sound of the sea and the people around her talking, she felt what she hadn't before: warm wetness between her legs. Dropping the water bottle, she put her hands to her bare inner thighs. When she lifted her hands to her face, her fingers were covered with bright blood.

27

Don't Go

Jarvis picked her up and carried her to the car, Posie hurrying after them. Romily didn't protest. She held her belly and tried to feel a movement, prayed to feel a movement.

He didn't say anything, laying her on the back seat, driving what she suspected was considerably over the speed limit. Posie sat quietly too, and all that Romily could hear was the sound of the engine and her heart beating.

Don't go, Thing, she thought as hard as she could. *Don't go.*

She found a packet of tissues in the back-seat pocket and shoved some of them in her pants. Borrowed car. Don't want to take it back with a stain on the seat. Her hand came out with more blood on it; she wiped it on her shirt.

Don't go.

It seemed to take a very long time to get to the hospital. Once they'd arrived, Jarvis said, 'Wait here,' and disappeared into the building. The silence in the stopped car was very large.

'It'll be fine, Posie,' said Romily. 'I'm okay, we're just a little worried about Thing.'

'I'm scared.'

'It's probably nothing. Babies are tough. They survive almost everything. And it's well-protected inside me. It's as if I wrapped you up in a whole load of pillows.'

But she could feel the cramping now, low in her stomach and in her back. It was hard to tell how bad it was, how much was her own pain and how much of it was from the baby, but she didn't think it was bad. Not yet.

'I'm sorry,' Romily said, though she wasn't certain which of her children she was saying it to.

Jarvis reappeared and opened the back door. 'Do you think you can get into this wheelchair?' he asked her.

He helped her out of the car. Her muscles had stiffened up from lying in the back of the car, and her ankle protested when she put her foot on the ground. Jarvis wheeled her into A&E, where they were met by a nurse who gave Jarvis a clip-board and took Romily into a cubicle. 'We are going to decide where to send you. You had a fall?' She had a kind face and a brisk Eastern European accent.

'Yes, on Great Knoll Beach, about thirty minutes ago, I think.'

'And you are bleeding? How much?'

'I – don't know.'

'Are you losing a lot of blood or is it more like a period, or is it just spotting?'

'I'm not pooling with it. I . . . used a tissue.'

'Let's see.'

Romily didn't want to see. She reached into her pants and pulled out the wad of tissue. It was less than she'd feared, but not by much.

'Okay. Your life is not in danger from it. We are mostly con-cerned about the baby.' She gave Romily some more tissues. 'Did you bang your head? Are you feeling sick?'

'No, I didn't bang my head. I'm fine. I'm worried about the baby.'

The nurse did a quick checkover. 'Yes. You have had a blow to your stomach. There is a bruise coming up already. How many weeks are you?'

'Twenty-one.'

'Over twenty weeks, you will go to the maternity ward. I will ring them to expect you. Your husband can take you in the wheelchair. There are signs to the ward. Here is a sanitary towel.' She dropped a light box onto Romily's lap, then adjusted the wheelchair so that her ankle was elevated and put a cold pack on the swelling before she wheeled her back out into Reception. 'She must go to the maternity ward,' she told Jarvis, who was waiting. He didn't have the clipboard any more.

'You don't know all my details,' she said to Jarvis.

'Posie did.' He immediately took the handles of the wheelchair and began wheeling her to the double doors at the back of A&E. Posie trotted along beside them, quiet.

It was out of her hands now. She was in the NHS machine. Whatever happened would happen and she would be helped as much as she could be. Romily closed her eyes and held on to the box containing a pad of cotton that would never, ever be enough to soak up everything that was inside her.

The maternity ward was much quieter than A&E. Jarvis wheeled her straight up to the desk and the receptionist said, 'Yes, you've been called through and we have your details on the computer. The midwife will be with you in just a moment.' He pointed them to a line of waiting chairs.

Jarvis parked her and sat beside her, Posie on his other side. 'This is my fault,' he said in a low voice.

'It is utterly and completely my own fault. I stepped in the wrong place and I slipped. You weren't even there.'

'I shouldn't have argued with you.'

'Don't.'

The procedure, the quiet, the silk flowers on the reception desk, were all there to take the edge off her panic, but she was still breathing quickly, her heart pounding, her fingers shaking. She wanted to run screaming down the hall demanding to be seen right now, right this minute. But that wouldn't do any good.

'What can I do?' asked Jarvis.

'We need to tell Ben and Claire.'

'I'll go outside and call them. What's the number?'

She gave Ben's mobile number to him from heart.

It wasn't going to be the most popular move having Jarvis call him, but she didn't dare leave this hospital, not even for a moment.

'And can you take Posie to the café or something? I don't know how long I'll be.'

He nodded. 'We'll come back and check on you. Posie? Your mum's going to be fine but it might be a long wait, so let's go get some cake.'

Posie gave her a swift kiss on the cheek before they went. It was all Romily could do not to clutch her and not let her go.

The midwife strapped a monitor to her belly and the sound of the heartbeat was immediate and strong. 'That's a good sign,' she said, smiling.

'I'll take all the good signs I can get.'

Waiting for the obstetrician, she lay on the table and looked at the poster on the wall, a cross-section of a pregnant woman. It wasn't unlike the animal specimens Romily had dissected herself.

The doctor bustled in, slender in a lab coat. 'Dr Summer,' she said, glancing at the computer screen. 'Throwing yourself off a sand dune, I hear?'

'It wasn't the best decision I've ever made.'

She checked Romily over. 'Still bleeding steadily. Any cramping or contractions?'

'I can feel some cramps. Though it's hard to make out what's cramp and what's the result of hitting the ground with my belly.'

'This isn't your first baby?'

'Second.'

She nodded and snapped off her gloves. 'It's difficult to tell at this stage what's going on. I'll send you for a scan immediately and that will give us more of an idea. There are a number of things that could be causing the bleed, which may or may not be related to the trauma. If you are actually miscarrying, there's very little we can do, of course, and as you know, sadly we can't resuscitate before twenty-four weeks.'

'I . . . no, I didn't know that.'

The obstetrician gave her a swift look. 'You're not a medical doctor?'

'An entomologist.'

'Oh.' She opened her mouth, and then closed it. 'Oh. I see. In any case, we'll send you for that scan, then. Good thing you did this during office hours, eh? Otherwise you'd have to wait till tomorrow. I'll get someone in here to help you.'

She left Romily with the cut-open pregnant woman.

The baby had grown since the last scan when both Ben and Claire had been with her. Romily wouldn't have thought she'd have noticed; she hadn't thought she'd looked that closely. But she did notice. She stared at the screen that was filled with the mystery inside her. She saw a head, a hand, two closed eyes and a nose and a mouth.

'It's sucking its thumb,' said the technician.

This is my baby. This is my baby with the only man I have ever loved.

'Is it going to be all right?'

'I'm sorry, I can't diagnose anything. The doctor will have a look at the scans.'

Two curled-up legs, crossed feet at the ankles. The cord attaching its body to hers, through which she was feeding it, giving it life.

'Is it a boy or a girl?' she asked. Ben and Claire wanted it to be a surprise. But if it were never born, how could Romily grieve if she knew it only as a thing?

'It's a little boy,' said the technician. 'Do you want a photograph?'

She clutched it in her hand all the way back to the maternity unit, as if holding on to it would keep her baby inside her. She traced it with her finger. Caressed her baby's cheek. Her little boy.

'Well,' said the obstetrician, her lab coat buttoned up this time, 'there's no placental abruption that I can see. Everything looks fine. Any contractions yet?'

'No.'

'Let's check the bleeding.'

Romily turned her head and looked at her photograph while the doctor pulled on another set of gloves. *Please*, she thought.

'It's old blood now.' The doctor chucked her gloves in the bin. 'Sometimes these things just happen. But we'll admit you to keep an eye on you, and keep you for twenty-four hours after the last bleed.' She turned to go.

'Is my baby going to be all right?' Romily wanted to scream the words, but they came out as a choked whisper.

The doctor paused. 'My best guess is yes. Shaken up, but fine.'

Romily burst into tears.

28

Maternity Ward

The first thing that Claire heard was the sound of a baby crying. It was a shared ward, with four beds on either side of the room, separated by curtains on rails; in the bed nearest the door, a woman nestled a downy head to her breast.

Ben rushed to the far bed where Romily lay. He flung himself onto his knees and put his ear to her stomach. 'The baby's all right, isn't it?' He laid his hand on Romily's stomach.

They'd had a call on the journey down to Poole to say so. But Romily looked slight and pale in the hospital bed, in a patterned white hospital nightgown. There was a scrape on the side of her face.

'They think it's going to be fine,' she said. Her voice was hoarse.

'Claire!' said Posie, running up to her and throwing her arms around her waist. Claire hugged her back.

'Come on, Thing,' said Ben to Romily's stomach. 'Kick your daddy. Show me you're all right.'

'It was going crazy a few minutes ago,' Romily told him.

'Have you stopped bleeding?' Claire asked over Posie's head.

'Pretty much. They have to keep me in for twenty-four hours, but then I should be okay to go.'

'Unless you start again,' said Claire.

'We were frantic,' said Ben. 'I'm sorry we couldn't get here earlier. I was in London and then there was an accident on the M3.'

It was a trip that Claire never cared to repeat: Ben swearing at the traffic, while she sat beside him, twisting her hands together, trying not to think about the blood. The pain. Happening to another woman this time, but with Claire's baby.

'Did they really have to put you in a ward with newborns?' she said. 'It seems a little . . . cruel.' She glanced at the woman beside Romily, who was reading a magazine. Her baby was asleep at the end of her bed in a plastic cot.

'I think it was the only bed they had. I'm not expecting to get a lot of sleep.'

'Romily fell straight down a sand dune on her face,' said Posie, detaching herself from Claire but taking her hand. 'You should have seen her! She looked dead.'

Ben raised his head. 'You fell off a sand dune? Is that what happened?'

'Didn't Jarvis tell you when he rang?'

For the first time, Claire noticed the man leaning against the windowsill. He was tall, lanky, with blond hair that needed a cut. He wore baggy shorts and sandals and had his arms crossed against his chest.

Ben seemed to notice him at the same time. His face hardened and he stood up. 'Where did you take her?'

'We went to the beach,' the man, Posie's father, said. 'Hello again, Ben.'

'You let her go climbing on sand dunes when she's twenty-one weeks pregnant?'

'The dune climbing wasn't on the agenda,' Jarvis said.

'I caught my foot in a hole,' said Romily. 'It could've happened anywhere.'

'And what was Posie doing?' Ben asked. 'Who was watching her?'

'I was,' said Jarvis.

'I was building a sandcastle,' said Posie. 'It had shells for windows and it was where we could all live if we were tiny people. And then suddenly, out of nowhere, I heard a scream.'

Claire squeezed her hand, though to be honest Posie seemed to be enjoying the drama. She was too young to understand the gravity of the situation or to pick up on the tension between the adults.

'Essentially, you decided to take your brand-new family for a jolly to the beach,' said Ben to Jarvis, 'and as a result, our child was put at risk.'

'I take full responsibility,' said Jarvis.

'That's new for you.'

'It was my fault,' said Romily firmly. 'I'm really sorry to worry you, Ben and Claire.'

'As long as everything is all right,' said Claire. 'I brought some fruit.' She put her canvas carrier on the little table and took out a bag of grapes and some oranges. It was what she'd had in her refrigerator. Posie took an orange and sat down on the only chair, peeling it.

'They gave me a scan,' Romily said. 'I saw the baby. The consultant said it looked absolutely fine, no injury at all. She said that these bleeds sometimes happen for no reason.'

'What about you?' Ben said, turning from Jarvis to her. 'Are you all right?'

'Sprained an ankle, bruised myself. It's fine.'

'Did you get a photo of the scan?' asked Claire. 'So we can see?'

'I . . . I forgot. Sorry.'

Romily reached for the bag of grapes, but Claire took it first. 'They need washing,' she said, and went to the communal bathroom on the other end of the ward.

Her head was spinning. She'd been on her way out to the gym when Ben had rung her, nearly frantic, on his way down the M4 already, coming to pick her up. Then the rush to get here, and the traffic, and the brief phone call from Romily to say that everything was looking all right, but by then Claire could hardly believe it. And then after all that worry and panic, to find out that Romily had been out with someone Claire didn't know, and had been careless enough to fall hard enough to endanger Claire's baby.

She tried not to let the bag touch any of the surfaces as she rinsed the fruit in the sink and took a few paper towels to place the bag on.

'I've cancelled everything,' Ben was saying to Romily when Claire came back. 'We'll stay down here until you're ready to come back home.'

'What about me?' asked Posie. Her fingers were covered with orange juice; Claire handed her a paper towel.

'My sister lives about twenty miles from here,' said Jarvis. 'I was thinking we could stay there tonight and take Romily home tomorrow.'

'Posie will stay with us,' said Ben. 'We'll find a hotel nearby.'

'Is your sister my auntie?' Posie asked Jarvis.

'Yes, she's your aunt. You've got three.'

'She's a stranger,' said Ben. 'We're Posie's godparents. We've known her since she was born.'

'Posie's had a hard day,' Claire said, as gently as she could.

'She should stay with Ben and Claire,' Romily said. 'Sorry, Jarvis, but you know it makes sense.'

'I want to stay with you,' Posie said to Claire. 'But Jarvis can get a room in the hotel too.'

'Jarvis can do whatever he wants. He always has.'

'Ben,' said Claire.

'I'll stay with my sister Sally,' Jarvis said to Posie, and Claire heard how his voice softened when he addressed her. 'But I'll be back tomorrow to see how your mum is doing and I'll see you then. Bye, Romily.'

He left, and everyone was silent for a moment.

'I had some clothes for Posie for the beach,' said Romily. 'There should be enough for tomorrow.'

'We'll go shopping for toothbrushes and nightgowns,' said Claire. 'And it looks like you could use some after-sun on your face and shoulders, too, Posie. Have you eaten any dinner?'

'I've had two double chocolate muffins in the café with Jarvis.'

'Don't worry,' Claire told Romily. 'We'll look after her.'

'I know you will.'

The baby next to them woke up and started crying. Claire saw Romily wince.

'Are you sure you're all right?' asked Ben.

'Yes. Yes, go before the shops close. I'll be fine. I'll see you all tomorrow.'

Ben kissed her forehead. 'Don't go giving us any more scares like this, lady.'

'I won't. I promise.'

Posie gave Romily a swift hug and then she took Ben and Claire's hands. 'I've never stayed in a hotel before,' she said. 'This is turning out to be the most exciting day *ever*.'

★

They turned down the lights in the ward early. Romily lay flat on her back in the bed. Her ankle throbbed. The woman next to her was sitting in her chair, her nightgown pulled aside, trying to breastfeed. The baby was making snuffling, rooting sounds, like a miniature pig. The woman across from Romily was the only other one in this ward without a baby with her; her twins were in special care. She'd gone to visit them and come back half an hour ago, crying. Now she was asleep.

Romily took the scan photograph out from underneath her pillow. In the dim light, alone, she looked at every detail.

'I don't like it,' said Claire in a low voice. In the other double bed, Posie lay asleep, breathing deeply. Her mouth was open and freckles scattered her nose and cheeks.

'I don't either.' Ben pulled off his tie and began unbuttoning his shirt. 'I was scared to death.'

'I mean, I know that Romily's entitled to have her own life, but I feel like a hostage to fortune. It's not that I don't trust her, but I can't help thinking that she's . . . being a little careless.'

'I don't think that she meant to fall.' He draped his trousers on a chair and climbed into bed beside Claire.

'No. No, of course not. But she's not . . . I'm not sure she thinks these things through.'

'And then there's Jarvis. How can you trust someone who abandons his pregnant girlfriend?'

'I don't know.' Claire glanced at Posie.

'Your first duty of care always has to be to your child. Always. And he left Romily to deal with it alone.'

'He seems to be trying to make up for it.'

Ben was quiet for a moment. 'You didn't see her after he

237

left her pregnant. She was trying to be brave. You know how she doesn't like to talk about how she feels. She was terrified.'

'She said . . . she said that you convinced her to keep Posie. You never told me that.'

'She asked me not to tell anyone, and besides, there was nothing to tell. I didn't convince her. I just talked with her. She made her own decision, and it was the right one. He had no interest in it whatsoever. Who knows what's going on now? Romily wouldn't have been at the beach in the first place if not for him.'

'I think climbing sand dunes is exactly what Romily *would* do,' said Claire. 'She was probably chasing butterflies or something. She doesn't think, Ben. She didn't even ask for a scan picture for us when we couldn't make it on time.'

'It's not Romily's fault. She was shaken up.'

'But we don't know anything. We couldn't talk to the doctors ourselves. We've had everything second-hand. If they're keeping her in hospital, they must be worried still.'

'We'll see. We'll wait and see. If the worst comes to the worst, we'll book a private scan.' Ben turned out the light. 'She needs looking after, that's clear enough.'

'I feel so powerless.'

'It's been a hard day. Let's get some sleep.' He kissed her and lay down.

Ben could always sleep at night. It was as if he put aside the worries and concerns of the day with the clothes he'd been wearing. Within minutes he was breathing deeply. They'd left the bathroom light on for Posie, in case she woke up, and in that half-light Claire lay staring at the blank ceiling, awake and alone.

29
A Million Times

Romily was just thinking about getting up off the sofa and going to bed when there was a tap at her door. She tucked the photograph back between the pages of her notebook, shoved the notebook under a sofa cushion, and struggled to her feet – or rather, to her foot, as she held her bandaged left ankle clear of the floor. She hopped to the armchair, steadied herself on the back of it, and then hopped the rest of the way to the door.

'You'd better not be a crazed murderer after I hopped all this way,' she muttered, sliding on the chain and opening the door.

It was Jarvis carrying a pizza. He'd changed clothes since she'd seen him at the hospital this morning, to jeans and a black jumper. An orange August Thorn moth fluttered near his hair, attracted by Romily's light.

'Requesting permission to enter,' he said.

She unfastened the chain. Two days ago she hadn't been ready to let him into her flat, but since then he'd carried her in his arms, admitted her to hospital, and watched their daughter while Romily spent some time

239

being more frightened than she'd ever been in her life.

Plus, she saw and smelled as soon as she opened the door, he had pizza.

The August Thorn followed him in; Romily reached up, captured it between her hands and released it gently outside before she shut the door.

'Posie's asleep,' she said.

'I didn't come to see Posie.' He put the pizza on the coffee table next to Romily's empty cocoa mug.

'I hope that's green pepper and mushroom.' She hobbled to the sofa and fell onto it. Jarvis took the armchair.

'Are you kidding? It's extra-meaty meat feast. I just brought it to taunt you. This flat isn't bad.'

'What a compliment from someone who's spent the last eight years in a tent.'

'When you wouldn't let me come in the other day I thought you were living in squalor. But this isn't squalid. It looks as if you even do the washing up occasionally.' He pointed to Posie's painting above the sofa. 'I like that.'

'I wouldn't let you come in because I wasn't sure I was ready to let you that close.'

'What changed your mind?'

She flipped open the lid of the pizza box. 'Ah. Green pepper and mushroom. There's your answer.' She helped herself to a gooey slice. 'I shouldn't even be hungry. We stopped for a huge meal on the way home from Poole.'

'How are you feeling?'

'Stiff. But okay. I had a full check-up before I left the hospital and the baby is fine. Ben and Claire have booked me in for a private scan.'

Jarvis took a slice for himself and ate half of it in one bite. She wondered what he'd been doing all day; he'd only stayed at the hospital that morning for half an hour, chatting with Posie and avoiding speaking to Ben.

'I was thinking that school starts next week and you're going to have trouble getting Posie there if that ankle isn't healed. I can help.'

'Ben's already sorted it. He's rearranging his schedule so he can do pick-up and drop-off while I take some time to recover.'

'They really look after you, don't they?'

'They're looking after their baby.'

'No,' he said, 'it's you. And Posie.'

'They're her godparents.'

'He got that too,' Jarvis said quietly. He put down the pizza and looked straight at Romily. 'Claire doesn't know how you feel about him, does she?'

She could deny it and bullshit him and herself all over again. But look where it had got her the last time. 'No, she doesn't have a clue. She can't. I don't feel great about it, before you ask. I've tried not to . . . care about him.'

'I genuinely thought that the two of you had got together. I thought that was why you'd never told me about Posie, and why you didn't want me to come into your flat.'

'How . . . how did you know that I felt that way about him?'

He laughed humourlessly. 'It wasn't difficult. When we were seeing each other, the first time you cancelled our plans together to see him instead, I thought, *Well, he's been her friend for longer than I've known her, fair enough.* But after the third time I started to think differently. And when I saw you together, I knew. You looked at him like . . .' He shook his head. 'Let's just say you never looked at me that way.'

'Do you think it's that obvious?'

241

'It is to me. Look, I'm sorry about what I said on the beach. I shouldn't have accused you of trying to steal Ben by having his child.'

'I'm not. He's married to Claire. I came to terms with that a long time ago.'

'I do, however, still reserve the right to think it was a stupid move to get pregnant with his baby.'

Romily bit her lip. 'Obviously,' she said, 'you can think whatever you like. But I'm fine.'

'Is that why you stayed in England? Because Ben was here?'

'Well, I had a kid to look after.'

'They do have children in other parts of the world. If you'd wanted to travel, to work, you could have done it with Posie.'

'Ben and Claire helped me look after her while I finished my PhD. And by then I was interested in Amity's insects. So I stayed.'

'I suppose that by that time, Ben and Claire had also decided to stay in Brickham.'

'Just outside.'

'And Posie loves them.'

'As if they were her parents. Sometimes she thinks they *are* her parents.'

He was silent. Romily had a flash of the kind of thought she'd had before on the beach, when she'd imagined what it would have been like if the two of them had stayed together. That would have been his armchair, and he'd have kicked his shoes off underneath it as they shared a pizza for the millionth time while their kid slept. It would have been nothing unusual.

When they were together their relationship had never been like that. It had never been everyday and ordinary.

242

They'd never moved in together, never got serious. He was always planning to go away, and so was she. That was what they'd agreed. They were only having fun.

But somewhere, sometime, she had seen him looking sad, as he did now. With a furrow between his brows, with the corners of his mouth turned down but not in a smile.

She couldn't quite remember when that had been. If they'd only been having fun.

'Can I look at her sleeping?' Jarvis asked.

'Go ahead.'

He got up from the armchair and went into the short corridor leading to their bedrooms. From the sofa, Romily could see him. He pushed open Posie's door and stood there in the doorway, with the blue of her night-light picking out his outline in the shadows. As he had never done a million times before.

He came back to the armchair. 'She sleeps all sprawled out.'

'Always has. Every time I share a bed with her I end up with an elbow in my face.'

'I should have fought,' he said.

Romily, who had reached for another piece of pizza to give her hands something to do, paused. 'Fought?'

Jarvis appeared to be weighing his words. 'It was a good job I left for,' he said. 'But it wasn't the only one. It was the furthest away.'

'I don't understand.'

'I didn't feel there was any point in staying. You were in love with Ben. I didn't want you to be stuck with me, stuck with my child, when you wanted to be with him.'

'You left because of *Ben*?'

'No,' Jarvis said. 'I left because you didn't love me.' He got up and went to the door. 'Ring me if you need any help with anything. I'll take Posie to the park on Saturday, if you haven't any plans.'

'We haven't.'

He nodded, and let himself out. The August Thorn, or maybe it was another, fluttered in and began circling the ceiling light. Romily watched it for a few moments. Then she turned off the light and went to crawl in beside Posie in her single bed. She tucked her arm around her, put her face in the hair at the nape of her neck, smelling child sweat and the sweetness of her breath.

'I am your mother,' she whispered to Posie, 'and I love you.'

It was always easier to say when Posie was asleep. And this time, she wasn't only talking to Posie.

30
New Term

'Thank Christ that hell is over.'

Claire looked up from where she was entering names into her new planner. She didn't try to hide the pleasure she felt from seeing Max, his hair awry, his school shirt-sleeves rolled up, his guitar slung over his back. He'd grown over the summer. She did say, mildly, 'I'm not sure Mrs Greasley would approve of your language.'

'It's not true, anyway. It's out of one hell and into another.'

Claire nodded at the stool beside her and Max sat down, arranging his guitar in his lap.

'You've got a new one,' she said.

'Guilt money. Again. At this rate I'll have a collection like Keith Richards'.' But Claire saw how he held the instrument with reverence.

'It's beautiful. Do you have anything new to play for me?'

His bravado faltered and his cheeks went pink. 'Yeah. I . . . I had quite a bit of time to write this summer. And I was thinking about what you said. That you thought I had talent?'

The rising inflection tugged at her heart. He cared so much what she thought. This one lonely boy.

'I think you have a lot of talent, Max, and what's more important, I think you're willing to work hard at it.' She shut her planner. 'I thought about your music this summer.'

'You did?'

'Yes. In fact, I was thinking that maybe you'd like to perform some of it at the end of term.'

'Not at the Christmas concert,' he said. 'No offence, Mrs L, but I don't think I can compete with the Year Sevens dressed up as angels.'

'I wasn't thinking the Christmas concert. I was thinking an individual recital.'

'But that's only for sixth-formers.'

'We have some GCSE students giving recitals too, occasionally. I could stretch a point for you.'

'I'm – I'm not even taking GCSE Music.'

'I noticed your name had been taken off the list. Did you decide against it?'

'My dad said I couldn't.' His face was bright red now.

'Well, we could work on a recital anyway. If you wanted to.'

'I don't know if I can.'

'You're certainly able enough. But you don't have to make your mind up now. You can think about it. Meanwhile, do you want to play me your new pieces? I'd like to hear them.'

His fingers fumbled. He played a chord, then laid his palm on the strings.

'I wish I had a mother like you,' he mumbled down to his guitar.

I would be lucky to have a child like you, she thought.

'Play for me.'

As usual, Romily kept her head down when she entered the playground. Because Ben had been doing the school run for the past week, she hadn't been here since before the summer holidays, but nothing had changed. The Mummies, with their pushchairs and toddlers, wearing smocks and summer dresses, lined the perimeter keeping up a constant chatter, while the Working Mums queued in traffic behind the wheels of their cars, desperate to drop off their charges and be away. By the gate a member of the PTA clutched a clipboard, looking for volunteers for something or other. Romily avoided her eye.

The bell rang and Posie flitted ahead and disappeared into a group of children. No kiss, then. Romily shrugged and went to turn round, only to find the PTA woman blocking her way.

'You're expecting!' she trilled joyously.

'Er. Yeah.'

Within seconds, the Mummies had gathered around. 'How far along are you?' one asked.

'Twenty-three weeks.'

'Oh, so plenty of time to go. You show more because you're so slim.'

'How are you feeling?'

'Do you need any maternity clothes? I've got loads left from Bobby.'

'What about a Moses basket? I've got one of those.'

'You're lucky you've got the summer over with before you're really big. I had Arjan in August and I was ready to drop.'

'Yes,' said Romily, confused about which question to respond to first. 'I'm feeling fine now. I was sick for quite a long time, though.'

'Oh, I know,' said one who had her baby strapped to her chest in a sling. 'I was sick all through it with this one, and then he didn't want to come out. Gave your mummy an

247

awful time, didn't you, sweetheart?' She dropped a kiss on its downy head.

'I had sciatica all down my leg,' said another.

'Had to spend the last three months in bed.'

'The acne! It was awful.'

'Still, you look great. It suits you.'

Romily doubted that anyone looked great with the equivalent of a football stuffed up their top, but she said, 'Thank you.'

'How are you sleeping? I could never get comfortable once the baby started poking me in the ribs.'

'Your little girl must be so excited to have a little brother or sister.'

'Was that Daddy dropping her off last week? I noticed she came in by car.'

'That's her godfather. I had a sprained ankle.'

An immediate collective outcry of concern. 'Have you tried arnica?'

'You can take paracetamol, you know. The pharmacist doesn't want you to but my midwife told me it was absolutely fine. Who's your midwife?'

'Er. Katya?'

'I had her! She's wonderful.'

'I had her too. Fourteen hours in labour.'

'Can I feel?' Without waiting for an answer, the Mummy put her hand on Romily's stomach. 'Ooh, lovely! It kicked.'

'Do you know what you're having?'

A boy. My boy. 'No, we don't.'

The first Mummy's hand was removed and replaced with another Mummy's. Romily was beginning to feel like a melon being tested for ripeness.

'We didn't know either,' said the Mummy who was

touching her. 'Not for the first one. Everyone says you need to know so you know what colour to paint the nursery but we just painted ours green. What about you?'

'Er. Yellow.'

'That's nice. It's good to avoid all this gender typing, isn't it?'

'You can't stop it!' said another. 'We put Joseph in a pink nursery because he came so quickly after Catarina that we couldn't be bothered to paint it again, and he still won't play with anything except for cars!'

'Do you need a place on an NCT course? I know the woman who runs them, I can give you her number.'

'Have you written up your birth-plan yet?'

'How are your iron levels?'

'How does it compare to your first pregnancy? Mine were totally different from each other.'

'You must have found it difficult to get your shoes on, with your ankle and your bump.'

Romily focused on the woman who'd said that. She had long hair, a handknitted jumper, a toddler in a pushchair. Her jumper had a hole in the sleeve and her toddler had a dried-on milk moustache.

'Yes,' she said. 'The shoes haven't been easy.'

A third woman put her hand on her stomach. 'Come back to mine for coffee if you like. We have a bit of a standing play-date on Mondays but bumps count.'

'Thanks, but I have to get to work.'

The baby wasn't kicking, so the woman took her hand away. 'Come when Baby's here, then. Everyone's welcome.'

'I'll bring those maternity clothes for you tomorrow.'

'I'll write down my NCT friend's number.'

'Have you chosen any names?'

Romily bit her lip. Quietly, very quietly, she said, 'My father's name was William.'

'Ooh, that's lovely. I love the old-fashioned names.'

And they were off, pushing high-tech prams in black and bright colours, chattering. The woman in the jumper lingered behind for a moment. She was smiling.

'Do you feel like a belly on legs?' she asked.

'A bit.'

'Everyone means well. It's what we all have in common, so we have to talk about it. As a conversational topic, it's like the weather, only it involves much more pain.'

Romily had to swallow twice before she answered. 'That's one way of thinking about it.' She tried a smile.

'And besides, it's important, probably one of the most important things we ever do, and no one else is interested. Are you all right? You look like you're about to cry.'

'Hormones,' Romily said roughly. 'It's just hormones.'

'Sorry love, I lost track of the time.'

Claire carried on scraping the ruined dinner into the compost bin. 'You could have rung.'

'I didn't think it was that late. Anyway, I had a sandwich at Romily's.'

She put the plate in the dishwasher before she turned to him. 'You were at Romily's?' she said, keeping her voice light.

'I dropped by on my way from work.'

'Brickham,' she said, lightly, lightly, 'is not on your way home from the site.'

'She had a leaky tap I wanted to take a look at.'

'We haven't had dinner together for over a week.' *And sex for longer than that*, she thought, but she didn't say it.

'It's busy at work. You know that.'

'But not so busy that you can't mend a leaky tap for Romily.'

Ben ran his hand through his hair. 'She's on her own, Claire.'

'I know how she feels.'

'You're busy, too. You've had meetings and auditions all week. You always do at the beginning of term.'

'Yes, but this is our last chance, Ben. We won't have time for quiet dinners on our own once the baby comes. This is supposed to be the time we can spend together.' The last time for quiet dinners, the last time for spontaneous sex, the last time to act as they did when they were first married, before all of this, back when they were still fully themselves.

'Romily needs me more right now. I'm sorry, Claire, but that's the way it is. Besides, you're the one who wanted me to keep an eye on her to make sure she didn't do anything silly again.' There were dark circles under his eyes, though he was sleeping at night. 'I'm trying to do my best for everyone, and sometimes that means I can't be here exactly on time for dinner.'

'All I'm saying,' she said, not so lightly now, but trying, 'is that you could have rung.'

Dear Thing,

I was listening to the radio today and a song came on: 'All You Need Is Love' by the Beatles.

What a load of rubbish.

Love isn't the answer. Love is the problem.

It would be so much easier if we worked on instinct. Letting someone else raise your offspring isn't a problem in nature. It happens all the time; for some species it's a positively advantageous evolutionary decision.

So why is it so hard for me?

Mating is a transaction. An exchange of genes. Most species don't pair-bond. They certainly don't pair-bond with someone else's mate and then spend years and years torturing themselves about it. They don't pass up pair-bonding opportunities with other mates because they can't have the one they've decided they want. Only humans do that, with their ridiculous dedication to love.

My love for Ben — for your father — has been an unchanged part of my existence for so long. Not because it's something I want to feel; quite the opposite. I'd be much happier if I woke up tomorrow and realized I didn't love him any more. I'd be free of this constant ache and yearning and guilt. It would be like being healed.

252

If I hadn't been in love with Ben, who knows what it might have been like with Jarvis? If I'm honest with myself, I chose him because he seemed to be the opposite of Ben. I was comparing him with Ben every moment from the start, and it made me blind. I certainly never saw how he felt about me. I never understood how his leaving me meant that he loved me.

If I hadn't always been comparing, if I'd seen him for who he was, could I have fallen in love with him? Could we have stayed together, raised Posie together?

Would I have loved Posie more before she was born?

You would think that love for your children would be the easiest of all. But I didn't love Posie when she was inside me. Not the way that I love you. I have lots of excuses — I was trying to work on my thesis, I was worried about my future, I hardly had any money — but in the end, nothing can excuse my failure. I tried my best to ignore the fact that she was happening. I didn't suffer for her like I have with you: I didn't puke, I didn't bleed, I didn't have to get up every five minutes at night to use the toilet. But I didn't marvel, either. I took each stage in my pregnancy as a matter of fact, as a natural process of reproduction that was happening to me and that I would get through. Even the birth was easy and quick. I felt some pain and then it was time to push, and she slipped out, eyes open. She looked wise already.

That was when I fell in love with her. Not before.

If I'd been in love with her before she was born, the way I'm in love with you, would I have found it easier to be a mother? All those sleepless nights; all the mistakes and messes and days over and over again that were the same. Everyone says that motherhood is so easy and instinctive. It

253

will be that way for the woman who wants to be your mother. For your real mother.

It wasn't for me. Maybe if I'd loved Posie more, maybe if I'd let myself love her father, it would have been easier.

You are my child who was meant to be. Made half of me and half of the man I have somehow, against all my better interests, decided to love. Your father has protected you, wondered at you. Your mother has dreamed about you, will find the cure for her own pain in you.

You will never be mine, dear Thing.

31

Parents' Evening

No matter how many times she told herself that she was having a baby, even though it was in another woman's body, Claire always felt her spirits plummet whenever her period started. It wasn't just that it reminded her of her miscarriage, or the embryos that didn't take. It was that the whole thing was so pathetic, her body cycling hopelessly, going on preparing itself for a child that would never come. It was a mess with no purpose, another month of plugging, mopping, washing, throwing away, all because her womb didn't know that she was a failure.

Parents' evening, too. The timing couldn't be worse. Still, at least she was prepared. She was always prepared.

From inside the cubicle she could hear the door to the staff toilet open and someone enter. Two someones, mid-conversation. Their voices were quiet, but easily loud enough for Claire to hear.

'I don't know if I could use another woman's body that way. Do you think they're paying her?'

'They must be. Why would anyone do it, otherwise?'

It was Georgette and Bonnie, who'd replaced Lacey. Claire

paused, wanting to call out, instead staying still and listening.

'How much, do you think?'

The tap went on. She could hear lipsticks being uncapped, hair being brushed.

'I'd be terrified the entire time. Do you remember that case in the papers, Baby T or M or something? When the surrogate mother wouldn't let the adoptive parents have the child? Whatever happened with that?'

'I don't know. You're right, it would be frightening.'

'Did you notice that she's gained weight? Do you think she's got sympathetic false pregnancy or whatever that's called? Or do you think it's the stress?'

'Poor Claire. Do you need the loo, or will you have a cup of tea first?'

'What have we got, five minutes? I'm seeing the Macleans first. I think I'm going to need a whisky, let alone a cup of tea.'

Poor Claire. Poor Claire hiding in the lavatory, listening to herself as the subject of gossip. Poor Claire, barren and sad and worried and scared, defined by this period, defined by her failure. She flushed the toilet and stepped out.

Georgette and Bonnie were at the row of sinks. Bonnie spotted her in the mirror and she had the good grace to blush.

'We're not paying her,' said Claire. 'It's illegal to do so in this country, but I wouldn't anyway. She volunteered. And I'm not afraid she's going to keep the baby. I'm more afraid it's not going to be born, to be honest. That's mostly what keeps me awake at night. Is there anything else you'd like to know?'

The two women averted their eyes. 'I'm so sorry,' said Bonnie.

'I'm happy to answer questions. Or just to talk. Preferably somewhere other than in a toilet.'

They didn't say anything. Claire washed her hands and left the staff loo, feeling their eyes on her.

Was this never going to end? What about when she had the baby, when it was legally, emotionally, unassailably hers? Would she be walking around with a pram hearing whispers about where the baby came from? Would she have to fall silent when other mothers chatted about their pregnancies? Would she still feel that her and Ben's world wasn't quite right because nothing had gone as they'd planned?

It will all be all right once the baby comes, she thought, and put her hand into her bag to touch the envelope she used to carry the most recent scan photo around. Even the touch of the paper calmed her. A bit. But now, of course, she felt guilty about flying off the handle.

Some ambassador for alternative birth methods she was. People were going to look at her even more strangely now. She not only couldn't have a child, she lurked in toilets and eavesdropped on other people's conversations.

Claire's hands were shaking. She rang Ben but it went straight to voicemail. She tried not to think that he might have turned off his phone on purpose because he didn't want to go through it any more.

Parents' evening was set up in the Hall, the high-ceilinged high-windowed space that used to be the nuns' refectory and now hosted assembly every day. Small tables had been lined up, each with a name card on it, with one chair behind and two chairs in front. Claire found hers and sat down, folding her hands together and glancing over the schedule on her desk. She had a dozen appointments, all of them with the parents of perfectly pleasant students, the keen ones and the conscientious ones who made appointments with every teacher. Thankfully, she'd be able to do them all on autopilot. The parents would be happy, the children would be happy, everyone could go home for the exeat and relax.

She wished she had a glass of water.

She opened her folder of reports and notes and began putting them in appointment order. Without looking, she could sense Georgette and Bonnie looking at her from across the room. She schooled her face to look calm.

'Oh, thank God for small favours, you're here.'

Claire looked up. A couple stood in front of her. He was tall and wide-shouldered, wearing a well-tailored suit and a patterned silk tie. His dark hair was greying at the temples. She was younger, very pretty, with the kind of glossy, tumbled hair that only came out of an hour's professional blow-dry. She wore high heels and a fitted blue dress which emphasized her baby bump.

'Hello,' Claire said, rising to her feet and extending a hand that still, to her dismay, trembled. 'Are you . . .' She glanced down. They weren't Mr and Mrs Hanley; she'd been teaching all the Hanleys for years now and Mrs Hanley's sister used to play first violin in the Philadelphia Symphony Orchestra.

'Martin Gore-Thomas,' he said, shaking her hand and flashing white teeth. 'We don't have an appointment, but Maximilian was insistent we see you. Wouldn't stop harping on about it. Ernest Doughty said you were here anyway, so we might as well pop down before we left.'

'You're Max's parents.' She glanced at Mrs Gore-Thomas's baby bump. So Max had been right.

'We've only a few minutes,' said the woman. 'We've a dinner in London.'

And is Max going to it, too? Claire thought. *Or are you leaving him at home with his guitar?*

'Please, sit down,' she said. 'I've only a few minutes myself. I'm meant to have an appointment with the Hanleys right now. But Max is an extraordinary student, and I'm pleased to talk with you about him.'

'Can't sit – no time, I'm afraid. The M4 is horrific this time of day.'

Max's stepmother had taken out her mobile phone and was scrolling through something.

'Well,' Claire began, 'as I'm sure you're aware, Max isn't actually one of my students—'

'What do you teach, then?'

'Music.'

'Ahh, charming. No, we paid for Max to take lessons in the hols, of course, but there's no question of him studying music as a subject. No offence to you, but he'll need a proper education rather than messing around on the guitar at all hours. Children his age always want to be pop stars, don't they?' Martin Gore-Thomas laughed.

'Actually,' said Claire, 'that's why I wrote to you at the beginning of the year. We're very willing to allow Max to do music as an extra GCSE on top of his current studies. It's not too late for him to start; I can help him with some catch-up sessions. He's also expressed an interest in taking it on as an extra AS level in a couple of years.'

Max's stepmother sniggered. Claire thought she was laughing at the suggestion, but then saw that she was reading something on her phone. She nudged her husband and showed him the screen, and he chuckled.

'Max is very talented,' said Claire, 'and he's shown that he's capable of the extra work.'

Mr Gore-Thomas glanced at her as if he'd forgotten what she was talking about. He gave her another of his wide smiles. 'No, no, it's a lovely idea, but as I said, it's out of the question. Max needs to concentrate on real subjects. He's no intellectual, as I'm sure you know. He has to work hard to get decent results, and the guitar will be a distraction. He'd only find some new fad anyway. Boy doesn't have an attention span longer than five minutes.'

'I think he's demonstrated that he does have the ability to focus, Mr Gore-Thomas. His compositions took an enormous effort.'

He chuckled again. 'Compositions. That's kind of you, Mrs—'

'Lawrence.'

'Lawrence. Look, I can understand what you're saying, but in my experience every teacher thinks their subject is the most important, which logically can't be true. A boy like Max needs to think about his exams if he's ever going to get any-where in life. He needs to find a bit of ambition instead of indulging fantasies of instant fame. You and I know that's not realistic, don't we?'

'Martin,' said Mrs Gore-Thomas, gazing at the door. 'It's half past.'

'Already? Time flies. Thank you so much for chatting with us, Mrs Lawrence, I've enjoyed—'

'Have you even heard Max's music? Have you asked him to play it for you?'

It came out quite loudly. Mrs Gore-Thomas sighed.

'Max is a talented composer,' Claire said, 'certainly with the most talent I've come across in someone his age. He doesn't want to be a pop star. He wants to be a musician. And even

260

if he weren't so talented, Mr Gore-Thomas, music makes Max happy.'

Mr Gore-Thomas had half-turned to the door, half-extended his hand for a goodbye shake. Now he paused. For the first time, he appeared to actually look at Claire.

'Are you implying that I don't know what's best for my own son?'

'I'm saying that if you took the time to listen to Max's music, if you took the time to listen to *him*—'

'Martin, we're going to be late.'

'Why do you even have children if you're not going to pay attention to them?'

It burst out of her. She saw Mrs Gore-Thomas's eyes widen, and Mr Gore-Thomas's expression grow stern. Behind them, the Hanleys waited politely for their turn, their faces astonished.

The sight should have stopped her, but it didn't. She turned to Mrs Gore-Thomas. 'What are you going to do with this new baby once it's not a stylish bump any more? Once it's a real person who makes demands on you? Are you going to shove this one off onto nannies and au pairs and into boarding school, too?'

Max's father had raised himself to his full height. 'I think it's time to discuss this with Mrs Greasley,' he said, putting his arm around his speechless wife and steering her towards the door.

'Why don't you discuss it with your son?' Claire called after them, across the silent room. 'Or will you be going straight to your dinner party without him?'

The carpet in Veronica Greasley's office was woven in a pattern of geometric lines. It looked almost like a maze in

261

a children's puzzle book. The kind that appeared to be a logical progression of paths that you could travel quite happily along with your pencil, until the path abruptly ended and you were lost.

Claire looked down at it. She traced the small bit of path in front of her with the toe of her shoe, like a child.

'Mr and Mrs Gore-Thomas were very upset,' said Veronica. 'They say they'll be writing a very strong letter of complaint.'

'It was totally unprofessional,' Claire said. 'I'm so sorry. I don't know what came over me.'

'I'm afraid that the Gore-Thomases will insist that we follow a formal disciplinary procedure. We don't like to have to do it here, but . . .' Veronica raised her hands as if it were out of her control.

'I know,' said Claire miserably. Her anger of half an hour ago had all deserted her now, as had the power it had given her. She felt empty, silent, grey.

'But I wanted to have a word with you myself tonight, before we initiated any of this. Can you give me your side of the story, Claire?'

Veronica's voice was kind, and Claire raised her head. 'I know I shouldn't have said it. But to be honest, Veronica, I don't think what I said was inaccurate. I don't think Max's parents do listen to him. I don't think they spend any time with him. He's a very unhappy boy. Music seems to be his only escape.'

'And why didn't you mention your concerns to Ernest Doughty, Max's head of house? We have a very efficient reporting procedure here.'

'Max asked me not to.'

Veronica made a little distressed sound.

'I know,' said Claire. 'But I thought if he could be allowed to study music, if he could grow his confidence, it might . . . help.'

'Claire, let me get this straight. You made up your own mind about what was best for a pupil, which is using your professional judgement, obviously, which I respect, but it happened to clash with what his parents wanted—'

'His tutor did agree with me that he'd be able to handle the extra work.'

'—and then took it on yourself to attack his parents' love for him when they disagreed with you.'

Veronica's voice had lost its kindness. Claire looked down at the maze again. 'Yes.'

'Many of our parents have busy lives. That doesn't mean they love their children any less; in fact, they have very close family relationships. It's an insult to all of our parents to refer to their sending their children to school here as "shoving them off".'

'I know that. But I wasn't talking about all of the parents. I was talking about Max's parents.'

The school was never silent, but it was now. All the children had gone and most of the staff, too.

Veronica sighed. 'I know you've had a very difficult year,' she said. 'A difficult few years. And though you've had some good news lately, there must be some emotional adjustments taking place.'

'I've wanted a child so badly,' said Claire to her lap. 'I can't understand how someone can have a child and not love it with everything they've got.' A tear hit her skirt. No, no crying. She tried to swallow it back.

'I have so much sympathy for you, Claire. And of course you can't magically leave your personal feelings behind when you step into school. We respect your teaching here at St

263

Dominick's, but sadly, if we're being honest, it's not the first time your personal situation has impacted on your professional behaviour.'

'It hasn't—'

'There have been medical absences, of course, and you're due those. But students have mentioned to me that you've seemed . . . distracted. And there's a noticeable effect in the staff room, too. I'm very sorry to have to mention it.'

'I've tried very hard not to—'

'Yes, of course.'

But not hard enough.

Veronica handed her the box of tissues from her desk. Claire took one and blew her nose. She didn't see a bin, so she held the wet tissue in her hand.

'The Gore-Thomases will insist that something is done,' Veronica said again. 'What do you suggest that we do?'

'I don't know.'

'I'm thinking that this might be a blessing in disguise of a sort, for you.'

'Sorry?'

'You were planning to take maternity leave after Christmas anyway. Perhaps we can bring it forward. Max's parents will see that something is being done, and you can spend the time getting ready for your child. It's a useful compromise.'

'But all my lessons! And I'm in charge of the Michaelmas concert.'

'We'll be able to take care of it. You should take some time for *you.*'

'And Max was going to—' She went silent. She was unlikely to be allowed to work with Max for the foreseeable future. Another thing she had messed up.

'It's not the only option, of course,' said Veronica. 'But it might be the easiest one. Why don't you take the weekend to think about it and we'll have a meeting first thing Monday morning.'

'I've got A-level in period one.'

'We'll cover it.' Veronica stood. 'And Claire, this leave might be an even better thing if the governors see that you've volunteered to take it. They might see it as your appreciating the gravity of your actions. Our parents are one hundred per cent the school's greatest asset. We would not have a school without parents choosing to send their children here.'

For all of the headmistress's friendly, concerned tone, it was a warning. Claire didn't want to take another tissue, but she had to.

'Are you all right to drive home?' Veronica asked. 'Would you like to ring your husband to come and get you?'

'I . . .' She wiped her eyes. She thought of how Ben's phone had been switched off when she'd tried to ring earlier. 'No. No. I'm fine by myself. I'll think about your suggestion.'

'Lovely.'

When Ben got home she was sitting in the darkened living room under a knitted throw, staring at *Wife Swap*. 'What on earth are you watching?' he said, standing in the doorway of the room.

'Where have you been? You had your phone off.'

'I was playing Monopoly with Romily and Posie. Is there anything to eat?'

Claire rested her chin on her knees. 'You turned off your phone to play Monopoly?'

He sighed. 'Let's not, Claire. I didn't mean to.'

'What if I needed to talk with you?'

'You had parents' evening. Besides, you could always have rung Romily if it was an emergency.'

'Do you not see how it might feel a little bit wrong for me to ring Romily to talk to my husband?'

'Okay. I'm sorry.' He began to move off to the kitchen.

'I might get sacked,' she said.

Ben stopped. 'Pardon?'

'I've . . . I said something foolish.'

'I don't understand. Why would St Dom's sack you? They love you.'

'I yelled at Max's parents.'

'Who's Max?' He was still standing up, but he put his hand on the back of the sofa. His face was lit up from the television.

'I told you about Max – the boy who's such a good guitarist? The one who I wanted to give a recital?'

'Why did you yell at his parents?'

She started at the beginning, with what Max had told her about his father and stepmother, his music and its yearning for love. The letter she'd written asking if he could study music, the recital, all the lunchtimes and break-times he'd spent with her. And then the conversation she'd overheard in the loo, the Gore-Thomases, that stylish, trim baby bump. How she'd lost control and said exactly what she was feeling.

'Oh, Claire,' he said.

She'd been about to mention the surge of power she'd felt – how exhilarating it had been in those few moments freed from the rules of playing nice. Instead, she said, 'But what I said was true, Ben. They're lousy parents. They don't really care about Max. If they did, they'd take the time to get to know him.'

'It sounds awful. But . . . it's not like you.'

'It was how I really feel.' But Ben was right; she didn't do these things. It made her stomach sick to think about it. 'Veronica said she doesn't think I've been doing a very good job teaching. She says that I've been letting my personal life affect how I am in the classroom. It's ridiculous.'

'Well, it would be surprising if it didn't affect your teaching. It's been a lot to get through.'

'Has it affected the way you've done your job?'

'I'm sure it has. I haven't been one hundred per cent, not lately. Especially since Romily had her accident. Listen, Claire, this is okay. It's got it all out in the open, anyway. And St Dominick's know what an asset you are to their school. It'll be fine.'

He put his arms around her and kissed the side of her forehead.

'Veronica says I should take my maternity leave early. She says I should start it right away. To get me out of the way, stop the Gore-Thomases baying for my blood. Veronica didn't mention that the father is an MP, but she must have been thinking about it.'

'It's not a bad idea, you know. You'll have some time to yourself.'

'I've just had lots of time to myself. Too much time to myself. I was going crazy over the summer holidays.'

He stroked her hair. 'It's going to be all right, Claire. This is because of the pressure you've been under. Take some time, get everything ready for the baby, and then once it's here, everything will be perfect. The last thing you'll want to do then is go back to school. You'll wonder why you thought it was so important. You'll be laughing about all of this, you'll see.'

'You think I'll be laughing about losing my job?'

'You were planning to leave anyway.'

'But not like this.'

'Claire,' said Ben, dropping his arms from her, 'what do you want me to say? I'm trying to make the best of this.'

'I don't want you to make the best of it.'

'Do you want me to agree that you made an awful mistake, then?'

Claire stood up. 'I just want you to be on my side.'

'I *am* on your side. I want what's best for you. I think you're not yourself lately, and you end up saying things and doing things that you don't really mean. Anybody would.'

Claire buried her face in her hands. 'I'm not anybody,' she said, her voice louder in her head because she was speaking to her hands. 'I'm me. I meant to say those things. And I want you to fight for me. I want you not to think that I'm irrational, or not coping, or out of control.'

'I don't. I don't think any of that.' He stroked her back.

But I do, she thought.

32
Funny and Horrible

When Claire opened the door on Tuesday, Romily was standing there balancing an umbrella and a cardboard box, which rested on her stomach.

'I heard what happened,' she said, with half an apologetic smile. 'I've taken the morning off. Want company?'

She didn't, but she let Romily in anyway. She was too shell-shocked with the fact that it was a Tuesday in the middle of term and she hadn't had to get up and get dressed for work. She was in leggings and one of Ben's old T-shirts, her decorating clothes, although there wasn't much left to decorate.

Romily had been letting her hair grow and the ends were wet. She handed the box to Claire and leaned down to untie her boots, grunting with the effort of getting round her belly.

'Ben told you,' Claire said.

'He told me, and I think it's totally ridiculous,' said Romily. 'How can they make you take leave just for saying what anybody with any common sense would think anyway?' She straightened up, putting her hand in the small of her back. 'These people should be falling down on their knees to thank you for taking the trouble to raise their kids properly when they can't be bothered.'

'You think I was right to say what I did?'

'I'm all for telling a few home truths every now and then at work. Stir it up, cause some controversy. It makes things interesting.'

This was so different from just about everyone else's attitude that Claire couldn't help but stare at Romily.

'Then again,' Romily said, 'what do I know? I work alone in a room full of dead bugs.'

'I never thought I'd say this, but I can see the appeal of a job like that right now. Cup of tea?' They went into the kitchen, where Claire had not yet washed up from breakfast. 'I wasn't expecting anyone today,' she said, as if she didn't do the washing-up first thing every morning whether she had guests or not.

Romily didn't seem to notice, and she realized that even if Romily did notice, she, out of nearly everyone Claire knew, was the most likely not to care.

As infuriatingly casual as Romily could be, as careless on sand dunes and as slapdash in matters of diet and tidiness, she did have one very appealing quality right now. She wouldn't judge Claire.

It must be so easy for Ben to be with her, she thought, and then she tried to crowd that thought out by bustling around with the kettle and the teapot.

'I hear Thing is fine,' she said. 'I've been getting updates practically every day from Ben.'

This was meant as a dig; it seemed that since Friday, when her brain had given her mouth permission to say what it wanted, she hadn't been able to help herself. It was as if some control switch had been turned off. Except unlike Friday, the barbed truths that escaped her didn't give her any feeling of power or freedom. They just made her tired.

Romily didn't seem to notice this, either. 'Thing is a kicker. I think you have a lot of football games and/or dance recitals in your future.' She shifted in her chair, trying to get comfortable. 'I wanted to check your schedule. One of the ladies at school has got me booked into an NCT class at the beginning of December and I thought you'd like to come.'

'My schedule is wide-open now. As you know.'

'How long have you got to stay off?'

'The governors accepted my proposal to take maternity leave effective immediately. Apparently they'd lined up a cover teacher over the weekend. Before all this happened I'd thought I'd go back part-time for the last few weeks of term in the summer, and then not come back in the autumn, but now I'm thinking I might have to resign first and not come back at all.'

'It might have all blown over by Easter.'

'Maybe. But I doubt it. The management were ... I wasn't made to feel very welcome yesterday.' Even Veronica, who had been reasonably supportive of her on Friday evening, had had a grim expression as she accepted what was tantamount to Claire's resignation. She'd had more communications from the Gore-Thomases over the weekend, Claire supposed. It was surprising they found so much time to complain between all the dinner parties.

'What did they do, jeer at you when you walked in?'

'No, they were all polite, but—'

'But they gave you a big box to pack up all your stuff, I bet.'

'Two small ones. I had to carry my aspidistra separately.'

Romily caught her eye. Incredibly, the two of them began to laugh.

'It's not funny,' Claire said. 'It's horrible.'

'Some things can be funny and horrible at the same time. Look in the box that I brought you, for example.'

Claire had put it on the table while she made the tea. Now, she opened up the flaps and gazed inside. The aroma of burnt chocolate greeted her.

'I made you some cupcakes,' Romily said. 'At least, I tried to make you some cupcakes. It went a bit wrong.'

Claire lifted out the plate. On it were nine misshapen blackish-brown lumps in pink cupcake papers. Each one had a half-melted marshmallow on the top of it.

'They're meant to be chocolate. The corner shop didn't have icing sugar so I tried to put the marshmallows on there while they were warm, but then they didn't do anything so I put them back in the oven to melt but that didn't really work either.'

'But Romily, that's so nice of you. Thank you.'

'You won't be thanking me once you try one of them. I am truly a terrible cook.' She picked one up and then dropped it back on the plate with a thunk. 'Still, not bad for my first-ever effort, I suppose.'

'If that's your first-ever effort, I'm getting out my grand-mother's porcelain in honour of it.' Claire went to fetch two flowered, gold-rimmed plates from the dresser and put a cake on each of them. They were quite heavy for their size.

'You don't have to actually eat them,' said Romily. 'It was purely a lame gesture.'

'I'm going to enjoy this thoroughly.'

'I hope you have a good dentist.'

Claire peeled the paper off and took a bite of her cake. The top was slightly burnt and the middle had settled into a dense, floury, cocoa-tinged brick. 'Interesting,' she said.

'Now that's a word for it. I do appreciate constructive criticism. Who knows, I might decide to make these again one day.'

Claire chewed, and chewed, and swallowed, and then spent a few moments trying to remove gluey cake from the sides of her teeth with her tongue. 'Next time, maybe set the oven a bit lower. If it's too hot, sometimes the top can burn and the middle doesn't cook through.'

'Noted.'

There was a chunk of something in her next bite that she couldn't quite identify. 'Did you put nuts in?'

'It might be a bit of eggshell,' Romily said, wincing on her behalf.

For the second time this morning, Claire surprised herself by laughing.

She was glad Romily was here. Glad to be rescued from the long, purposeless day stretching ahead of her.

'As long as it's not a bit of a cricket,' she said.

'It's definitely not cricket, though I hear they are delicious and full of protein.' Romily took a bite of her own cake. 'It's not as bad as I feared. Nearly, but not quite.'

'They're good,' said Claire. 'And I'm honoured that you went to the trouble for me.'

'Oh well, you know Hal is still talking about the ones you brought me.'

'I'll make him some more.'

'No no, don't do that. I'm sure you have many more important things to do.'

'Not really,' said Claire sadly. 'I finished the nursery over the summer.'

'Did you?' Romily turned her tea mug around and around in her hands. 'I'm sorry we haven't been able to get together very often recently. I sent you some texts about the yoga, but you must not have got them.'

'I did,' said Claire's mouth without her brain's permission, again. 'But I didn't answer them because I was angry with you.'

Romily's hands stilled. 'Why?'

'I felt that you were taking stupid risks with yourself and by extension, with our baby.'

'Claire, I'm so sorry about the accident. I didn't mean to—'

'I know.'

Both of them poked at their misshapen cakes.

'I was upset,' Romily said, at last. 'I'd had an argument with Jarvis.'

'Oh no. About Posie?'

'It wasn't about anything important. I wasn't looking where I was going. Believe me, Claire, it won't happen again. I know how precious this baby is.'

'I know you do,' said Claire, because it was obvious in everything about Romily right at this moment. 'And it was rude of me not to answer your texts. How are you feeling in yourself?'

'Fat and awkward.'

'Ben says that once the baby is here, everything is going to be perfect and we won't have to worry about anything any more.'

Romily smiled. 'Oh Claire, your worries are only just beginning. You've got nappy rash, and colic, and sleepless nights, and children's television, and potty training, and the naughty step, and nits, and tantrums, and bedwetting, and mystery illnesses, and dribble, and oh, and you can never watch horror movies again because you'll completely

274

imagine that everyone who gets killed in them might be your child.'

'I think it will be worth it.'

'Yes,' said Romily. 'It is.'

'Can I ask you a question? As a mother?'

'Of course.'

'Do you think I should email Max? That's the boy who the trouble was about. He's very lonely and he's very talented. I'm afraid that without me in the school to encourage him, he'll give up music altogether.'

'Are you joking? Of course you should. Otherwise he'll feel abandoned.'

'I'm not sure it's professional. His parents wouldn't like it.'

'Well, as you're saying you've pretty much lost your job anyway, it doesn't seem like you have anything to lose by being a little unprofessional. But I think it's exactly the thing that a good teacher would do. My biology teacher from school used to send me notes after I went to uni. I met up with him a few times. He was great.'

'Max is only fourteen. I don't want people to think it's weird.'

'You're not weird. You'd be trying to help him. A good teacher like you can change a kid's life. And you wouldn't write anything that you'd be ashamed for his parents to see, anyway.'

'No. I wouldn't. Okay, I will email him, then. Thanks for the vote of confidence, Romily.'

'No worries. I'm glad I could do something more useful and appealing than my baking.'

'Do you want to see the nursery?'

'Go on.' They abandoned their cakes.

'How are things with Jarvis?' Claire asked as they climbed the staircase.

'Um . . . unexpected.'

'How so? Besides the obvious, of course.'

'He's his own person. He's not just a memory or a set of genes. He's got his own wants and opinions, and he sees everything differently.'

'Do you think he's a good father? Potentially?'

Romily paused at the top of the stairs. 'He's trying hard. Posie likes him.'

'What about you?'

'That doesn't really matter.'

'Posie favours him. He's quite good-looking.'

Romily made a non-committal sound, probably amused that Claire was trying to set her up with the father of her own child. It was none of Claire's business. But wouldn't it be neat, if it tied up that way?

'Sorry,' said Claire. 'I suppose if you're happily married you just want to see everyone else paired up too.'

'It's fine,' said Romily, though her voice was a little off, and Claire instantly wondered if Ben had been confiding in her. If she knew about the arguments they'd been having.

But she couldn't ask, and Romily didn't say anything more, just went to the nursery and stood there looking around.

Outside it was still raining but this room was full of sunshine. The yellow walls, the bright yellow curtains with their crisp white ribbon trim. The soft carpet, the cuddly bears, the changing table and the honey-coloured cot with its light green blankets and its mobile of sheep and clouds.

'It's beautiful,' said Romily. She picked up a cushion from the rocking chair, the chair where Claire would hold the baby and sing. She ran her hand over the crisp soft cotton and then she put it down carefully where it had been before. She looked at the baby monitor, ready to go; the wicker baskets where Claire had already stashed nappies and cotton balls. 'You've thought of everything.'

'I wasn't sure. I felt as if I were tempting fate.'

Romily shook her head. 'No. This is perfect. This is how it's meant to be.' She touched the mobile and sent it twirling gently in the air. 'Posie never had any of this. Do you remember? She slept with me for so long until we could find a flat with two bedrooms.' She stopped the mobile. 'But even if I'd had a bigger house and more money, I could never have done anything like this. I haven't got the gift for it. Not like you.'

'Oh.' Claire shrugged self-consciously. 'It was my project.'

'The baby is going to be very happy here.'

'I hope so.'

Romily took Claire's hand. She put it on her belly.

'You're all going to be very happy,' she said.

33

A Secret Mission

'Okay, now I need you to come in here with me.'

Claire hesitated. They were at a motorway services, having stopped after being on the M4 for only fifteen minutes, and Romily was pointing to the baby changing room. She was holding a large rucksack which she'd excavated from the boot of her Golf when they'd pulled in.

'You want me to go into the baby changing room?' Claire asked. 'Why?'

'Trust me,' said Romily. 'It's all part of the secret mission.'

She'd shown up at Claire's house this morning with Posie in tow. Claire hadn't had a clue that she was coming, but from the way Ben scooped up Posie and immediately went upstairs with her to play knights and queens with her toy castle, she knew that he had helped to plan whatever it was. All Romily would say was that it was a top-secret mission and that Claire had to get into the car with her. She refused to answer any questions about where they were going, just smiled and shook her head.

And now the baby changing room. Claire had a quick look around to make certain there weren't any desperate parents with bulging nappy bags before she went in. Romily closed the door behind them and plopped her bag down on the changing table.

'Now take off your top,' she said.

'Pardon?'

'You'll understand in a minute. I promise.'

Claire unbuttoned her shirt and slipped it off. Romily immediately took out several scarves and a cushion from her rucksack. Claire recognized the cushion as being from Romily's sofa.

'What are you doing?' she asked for the dozenth time, beginning to laugh.

'I'm making you pregnant. Turn around.' Romily placed the cushion on Claire's stomach and quickly tied the scarves around her waist to keep it in place. She did some adjustments and then stood back to survey her work.

'My shirt is never going to fit over this,' said Claire.

'No worries. I've just the thing.' Romily pulled out a pink T-shirt and handed it to her. It had BABY printed across the chest, with an arrow pointing down to the belly. 'I bought it specially. Just to banish any lingering doubts.'

Claire would never wear such a thing in a million years. She put it on.

'Perfect,' said Romily. 'You are now, officially, knocked up.'

There wasn't a mirror in the room. Claire looked down at herself. 'This must look fake.'

'No, it's pretty convincing. As long as no one pulls up your T-shirt, you should be fine. Come on.' She opened the door.

Claire hesitated again. 'I see what you're trying to do, Romily, and I appreciate the gesture, but I don't really think this is a good idea.'

'Nobody knows you out there. You're among strangers.

Nobody knows anything about you, nobody's going to think twice about it.'

'I don't know.'

'Trust me,' said Romily.

Claire followed her out, feeling extremely self-conscious, expecting stares and questions. Nobody appeared to notice them at all.

On their way out of the services, Claire caught sight of her reflection in the glass door. She stopped and stared at herself. It wasn't a clear reflection, not like in a mirror, but it was clear enough.

She looked pregnant. This was the way she would look if she were pregnant. She was rounded and flushed and pretty. She looked happy.

'You look great,' Romily told her. 'Even I would give up my seat to you on a bus. Are you ready for the next stage?'

'You even have to sit differently,' Claire was saying as they arrived at the address Romily had looked up on the internet. 'Your legs have to go wider. It affects absolutely every movement you take.'

'The first time I was pregnant I kept on getting stuck between things. I forgot I couldn't fit through.' Romily turned off the ignition. So far the experiment was a success; Claire had been exclaiming for the past half an hour about how strange it felt to have an enormous belly. She looked younger and more vulnerable when she smiled. Romily could understand why Ben liked making her do it.

Though Ben made Claire smile because he loved her. Unlike Romily, who was trying to expiate her guilt.

'What are we doing here? Where are we – Marlborough?' Claire asked, and then she looked out of her window. 'Oh.'

'It's a baby boutique and it's far enough away from where you live and work that nobody is going to know you.' Romily gestured to the front door of the boutique, painted a pastel blue. There were fluffy cotton clouds hanging in the window. 'Go ahead. It's Thing shopping-time. After that, if you want, we can find the café with the most yummy mummies in it and sit right in the middle of them.'

'Do you – do you think it's bad luck to buy clothes for the baby?'

'You've decorated the nursery. How can this hurt? Go on, enjoy yourself.'

Claire opened the car door and got out. She bent, clearly with some difficulty, and looked back in at Romily. 'Aren't you coming?'

'You don't need me. I'd be surplus to requirements.'

'I'd like you to come too.'

'No no, I'd be a distraction. This is for you.'

'It'll be much more fun with two of us. And I'd feel less of a fool.'

It was Romily's turn to hesitate. This was the downside to her plan. She'd thought she'd be able to stay in the car. Not have to look at the little things.

'What if one of the scarves slips and I need you to tie it up again?' said Claire. Romily gave in and got out of the car.

'I'll just buy one or two bits,' said Claire. 'Maybe a hat or a cardigan, if they have them in yellow or green or white.'

The boutique was exactly what Romily had pictured. It was painted white inside, white walls and off-white floorboards, with tiny beautiful clothes hanging everywhere. Teddy bears. Cuddly lambs. Handmade rag dolls. Everything safe and soft, in the colours of jewels and nature. A woman folding clothes near the front greeted them both.

'Good morning,' said Claire, bright and cheerful, and began looking around. She obviously had a talent for shopping that Romily didn't possess. Romily glanced at a price tag. *That much* for something that was just going to get baby poop on it?

She tried to glide around looking noncommittal, while Claire examined everything, exclaiming over the gorgeous little dresses and darling little trousers. She picked out a knitted green cardigan and considered a pack of organic cotton Babygros. The sales assistant gravitated towards her, judging her the more likely of the two of them to make purchases.

'When's Baby due?' she asked.

'The sixth of January,' Claire answered.

'You look great.'

'Thank you.'

'Is it your first? How have you been feeling?'

Claire glanced briefly at Romily before she answered. 'I had quite a bit of sickness until I was seventeen weeks, but aside from that it's been fine.'

'That's awful. I was really sick with my first pregnancy, too.'

'And now I keep on getting stuck between things! I think I'll fit through and then I don't.'

This was what Romily should concentrate on: Claire's joy. How Romily was helping to create it. Not the little clothes that Romily did not need to buy. The tops she would not pull over a downy head, the sleeves she would not arrange on chubby arms. Surreptitiously, she picked up a blanket with a duck on it and rubbed it between her fingers. She put it down on the shelf next to a small pair of white shoes.

Baby shoes. What a useless item. But these were embroidered, exquisite, unsoiled and empty. They both fitted into the palm of one hand. Tiny feet with that curling reflex when you ran your finger up a bare sole.

'And are you looking for anything special?' the sales assistant asked, and it took a moment before Romily realized she was speaking to her.

'Oh no. No, I'm just here with my friend.' She put down the shoes.

'You should choose something too.' Claire had added a hat and some white pyjamas to her pile of small clothes, which was now quite tall.

'I think this place is a little out of my price bracket,' Romily said.

'Don't worry about that. It'll be my gift. I think the baby should have something special that you've chosen yourself. Don't you?'

'Oh no, that's not necessary.'

'Aren't those shoes adorable?' said the sales assistant. 'They're handmade locally.'

Claire came over and picked them up. She cradled them. 'They're wonderful. Can you just imagine?' She met Romily's eyes. Romily bit her lip, inside her mouth where Claire wouldn't see it, and nodded.

Claire brought everything to the till and chatted with the assistant as she rang it all up. An affluent mum, overspending maybe, but who could blame her when it was for her first-born, who anyone could see would have a charmed life? She slipped into the role effortlessly and Romily knew it was because Claire had imagined it, rehearsed it in her head, the stance, the words, the rueful, happy smile as she passed over her credit card. She'd imagined it just like Romily was imagining buckling those little shoes on her little boy, those little shoes that would not get dirty.

'Thank you,' Claire whispered to her as they stepped onto the pavement outside. She hugged Romily and their bellies, one real and one pretend, pressed together. Only Romily knew that they were both pretending to be something they weren't.

Dear Thing,

But oh, how I want you. How I want you so much.

34
Threads

Dear Mrs Lawrence,

Yes I did work on that Alan piece some more. I recorded it for you on my phone, here it is. Mrs Radcliffe who they have brought in to replace you is letting me use the practice rooms if I ask but most of the time I've found somewhere I can play where people don't bother me (the cricket pavilion tho it is cold and full of fag ends).

Look I'm sorry again that my dad is such a pig. Everyone says you're not coming back and it's all his fault. Thank you for writing to Mr Doughty about my recital tho. There's less than 4 weeks left and I'm not sure I won't bottle out. I feel a little sick when I think about it. Maybe you will come if you can? I hope you can find another damn job, you deserve a place with nicer parents.

Max xx

Dear Claire,

Thank you so much for your lovely and very comprehensive lesson plans since you have left. It is so good to know that the students have enjoyed continuity over this term. I'm writing, however, to say that Helena Radcliffe has indicated that she'd prefer to start with her own lesson plans in the Easter term. She comes to us from Cape Town, where she was Head of Music at the International School.

I hope you are well. Please let us know when your lovely baby has arrived!

Yours

Veronica Greasley, Head, St Dominick's School

Claire saved Max's music files to listen to later, got up from her laptop and went to find Ben, who was spending the evening working on the sofa, his own laptop open and the football on the telly in front of him.

'They've already found my permanent replacement,' she said. 'Mrs Helena Radcliffe. Head of Music from Cape Town.'

'That's good, isn't it?' said Ben, still scrolling down pages. 'Now you don't have to worry.'

'I like worrying.'

'I've noticed.' He reached for a folder, checking the score on the telly. Claire considered joining him on the sofa, cuddling under his arm while he worked. Once, she'd have done it without a second thought. She'd have her own stack of marking to do, her own work to get on with. They would sit together in their own worlds, sharing.

But she didn't have anything of her own and she didn't want to seem needy.

'Would you like a cup of—' she began, and then she heard her phone ringing.

'Yes, please,' Ben said absently, not seeming to notice that she was heading for the front door where she'd left her handbag, rather than the kitchen. When she answered, it was Romily.

'I need a favour,' Romily said, her voice hushed. 'Is Ben there?'

'Yes, he's just here.' Claire hesitated. 'Do you want me to hand you over?'

'No! No, I wanted to talk to you. Can Ben hear you?'

Claire sat on the stairs, lowering her own voice. 'What's the matter?'

'Nothing. Jarvis wants to have dinner with me next Friday.'

'That's great!'

'He wants to talk about more formal visiting arrangements with Posie.'

'Oh.'

'So I need someone to look after Pose, and Mrs Spencer has got bingo.'

'I'll look after Posie, that's no problem at all.'

'The thing is, can you come over here? Because I don't really want Ben . . .'

'I see.'

'I mean, obviously he'll have to know sometime, but he's got a thing against Jarvis and I think it would be much easier just to present him with . . .'

'It's your decision,' Claire said. 'I don't expect you to be telling us how to raise our child either. I mean, once we . . .'

'Yes. So . . .'

'I'll come over at half six next Friday. Is that all right?'

'And you won't tell Ben, will you?'

She glanced through the banisters at Ben. He was absorbed in his work. He probably didn't remember the cup of tea she'd offered, let alone their conversation about her being replaced at school. 'No,' she said. 'I won't.'

'Girls together, eh?' Romily sounded relieved.

'Girls together.'

There was no way around it: she looked like a fat cow. Breeding someone else's calf.

But the dress wasn't bad, she supposed. Romily turned around, trying to see her arse, but the mirror wasn't long enough. She stood on tiptoes.

'Nice threads,' said Posie, coming into the bedroom and throwing herself on the bed.

'Where did you learn to say that?'

She shrugged. 'Is Jarvis taking you somewhere expensive? Is that why you've got a new dress?'

'No. Sasha's mum gave me this dress. It was hers. So it's not new.'

'It wasn't Sasha's mum, it was Alexa's mum.'

'Alexa. Right. How do you know? Is Alexa one of your friends?'

'No.' Posie stretched her arms out over her head. 'Do you think Claire will bring that *Swan Lake* DVD?'

'I didn't know you liked ballet.'

'I think I might be a ballerina every now and then, in between exploring.'

'That's an idea.' Romily gave up tugging at her hem and started tugging at her neckline instead. She wasn't used to showing quite so much cleavage. She wasn't used to owning quite so much cleavage. 'Maybe I should just wear jeans and a T-shirt.'

'Nah, wear the dress. It's pretty.' The knocker went, and Posie leaped off the bed and ran to the door like a shot. Romily heard her greeting Claire.

Romily redirected her fussing to her hair. She'd not had her hair this long in ages; she'd had to borrow Posie's brush. She'd never have agreed to go out with Jarvis if she'd known she'd be so uptight about it. It would be the first time they'd been alone together since they'd had that conversation about who she loved and why he'd gone away; and even then, Posie had been in the next room. This was the first time she'd really be alone with him, without Posie at all, since the time he'd walked into the museum, taken her completely by surprise, and made her throw up. That was probably why she was paying so much attention to how she looked: she was trying to distract herself from anticipating an evening full of long, awkward silences where they realized that they had nothing in common except for the child they'd made. Or an evening where he continually berated her for getting pregnant with the child of the married man she was in love with. Or an evening where they coldly compared diaries and worked out when they could safely exchange custody of their daughter. None of these was a particularly appealing prospect. At least she could look like a nicely dressed fat cow. It might make her feel a little better.

And it wasn't only the evening she felt uptight about, either. She'd been cleaning the flat for three days straight to get it up to Claire's standard. Not that she could get it remotely close, with the amount of stuff they had in this tiny place. If Claire opened any of the cupboards she'd be in for a nasty surprise or two.

But the flat and herself were the best she could make them. They were going to have to do.

The story of her life.

When she emerged from the bedroom, Claire and Posie were already on the sofa together, poring over a book of colourful paper dolls. Claire looked up at Romily and smiled. 'You look pretty. Is that a new dress?'

'No. One of the mums at school gave it to me. I don't know why, but when people see that you're pregnant, they just give you stuff whether you even know them or not.'

The mums kept on trying to give her baby clothes as well. Sooner or later she was going to have to say something.

She just hadn't found the right moment, that was all.

'It really suits you,' said Claire. 'Blue is your colour.'

'She's dressing up for Jarvis,' Posie told Claire. They exchanged a not-so-secret smile.

'Oh, for God's sake, I'm going to change into jeans,' said Romily, turning around. Someone else knocked on the door, and Posie jumped up to answer that too.

It was Jarvis. Early. Of course. Posie hugged him and he said, 'Hello Claire,' in a neutral, friendly tone. Romily grabbed her handbag.

'Have a wonderful time,' Claire called after them.

They walked down the pavement together. Jarvis was wearing actual trousers without large pockets on the sides of them. His shirt was untucked, but it looked as if it might have been ironed. He glanced at her sideways. 'You look nice.'

'It's not a new dress,' Romily said.

'Can I have another pillow?'

Posie already had three of them piled up under her head. 'Do you have any more?' asked Claire.

'Romily won't mind if you take one from her bed.' Posie smiled at her appealingly. 'She lets me use all of them when I want to play Princess and the Pea.'

Claire went to Romily's bedroom, where a rumpled duvet had been spread out over the bed. She knew full well that Posie was playing her, but she didn't mind spoiling her occasionally. She was going to have to watch out with her own child, though.

She caught a glimpse of herself in the mirror over the chest of drawers. Look at her, worrying about spoiling a child she didn't have yet. Playing Mummy while Ben thought she was at book club. She should feel guilty; she should feel worried. Tonight, she didn't. Being with a child took her out of herself. It let her relax and be in the present. They'd spent the entire evening watching *Swan Lake* and then pretending to dance. Her hair was in disarray; her cheeks were pink. She had a bit of toothpaste on her blouse from helping Posie.

She grinned at her reflection and took a pillow off the bed. On second thoughts she took both of them. There was a collection of objects hidden under them: a balled-up nightgown, a plastic bottle of hand cream, a novel, a notebook, a black-and-white photograph.

A black-and-white ultrasound scan photograph.

She hadn't known that Romily had kept any of the scan pictures. She peered more closely, and realized this wasn't the same as any of the ones she had herself, the ones she'd memorized and carried around with her.

It must be of Posie. Still kept treasured, all these years later. Claire smiled and picked it up, wondering what Posie had looked like in the womb. If she'd resembled her half-sister or brother. If all babies looked the same before they were born, or if they were different, individual, already themselves. This one showed half a face. The baby had its thumb in its mouth.

The date was printed across the bottom.

'Claire?' called Posie. 'I've chosen my bedtime stories.'

Claire put the photograph back where she'd found it, on top of the notebook. Biting her lip, she went back into Posie's room with the pillows.

'Thank you,' said Posie happily, arranging the pillows behind her. She had a stack of books on the bed.

Why did Romily have a scan photograph from 29 August this year?

'Let's start with *Peter Pan*,' said Posie, handing her a book. Automatically, Claire opened the cover and began to read aloud.

That was the scan that had been done in the hospital. After the fall. Romily had said she hadn't asked for a printout.

Why would she do that?

She read about Neverland without understanding a word of it. Then something about a witch, something about a bear, something about the Mayans. She found herself closing the next-to-last book and looking down to see Posie fast asleep on her tower of pillows, her hand tucked under her cheek.

She kissed Posie's forehead and smoothed back her hair. She turned on her night-light and gently closed her door. Then she went back into Romily's bedroom.

She wasn't snooping. She'd found this by accident. And it was a photograph of her own child, after all.

Claire sat down on the bed and picked up the photograph again.

Romily had never seemed particularly interested in the scans. Unlike Claire and Ben, she hadn't been glued to the screen. Claire had always had the impression that she wanted to act as if she wasn't actually there, to try to give the illusion that Ben and Claire were alone in the room. '*That's your baby,*' she'd said several times.

And yet she'd kept this one picture, taken the one time that Ben and Claire hadn't been with her.

And then lied about it.

And hidden it.

Claire looked around the room as if it would give her a clue about why Romily would do all that. Romily, who seemed to Claire to be one of the most straightforward people she'd ever met. Who said what she thought, who'd cheered Claire for doing the same thing. Who was honest to the point of tactlessness, sometimes.

Who'd asked her to hide her dinner with Jarvis from Ben.

The room didn't reveal anything except for the fact that Romily'd been tidying up. She'd probably shoved all this stuff underneath the pillows to get it out of sight. Or did she sleep with this photograph under her pillow every night? While Claire's baby slept inside of her?

Claire touched the notebook that the photograph had lain on. It was a plain paper-backed notebook, spiral-bound, A5, with a green cover. There wasn't anything written on the front.

And hadn't the photograph been partly *inside* it? With the corner just underneath the cover? As if it had fallen out when Romily was tidying?

She tried to remember, tried to picture it as it had been when she'd first seen it.

Claire glanced around the room again. This other woman's room, this other woman's life. She picked up the notebook and opened it.

Dear Thing, she read.

35

What Could Have Been

It really hadn't been that bad after all, Romily thought. They'd had plenty to talk about: mutual acquaintances, music, Jarvis's travel, Romily's work, the field uses of Vaseline and string. Books. How they both missed seeing proper films on a proper screen and had to make do with DVDs or aeroplane entertainment systems. The Kyoto Agreement. Fleas and bedbugs. They'd talked all through dinner, which was not at an expensive restaurant but at a newish pub by the river that did good food with plenty of vegetarian options — over Jarvis's glass of wine and her glass of lemonade, over his steak pie and her beetroot tart, the sticky toffee pudding that she ate while he had two cups of coffee. He preferred his sugar to be accompanied by caffeine. She remembered that about him from years ago.

She'd forgotten about all the conversations they used to have.

And they talked about Posie, of course.

'If we agree on some definite dates, I can arrange my year's work around them,' Jarvis had said, stirring his coffee. 'A few days at Easter, maybe. And a week in the summer when I can take her camping.'

'You can do that? I thought you had to go when the work came up.'

'I can have a few times a year which are non-negotiable. What about Boxing Day?' He smiled. 'I'd like some Christmas with her.'

'I didn't think you'd like that sort of thing.'

'I liked it when I was a kid. As an adult, the magic rubs a little thin. Especially when everyone else in your family is paired off.'

'It's usually just me and Posie. We stay in our pyjamas all day and eat nothing but chocolate.'

'It's fun as an uncle. I think it would be more fun as a dad. I might be able to arrange for all my nieces and nephews to be there.'

That was yet another thing Posie had missed out on: big family Christmases. Something Jarvis could give her and Romily could not.

'That should all be fine,' Romily said at last. 'I think she'd like it.'

He looked up from his coffee. 'You'd trust me with her? Overnight? Or for a week camping?'

'You've kept yourself alive for this long, and you've demonstrated that you can shift it to the nearest hospital in an emergency. I think you'll keep her safe. But . . .'

'But what?'

'Oh, nothing. I was just thinking – it just occurred to me that with her gone for that long, I'd be lonely.' Romily laughed. 'Silly. I'll be able to sleep late and get loads done.'

'But you'd still be lonely.'

She shrugged and ran her spoon around her plate to pick up the last bit of sticky toffee.

'I don't mind being alone,' Jarvis said. 'I quite like it. I used to think that since I liked being alone, I could never get lonely.'

She caught his eye for a moment, and then looked down again at her plate.

'So Boxing Day, and we can set dates during the school holidays,' she said hurriedly, 'which you'll work around, and then some weekends and evenings, to be decided according to our work schedules as we go. Does that sound right?'

'It sounds good. I was thinking it's time I did more work in this country, so that will make it easier.'

'You don't have to stay around. Our lives aren't that complicated. I'm happy for you to ring when you're heading back to England and give us a few days' notice.'

'I want to stay,' he said, and stood up. 'Done?'

They walked back on the towpath along the Thames. The streetlamps reflected off the black surface of the water in undulations of orange light. An unseen duck protested at the shadows. She remembered one evening in London, years and miles away but on the bank of this same river, when they had walked together and he had taken her hand.

He kept his hands in his pockets and she held her handbag strap on the side facing him. '*You don't have to be alone to be lonely*,' she thought about saying to him. '*You don't have to be alone at all.*'

But she didn't say it.

They turned up onto her street. The curtains of her flat had been drawn. The two of them stopped in front, and when Romily turned to say goodbye to Jarvis, he was much closer than she'd expected him to be. She could smell the faint scent of his shaving lotion and hear the rustle of his clothing and her eyes met his and her heart thumped and Romily forgot the facts of her life. Her hand loosened on her bag and she tilted her face up towards his. His breath touched her cheek.

The baby kicked.

'Oh,' said Romily, putting her hand on her stomach. 'Um. Well. Thank you.'

'Thank you. That was fun. A bit like old times.'

In old times he would have kissed her goodnight. She ducked her head. 'I'll ring you about next weekend.'

'All right. Goodnight, Romily.'

He didn't move, though, and Romily hesitated before she realized that he was waiting for her to get safely inside before he walked to the station.

It only took the short flight of steps to her front door for her to travel from what had been and what could have been, to what was. By the time she opened her door and looked up at Jarvis, he was already walking away.

Claire had all the lights on inside and she was sitting on the armchair that Ben always used. Romily put a big smile on her face.

'Good news,' she said. 'I didn't spill anything on the dre—'

Claire looked up. Her face was white. On her lap was Romily's notebook.

'I found,' she said, and swallowed. 'I found the scan picture.'

Romily stood where she was, the door swinging shut behind her.

'You read my notebook.' *Oh no. Oh dear Lord no, no no no.* 'Why are you reading my notebook?'

'I saw the picture,' Claire said. She was speaking as if she were in a dream. 'I borrowed a pillow for Posie and I saw it, and I was putting it back inside the notebook and I saw the letters you've been writing. To my baby.'

'That's private.' Romily strode over and snatched the notebook from Claire's lap. The scan photograph fluttered to the floor. Romily shut the book and held it close to her chest, all the words she'd written flashing through her head at once. All the secrets.

'You were doing what I'd asked you to do,' said Claire. 'Writing letters to the baby. To let him know he was wanted. You said it was a stupid idea.'

'It was just silly stuff, just feelings. No one was meant to read it. I was going to rip it up.'

Claire didn't sound angry; she sounded stunned. Maybe she hadn't read all that far. Maybe she'd only just started reading it. It wasn't that bad at the beginning, was it?

And then Romily realized what Claire had said. She had called the baby 'him', even though she and Ben had been so careful not to learn the sex.'

'"Love isn't the answer",' said Claire. '"Love is the problem". How long have you been in love with my husband, Romily?'

'I'm not,' Romily said automatically. 'I never was. I only wrote that because I – I was making up a story. Once upon a time. Like it says at the beginning.'

'It's not a story. It's true.'

'It's not. I'm not in love with Ben.'

'So why do you have a whole page where you tell yourself not to be in love with him? Over and over and over again?'

'It's . . .' Romily couldn't breathe. It was as if the room were shrinking in on her, crushing her. 'It's just the hormones. They want me to pair-bond with the father of the child I'm carrying. It's nothing, nothing at all, and I'll get over it as soon as the baby is born.'

'You're a horrible liar.'

Claire's voice was cold. She stood up, her body straight as an arrow.

'Did you volunteer to carry Ben's baby because you loved him? Was it your idea that once you were carrying his child, he'd fall in love with you too, and you'd get to keep him *and* the baby?'

'No! No, it wasn't like that at all. It's not like that.'

'But you loved him when you said you'd carry his baby. That's why you said you'd do it.'

'I . . . no.'

'And it was even easier for you because I couldn't conceive. So the baby is half yours.'

'Claire, please.'

'I trusted you,' said Claire. 'I trusted you with the most important part of my life. The part I felt weakest in, the part I was most afraid of going wrong. And you *knew* that.'

'I trusted *you*,' said Romily, on a sudden surge of anger. She welcomed it. Anger was better than panic. 'I trusted you to be in my house and look after my daughter and not go snooping through my life.'

Claire pointed to the notebook in Romily's hand. 'That's about *my* life. My baby. My husband. You want them both.' A tear rolled down her cheek. 'Have you been laughing at me this entire time?'

'It's not about you, Claire. It doesn't all revolve around you. Every minute since I've got pregnant, I've been examined and looked at and questioned and told what to do, what to eat, how to behave. I don't belong to you. Not my body, not my feelings. They're mine and they're private and they're none of your business.'

'Everything you've done has been an act. It's all been to lull me into a sense of security. You kept telling me the baby was mine. You saw the nursery. I liked you. And all the time . . .' She choked.

'You were never much bothered with me before. Did you like me, or did you like what I was doing for you? The service I was providing?'

Claire hurried to the sofa and scooped up her jacket and her handbag from where they lay. She slammed the door after her. Romily dropped the notebook and leaned back against the wall, her hands over her mouth. Her heart pounded.

Posie appeared, rubbing her eyes, her hair mussed from sleep. 'What's going on?'

'Nothing,' said Romily. 'Nothing's going on. Claire had to leave quickly because she forgot to do something. Go back to sleep, Pose.'

Posie nodded and padded back to her room. Romily picked up the notebook and, as quietly as she could, ripped every single page out of it. She tore each letter to shreds, tinier and tinier until she could barely see the writing any more. And then tore it tinier still.

36
All There Is

Ben had spread his blueprints all over the kitchen table. A half-empty glass of milk and a crumb-littered plate sat in front of him. He barely glanced up when she came in. 'Good book club? You're home early.'

'I wasn't at book club.'

'Sorry, was it something else? I'll do the washing-up before I go to bed, promise.'

'I was at Romily's.'

He did look up at that. 'Is she all right?' Claire's face must have been broadcasting her feelings, because he pushed his chair back and stood. 'What's wrong? Is the baby okay? I had my phone right here, why didn't you ring?'

'The baby is fine. I was babysitting Posie.'

'That's all? Why didn't she tell me?'

Romily's little secret about dinner with Jarvis seemed so faraway and trivial now. Compared with her big secret. 'I found something while I was in her flat. She's been writing letters to the baby.'

'That's what you wanted her to do.'

'She's written all her feelings down in them. *All* her feelings.'

Ben stood in their kitchen, wearing jeans and a rugby top she'd bought him. His hair was rumpled where he'd run his fingers through it as he worked; he still wore his reading glasses. He looked familiar in every way. The way the world had looked before she'd opened that notebook and discovered that nothing was familiar any more.

She had gone through it in her head, over and over and over again on the way home, stopping carefully at red lights, looking both ways before she pulled out at junctions.

How could Romily be in love with Ben if he'd never encouraged her? All these years without a single sign back? You didn't fall in love with someone who was indifferent to you, someone who was just your friend. Someone who was in love with his wife.

But Ben couldn't know. He'd never have let Romily get pregnant with his baby if he'd known. He'd never have kept seeing Romily, spent so much time alone with her.

Unless all this time, when she'd thought of nothing but a baby, when she'd been blind to everything except the failure of her own body, unless all this time Romily and Ben had been . . .

'There's something wrong,' he said. 'You look like there's something wrong. I don't understand.'

'Don't you? Not at all?'

If he didn't know how Romily felt, she could keep going. She could handle this. They could make a plan together. They could see a solicitor, they could draw up the agreement Romily and Ben had said they didn't need.

Had they dismissed it because . . .

'Claire. Don't make me guess. If this is something about Romily and our baby, it affects me too.'

'Romily is in love with you.'

She held her breath. She waited for him to laugh it away. She waited for him to react in horror.

'Oh,' he said.

'Did you hear what I said?'

'She wrote that?' he asked. 'In her letters to the baby?'

'She wrote that she's been in love with you for a long time.'

'Oh,' he said. He sat back down in his chair.

'Is that all you have to say about it? "Oh"?'

He chewed on his lip. 'I'm not sure what to say about it.'

'You mean that you knew?'

Ben paused. His whole manner was thoughtful, as if he were sifting through evidence, memory and emotion. Claire, on the other hand, was trembling. She held on to the back of a chair, her fingers pressing against the wood.

'No. I didn't know. But now that you say it, it's not a surprise. Oh God. It's not a surprise.'

'It was to me!'

'You don't know her as well as I do.' He was looking off into the distance. 'She's been single for a long time. I've been more or less the only man in her life. Objectively, it makes sense.'

'Objectively? I'm telling you that another woman is in love with you and you're talking objectively?'

'I'm trying to explain it to you. I'm trying to understand it myself.' He rubbed his hands in his hair. 'I wasn't expecting this conversation tonight.'

'Ben, she's in love with you and you're my husband.'

'It must have been very difficult for her. It must still be, with the baby. My baby.' He frowned.

'You're worried about *her*?'

'Yes. She's got the worst of it.'

She stared at Ben, the man she had thought she knew better than anyone else in the world. 'Didn't you think that she must be in love with you when she offered to carry the baby? To do this huge thing for you?'

'No. That is, I was so excited, so happy, I . . .' He sighed. 'You're right. It was cruel of me. I didn't mean it to be, but it was cruel. I just thought it would be all right.'

'How could it ever be all right?'

'I didn't think about Romily being in love with me. It's only now, when I think about it. When I have all the facts. It's—'

And now, now, his face crumpled into sorrow and regret. He put his head in his hands.

'It's the worst thing I've ever done,' he said.

It felt as if her fingers were going to bore through the back of the chair, straight into her own palms.

'I don't understand,' she said. 'You're acting like this is all about Romily. I'm your wife. It's my baby too.'

'Yes,' he said. 'I've done this to both of you. I'm so sorry.'

'What's going to happen?'

'I don't know,' he said into his hands. 'Oh God. She trusted me. You trusted me. I've let both of you down.'

She wanted him to look at her. To see her. To know what this was doing to her.

'Have you had an affair with her?' she asked.

'No,' he said. 'In some ways it would have been less cruel if I had.'

'What? How can you say that?'

He raised his head, but his attention was still far away, still deep in his thoughts. 'I don't mean less cruel. That was wrong. I mean it would have been more honest.'

'More honest?'

She couldn't stand. She pulled out the chair and sank into it. Her fingers throbbed.

'Ben,' she asked, not even trying to keep her voice steady any more, 'are you in love with Romily?'

'I care about her a great deal. I don't know if it's love. My feelings have changed towards her over the past few months. I've been trying to ignore it, but it's true.' He swallowed. 'I think about her first thing in the morning when I wake up. She's carrying my child. I feel protective of her. I think she's precious. I would do anything for her.'

Now he looked at Claire.

'That sounds like love to me,' she said.

'I'm trying to be honest with you,' he said. 'I'm sorry if it hurts. But we need to get it out in the open now. Don't we?'

'You,' she said, 'are the only man I have ever loved. Ever.'

'I know.'

'Do you still love me?'

'Yes. I'll always love you.'

'But you love her too.'

He looked away. 'I don't know.'

'Is that why you've been spending so much time with her?'

'Yes. Probably. I keep feeling that I've failed you, Claire. That I can't do or say what you want me to. It's easier with Romily. I know that makes me sound . . . I'm a coward. But I owe her something too, don't I?'

'Is it her, or the fact that she's pregnant with your child?'

'I don't know. Can you separate them? I've never felt like this before.'

Because I couldn't have your child. And she can.

That's what it came down to. Again, and again, and again.

'I think you need to leave,' Claire said.

'Okay.' He stood up. 'I'll sleep in the spare bedroom.'

306

'No. I want you to leave the house. I want you to leave me alone. I don't want to live with a man who says that he loves me and falls in love with another woman who can do what I can't.'

The pain was so naked on his face that she had to look away.

'If that's what you want,' he said.

And it was that easy, to uproot her entire existence. She sat at the kitchen table and listened to him going upstairs, putting a few things into a bag. When he came back into the kitchen to gather his laptop and work, she didn't look at him.

'Claire,' he said. 'Are you sure?'

'Everything that we have is a lie.'

'It's not a lie,' he said. 'But maybe it's not all there is.'

She didn't answer.

'I'll ring you,' he said at last. And then he was gone.

37

The Truth

'If you don't mind my saying so, you look absolutely awful.'

Romily rubbed her eyes and turned to the woman who'd spoken. It was the one with the scruffy toddler, the one who'd been kind to her before. She had on a scarf with crocheted flowers sewn into it.

'I haven't slept,' Romily said. 'That's all.' She edged towards the school gates, to make her quick escape. She thought she'd perfected the art of dropping off Posie without being trapped into a conversation, but maybe she hadn't.

'Heartburn?'

'Something like that.'

'Better than heartbreak, that's what I say. Though not by much.'

The woman's voice was cheerful but it was the word that did it. Heartbreak.

The sob she'd been holding down all weekend, so as not to show Posie, erupted. It sounded like the wail of a sick animal. Romily clapped her hand to her mouth, but the tears had already started flowing down her cheeks.

'Oh, shit,' said the woman. 'Oh no, I'm sorry. I've said something wrong. I've been an idiot. I'm sorry.'

'No,' sobbed Romily. 'No, it's not you. It's me. It's okay.'

She went to wipe her nose on her sleeve but the woman handed her a muslin square before she could do so.

'I always misread situations,' the woman said. 'Everyone tells me so. I have some chocolate here somewhere. Here.' She held out a packet of chocolate buttons. 'Just don't show Daniel you're eating them or you'll have to share.'

Romily shook her head. 'It's okay.'

'Well, obviously it's not. Is there anything I can do to help you?'

Romily shook her head, wiping her face. The muslin smelled of baby lotion.

'Come on. I'm doing my best here. If you can't take chocolate buttons, at least tell me what's wrong.'

'I'm not keeping the baby,' Romily blurted out.

'Oh.'

'It's not mine. I'm a surrogate. But I didn't say anything because . . .'

'Oh. Well, that's a really nice thing you're doing. It's incredible, in fact.'

'I don't want to give it up.'

'Oh.'

'So that's one reason why I'm crying. I can't tell you the other one.'

'I think you had better take the chocolate buttons. My name is Eleanor, by the way.'

Romily felt the packet being pressed into her hand.

'You must think I'm a terrible person,' she said.

'No, I think it's pretty understandable, actually. You're heartbroken. Like I said. I take it back: heartburn is *much*

309

better. You can go ahead and blow your nose on that. I've got a million of them.'

Romily blew her nose. She looked at the woman blearily.

'Will you tell them?' Romily asked. 'The other mothers? I don't think I can.'

'Okay. Are you sure you want me to?'

'Yeah,' said Romily. 'It's time for the truth.' She shoved the muslin into her jacket pocket. 'I'll give this back to you after I've washed it.'

The truth, she thought as she hurried to the museum. She was supposed to be a scientist. She was supposed to relish facts, recognizable behaviour patterns, data. She knew that the truth was objective, the truth was the way the world worked. The truth was that Ben was married to Claire and that she had promised to give this baby to them. She had always known the truth.

And all the time she was busily writing down her inner feelings, her illogical, untenable, unbearable feelings, as if that was going to help anything.

Feelings hurt. Even though writing them down gave some sort of momentary relief, it wasn't worth it. Because once feelings were out there in the world, they became real. They became part of the truth.

And then you had to deal with them. You had to feel the humiliation when another woman discovered you wanted what was hers. The shame, the self-hatred, the anger, the desperation to cover up your shabby secret; the sickly, stunted, hopeless love you had nurtured for no reason at all.

Hal looked up as she passed his desk. 'How's the Queen Bee today?'

'Queen Bees control the colony as well as serve it,' she said. 'They work purely on biological imperative with no

310

free will. I don't think the metaphor is particularly apt.'

'Cranky.'

'If you were thirty-five weeks pregnant, you would be cranky too.'

'If I were thirty-five weeks pregnant, I would have taken maternity leave by now and would be lying on a sofa watching *Bargain Hunt*.'

'I'm not taking maternity leave. I don't need to.' All that time, by herself. With no work to distract her.

Like Claire.

She went to the collection store room and shut the door. She lay her head on Amity's rosewood cabinet, atop the corpses of hundreds of insects.

Claire had promised herself, when she got on the train to London, that she would not answer her phone. She would not talk to Ben if he rang; she would not speak to Romily. She would not trust herself to talk with her mother or her sister. She would take a weekend in London, away from her empty house, in a pretty hotel. She would go to galleries and concerts, she would spend money on her credit card, she would lick her wounds and fill herself up with other people's art and music and food and she would have space, good space, constructive space, to work out what she wanted. How she could possibly go forward, with a husband who was in love with another woman and a baby who was still in that other woman's womb.

In the end, her phone only rang once. It was her sister. Claire remembered with guilt that she was meant to be discussing with her what to get their parents for Christmas. But she couldn't talk without giving herself away. She wasn't even certain that she'd be able to go home for the holiday. She

311

couldn't picture herself going without Ben. Surrounding herself with concerned family, exposing her wounds for everyone to see. Her mother might not say *I told you so* – she probably wouldn't, she was too kind – but Claire would think it. Her mother had never had to discipline her as a child, not as she'd had to with Helen and Ian. Claire would send herself to the corner.

Christmas is over three weeks away. Everything could be back to normal by then, a small hopeful voice said to her as she walked through Tate Britain without seeing anything, as she sat through Brahms and Chopin.

But she didn't know how it could be.

There was too much space in London, none of it hers. Being away from home didn't let her think; it untethered her, set her adrift among too many conversations and carols, too much traffic, too many ideas. She didn't like eating alone in restaurants, and room service was too quiet unless she put on the television. She wrote a dozen texts to Ben and deleted them all. She brought up his number but did not call it, as if that would magically make him ring her so she could refuse to answer it. So she would know that he was thinking of her. That he was not with Romily.

Because where else would he go?

London was intolerable, but getting on the train home didn't make her feel any better. She picked up her car from the underground car park beneath the station and drove home. Ben's BMW was in the drive, exactly as normal, and that small signifier made her heart leap then sink. Before she could go in the house he opened the front door from the inside and they stood there on either side of the threshold of their home. She held her weekend bag and he held a suitcase.

'Hi,' he said. It was Ben, it was Ben, her husband, her only love, looking the same as he always did. He didn't reach forward to kiss her. He looked wary, as if caught doing something wrong.

'I've been in London,' she said.

'Did you have a good time?'

'I . . .'

He nodded. 'I came to pack some things.'

'Where . . . have you been?'

'The George, in town.'

It was on the other side of Brickham from Romily's flat. 'Have you seen . . .'

'I haven't seen anyone. All I've done all weekend is think.'

It was unbelievable that he could look the same. Claire felt that if she smiled, if she touched him, they could carry on just the same as they always had. But there was something between them, some membrane she couldn't push through. A mutual agreement that all the years didn't count for anything. It was as if they'd lost the habit of being married, as if that had been all that was keeping them together and now that they'd broken it, they couldn't get it back.

'This is strange,' said Ben. 'It's awful.'

Since he'd said it, she couldn't agree with it, even though it was what she'd been thinking too. She'd been the one to kick him out, after all.

'What are you going to do?' she asked.

'I don't know. I can't stay at the George for ever. The breakfast is horrible.'

It was meant to be a little joke. It would be so easy to smile.

'I could come back here,' he said. 'If you wanted. It doesn't feel right without you. Please let me come back, Claire. I love you. This thing with Romily . . . I said it all wrong. I was taken by surprise. I didn't mean what I said about an affair being more honest. I wouldn't have an affair with her. It never even occurred to me. It's you that I love.'

'But you do have feelings for her.'

'They don't count. I swear to you, they don't.'

'What if you had to choose between me, or Romily and the baby?'

'What do you mean?'

'It's her baby. She wants to keep it.'

'She does?'

She had thought he looked just the same. But at that, he changed. He became somehow less, as if something inside him, something holding him up, had collapsed.

'I didn't know that. She said that she wants to keep it? She said that to you?'

'She wrote it in the letters.'

'What did she say? Do you remember, exactly?'

'She wrote that she was in love with him, with the baby. That he was her baby who was meant to be. Half her and half of the man she loves.'

'And when you asked her about it she said—'

'She didn't deny it. How could she give him up if she loves him?'

'If she says she'll give the baby to us, she will,' Ben said. But his voice was shaky.

'I don't see how she could. She wrote it all down. It was how she really felt.'

'It's a boy?' Ben said. 'Is it a boy? Does she know?'

'They must have told her when she had the scan after her fall. She never showed us the photo.'

'I have a son,' he said quietly.

'Who would you choose?' she asked him again. 'I need to

know, Ben. If she keeps the baby, who would you choose?'

'I can't choose between my wife and my son.'

'So you'd choose to be with her and the baby.'

'Don't make me choose,' he said. 'I can't.'

It was so wrong to see him hurting and not go to him, not hold him.

'Then you've already chosen,' she said.

'Romily? Why can't we see Ben and Claire this weekend?'

'I think they're busy, Pose.'

'But we haven't seen them since last week. And Claire promised to play me some more ballet music. I've been practising.'

'I know you have. You look very graceful. I'm proud of you. It's your turn to deal.'

'I'm bored with this game.'

'We can go to the park if you want.'

'Is Jarvis coming?'

'I think he's busy, too.'

'Everyone is busy except for us.'

'I'm sorry, Pose.'

'And you look sick. Have you been throwing up again?'

'No. It's the baby. I can't sleep properly. It's okay. Don't worry, please.'

'Is Thing close to being born?'

'Not too far off now. After Christmas, in the New Year.'

'Are we all going to be there, in the hospital, with you? Does it get all yucky when a baby is born? Do you poo if you're pushing really hard?'

'Are you going to deal, or should we go to the park?'

'What are we doing for Christmas Day, anyway?'

'I don't know yet, Posie. Why don't we plan on one of

315

those lazy days, just you and me together. The way we like it.'

'Maybe all of us can go to Ben and Claire's house. Jarvis says he has lots of brothers and sisters. Maybe they can come, too. Do you think Claire knows how to make figgy pudding?'

'I don't know. But I'll get a special pudding from Marks. One of the ones we can do in the microwave.'

'I think I should call Claire and ask her.'

'No! Don't do that. Why don't you and I just spend some time together? Isn't that enough?'

38
Ergo

Romily had turned off her phone before for quite long periods when she was working, or more recently, when she'd been dreading Jarvis getting in touch. But she had never quite reached the level of phone-turned-offedness that she reached now. She carried it with her – she'd be foolish not to, in this stage of pregnancy and with the scare she'd had on the beach. In an emergency she could turn it on and be ringing a midwife on the maternity ward within seconds. In a different kind of emergency, she could have a pizza delivered to her flat within twenty minutes.

She knew that Claire would have told Ben what she'd discovered. That the two of them would be talking, horrified, trying to figure out how they would get through this latest threat to their having a child. The thought of it made her panicky and sick. If she knew Ben and Claire, they'd have come up with several strategies by now.

She didn't want to be part of a strategy. She wanted all this to be over. She wanted to be able to hop on a ship to Madagascar, for her and Posie to disappear off together and have wonderful mother-and-daughter adventures of the type you read about in travel magazines. Of the type Amity would have had if she'd had an intrepid offspring.

But she was thirty-six weeks pregnant. The baby weighed down everything that she did. Her ankles were swollen and she couldn't tie the laces of her Converses. She had the concentration of a— well, of a woman most of whose bodily resources were going to the child curled up in her womb. She was useless in almost every way except for being an incubator.

She was trapped here in this situation, at least until she gave birth. And what was going to happen after she gave birth was so huge and unbearable that she couldn't look forward to that, either.

Her only choice was to keep her head down. Quite literally, when it came to dropping off and picking up Posie from school. She hunched her shoulders up around her and looked at the pavement. Today, she was wearing a hat.

She imagined that Eleanor would have told everyone by now that the baby wasn't hers. That she wasn't really one of them and that she had lied, if only by omission. So they were probably keeping their distance, too. In any case she avoided their eyes and she hovered outside the school gates, not going in, waiting for Posie to emerge. She was pretty sure they were looking at her. She was pretty sure they were talking about her.

She bit her lip and thought about a documentary she'd seen about caves in Borneo, piled with bat guano, seething with all those lovely, lovely cockroaches. Now *there* was a creature which could survive anything. A lot to admire there.

'Romily.' A hand touched her shoulder and she turned around.

It was Jarvis. He looked angry.

'What are you doing here?' she asked.

'You're not answering your phone. I've left messages.'

'I don't feel like talking.'

'What's wrong?'

She folded her arms. 'You mean besides your turning up uninvited?'

'I want to see my daughter. You said I could whenever I liked. Ergo, I'm turning up to collect her from school and take her to the park.'

'Ergo.' Romily snorted.

'I don't understand. You haven't talked to me for days. What's going on?'

She felt the weight of attention from the school playground. Here she was with another man, a different man from the one the mothers had seen with Posie before. She shouldn't care – who were these people, after all, to judge her? But the fact was, she was guilty. She couldn't think of a single thing she'd done right.

'She'll be glad to see you,' she said grudgingly. 'She's been asking.'

'So why have you got your phone turned off?'

'Jarvis!'

She saw Jarvis's face light up at the sight of Posie. Their daughter tripped, smiling, into his arms.

'I thought we'd go to the park, Butterfly,' said Jarvis, taking her hand.

'Scintillating.'

'Pardon me, are you Posie's parents?' A young woman stood just inside the school gates, wearing a staff security pass around her neck.

'Yes,' said Jarvis.

'I'm Posie's teacher, Mrs Kapoor. I wonder if I could have a quick word?'

'Oh. Okay.' Romily turned to Posie. 'Is there something you need to tell me, Posie?'

But Posie had scooted behind Jarvis, and only the hem of her skirt was visible. 'I'll take her to the park,' Jarvis said, 'and you can meet us there.'

Romily followed the teacher into the school, trying not to notice the staring mothers, and into the classroom. Brightly coloured paper displays plastered the walls. 'Please have a seat, Mrs Summer,' said Mrs Kapoor.

'Dr Summer,' said Romily, to cover up. She didn't even recognize her daughter's class teacher; she'd never made an effort to meet her. Yet another thing she'd done wrong. The only seats were child-size plastic chairs. She took one. It made her about half a foot shorter than the teacher, which she supposed was the point.

'I know we have a parents' evening coming up after the holidays but I thought this was important enough to warrant a little chat. I'm concerned about Posie's behaviour.'

'She's always been quite an . . . individualistic child.'

'She's very bright. At the beginning of the year her work was in many ways outstanding. She's very creative.'

'You're telling me.'

'I think she spends a lot of time in her own imaginary world. Am I right?'

'Yes.'

'And she's very shy.'

'Shy? No, I wouldn't call her shy.'

'She finds it difficult to work in groups. When I ask her to work with another child, she refuses. Not in a rude way, you understand. She just carries on as if the other child isn't there. Does she have an active social life outside of school?'

'You mean, does she have any friends.' Romily sighed. 'I've

320

tried to encourage her, and she did use to have some. They've sort of . . . faded away. She prefers to spend her time with grown-ups, or doing her own thing. I used to be the same when I was little.'

'Some children are more naturally solitary, but over the past week or so Posie has completely withdrawn into herself. She doesn't interact with any of the other children and when I ask her a question she acts as if she hasn't heard me. She's not done any schoolwork at all. She gives in blank sheets, or with a doodle on them at most. Her homework is non-existent.'

'She tells me she's done it.'

'Don't you check?'

Romily began to know what the parents of that teenager at Claire's school must have felt like, told by a teacher that they were doing a horrible job. 'It's sort of fallen by the wayside recently. I'll do better.'

'The homework is the least of it. She's almost unresponsive. Sometimes this can happen in cases of bullying so I've made some discreet enquiries, but I haven't uncovered anything so far. Has Posie said anything to you?'

'No.' Would she even have been listening if Posie had said something?

'Is there something going on at home?'

Romily wondered how much of playground gossip made it to the teachers. She swallowed. 'There are one or two things. I didn't think Posie was affected.'

'That might be what's causing it. She may be worried. Children often know more than we think they do.'

'I'll talk with her.'

'It would be good if we could get to the bottom of it. It's disrupting a lot of lessons.'

'I'm sorry.'

'And she seems like a very unhappy little girl at the moment.'

A very unhappy little girl.

Posie sat on the swings, her feet drooping. She dragged her toes in the dirt as Jarvis pushed her. Her fringe, which Romily had let get even longer than usual, flopped over her face, hiding it.

'What's up?' asked Jarvis as soon as Romily got close enough. Posie stopped the swing and began twisting it round. Romily took hold of the chains and held it still, so she could see Posie's face.

'Mrs Kapoor says you've stopped talking to everyone at school,' she said. 'She thinks something is wrong. Can you tell me what's wrong, Posie?'

Posie kicked. 'Nobody has anything interesting to say.'

'I think it's more than that,' Romily said gently. 'Are you worried about something?'

'It's more fun just to think things. Like today I was thinking, you know when the sun shines off the water and it looks like a ladder or a path? What do you think it would be like to walk on that? A sparkly path of light all the way to the sun?'

'Pose.' Romily cupped Posie's face in her hand, but Posie turned away.

'I just don't feel like talking. Nobody wants to talk about anything except for what's real. And I don't like what's real.'

'What about it don't you like?' asked Jarvis. His eyes met Romily's briefly before they both focused on Posie.

'I don't like, I don't like . . . why do you think it's called December? It sounds a little like a decent cucumber, don't you think?'

322

'Posie. Please tell us.' Although Romily knew. Of course she knew. It was a small flat; Posie had probably woken up long before she appeared in the room that night, the night that Claire had found Romily's notebook. She'd probably heard every word of Claire and Romily's argument.

'It was Ben's text.' Posie mumbled it into her lap.

'What are you talking about?' Romily asked.

'I used your phone. I know you've had it turned off but I turned it on and sent him a text to ask when we were going to see him.'

'Oh.' Cold flooded Romily. 'Did you sign it, Posie? Did he know it was from you or did he think it was from me?'

'Romily,' said Jarvis, 'what is going on?'

'I don't remember if I signed it,' said Posie. 'I just borrowed your phone one night when you were in the shower and he texted back and then I turned your phone off again.'

Romily dug in her bag for her phone.

'What did his text say that's upset you so much?' asked Jarvis.

'He said he'd moved out of Auntie Claire's and his house. And that they had a big argument and that he thinks they've split up. And that he's got a flat by himself, and Romily, does this mean that Ben and Claire aren't married any more? Does this mean they're not my godparents and they're going to sell their house and move away?'

Posie had started crying. Romily stopped searching for her phone and that text and gathered Posie up into her arms. Posie turned her face into Romily's neck.

'Was it because Auntie Claire had to look after me in secret when you went out with Jarvis?' Posie asked, her words muffled. 'Is it my fault?'

'It is one hundred per cent not your fault,' said Romily. 'One thousand per cent.'

323

'You can't have one thousand per cent,' said Posie.

'You can in this instance.' Romily squeezed her eyes tight shut, keeping her own tears inside. She was causing her own daughter pain, now. Again.

'Let's go home,' said Jarvis.

'Has this happened before?' Jarvis draped the tea towel over the side of the sink and came to join Romily on the sofa. He had made them all beans on toast with what he insisted was his special mystery ingredient (it was ketchup) and lost to Posie twice at Scrabble. It was enough to raise a smile before she went to bed.

'She's always been a little on-and-off about kids her own age. It's probably my fault; I never took her to playgroups or activities or any of those things. We just hung out. And she loves playing at Ben and Claire's.'

'But she's never completely shut off before?'

'She's never completely shut off.' Romily bit her lip. 'She's learned that from me lately.'

'And Ben and Claire splitting up?'

'Surprise, surprise. That's also my fault.'

Jarvis waited.

'I wrote some letters. To the baby. It was Claire's idea, so the baby would know it was wanted from the beginning, I suppose so it would have some sort of insight when it was older about why we did everything this roundabout, weird way. Anyway, I wasn't into the idea at first but I found that it was useful. It felt good to get all of my feelings out on paper. I'd been bottling everything up for so long.'

'Tell me you didn't write about being in love with Ben.'

'I did. I've— it's not been easy, Jarvis. I didn't think I'd feel anything about this baby. But I do. I know it's not mine to

324

keep. But . . . well, when I wrote the letters, sometimes I could pretend for a little bit.'

'What a bloody stupid thing to do.'

'I know it. I really know it.'

'And of course Ben found them.'

'No, it was Claire.'

'Why would that split them up?'

'I don't know.' She got up, fished her phone out of her bag and turned it on. Almost immediately, it started vibrating and pinging with messages. 'Claire and I had a huge row, but that was between us. I didn't mean for them to split up. I only wrote all of that stuff down for myself. I pretended it was letters to the baby, but it wasn't really, not after the first few. It wasn't part of a scheme or anything.'

'I never really thought you were trying to steal Ben. But I stand by my original opinion, that you've let yourself into a whole hell of a mess, Romily.'

'I'm very good at making mistakes.' There it was, in the read messages. It was the only text from Ben at all, although there were several messages from Jarvis.

Been waiting for you to get in touch. Hope you are all right. Have moved out, got flat in London St for now. C unhappy and angry, doesn't want to see me. I'm worried it's over. So sorry for what I have done. Can talk when you are ready. B

There seemed no reason not to show it to Jarvis, so she passed the phone to him. 'He didn't know he was texting Posie,' he said. Then: 'He must be staying in those serviced apartments in London Street. I looked into them.'

'You did?'

'A season train ticket is cheaper. And I thought you probably didn't want me in your neighbourhood.'

Ben was in her neighbourhood. Less than a mile from her

flat. If he'd moved out right after Claire had found the letters, he'd been very close to her, geographically, for the past several days.

Had he stayed away from her because he was so angry with her? It seemed likely, but then in his text he said he was sorry. And that he'd talk when she wanted to.

'I don't understand any of it,' Romily said. 'Why would Claire kick him out because I'm in love with him? It's not his fault.'

'I'm not going to comment on that,' said Jarvis. 'Much as I would like to. The important thing is Posie. You can't shut down, Romily.'

'I know.'

'You might be able to escape into your insect world, but it's not good for a little girl.'

'I did it when I was a little girl,' said Romily. 'It meant I didn't have to think about missing my mum.'

'I've been doing something similar for eight years.'

His words startled her. She met his gaze. The blue eyes that were like Posie's, the face she'd imagined, for that split second that one night, kissing again.

'I can help you,' said Jarvis. 'But you have to let me.'

'Okay,' she said. 'Yes.'

39
Home

Sonning had the scent of hedgerows and woodsmoke, pollen and cut grass and rain and traffic, wet thatch and warm stone and manure on the fields and the distant smell of baking. But there was something missing, every day, every breath. Claire tuned out the missing part so she barely noticed, until she came back to Suffolk and there it was: salty, fetid, fecund.

Her parents lived in a white detached Georgian house on the outskirts of town. The sea air blew up on the breeze into the garden. She had breathed it in her cot as a baby, brought home sand and seaweed and shells as a child.

She parked the car down the lane in a layby; the sea glistened in the distance between gaps left by branches empty of leaves. She should probably drive right up to the house. But she wanted a few minutes to breathe and to walk. To be able to change her mind if she wanted to. She hadn't called her parents before she set off from Sonning. She hadn't talked to them at all in weeks. They might not be home; they might be busy and not pleased to see her. It had never been precisely stated, that their grown-up children should ring before coming for a visit, but nevertheless Claire always did. It showed consideration.

But this morning she had had enough of emptiness, the empty house that the central heating didn't seem to warm. She wanted to breathe in the thing she was missing. She wanted to go home.

Winter sunshine warmed her shoulders and cheeks, and leaves rustled underfoot as she walked. The house came into view around the corner of the hedges. All of the flowerbeds had been tidied up and winter jasmine blossomed against the wall. The car was gone, though that didn't mean both of them were out. Claire paused, staying behind the hedge so she couldn't be seen through the windows, and gazed at the house where she'd grown up.

It had been warm and bright. It had echoed with children. She remembered being tucked into bed by her mother, sung songs by her father. There was always a kettle singing on the Aga, always something delicious cooking, flowers in vases all year round. Claire and Helen and Ian had always felt safe at home, always loved bringing friends there to see how welcoming it was, how cheerful and neat and tidy. Each child had their own place. Helen was good at sport, Ian was good at school, Claire was good at music but really she was good at everything, anything she could do to please her parents whom she loved so much. Especially her mother, who was always at the centre.

Even now that they had grown up it was the same, every Christmas, at weekends and holidays. The house was full of food, warmth, beautiful objects. Sometimes Claire picked up glossy magazines about home and entertaining, and in their slick promotion of spending and buying, consuming and making, she glimpsed the ideal they were trying to capture. It was the ideal her own mother had created for her children.

When Claire and Ben had bought the house in Sonning, Claire had pictured it exactly the same. It would be a haven, a warm place for her family. It would give their children the glowing, loving start that Claire herself had had. Idyllic and perfect. Always there, never changing, the mother at school pick-up and drop-off, homemade cookies waiting with creamy milk, kisses and plasters for small injuries, stories at bedtime.

She worked hard at creating what her mother had made with seemingly no effort at all. Sometimes she didn't get to bed until long after Ben did. And all for nothing. A house with too many spare rooms. No husband. No child.

Only herself, empty-handed, coming home.

She should go back to Sonning. Her parents might not mean her to, but she would only compare her failure with their success. She would only look for wisps of *I told you so* in their sympathy. It was so much safer to pretend that everything was perfect.

But it would be such a relief not to have to pretend at all.

Claire stood half in the hedge, poised to go or to stay, when she saw a silhouette pass inside the front window and caught a glimpse of pale hair.

Suddenly there was no choice any more. Perfection didn't matter. She needed the kiss and the cuddle, the soothing and her mother's arms. Claire ran, her shoes slipping on the gravel and grass, her hands outstretched in front of her. She reached the door and she wrenched it open and she raced to the front room where her mother stood in a house-dress and slippers, humming. Stacks of ironing lined the sofa and the chairs. The light slanting through the window caught the colour of her hair, once blonde, now pale grey.

'Mum,' said Claire and her mother looked up, startled.

Her face immediately melted into a smile. No surprise, no questions, only joy. She put down the iron.

'Darling!' she said, and opened her arms.

When Claire's father came home from the shops, her mother sent him out again to the pub, telling him that he should come back much later with fish and chips. They left the ironing undone and they settled in the kitchen. Everyone settled in Louisa Hardy's kitchen with the big farmhouse sink, the Aga radiating heat, the fresh flowers and vegetables and the scarred wooden table with its bright cloth. It was very much like Claire's kitchen. It seemed like the correct way for a kitchen to be. Her mother took some tea cakes out of the freezer and they toasted them and went through several pots of tea and more tissues as Claire told her mother everything that had happened. Romily's accident, Ben's protectiveness, all the time he'd spent working and with Romily instead of her. The photograph, the letters, the way she had sent Ben away.

Louisa held Claire's hand the entire time, running her soft thumb over the back of it. Claire talked and talked and talked, surprised at how she could say so much when she thought she had been empty.

When Claire had run out of words, her mother sighed.

'What are you going to do about the baby, love?'

'You said it was a bad idea. I didn't listen to you.'

'I take no satisfaction in being right.' She squeezed Claire's hand.

'You weren't the only one. I was really worried myself. But then I got to know Romily. I . . . liked her.'

'You're a good person, Claire. You like people.'

'Then how come I don't have any friends?'

'You have friends.'

'Not really. I haven't opened myself up to anyone in so long, Mum. I couldn't bear to be around children. I've even found it difficult to be around Helen.'

'Oh, sweetheart. I know.'

'Getting pregnant was always the unobtainable goal. For years I thought of nothing else. I don't know what else to think of.'

'Think of yourself,' her mother said firmly. 'A baby doesn't stay a baby for ever. It grows up and moves away and you want that to happen, of course, but then all you have is yourself. When you and Ian and Helen moved out, I was lost. I didn't know who I was any more. Your father missed you too, of course, but he had his office, his hobbies. I didn't have anything of my own. All I had was you and this house. The house was empty, and you had your own lives.'

Claire stared at her mother. This was something new, like the not-yet-ironed sheets and the request for fish and chips. 'I . . . I didn't know. I'm sorry.'

Louisa fluttered her free hand in the air. 'It's got better. I'm still in the process. But Claire darling, this is what I'm trying to tell you. A baby isn't a solution. It isn't something you have because you think it will make you happy. It will keep you busy, but that's not the same as happy. You have to want the baby for itself, not because it's something that's expected of you or something that you think you need. I've watched you pining and pining for so long. It can make you forget the good things you have.'

'What good things have I got, now?'

'You're a wonderful woman. A gifted musician and a talented teacher. I'm so proud of you, Claire.'

'You have to say that. You're my mother.'

'And that's why I know you better than anyone else.' She lifted Claire's hand and kissed it.

331

'But why did she do it?' Claire asked, as if her mother could give her the answer. 'How could Romily offer to get pregnant with Ben's baby if she was in love with him? Why did she pretend to be my friend?'

'Do you think that she did it deliberately, to make Ben care for her?'

'In her letters she said she didn't want to be in love with him. But I can't believe that there wasn't an element of that. It doesn't make any sense to me, otherwise.' Claire hit the table with her free hand. 'She's been playing with all of our lives, intentionally or not.'

'What do you think is the best thing for this baby?'

Claire opened her mouth to say *Me*. But then she thought again.

If she were fair, if she put her own feelings aside and faced the things that her despair had been telling her, she had to admit that Romily wasn't a bad mother. An unconventional mother, maybe, but Posie was happy and secure and Romily loved her. Romily was experienced, too, which Claire was not. And Romily did love this baby. She had made it. It was part of her, in a way that it would never be part of Claire.

Not long ago, Claire would have said that it was one hundred per cent better for a child to have two loving parents rather than just one. But what if she and Ben never got back together? Did she want to be a single mother? *Could* she be a single mother? And even if Romily stuck to their agreement, despite her feelings, would Claire be able to take Ben back purely so that they could be parents?

She loved the baby, but she had no idea how she would go it alone. She couldn't work out any way that this could end happily for everyone.

'I'm the only one of the three of us who has no legal right

to the baby,' she said. 'So it doesn't really matter what I think.'

Her mother sat down again and took both of Claire's hands in hers. 'If you believe that you are the best mother for this baby, and I can't see how you wouldn't be, then you must fight for him.'

'I should see my lawyer.'

'You should definitely see your lawyer. Do you want to talk with Mr Fredericks? Your father can give him a ring for you.'

'It's tempting, Mum. But I need to get used to doing things for myself. I just wish— I wish I didn't understand her.'

'You understand her?'

'Of course I understand her. She wants all of the same things I want.'

'You're a better person than I am, darling. I want to rip her face off with my nails.'

'Mum!'

'I'm just calling it as I see it. When someone threatens your child, you become a mother bear. But you were always fair-minded.'

'I wish I wasn't,' said Claire unhappily. 'I love this baby, Mum. I was frantic when I thought we might lose him. And I dream about him, and think about holding him, and make plans for him. He was promised to me and I want him very, very much.' She swallowed. 'But I don't want him more than Romily does. When I read Romily's letters, he was there inside her words. She knows him. Much better than I do.'

'You can learn to know a baby. You can learn to love him.'

'But can you learn *not* to love him?'

'I don't think so,' said her mother. 'I'm so sorry, Claire. But I don't think you can.'

40
The Question

All things considered, being thirty-seven weeks pregnant was fairly awful. Romily could barely fit in the shower, she couldn't put on any shoes with laces, she huffed and puffed whenever she walked or climbed stairs, her bum hurt when she sat down and her ankles swelled when she stood up. She had itchy red stretchmarks on her belly, she had developed odd tags of skin on her neck, she needed an industrial-strength bra and she could not stop eating mince pies. She had to go to the toilet every five minutes and her back had been aching continuously for two days. She also cried at nappy ads – so much so that she had stopped watching any telly at all.

The nappy ad crying was worrying her. She had dealt with many gross things in the course of her career – some might say many extremely gross things – but a disposable absorbent wrapper filled to the brim with mushy baby poo was worse. She'd spent two years gagging every day until she had Posie safely potty-trained. She should not feel sentimental about nappies. But once this baby needed nappies, he wouldn't be hers any more.

And then she was so very pregnant that every unavoidable

encounter with a stranger prompted questions about the baby's due date, its name, its sex. Everyone was being kind, but her breezy 'Oh, I'm a surrogate' response had vanished, and it was torture to have to mumble a non-committal answer and move on as quickly as possible.

It was, she knew, the same way Claire had felt every time she saw someone else's children.

Jarvis had offered to look after Posie tonight so that Romily could go out and relax, but she'd declined. She didn't have anyone to go out with, for one thing. Even Hal was busy on Friday nights. And she hadn't invited Jarvis to stay in with her after Posie went to bed, either. She didn't need any more confusion in her life. Not now.

Instead she sat on the sofa with her feet up on a cushion and her laptop balanced on her belly, pretending to look for new research jobs by the light of their sparse artificial Christmas tree. When Thing kicked, the laptop jumped.

She'd promised Jarvis she wouldn't shut down and avoid reality, for Posie's sake. The problem was, what should she be doing instead? She'd helped Posie with her homework and spent as much time with her as she could. Jarvis had met them from school every day; this afternoon they'd done some Christmas shopping and decorated the tree, such as it was. She'd given Posie extra cuddles at bedtime, lying beside her in her single bed and talking. She'd tried to explain that Ben and Claire splitting up had nothing to do with Posie, and that probably it was temporary – but it was nearly impossible to explain to a seven year old what was really going on. It would help if Posie could see Ben or Claire, but Romily wasn't brave enough to answer Ben's text. She would. But not quite yet.

She should set up a playdate with someone from Posie's class. She could screw her courage to the sticking point and ask Eleanor about that. Posie had never mentioned being friendly with Eleanor's daughter Emily, though at this point, that probably didn't make much difference. But again . . . courage.

How could she get up the courage when she couldn't even face turning on the television?

A knock at the door. Ben's knock.

She had enough time to feel elation, panic, fear, longing as she carefully put the laptop on the coffee table, hauled her bulk off the sofa, bracing her aching back with her hand. It still didn't prepare her for seeing him standing there, the punch of emotion.

His chin was rough. There were dark circles under his eyes. He didn't wear a coat.

'You look awful,' she said.

'I've got to talk with you.'

He came in. She could smell alcohol on him. 'I've been to the pub,' he said. 'I needed a bit of courage.'

'Don't we all.'

'I wanted to say that— I just wanted to say— Where's Posie? Is she asleep?' Before Romily could answer, he went to the doorway of her room and looked in. After a long moment, he shut the door and came back. 'I've missed her. God, so much.'

'She's missed you. She's the one who sent you that text.'

'Oh? Oh.' He frowned, but didn't say anything more. Romily waited, her heart thudding.

Ben knew everything about how she felt. For the first time since she'd met him, he knew.

It should be happy when someone knew you loved them. It should be the beginning of something. Not the end of everything.

'How's the baby?' he asked, at last. 'It's a boy?'

336

'Yes. He's fine.'

'You're huge.'

'Thank you.'

He sank into his chair, his head hanging, rubbing his face. Romily remembered another time when he'd looked like this, half-drunk and full of despair, that night in the pub when she'd offered to carry his baby. That was when this had all started.

Though if she wanted to be honest, this had all started years and years ago, when she'd realized she felt something more than he did, and instead of walking away, she'd stayed and hidden it as deep as she could. When she'd started lying.

'I'm so sorry,' she said.

'You're sorry? No. No, Romily, it's me. I'm sorry. I'm so, so sorry about what I've done to you.'

'What *you've* done to *me*?'

'I saw Jarvis.'

'Oh God. This is really messed up.' The baby, responding to his father's voice or to Romily's adrenaline rush, kicked her in the ribs and she winced. She perched on the sofa, upright so as to give her belly more room. 'Jarvis found you?'

'I ran into him at the station a couple of hours ago. I think he wanted to give me a pounding.'

'Oh no.' Romily dropped her head into her hands. 'Please tell me you didn't have a fist-fight on the concourse of Brickham station. I'm thirty-seven weeks pregnant and I have enough drama in my life right now.'

'No. He told me very quietly, very calmly, just what he thought of me. He told me that I've been stringing you along for years. He said that you could be happy right now, if not for me.'

'You haven't been stringing me along. I had no hope that

337

you would ever be . . .' *In love with me.* She couldn't say it. It was bad enough that he knew it.

'I've known you for years, Rom. How could I not sense how you felt? Why didn't I?' He pushed his hands through his hair.

'I never meant for those letters to be seen. I wrote most of them late at night, when I couldn't sleep. I think some of the language got pretty flowery. I probably exaggerated a lot.'

'Did you? Did you exaggerate how you felt about me, Romily?' He was looking directly at her in a way he'd only done a handful of times.

'No,' she said. She bowed her head.

'I've had a lot of time to think,' he said. 'More time than I've had for years. Claire wanted to give up. She said we could be happy without children and I didn't listen. And then there was you. I never even thought about how it would affect you.'

'Listen, I knew the situation. I knew there was never going to be anything between us. It was okay.'

'Jarvis didn't think so. Jarvis thinks that you chose to stay in Brickham because of me. Jarvis thinks you could have had chances for better jobs and more money elsewhere.'

'I couldn't leave Amity's bugs.'

'He thinks you might have found someone to be a proper father to Posie. I think he means himself, by the way, but other than that, he has a point, right?'

She just kept on looking down. The carpet had a Ribena stain on it.

'God, I am such a wanker,' Ben said. 'And I thought I had everything. Perfect wife, perfect house, perfect job. The only thing I didn't have was a child, so I went about finding a solution to the problem. Letting my wife be subjected to every procedure under the sun and then when she didn't

338

want to do it any more, I pushed her harder. And then you offered to get pregnant for us and I jumped on it. I didn't think it through. It was all about what *I* wanted.'

Romily sat up straight, ignoring a twinge from her back. 'Stop it. I'm a big girl. I can make my own decisions. Claire can, too. You didn't make me fall in love with you. I did it all by my stupid self. I knew that you loved Claire and that I never had a chance. I stayed anyway.'

'It's my fault.'

'Because you're so irresistible? Give me a break.'

He was staring at her. 'Why did you fall for me? How long has it been going on?'

'I am not going to talk about that.' She swept her hands briskly in the air, as if clearing the topic out of the room. 'The important thing is what happens next. You have to get back together with Claire because this baby needs its parents.'

'It's not that easy.'

'Of course it is. The baby's the most important thing. We have to do what's best for him.'

'Claire says that you want to keep the baby. That you love him.'

Romily set her jaw. 'That doesn't matter.'

'Why do everyone's feelings matter except for yours, Rom?' She shook her head.

'It's our baby, too,' Ben said. 'Yours and mine. We made it because we trusted each other and because of how we felt about each other. That's what I can't get out of my head. People stay together for a lifetime for less reason than that. And when I see you, like this, with the life that we created growing inside you, I feel . . .' He took a deep breath. 'I've never felt quite like it before. That's why when Claire asked me if I loved you, I couldn't say no.'

Romily felt every cubic centimetre of air leaving her lungs. It was thick, heavy.

'Maybe I shouldn't have said anything,' he went on. 'Maybe I should have ignored everything and concentrated on making a perfect home for the baby. But I owe Claire the truth. I owe you, Romily. If I've made a mistake, I need to try to fix it. But whatever I do, someone is going to be hurt. I feel like it's up to me to choose which one, and I can't do that.'

'You love Claire,' she whispered. 'Claire.'

'Yes. But look at what you're doing for me. And then when Jarvis showed me how much you've given up for me . . . I can't ignore that. I can't just take the baby and leave you behind. He's yours too.' He raked his hair again. 'It's going through my head and through my head and it's driving me mad. I don't know what to do for the best. I don't know how to make it better.'

The pain on his face was so naked that Romily had to hold tight to the sofa cushion she sat on, plant her feet hard on the floor.

'I think I might have ruined everything with Claire. I don't know if she can trust me any more. Last time I saw her, she was like a stranger. She looked as if she hated me. And I can't blame her. But you – I can't disappoint you, can I? I've already done the worst thing to you that I can do.'

'No.'

'She asked me to choose and I can't. It has to be your choice, Romily. You've got the most at stake. You've got our son. He belongs to you. Do you want him?' He gripped his hair, as if he were going to tear it out by the roots. 'And if you want him . . . do you want me, too?'

41
Listening

There were no seats left in the back rows, but Claire slipped into a lone chair against the back wall while everyone was chatting. The hall was decorated for Christmas; a large tree sparkled on the side of the stage. Paper chains made by Year Seven festooned the walls. Beside Claire's seat, a long table covered with a green cloth and tinsel held rows of glasses waiting to be filled with wine and squash. It was tended by Octavia and Felicity, two of Claire's former A-level students. When they spotted Claire their eyes widened in surprise but they recovered themselves quickly and smiled at her. She'd go and speak with them before she left, ask them about their lives, and never mind about the gossip in the sixth-form common room.

She had been to dozens of these, maybe hundreds. Usually she sat up at the front with the rest of the music department where she would be visible to the students in case they needed her. Over the heads of the audience, Claire could see a woman with short iron-grey hair sitting in the front row beside Lindsay. She was wearing a navy-blue jacket with visibly padded shoulders. Claire would speak with her, too;

she wouldn't want her replacement, Mrs Radcliffe, to think she was afraid of her.

Claire had changed three times before she left the house. She had scheduled an appointment for a trim and blow-dry at a salon in a Brickham department store where she had never been before. She had painted her nails carefully with transparent lacquer and she had spent a full forty-five minutes applying make-up, trying for a well-groomed effect that would mask the shadows of weariness on her face and yet still look natural and effortless. War paint, all of it. A necessary façade. Nevertheless, when she reached the St Dominick's car park she still had to sit for five minutes before she got out of the car. She had to remind herself of Max's latest email. *I'd love it if you could come. I wouldn't be doing this if not for you. PS I am scared shitless.*

She didn't see Mr and Mrs Gore-Thomas. That was good for her, and sad for Max. But there were quite a few members of staff, even apart from the music department and the housemothers, who went to almost every concert; it was compulsory for the Music A-level and GCSE students to attend, but there were more than she would have expected filling the rows of chairs, boys and girls wearing their slouchy home clothes, their hair waxed into messiness or pulled into sloppy ponytails. She wondered if Max had invited them, if he had started spending more time with his classmates. Or if they had come out of curiosity, to see what he'd been doing with that guitar, to see what all the fuss had been about in October.

The programme was a white A5 sheet, printed off the computer with no pretence of decoration. MAX GORE-THOMAS it said at the top, followed by a list of names: *Mr Doughty, Angel, Max, Alan, Mrs Greasley*. Most of them she recognized, and she had heard the pieces here in school, or he had sent her a recording. Her own name was at the bottom of the page, after Alan. *Claire Lawrence.* No Mrs. He hadn't told her about that piece.

The curtains rustled and Max emerged from between them carrying his guitar. He didn't make eye-contact with the audience, just sat down and arranged the guitar on his lap. His head hung down in that familiar posture. He began to play.

The music struck Claire, bright and clear and perfect. He had been practising. And he'd grown musically as well as physically. The mp3 files he'd sent hadn't captured it. Claire closed her eyes and the people emerged from his music. With her eyes closed she could see them as well: the newsagent with his aggressive stare, the wandering dreamer, the skipping child. Max himself, sullen and angry, shot through with jagged shocks of clarity. When he played Mrs Greasley Claire heard the audience's laughter of recognition, but she didn't laugh. She listened. That was what Max needed of her, for her to listen with her entire mind and her entire heart.

Between pieces there was silence. Claire listened to that as well: to the wonder that this boy was creating in the audience. She listened to what she, his teacher, had done for him, not by teaching him, not by standing up for him. Merely by giving him his own space, letting him find his own way.

When the mother theme came at last, she recognized it: slow and soft, warm and sweet, hopeful and longing, full of the smell of a baby's head, a cheek tilted against hers, the brush of eyelashes. The papery skin of her mother's hand, which had once been the most beautiful hand she had known.

A tear fell on her lap.

The song finished, and in the still moment when it ended, Claire looked up at Max on the stage. He was gazing straight at her.

And then she realized: this was the last song. The mother song was her song. He'd named it for her.

Claire stood up and she smiled at him. With the rest of the room, she applauded this gifted, determined, lonely boy. Her lonely boy. She wiped her eyes with her arm as the audience clapped and clapped and clapped and Max stood up, bowed slightly, and went through the curtains again.

The applause lasted quite a long time, far past the time when Claire realized that Max wouldn't be coming back out to take another bow. She wanted to rush backstage to congratulate him, but with something like this, there would be a crush back there. He'd have enough to be thinking about. She'd have a glass of the school's half-warm white wine and wait for him. She remembered how it had used to be at her own school concerts: afterwards she wanted to talk with her friends, go through it point-by-point. But she always wanted her mother to be there too, waiting.

Being where she was, she was one of the first to take a glass, and she could exchange no more than a few enthusiastic words of praise with Felicity before the rush for drinks began. She stepped back, half in the corner. It was a good place to observe. She sipped her wine and listened to what people were saying about the concert.

Amazing. So talented. I could see Mrs Greasley when he was playing! I thought he was a bit of a freak, you know – but now I understand.

'I had no idea,' said a man not far from her, a tall man with dark hair. From the back, she could make out that he was greying at the temples; she recognized the voice. She stepped a little bit further back into the corner, in case Mr Gore-Thomas turned around. He was talking to Max's head of house, Ernest Doughty. 'No bloody idea he could play like that. I don't know music, but I know what I like. Astounding. Truly astounding.'

'I'm so glad you could come for drinks tonight,' said Ernest. 'I know how busy this time of year is for you.'

'No, no, think nothing of it. Had to be done, as you say.'

Ernest caught Claire's eye over Gore-Thomas's shoulder. He nodded and Claire thought she saw him wink.

'Dad?'

Max's voice rang out over the chatter. He was still holding his guitar and he was staring at his father. Mr Gore-Thomas went straight to him through the crowd. He put his arm around Max's shoulders. 'Proud of you, son,' Claire heard him say, as Max flushed a deep red.

She put her drink quietly on the table and made her way out of the Hall.

Veronica was coming the other way up the corridor, holding two more bottles of wine. 'Claire!' she said. 'Wasn't that extraordinary?'

'Yes, it was.'

'I'm so glad you came to see it. Hasn't it all turned out so well? Listen, you must come in very soon so we can talk about when you'll be returning to us.' She smiled broadly.

'Actually,' said Claire, 'I don't think I will be returning to St Dominick's.'

'You're going to be a full-time mum?'

'No,' she said. 'I'll be applying elsewhere. I'd really appreciate a good reference from you, if you feel you can write one.'

Veronica frowned. 'When did you decide this?'

'Just now. Have a lovely evening.' She nodded cordially at Veronica and left the school.

She felt strangely calm as she drove back to Sonning, calmer than she had felt in weeks, months – maybe even years. When she got to the house, she first put Bach on the stereo, as loud as she liked, and then she opened the kitchen drawer and found a screwdriver and an Allen key. She went upstairs, where the music filtered through the floorboards and the walls of the old house and became muted and mellow.

Max had needed her. And that had been truly wondrous, a small miracle of giving and listening. He had thought of her, at least for a little while, as something like a mother. But now he had come into his own. His father, at last, had heard him. Max didn't need her any more. She would still be his friend, still be his former teacher, but the mother theme wasn't really hers. She had only borrowed it.

And that was all right, too. It was the natural order of things. There were many ways for her to be needed again. There were other lives than the one she had imagined for herself.

It took her until nearly three o'clock in the morning to dismantle the cot, the chest of drawers, the changing table. To take down the curtains, the mobile; to fold up the blankets and the clothes and to roll up the rug. In the dark, with all the front lights on and the door open so that she could still hear the Brandenburg Concertos, she fitted each piece carefully into her car. It filled every space aside from the driver's seat, but packed away like this, it didn't seem like so much after all.

And then she went to her bed, lay down, and went to sleep to wait until the sun came up.

346

42
The Answer

He asked her if she wanted him. And then he looked at her, straight on, right into her eyes.

In her dreams, they hadn't been here in the front room of her poky flat with its listing Christmas tree. They'd been in a field, maybe. Or on top of a mountain. It was always in an alternative universe where Claire didn't exist, or where he'd never met her. Where they'd hung out together as friends until one day he had turned to her, in a field or on the mountain or maybe just in the student union, and looked at her just like this. Straight on, right into her eyes.

She could taste his kiss. She'd tasted it thousands of times in her imagination, always with guilt. She knew what he would feel like in her arms, the large strong length of him. She knew him for a good father, for a loyal friend, for a dreamer and an optimist, for a man whose smile and force of will could make anything happen. For the man her daughter wanted as a parent.

Eleven years she had loved him. Eleven years that had to be worth something more than yearning and missed chances. And now he had asked her if she wanted him.

And now he was holding his breath waiting for her answer. Waiting to hear how she felt.

Why do everyone's feelings matter except for yours, Rom? he had asked.

In her dreams, he had always chosen her.

'No,' she said.

He let his breath out. She knew she was not imagining that it was in relief.

43
Now

Now that she'd made her decision, Claire wanted to get it over with as soon as possible, but Romily's flat was in the middle of town, around the corner from Berkshire's biggest shopping centre, and it was the last weekend before Christmas. She'd meant to get up at the crack of dawn, but she'd slept too late and now the traffic queues began on the outskirts of town and snarled up every road leading in the direction of the car parks. She sat in her car, which was filled to the brim, and tapped her fingers against the steering wheel. With Brickham's one-way system she couldn't even change her mind and turn around. It was raining a grey icy rain, and though the town Christmas lights blazed from every building, they seemed dim and flimsy.

She crawled past the building where Ben was staying. The traffic was slow enough that she had time to look at all of the windows and wonder which flat was his. She couldn't picture herself going there to visit him. But they'd have to talk at some point. Perhaps a neutral location would be best.

Were there any neutral locations in the world? Everywhere, in her mind, would from now on be defined as a place she had been before she split up with Ben, or afterwards. She had thought of herself as Ben's beloved, as half of their partnership, for so many years that it was going to take a very long time to find her own identity as someone separate. If she ever did.

It took forty-five minutes to travel three miles. By the time she pulled into Romily's road it was mid-morning. Distantly, she noticed that her stomach was grumbling. She hadn't had any breakfast, and only a light snack before the concert last night. Funny to think that even though she didn't know how to define herself any more – the wife without a husband, the teacher without any students, the mother without a child – her body kept on going, kept on demanding the same things it always had. Perhaps she should define herself by her body, her faulty body that was able to play music and bake cakes and assemble and disassemble an entire room of furniture but wasn't able to create life.

Miraculously, a car pulled away from the parking space in front of Romily's flat as she drove up. Claire manoeuvred into it with difficulty, since she couldn't see very well out of her back or side windows. It was only when she'd stopped the car that she realized that Romily, at thirty-seven weeks pregnant, wasn't going to be able to carry any of the nursery things into her flat.

Well, she'd do it herself. Claire opened the back door and took out the first thing she came across, which was a wicker basket of baby clothes. She balanced it on one hip, went down the slippery steps to Romily's flat, and rapped on the door.

It was several minutes before Romily answered it. She was dressed in a big T-shirt and tracksuit bottoms, her hair was rumpled, and she looked bleary, as if she'd just woken up from a not very satisfying sleep. 'Claire?' she said. Claire did not miss the expression of guilty surprise that crossed her face.

'You should put some sand or something on these steps,' Claire said. 'I'm amazed that you and Posie don't fall down them on a daily basis.'

'What are you— I mean, it's good to see you. Come in.' She stepped back, and winced and rubbed at her back.

'Are you okay?'

'Backache. It's worse than last night. My mattress is awful.'

The front room of the flat looked even smaller because of an artificial Christmas tree taking up a whole corner, leaning slightly to one side. Claire caught sight of Posie's school shoes lying on the mat. She had forgotten all about Posie. The little girl must be confused. She'd had one night of fun with Claire and then all of a sudden: nothing.

But surely she'd seen Ben since then. He would have explained it to her, somehow. Claire's heart squeezed at the thought.

'Posie isn't here,' Romily said. 'Jarvis took her for the day to meet his brother and his kids. We thought it would be good for her to spend some time with children her own age. And I needed a rest.' She winced again. 'Ouch.'

'I brought you some things,' said Claire. 'I won't disturb you. I'll drop them off and go.'

Romily looked at the basket and frowned. 'Those are the baby clothes you bought.'

'Yes.' Claire put the basket down on the sofa. 'I'll just get the other things.'

'Why would I need baby clothes?' Romily said, following her to the door and up the steps.

'Be careful. It's icy. You'll fall.'

351

Romily put her hand on the railing. 'Why are you bringing me baby clothes?'

'I bought a few other clothes that you haven't seen. And friends gave me some, too. They're mostly white. There are some nappies in there, too.' She went to the car and pulled out a canvas shopping bag full of bottles and sterilizing equipment. When she turned around, Romily was standing on the pavement, both hands in the small of her back, staring.

'That's— Why have you brought all that furniture?'

'It's all of the nursery furniture.' Claire walked past Romily and into the flat. She put the bag on the sofa next to the basket and went back up to the car.

'Claire,' said Romily, 'I don't need nursery furniture.'

'You're going to need somewhere for the baby to sleep, right? And something for the baby to wear? Unless you've bought all of this already yourself.'

'Of course I haven't. I'm not keeping the baby. It's yours.'

Claire slid out the cot sides. She could just about carry two at once. 'No it's not,' she said. 'The baby is yours. It's your egg. Your body. You created him. And you love him.'

'Are you crazy?'

'I've been to see a lawyer. I'm sure you know this already, but I have no legal rights to this baby at all unless you voluntarily sign them over to me. Even though I'm the wife of his father – for the moment, at least – I have no connection with this child. You don't have to give him up, Romily. There's nothing making you. If you love him, he's yours.'

She walked past Romily again and back down into the flat. She heard Romily coming after her; she was puffing a bit and her footsteps were heavy.

'Let me get this straight,' she said. 'You think you're going to give me the baby?'

'I don't have to give him to you. He already belongs to you. Where do you want me to put these? Posie's room, or your room?'

'There's no space in either.'

'You'll have to work that out.' She leaned the cot sides against the kitchen cabinets and started for the door again. Romily was blocking her way.

'Stop it,' Romily said. 'I don't want all this stuff.'

'I have no use for it. I don't want to look at it any more.'

'Claire, I am carrying this baby for you.'

'No, you're not!' cried Claire. 'You're carrying it for Ben, because you love him! And he loves the baby, and he loves you. I'm giving you what you want, Romily. I'm giving you what you've always wanted. Don't you understand?'

Romily's eyes widened. The colour drained, all at once, out of her face.

'Oh, shit,' she said.

Claire wasn't sure how she'd been expecting Romily to react when she handed over all of her own dreams. But this wasn't quite it.

'Romily?'

'I think my waters just broke.'

'The baby isn't due for three more weeks!'

'Tell that to him. There's definitely something going on down there.' Romily abandoned the doorway and headed for the loo. At the threshold, she paused and held on to the doorframe.

'Are you okay?' There was a dark stain on the back of Romily's tracksuit bottoms. Claire hurried after her and put her hand on her shoulder. Romily's eyes were closed and she looked as if she were concentrating hard.

'That's a contraction there,' she gasped.

'Are you sure?'

'They're hard to mistake.'

'Do we need to ring the hospital? Are they regular and frequent?'

'I've only had the one, though I'm starting to wonder about that backache.' Romily straightened up and went into the loo. Claire stood outside the door, fretting.

'Are you all right?' she called.

'Don't panic,' said Romily through the door. 'Though my waters have definitely broken. Wow.'

'We need to time the contractions. Then we'll know if it's right to go to the hospital or not.' Claire looked down at her wrist, but she wasn't wearing her watch. She went into the bedroom (bed unmade, dressing-gown on the floor) and picked up Romily's alarm clock. When had the last contraction been? Thirty seconds ago? Two minutes?

'We'll start timing from the next one,' she called. Romily didn't reply. 'Romily? Romily?' Claire began knocking on the door.

Romily opened it. She was wearing a pair of pyjama trousers that looked as if they'd come from the bottom of the laundry basket. She smiled at Claire and took Claire's hand. Her hand was very warm. 'The baby's on his way.'

'You mean right this minute?' Claire's voice rose to a squeak.

'No. But he's on his way to being born. It's pretty incredible.'

Claire breathed deeply. 'Okay. Okay – well, that's great. We'll keep calm, and time the contractions, and when they're every five minutes—'

Romily's hand tightened on hers, so hard it hurt. Her eyes were wide this time, her face frozen.

'Breathe,' Claire said. 'Breathe through it, Romily.'

Romily let out a great whoosh of air through her mouth, and then sucked another in through her nose.

'That's it. Good girl. Well done.' After what felt like an eternity, Romily's grip loosened. 'That was less than five minutes since the last one.'

'Posie was born pretty quickly, once I got going. Maybe we should forget about ringing first and just go to the hospital.'

'Okay. Good idea. I'll drive. Do you have a bag?'

'No. It's okay. I don't think I'll be staying there long.'

Claire took a string bag off the door handle of Posie's room. It appeared to have Posie's PE kit in it. She emptied it onto the floor. 'I'll grab some clothes for the baby and a spare outfit for you. And a toothbrush and a hairbrush. Sit down, I'll only be a minute.'

'You weren't quite expecting this, were you?' Romily went into the front room while Claire ransacked her drawers for some clothes. When she emerged a few moments later, Romily was on all fours on the floor with her head under the coffee table.

'Romily!'

Romily raised her head. 'It's okay. I'm looking for my keys. But this position also feels pretty good.' She held up her hand. 'Got 'em. And my phone.'

'We can ring the hospital while we're on our way,' Claire said, and went to the front door, which was still open.

'And Ben.'

'And Ben.' Claire swallowed. 'And Posie,' she said more brightly. 'She'll want to know that little Thing is on his way, won't she?'

Romily slowly got to her feet. 'Claire,' she said. 'We have a lot to talk about.'

'Afterwards. Right now we have to get you safely to hospital. Come on.' She started out through the front door, holding out her hand to help Romily up the steps.

Romily didn't follow. 'I think I need some help with my shoes.' She was in her stockinged feet.

'Of course,' Claire said, and came back inside. Romily pointed to a pair of trainers near the sofa and Claire helped slide them on to her feet.

'I never wanted to hurt you,' Romily said to her when she stood up.

'Let's go.'

When they got to Claire's car, though, and Claire opened the door for her, she realized that it was still packed full of furniture. There was hardly room for the string bag, let alone a thirty-seven-weeks-pregnant woman in labour.

'We can take my car,' said Romily, and then she had to stand still and hold on to the car roof, weathering another contraction. Droplets of rain clung to her hair. 'If it starts,' she said when she'd finished. 'The electrics are a little temperamental in the damp.'

'The traffic,' Claire said, remembering. 'It's chock-a-block because of the shopping centre. I don't think driving is such a good idea after all.'

'The hospital is less than a mile away.'

'I think we'd be taking a chance of you giving birth in the car. It would be much quicker to walk.'

'I don't think that's a good idea either. I don't fancy having this baby on the pavement.'

'Right. Let's go inside where it's dry and warm, and let's ring the hospital after all. Maybe they can send an ambulance.'

Inside, Claire helped Romily off with her trainers again

and then Romily got back into her position on the rug, on all fours. While Romily rang the hospital, Claire boiled the kettle. She didn't precisely know whether tea would help in this situation, but she didn't have many other ideas. Plus, weren't you supposed to have boiling water on hand if you had to deliver a baby at home?

There was probably a section about this in one of the baby books she'd given Romily. She scanned the bookshelves while listening to the conversation Romily was having. 'Every five minutes, if not more frequent. Yes, it's my second delivery. The first was really quick. No, no complications at all. Well, we would, except the traffic is so bad that we're afraid . . . Oh. Okay then, that's great. Yes, I've got my . . . my friend with me. All right. All right, yes. Okay. Yes. Yes.' She repeated her address, and put down the phone. 'They said they can send an ambulance, but then as it's a second delivery and it appears to be low-risk they thought it might be quicker just to send a community midwife over on foot.'

The last word came out as 'foooot' as another contraction hit.

'Breathe,' said Claire, and she abandoned her search for the book to put her hand on Romily's back and soothe her through it.

'Ring Ben,' Romily panted. 'He needs to know.'

Claire was very aware, as she selected Ben's number on her own phone, that she hadn't rung it in what felt like a very long time. She listened as it rang and rang.

'He's not answering,' she said. 'Do you know where he is?'

Romily shook her head. Claire left a message telling him the essentials. As Romily rang Jarvis, Claire made tea, trying not to listen, but she did notice how Romily spoke with Jarvis in a kind of shorthand, as if they knew each other well.

She herself spoke that way with Ben, sometimes, when they were working together on something around the house. Claire could tell when Posie came on the line because Romily's voice became light and cheerful, though she wrapped up the conversation quickly and hung up before the next contraction started.

'She thinks it's incredibly cool that I might give birth in our living room,' Romily said when she'd caught her breath. 'She asked if I couldn't hold on a little while so they could get back from London first.'

'Do you think,' said Claire, pushing the mug of tea towards Romily, 'that you *can* hold on for a little while? At least until the midwife gets here?' The contractions were rapidly getting closer together, and she could tell they were stronger, too. She had no idea if this was the correct thing or not. It all seemed incredibly fast.

'I don't know.'

'I'm not sure what to do,' said Claire. 'It's— maybe I should get the bed ready.'

'I think I'd prefer the floor in here. That mattress is so lumpy. I've cursed it a million times in the past few months. It probably doesn't have very good vibes.'

'Okay. You stay right there. Do whatever you need to, to make yourself comfortable.' Claire pushed the coffee table up against the far wall, clearing the centre of the room. The Christmas tree had to be pushed back too. With her foot, she shoved whatever else movable she could find underneath the sofa: Posie's shoes, Romily's handbag, several books and jumpers and Jemima, the stuffed tiger. Then she went to the bathroom airing cupboard and came back with armfuls of bed linen and towels.

'Do you have anything like a plastic tablecloth?'

Romily, who was grimacing and breathing deeply, nodded her head at a kitchen cabinet. Claire found an oilskin pouch on a shelf. Inside, carefully rolled, was a heavy, high-quality picnic blanket, lined on one side with oilskin.

'My dad's fishing blanket,' Romily gasped. 'He wouldn't mind.'

Claire spread it out over the carpet, and then layered sheets and duvet covers and towels over the top. 'Okay,' she said doubtfully. 'That should do it, I think.'

'Thank you, Claire. Thank you. I know I don't deserve to have you helping me, but I'm glad you're here.'

'I'm glad I am!' said Claire, although she was anything but. 'It would be horrible if you were on your own. Do you know— have you seen Ben?'

'He came over for a little while last night to fill me in on what was going on.' Romily got to her feet, holding her belly with one hand and her back with the other. 'He didn't tell me what he was doing today.'

'Well, I hope he's not in a car, or else he'll never get here in time,' Claire said briskly. She put her arm around Romily's shoulders and guided her to the nest she'd made on the floor. 'What do you think would help you? Do you want a shoulder rub or a back massage? Is there any particular music you'd like playing? Do you have your birth plan here?'

'I never got around to making a birth plan.' Abruptly, Romily doubled over and screamed.

Claire held on to her. 'You're doing fine,' she murmured, 'absolutely fine, just keep breathing, keep on breathing.'

Romily looked up at her, panting, her face red and her hair hanging over it. 'Probably just as well I didn't make a birth plan,' she said. She began tugging down her pyjama bottoms.

'What are you doing?'

'Taking off my trousers because I really, really want to push now.'

'You can't push yet! The midwife isn't here!'

'Tell that to the baby. Can you help me with these?'

Claire dropped to her knees and pulled off Romily's pyjamas. 'But you know what to do, right? You've had a baby before. And you've gone to those NCT classes too, right?'

'I didn't go to them. I didn't want to go alone.'

'But I don't know how to do this!'

'It'll be okay. Can you help me with my knickers?'

'There's a book! One of those books I gave you, they have a chapter on what to do in an emergency!' Claire tried to jump to her feet to find it, but Romily grabbed her hand and held tight.

'You can do it, Claire. You will figure it out.' She took Claire's other hand and looked her straight in the eyes. 'I can't think of a single person who I would rather have helping me right now than you.'

'But I don't—'

'I trust you,' said Romily. 'I trust you more than anyone else I know.'

She held Claire's gaze. A clock ticked, loud and slow. At any moment there would be another contraction but, right now, it was calm. The baby was waiting.

Romily was waiting.

'All right,' Claire said. 'I'll try.'

Romily grinned. Her face was sweaty. 'Good. Now help me take off my pants.'

'You're going to be fine,' Claire said as she pulled Romily's pants down for her. They were damp and there was a smell, not unpleasant, slightly sweet and acidic.

'Amniotic fluid,' Romily told her. 'It's not wee. At least I don't think so. There's a lot going on down there, so it's difficult to tell. Argh!'

Claire was putting Romily's clothes safely to one side but she dropped them and put her arms around Romily again, urging her to breathe through the contraction. Despite the pain, she realized, Romily was calm. There was nothing either of them could do to stop this birth happening. Every move they made was inevitable and necessary, exactly what needed to happen. The midwife might knock on the door at any moment; Ben might turn up, or Jarvis, or the postman. She couldn't do anything to make those things happen or to prevent them. She needed to be right here, in the now, where she was.

Six years of Yoga for Fertility, every Wednesday night without fail, and she'd never lived in the now before this moment.

When the contraction was over, Romily arranged herself on the floor on all fours. 'I need you behind me,' she panted.

'Right.' Claire moved straight away, placing herself in position with her hands out as if she were trying to catch a ball. She stared. She wasn't quite sure what she was seeing.

'Romily,' she said. 'I think – I think I can see the top of his head.'

'Is he bald?'

'No.'

'That's good news.'

Claire couldn't help it – she laughed. Romily, looking over her shoulder, laughed too, until she was overtaken mid-breath by another contraction.

A quick tap on the door. 'Hello?' called a female voice.

Claire looked rapidly from Romily, head down, pushing, the baby's head emerging a little bit more, to the door, where she could see a silhouette in the glass panel.

'Does someone need a midwife?'

Claire jumped up and rushed to the door. The woman waiting outside was young-looking, blonde, competently dressed in hospital scrubs covered by a mac. She carried a bag and her hair was tied back. 'She's about to have the baby,' Claire said.

The midwife took in the room: the towels, the blankets, the furniture pushed aside, and Romily in the middle of it on all fours, pushing.

'You're not kidding,' she said and, shedding her mac, went to the sink to wash her hands. She pulled on a pair of gloves from her bag. 'What's your name, love?'

'Romily,' said Claire. 'Her name's Romily and she's having a baby boy.'

'That's wonderful. You're doing a great job, Romily. I can see your baby already. Lovely to have him here at home.'

Romily came out of the contraction with a whoosh of air. 'Claire,' she gasped. She held out her hand.

'Looks like you're a brilliant coach,' said the midwife. 'Romily, my name is Harriet and I'm here to help you. Though it doesn't seem like you need me at all, to be honest.'

'Don't you dare leave,' Claire told the midwife, taking Romily's hand. She crouched beside her, stroking her hair back from her face.

'Don't *you* dare leave,' said Romily. 'I need you.'

'I won't.'

'I was alone when Posie was born. I was so lonely, Claire. I didn't know what I was going to do at all. I didn't know how to be a mother. I didn't know you could learn it.'

'Everything is going to be okay.'

'Yes. Yes, it is. And everyone is going to be happy. I swear to you, Claire. Just don't leave me.'

'Go ahead and push, Romily, as hard as you can, when the contraction comes,' said Harriet. 'That's it. Nice and steady, now. Have a little rest, you're doing wonderfully.'

'I didn't mean to fall in love with him,' Romily said. 'I didn't want to. You never would have known if you hadn't found the letters. I wouldn't have said anything.'

'It's okay,' said Claire, rubbing her back.

'It's not okay. I like you so much. I used to be a little afraid of you, to be honest. You were so together, so beautiful.'

She screwed her eyes up and groaned, a deep uninhibited sound, and squeezed Claire's hand so hard it hurt.

'Good, Romily, good work, that's the head delivered. He's lovely. Just one more hard bit left to deliver the shoulders, and we're all set. You're doing my work for me today.'

Romily panted. She hung her head. Then she took a deep breath and looked at Claire.

'This isn't the hard bit,' she said. 'This isn't the hard bit at all. But you'll be good at it. Wait and see.'

'Wait for the contraction, Romily, and go with it, and we'll be nearly done.'

'Wait and see,' said Romily again.

'Romily, breathe,' said Claire. There were tears in her eyes. 'Keep calm and breathe. You're doing so well.'

The baby. The baby was nearly here. The baby that had changed everything, that would change everything again.

The contraction came. Romily pushed. Claire held her. And the midwife said, 'Here he is!'

Romily sagged on her hands and knees and Claire supported her. Behind them, she heard a snuffle and a hiccup, impossibly high-pitched and small. And then a wail.

She looked over her shoulder. The midwife held the baby. He was all red legs and arms, hands splayed, dark hair and an open mouth. He cried, the strongest sound she had ever heard.

'Here he is,' said the midwife again, 'a lovely and healthy baby boy. He looks great. Couldn't be better. I'll help you lie on your back, Mum, so I can hand him over and you can have a cuddle while I finish off.'

Romily shook her head. Her eyes were closed.

'Give him to Claire,' she said.

'Oh, are there two mummies?' said the midwife brightly. She picked up a towel from the ones Claire had scattered around and partly wrapped the baby in it. His eyes were half-open; his nose was a smudge. He looked like Ben sometimes when he was waking up in the mornings.

'No,' said Claire, unable to tear her eyes away. 'There's only one mummy. He's Romily's baby.'

'I'm a surrogate,' said Romily. 'I don't want to hold him. Please, give him to Claire.'

'I can't hold him,' said Claire. She knew just how he would feel, this crying, squirming, beautiful baby. Strong and alive and real and only minutes old. If she held him, even for a moment, she would believe he belonged to her. His warm, smooth skin, still too loose for his body, his damp hair, the skinny limbs, the papery fingernails.

'Please,' said Romily. Something hot and wet, a tear, landed on Claire's arm. Romily had her eyes closed, her head averted. Claire was still supporting her.

'Well, *somebody* needs to take him,' said the midwife. 'I have to deliver the placenta.'

'I can't,' said Claire, every fibre of her body wanting to.

'If I hold him, I'll want to keep him,' said Romily. 'Don't make me.'

'He's yours.'

'No.'

Behind them both, the baby cried for his mother. It was the most wonderful, the most terrible, sound in the world. The first few minutes of life could set the tone for everything that followed. Claire knew. She'd read the books. This baby had been thrust into a cold, confusing world and he wanted comfort, warmth, the person who loved him the most.

'Romily,' she pleaded.

There was a knock on the door, a triple rap. Romily raised her head.

'Ben's here,' she said. 'Thank God.'

Claire jumped up and opened the door. He was frantic, wild-eyed, unshaven, in running clothes. He grabbed her shoulders. 'I just got your message. What's happening? Are they all right?'

'Everything is all right but we need you to take the baby.' She pulled him into the room. She heard Ben gasp at the sight of his son, wrapped in a white towel, in the midwife's hands.

'Is this Daddy, then?' the midwife asked. For the first time, a note of exasperation was in her voice.

'This is Daddy,' said Romily, her eyes closed again. 'He'll take the baby.'

Ben held out his hands. 'Is it— is he— oh.'

Claire watched as the midwife gave him the baby. The awe on Ben's face, the way he instantly cuddled the bundle to his chest.

'Oh,' he said again. He stroked a finger down his son's cheek and the baby stopped crying and instinctively turned his head towards it. Claire could feel the softness in her imagination, the downy hair. She backed up so that she was pressed against the door. 'Hello, little one,' whispered Ben. It

365

was by far the loudest sound in the room. 'Hello, my little boy.'

In the periphery, the midwife was busy with Romily again. They had a murmured conversation and the midwife helped Romily to her feet and to her bedroom. The real world was here, with Claire's husband holding his child. The baby gazed up into Ben's face; she could see that his eyes looked like Ben's.

The baby clothes were still on the sofa, along with the bag of bottles. The midwife was in the bedroom to help. Everyone was safe, they were happy. No one needed her.

'Oh Claire,' said Ben. 'Look at him, darling.'

But he didn't look up, wrapped in his world of two.

Claire opened the door and slipped away. Outside, the rain had turned into snow.

44
Milk

Romily was alone. She sat propped up on pillows in her bed, the duvet pooled around her waist, with The Jam in the CD player to mask the silence and the whooshing sound of the breast pump.

She was fine. She was a little sore, and very tired, but the midwife had checked her out thoroughly and she was absolutely fine. She had lain on the bed listening as the midwife had talked with Ben about the baby – how healthy he was, how beautiful, how they should care for his cord and when he should have his first feed – all the advice Romily had probably been given in the moments after Posie was born and which she couldn't remember now because she'd been too drunk with sudden love for her daughter to take it in. And then she had heard the front door closing after the midwife and Ben coming to her room, carrying the baby.

She'd jumped off the bed and closed the door before he could get there. 'I can't see him,' she said through it.

'He's perfect, Romily.'

'He's not mine.'

'Claire's left. I don't think she wants to see me.'

Romily leaned her forehead against the door. 'You have to take him away, Ben. Please.'

There was a pause. Through the flimsy wooden door she could hear rustles of clothing, a tiny faint grunt. She spread her hand on the door as if she could reach through it, through the few inches, to touch them both.

Ben walked away. She listened to him gathering things in the front room, talking in a soft voice to the baby. She imagined Ben wrapping him up warm in the clothes Claire had left. And then the front door shut behind them and there was silence.

She had not been alone, never fully alone, for thirty-seven weeks. Even before that, even when Posie was not with her, even before Posie had been born, she had carried a sort of image of Ben around with her every minute. She had held him in her heart, a fictional version of her best friend who could be hers in some way. Even though it had hurt her; even though it would hurt those she cared about; even though it had driven other real people away.

Now she couldn't carry him any more. Not even a version of him that would never exist. She had lost Ben and his son in one fell swoop, in one last push, in one birthing.

Romily sat in her bed and worked the breast pump. Her hand was beginning to ache, but so far nothing had come out. Mammals were built to feed their children with their bodies. It was a defining characteristic. Any horse could do it; any antelope, any mouse. Giving birth activated the hormone prolactin, which stimulated milk production. It was stimulated more by an infant's sucking motion, which this pump, of rubber and plastic, had been specially designed to emulate.

It was not the same.

When Posie had been a baby, it would only take one cry and Romily's breasts would be leaking. The front of her shirt would darken in wet patches of milk. Not even a cry; a sniffle, or the way she turned her face, when stroked, to root. The way she opened her mouth at the scent of milk when Romily held her. The tiniest movement or sound was enough to prompt Romily's body to hold her close, skin to skin, and nourish her.

Romily closed her eyes. She felt as if she'd barely opened them today. She thought of those small sounds, through the door. She thought of the small head, with its downy dark hair – she knew, without looking, that it was dark – nestled in the crook of his father's arm. The unfurled mouth, the squashed red cheeks, the toothless gums. The scent of his skin, still pungent from her womb. Her hands ached from pumping, her arms ached from not holding him. Her dear thing.

The milk wasn't coming. On her lips, she tasted salt. The bottle was sealed, safe and sterile, but Romily still turned her head aside so that when the milk did come, it would not be touched by her tears.

The CD had finished playing a long time ago. Only a few drops of milk had come out, what the midwife had called the colostrum, but it was something. It would be good for the baby. She put the bottle into the refrigerator next to the strawberry jam. The midwife, kindly, had put the towels into the washing machine, so Romily hung them up. She put in her father's blanket to wash. Half an inch of snow sat on the windowsill. Outside, all was silent. It would be a white Christmas.

If she thought of the snow, she would think of the long queue of cars that had stopped her getting to hospital. She would think of the shoppers waiting in traffic, she would think of Claire driving in the other direction, she would think of Jarvis and Posie on a delayed train, she would think of Ben shielding the baby's face from flakes of snow. She would think about being alone, about being drained and empty.

She would not think of the snow. She turned on the lights on the tree and went back to bed.

As soon as she'd pulled the duvet up around her, she heard a key in the door. 'Romily?' called Jarvis. Posie didn't say anything but Romily knew her footsteps, knew her movements, felt her in the deep instinctive part of her that made milk, that had no words, where there was love.

'Mum?'

Her daughter's face was flushed. There were flakes of snow in her hair. She still wore her wellies and her coat. Romily opened her arms to her and Posie came into them and Romily held her. Her cold skin, warming. Her child-smell and the beating of her heart.

'I love you,' Romily told her. 'I am your mother and I love you.'

'Are you okay? Have you had the baby?'

'I'm fine. I've had the baby. He's with Ben. You can see him soon.'

'The train was delayed. We ran from the station. I was scared, Mummy.'

Romily held her. She rocked her and she breathed her. She had been so small. Now she was so tall and clever and tender. Romily kissed her forehead.

She felt Jarvis watching from the doorway. She held her hand out to him and silently, he climbed onto the bed with them and put his arms around them both.

45

A Piece in the Puzzle

When the doorbell went, she nearly didn't answer it. She was busy, anyway, using a small brush to paint the edges and corners of the room that was a spare bedroom again, with a half-full tin of paint that she'd found in the back of the shed, left over from decorating the downstairs loo. It was a sort of indeterminate blueish slatey grey with the name of Providence Harbour, and Claire had chosen it because it was not sunshine yellow, and because it seemed to have the most paint left in it. And because she could not sit still, and because she kept being drawn back to this room, stripped of its furniture and its hopes.

Painting, as always, had its own momentum: you finished doing one edge, and then you couldn't resist doing the next, and the next. The fiddly bits around the window and the light switches were particularly satisfying, and Claire was stooping on the floor, doing the last stretch above the skirting board, when the doorbell rang.

She could not imagine who it was. No one had rung her or texted her since she'd left Romily's flat. She glanced at her watch: 9 a.m. Somehow it had become the next morning after the baby's birthday without her noticing it. It had seemed like for ever and like no time at all, without other people to measure it against.

The doorbell rang again. It could be the postman, she supposed. No, it was Sunday. Maybe it was her mother, who had somehow sensed that Claire needed her, and come. Hope surged at the thought and made Claire stand up, push her hair behind her ears and go downstairs, still holding the paintbrush.

It was not her mother; it was an unfamiliar woman, her hair scraped back from her forehead and trapped in a plait, her face stretched in a smile. She held a big vase of flowers. 'Phew, the roads are a bugger out there. Delivery for Claire Lawrence?'

Claire took them, using her wrist to keep them steady as she held the paintbrush. They'd sent her flowers? Ben? As a sort of consolation prize for not becoming a mother?

'Wish someone would send me a bunch of these,' said the delivery woman cheerfully. Her chuckle faltered when Claire didn't respond at all. 'Well, anyway, have a nice day.'

Without bothering to shut the door to keep the cold air out, Claire put the bouquet on the hall table. She shoved the paintbrush under her arm, unmindful of the stains on her clothes, and opened the tiny attached envelope.

Thank you so much for being there for me. I couldn't have done it without you. I hope you liked your song. Max

Incredibly, Claire smiled. He'd noticed. He'd remembered. Two days late, maybe, but he was a teenager. Even with his father there, even with the parental attention and approval he'd always wanted, Max had thought of her, too.

She was not irrelevant.

Holding the card in her hand, she walked out through the open door without a coat. The air was fresh and cold. Snow lay over the garden, broken only by the footsteps of the delivery woman. It clung to the branches of the trees in a soft filigree.

In this moment she was not a wife, nor a mother. She was a person, a piece in the puzzle.

She remembered Romily's hand clamped on hers so hard it hurt. She remembered breathing with her, answering the door for the midwife. Seeing that small head emerging. She remembered the baby, perfect and beautiful, calming in his father's arms.

She wasn't the baby's mother. But he existed, in part, because of her. He had been conceived because she wanted him. She had helped him to be born. She had given him to a person who would love him and keep him safe. Even her failures had led, ultimately, to his birth. Wasn't that part of creating life?

And he was out there, somewhere in this vast quiet and calm. He was healthy and he would grow. He was a new, complete person. He was a marvel of the world, like this innocent snow.

He wasn't hers. But he *existed*.

Claire cupped the card in her hand and she smiled upwards to the sky.

The battered green Golf braked and skidded a few inches on the drive. The back door opened almost before it had stopped and Posie jumped out and ran across the snow to Claire. 'He's so gorgeous!' the little girl cried, barrelling into her and wrapping her arms around her waist. 'You have to see him, Auntie Claire, it's just incredible!'

Claire put her hands on either side of Posie's face and lifted it. 'You must be so excited about the baby.'

'He can hold your finger and everything, and he has funny toes just like mine!'

Claire's smile had faltered, but it came back at this, the simple reminder that the baby had toes. 'You're a wonderful big sister, do you know that?'

'I know! I'm going to do everything with him. I'm going to teach him how to read.'

The passenger door opened and Romily climbed out. Claire couldn't help it; she immediately looked past her to see whether Ben was driving the car; whether the baby was in the back seat. Instead she saw Jarvis's blond hair.

'How are you doing?' Romily asked her. Even wrapped in her navy duffel coat, she was noticeably slimmer than the last time Claire had seen her.

'Shouldn't I be the one asking you that?'

Romily shrugged. 'The birth wasn't the difficult bit. As you know.'

'How is the baby?'

'Ben says he's doing really well. He's been sleeping and he's fed a bit, too.'

'Ben says?'

'Romily won't go over to see them,' said Posie. 'I think it's silly. But Jarvis took me over to the flat last night.'

Claire's heart thumped. 'The baby's with Ben in his flat? They're not with you?'

Romily shook her head.

'He— I haven't heard from him,' Claire said.

Romily held out a canvas shopping bag to Claire. 'That's probably because you left your mobile at my flat. It's been ringing nonstop. Don't you ever answer your landline?'

'I . . .' She couldn't recall if the house phone had rung at all. She couldn't say she would have heard it from upstairs if it had. She was still trying to process the information that Ben and the baby weren't with Romily.

She glanced at the bag. 'It's not just my phone in here.'

'No. There's a Cool Bag with expressed breast milk.'

'She uses this icky pump-type thing,' said Posie. 'It looks like a loudhailer with a bottle attached. Jarvis says it reminds him of what you attach to a dairy cow. There isn't that much milk coming out right now, but Romily says that's normal because the baby ate so much when he was inside her that he doesn't need lots, he just needs little bits of the good stuff, and later on there will be plenty of milk.'

'Posie,' said Romily, 'I dare you to make a snowball without Jarvis seeing and then get him to wind down his window so you can throw it at him.'

'Yeah!' cried Posie and ran off back towards the car.

'The baby isn't with you,' said Claire. 'You're not breast-feeding him.'

'No, I've been experiencing an intimate relationship with a plastic pump.'

'Why— why aren't you together?'

'Ben doesn't love me. He loves you.'

'But he said—'

'I don't know what he said. But any fool, including me, can see that Ben and you are meant to be together.'

Claire stared at Romily. Her cheeks were flushed with the cold; she looked as if she had probably been crying. 'Ben would have stayed with you,' Claire said. 'He wouldn't have left you, not after you'd just had his baby.'

'He doesn't love me.'

Claire hesitated, not able to believe it.

'I was stupid to fall in love with your husband,' said Romily. 'And I did deceive you, Claire, about how I felt about him. I'm sorry about that. I never meant you and Ben to split up because of it. I never meant for anyone to know.'

There was a yell from the car and Jarvis jumped out. He scooped up a handful of snow and immediately started throwing snowballs at Posie, who shrieked and returned fire.

'The thing is,' Romily continued, 'that even though you have a good reason to hate me, you still helped me. You were amazing, Claire. I couldn't have done it without you.'

'I think you would have done it whether I was there or not.'

'But with you there, I wasn't afraid. Not for a single minute. I knew you were there, and I knew that you cared about what happened. I knew that you loved that baby as much as I did.' Romily's voice broke, but she recovered herself quickly. 'And I know that right now, you're the only person in the world who feels exactly the same way as I do.'

This time, her gaze definitely did not waver. And Claire could see all the pain in her eyes, all the emptiness and loss that Claire knew so well.

From a distance, Claire heard the wet thump of a snowball hitting its target, followed by triumphant laughter from Posie. 'Good shot, Miss Mariposa,' called Jarvis.

'You have a family,' Claire said to Romily.

'So do you. They're waiting for you.' Romily held out the bag to her.

'I can't take a husband and child from you like a gift,' Claire said. 'That's not how things work.'

'They're yours already. You just have to go to them.' Romily shrugged. 'Or don't. It's up to you. But it looks to me like you've got a car full of baby furniture, and there's a baby in a flat in Brickham without a cot.'

'Those are things.'

'Well, yes. Ben could buy another one. But he probably wants this one.'

A snowball sailed by their heads.

'Listen,' said Romily. 'Someone needs to deliver this breast milk, and I'm not going to do it. What's more, Jarvis and Posie are going to be absolutely soaked after this and they'll need a hot bath and a bit of calming down. You're the best person to go.'

'Romily—'

'Just try it. See what happens. All those books you gave me strongly recommend breast milk during the first few days of life. This is the colostrum, which is specially tailored for a baby's first days. It can help with immunity and some studies say it leads to better brain development. It's the most perfect food on earth for a baby, especially with all these organic vegetables I've been eating. But hey, you can leave this to spoil and let the baby have the powdered artificial stuff. Lots of babies do fine on that.'

'You're trying to manipulate me.'

'I'm doing whatever might work to get you your happy ending.' Romily put the bag down on the snow between them. 'It's in your hands. Right now I have to stop my daughter from killing her father.'

She turned and walked away. Posie ran over to give Claire another swift, snowy hug and Jarvis waved to her, too. Then they all got back into the car and drove off, slipping down the drive. She heard their tyres on the wet road.

Inside the bag, her phone beeped. It was probably a message from Romily, trying to get her to look. Trying whatever might work.

She looked. It was from Ben.

We miss you.

46
Natural

The door to number 4 looked like all the others in the block of flats – beech, with gold numbers and a small Yale lock. Claire knocked.

Ben opened the door a little way. He was unshaven and more rumpled than he'd been yesterday. He appeared to have neither showered nor slept.

He looked unbelievably happy and calm. The way he'd looked on their honeymoon, when they'd gone to Venice and stayed out late watching the lights on the canals and then spent all night making love.

'Claire,' he said, and his face creased into a tired smile. 'I'm so glad it's you.'

'I . . . got all your messages.' Half an hour's worth, when she'd listened to them. And a text for every hour that Thing had been alive.

'Good. Come in.' He stepped back and Claire saw for the first time that he had his shirt unbuttoned halfway and that the baby was nestled inside against his bare chest. The shirt formed a sort of pouch. Thing's eyes were closed, his hands in fists near his face.

'It's good for him to have skin-to-skin contact,' Ben explained. 'The midwife told me.'

'I know,' said Claire. 'I read about it.'

'I keep thinking he'll get tickled by my chest hair and have to sneeze. But he seems okay with it. He likes it. He wants to be held.'

'Have you slept at all?'

'A little while. Maybe an hour. I know I'll regret it later, but I'm too excited.' He laughed and rubbed his forehead. 'I don't want to miss anything. Which is silly, because mostly he's been sleeping. I've just been watching him sleep.'

The baby heaved in a deep breath and then let it out. His eyes were wrinkled, his eyebrows little pencil sketches. Claire could understand how Ben had spent hours watching him sleep. He had described it, in one of his phone messages, in hushed tones. As if the experience was so wonderful that he couldn't bear not to share it with her.

'You could probably use some coffee,' she said.

'God yes. I haven't got it together enough to make any.'

'You probably haven't eaten either.' The practicality, the immediate task to be done, allowed her to look away from the baby and realize they were still standing in the tiny entranceway between the door and the living room. She stepped into the flat proper and went to the kitchenette to put the kettle on. Ben followed her.

'Romily gave me some expressed milk,' she said.

'I don't know whether to wake him up or let him sleep.' Ben looked from the baby to her and back again. 'What do you think?'

'I don't know.'

'God.' Ben sank down into a chair. 'It's such a responsibility. Every decision is entirely yours, and it affects this little person. I don't think I really appreciated before how huge it is.'

'What's— what's his name?' She tried to keep her voice neutral, cheerful. It was a question you asked of a stranger.

'I don't know. That's something else that's a responsibility.'

She thought back to all their discussions about names over the years. They'd bandied them back and forth as if they were words, rather than a person's identity.

Claire got down mugs. He kept his coffee in the same place they did at home, in the cabinet to the left of the cooker. She spooned it into the cafetière, good and strong.

Ben watched her. 'So you got my messages?' he said. 'You didn't call back.'

'I left my phone at Romily's flat. I . . . thought you were there.'

'No. I don't want to be with Romily. I want to be with you. I was so mixed up with love for this baby that I didn't know what to think. And I was feeling guilty, too, about Romily. But being away from you made me realize that I'd wanted a baby so badly I'd forgotten that I wanted it with you. I'm sorry, Claire.'

The baby stirred. Ben adjusted him in his shirt.

She remembered Ben walking around with Posie when she'd been an infant. He'd lain her down the length of his arm; it was a position that seemed to alleviate her colic. She remembered feeling her heart melt a little bit inside and thinking, *This is what he will be like with our own child, one day.*

'He's awake,' said Ben. 'Do you want to hold him?'

Claire stepped back. 'I can't, Ben. Not yet.'

'But soon?'

'I don't know.' She went to the door and put her hand on the knob. 'You've got the milk, anyway. For when you need it.'

'Come back later,' he said. 'Or tomorrow.'

Thing's face peeped out of the gap in Ben's shirt. He was looking up at his father.

'I will,' she said.

Romily got down on her hands and knees, grunting, to look underneath the sofa and pulled out Posie's school bag. It had dust balls clinging to it. Romily dumped out the contents: homework folder, reading book and a crumpled envelope.

'Pose?' she called. 'You didn't tell me you had any letters home?' They had had a discussion about this.

'What?' Posie's voice was muffled, as if she was also clearing out underneath something. Romily opened the envelope.

It was an invitation to a Christmas party for Emily and Daniel, for today. Written at the bottom in an untidy hand was a message: *Dear Posie, please make sure your mum comes to the party, too. There will be chocolate. Eleanor x*

Romily jumped up. It was the first time she'd done that in a while, and it felt pretty good. She was getting stronger. 'Posie!' she called. 'Hurry up! We've got to go to a party.' She checked the time on the invitation. 'Now!'

Posie trailed out of her room. She was wearing a princess dress and a woollen hat. 'What party?' she said.

'Emily's having a Christmas party. The invitation was in your bag.'

'Oh. But I don't really know Emily.'

'That doesn't matter. You need friends, Posie. Real friends. You need to spend time with children your own age.'

'I don't think I want to.'

'You've got a choice. You can go to a party, or I can stand over you while you clean that bedroom *properly*.'

Posie twisted her toe on the carpet. 'All right, we can go to the party.'

The address was only ten minutes' walk from their flat, and was two terraced houses both identically decorated for Christmas. Romily knocked on the blue door, number 14, and the red door at number 16 opened. Eleanor beckoned them in with a big smile.

'I'm so pleased you could make it!' she said, taking their coats and the bottle of orange juice that Romily had brought from her refrigerator. 'I was going to pop by and make sure you got the invitation, but I wasn't certain where you lived. Posie, the children are in the next room making Christmas decorations. Romily, come through to the kitchen for the grown-up activities.'

The terraces had been knocked together inside, and the kitchen took up what would have been one entire reception room. Pastries covered the table and lots of people crowded together, holding glasses and talking. Cinnamon and mulled wine scented the air and, in the background, a tall man circulated with a bottle in one hand and a plate in the other.

'Are you drinking?' Eleanor hesitated over a vat of mulled wine and a similar one of hot chocolate. Romily shook her head and Eleanor ladled up a mug of the chocolate.

'You've had the baby!' One of the Mummies from school sidled up to Romily. 'That's wonderful! How is— I mean, how are the parents doing? Do you know?'

'They're doing pretty well,' Romily said.

'We think you are so brave,' said another Mummy. Eleanor handed Romily her mug, and winked.

'Not brave,' said Romily. 'Sort of foolish, really. I'd forgotten how tough pregnancy is.'

'So what's this I hear about you working at the museum?'

Eleanor cut in deftly. 'We love it there. Daniel goes in every week to stroke the stuffed badger.'

A chorus of praise for the stuffed badger.

'He's called Gavin the Badger,' said Romily. She tapped her nose. 'Insider knowledge.'

Some time later when Posie didn't reappear asking to go home, Romily went to find her. She was sitting next to Emily halfway up the stairs, their hands over their eyes, counting.

'Hide and Seek?' she asked.

'We're busy.'

Giggles from upstairs. 'Ready or not, here we come!' cried Emily, and she and Posie both dropped their hands and stood up at the same time.

Romily couldn't help it. She grabbed Posie and hugged her.

'I am your mother and I love you,' she said to her, her face buried in her hair.

'Yes, I *know*, you keep saying that. Go back to the parents where you belong.'

But Romily held on to her for a moment more, while Emily started up the stairs. 'Are you and Emily friends now?' she whispered.

'I don't know. She's all right. Do you know she has two daddies? One who really made her and one who lives with her? I told her about Thing and she wants to come and visit him sometime.'

'That sounds great.'

Posie gave her a swift kiss back and then she ran away up the stairs, after her friend.

You give birth to children so that they will go away from you, Romily thought. *So that they'll grow up and have their own lives with people they've chosen. It's natural. And the hurting is natural, too.*

47
A Window Out

By the morning of Christmas Eve the snow had melted to patches here and there in Claire's front garden, and it was already gone in Brickham. When Claire got to the door of Ben's flat, balancing the shopping bags and the live little tree in its pot, she found a stack of wrapped gifts waiting on the doormat. She recognized Posie's handwriting on the tags.

Through the door she could hear the baby wailing.

Ben had given her a key; she opened the door and slipped inside. The flat looked as if a bomb had exploded in it. Every light was on and the television played Christmas carols. Among the wreckage, Ben strode with Thing on his shoulder, patting his back and gently bouncing his body.

'He's been crying all night,' Ben said. 'I don't know what to do. I nearly called A&E. What if something is wrong?'

The baby's face was red, screwed up into a tight little ball of anger with an open toothless mouth.

Claire put down the bags: a small turkey, potatoes, vegetables. She didn't think Ben should be without Christmas dinner. She hadn't decided yet whether she would cook it for him, or if she was going to her parents' house. 'Does he have a fever?'

'I don't think so. The health visitor was here yesterday and she said he was fine. He started crying at about two this morning and he hasn't stopped. Nothing works. He won't eat, he won't sleep, he just cries.' Ben kept walking in circles round the perimeter of the flat, kept bouncing, skirting nappies and cuddly animals. The television was playing 'Silent Night'.

The flat smelled of stale coffee and posset. The central heating was on high. Ben was in the same clothes he'd been wearing yesterday. And, come to think of it, the day before. 'When was the last time you were outside?' she asked.

'Outside?'

'Let's go for a walk. It always used to work with Posie.'

'Isn't it too cold?'

She rummaged through the untidy piles of clothing, finding socks, a hat, a sleep suit, the green cardigan and tiny white shoes she'd bought with Romily. 'Here,' she said. 'Layer him up. I'll pack a bag.'

She'd noticed that Ben had become practised at changing the baby, but with Thing shouting and curling up his limbs it took some time to get him dressed. By the time he was, Claire had found the sling and was untangling its long straps. 'Let me put this on you so you can carry him.'

'Do you remember how it works?'

'It's marketed for new parents, how hard can it be?'

She looped the straps around his arms and connected them in front, making a pocket ready to hold the baby. Fastened up, Thing lay against Ben's chest, legs dangling like a frog's, crying into the front of his shirt. Ben wrapped his coat around the baby and they went out of the flat together, downstairs and outside.

The baby paused for a moment, sensing the fresh air, but

then began crying again. 'Do you think he's in pain?' Ben asked her.

She understood Ben's anguish. Every cry wrenched her insides, called on all her instincts to soothe and protect. 'Let's walk for a little while and see if he settles down. If he doesn't, we can ring the health visitor or go to the hospital.'

Without discussing it they headed for the town centre. Brickham was crowded with people clutching bags and parcels; coloured lights dripped from the buildings. 'I'd forgotten that all of this was going on without us,' said Ben.

A couple pushing a pram passed them. The mother, hearing the baby crying and seeing Ben with the sling, smiled at Ben and then at Claire. A smile of sympathy and complicity, the sort of smile Claire had seen mothers giving each other.

This woman thought Ben and Claire were normal parents with their normal newborn. A normal family.

As simple and as complicated, as everyday and as extraordinary, as that.

They entered Brickham's main pedestrianized shopping area. The shop windows sparkled with artificial snow and gleamed with goods for sale. Claire smelled coffee and baking bread.

'I haven't got you a present,' said Ben. 'I'm sorry.'

'I think,' said Claire, 'that if we're going to be a family, you're going to have to stop saying you're sorry.'

He stopped walking and looked at her over the down of the baby's head.

'Claire,' he said, reaching for her. The volume of the baby's cries suddenly rose up into a scream, and then subsided into a grunt. And then silence.

Alarmed, they both bent towards him. His cheeks were pink, not red, and he gazed calmly back at them, as if wondering why they were making such a fuss.

'What happened—' Claire began, but then the scent struck both of them at the same time.

'Ugh, that smells like a big one,' said Ben. 'No wonder you were shouting about it, mate.' He began to laugh. 'Imagine if I'd gone to A&E.'

'We should get him changed.' She pointed at the café on the corner. He held the door open for her, as he always did.

She gave him a nappy, wipes and a change of clothing from the bag she'd packed and he headed to the baby changing room. She bought them each a coffee and a mince pie and found the last unoccupied table, squeezed against the window between a group of squabbling children and four pensioners with their wheeled shopping bags. Over the speakers, Slade was singing about Christmas and looking to the future. She wiped sugar and coffee off the table with a paper napkin and when she spotted Ben coming out of the changing room she raised her hand so he'd find her.

And she had to catch her breath.

The man she'd chosen to share her life with was coming towards her through the crowded room. In his hands he cradled a child with his hair and his eyes, their dream come true.

Had she been afraid of Ben loving someone more than he loved her? This was *miraculous*.

Swiftly, holding the baby safe against him, he leaned over and kissed her on the lips. She took it like a breath of sweet air.

'Happy Christmas, love,' he said and just as quickly as he'd kissed her, he deposited the baby in her arms.

Her body adjusted to hold him by itself. His legs were curled up like the tops of grace notes, and his body was more solid than Claire had expected. She touched his cheek, his soft glorious cheek, and he turned his head. His dark eyes looked straight into her. He fitted against her breast as if he'd always been meant to be there. She saw how his hair whorled around his forehead, how his lips puckered out.

'He's so beautiful,' she said.

'He needs his mother. We both do.'

A little person, wholly new. It was the busiest part of the year but she had nothing to do but to hold him, nowhere else to be but right here and right now. He looked up at her and he knew her and she knew him.

She was in love, in all its danger and its wonder.

'Matthew,' she said. 'His name is Matthew.'

Posie was riding on Jarvis's shoulders, so Romily was rolling their suitcase along behind them. The London train was going to be crowded but they weren't in a hurry and Posie was singing a song of her own invention about reindeer and motorcycles, and it was making Jarvis laugh. Neither of them saw Claire and Ben and the baby through the window of the café, but Romily did.

Claire was holding the baby. She was stroking his cheek with one finger. Ben sat close. His world was no larger than his wife and his child. The pane of glass between them and Romily reflected a galaxy's worth of twinkling fairy-lights.

Through the window, Claire said something unheard, and Ben nodded. They did not glance up to see Romily where she stood not two feet distant.

Romily looked, but she did not pause. She caught up with the other two and slipped her free hand inside the pocket of Jarvis's coat, where it was warm. He put his hand inside with hers.

Dear Matthew,

Romily says that I should write you letters even though you can't read yet. I think this is a little silly because you're never going to forget me even if I'm away for the whole summer, but then she said that you could read them when you were older and it would help you remember things that happened when you were a baby and were too young to make proper memories.

So anyway, this is what happened today. We had a Bon Voyage picnic in our back garden at the flat. Bon Voyage is French and it means good journey – it's a nice thing to say to people before they go on a trip. You were sitting on a blue blanket on the grass and I made you a daisy chain and put it around your neck and you laughed. Do you remember that, now that I've written it? You poured your beaker of water over your head and Uncle Ben had to change you, and then I let you try a bit of the cake that Auntie Claire had made specially and you got it all down your front. Claire pretended she was cross but she wasn't.

Grown-ups say that pretending is just for children but they pretend things all the time even when they know that nobody believes them. Mrs Kapoor says you should always give examples when you are trying to prove something and my example is this morning when I got

389

up and Jarvis was pretending that he'd arrived at the flat really early, when any fool could tell he had been there all night. I have counted that he has done this four times that I have noticed. I don't mind. I like it, actually, and so does Romily because she is smiling a lot.

Anyway, we have to get used to being together all the time because we are going on a real proper adventure together. All week for the past week I've been closing my eyes and picturing what it will be like when we get to Brazil. It will be worth all those injections we had. Jarvis has promised to teach me how to use his camera when he's not working, and Romily promises that we won't spend too much time looking at beetles.

You will have to look after Ben and Claire for me while we are gone. I know you don't mind doing this because they're your mummy and daddy. I used to pretend that they were my mummy and daddy, back when we used to see them all the time, more than we do now. I also used to pretend that my name was Prunella Ferrari and I owned fourteen cats. I never told anyone about that one. I didn't believe it but I did believe it too, and I think this is the difference in pretending between children and grown-ups. But I could be wrong.

When I see you again in the autumn you'll be older and maybe crawling. I'll show you my photographs and I can teach you some more French if I learn any, and I'll tell you all the stories about our adventures.

I love you,
Your godsister,
Mariposa Jane Summer, Esq.

Acknowledgments

Special thanks to my agent, Teresa Chris, and my UK editors, Cat Cobain and Harriet Bourton, who have taught me so much. Thanks to Richard Madeley and Judy Finnigan, who brought *Dear Thing* to a wide UK audience. And thank you to Patty Moosbrugger, and to Alicia Clancy and the team at St. Martin's for giving my beloved book a home in the United States.

Thanks to midwife Harriet Neville for answering my endless questions about pregnancy and childbirth. For information on surrogacy, thanks to COTS (www.surrogacy.org.uk) and Surrogacy UK (www.surrogacyuk.org). I'm also indebted to Elly Teman's book, *Birthing a Mother.* For information on fertility, thanks to Fertility Friends (www.fertilityfriends.co.uk) and to several of my own friends for sharing their private struggles with me.

Thanks to Matthew Williams and Angela Houghton for the tour of Reading Museum and particularly of the entomology store. Fond thanks to the staff and students of St. Mary's School, from which I have borrowed the grounds, graves, and guinea pigs, but not the people. As always, thanks to friends and fellow writers Ruth Ng, Anna Scamans, Brigid Coady, and Lee Weatherly.

Last but not least, thanks to my parents, my husband, and most of all to my son, who's taught me everything I know about identifying ladybirds.

DEAR THING

by Julie Cohen

About the Author

- A Conversation with Julie Cohen

Behind the Novel

- Author's Note

Keep on Reading

- Recommended Reading
- Reading Group Questions

Also available as an audiobook
from Macmillan Audio

For more reading group suggestions
visit www.readinggroupgold.com.

 ST. MARTIN'S GRIFFIN

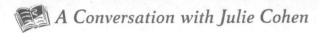 *A Conversation with Julie Cohen*

What was the inspiration for Dear Thing?

I miscarried three times before I had my son. It was the darkest period of my life so far, and I will never forget the children, and the hopes of children, that my family and I lost. Several of my friends were also suffering infertility at that time; we spent a lot of time hoping and grieving together. After my son was born, a dear friend of mine rang me to tell me that she and her husband had decided to give up on IVF treatment, after their third failed cycle. My first impulse was to offer to be a surrogate for her—but then I remembered my own failed pregnancies, and held my tongue. But the idea spawned a book idea, to write about an infertile mother and a surrogate mother, both wanting the same baby, and both as heroines for one book—because I could sympathize with both of them. (My friend has since adopted a little boy and is planning to adopt another child—*Dear Thing* is dedicated to her and her family.)

"I did a lot of crying and laughing as I wrote."

What kind of experience did you have writing this book?

Writing *Dear Thing* was quite a new experience for me as it was a new type of fiction, and also because I had to write a synopsis for it beforehand, which I had never done. So in some ways it was easy, as I had already planned the book out. On the other hand, the emotions of the characters (particularly Claire, but Romily, too) were so close to the emotions I had felt myself that at times it was quite difficult to write. Claire's miscarriage at the beginning of the book, which takes place at a baby shower, is based very closely on my own miscarriage on Christmas morning several years before. And Romily's pregnancy was quite similar to mine as well; she fears losing her beloved baby to another couple, and I feared losing mine to miscarriage. So at times it was close to the bone. It's also set in the town where I live, and includes many of my own experiences of motherhood—Posie is quite similar to my son. I did a lot of crying and laughing as I wrote it.

*Did you have any interesting experiences where you
were researching your book, or getting it published?*

Because of the subject matter, I've been contacted by
many women who have suffered infertility or miscarriage, or I've spoken with them during events, and it
has been both humbling and poignant to hear their
experiences. I've found that the book can prompt
heartbreaking and yet valuable discussions. When
I was interviewed by Richard and Judy for their Book
Club, they told me about their own experience of
baby loss and it was absolutely devastating.

*Tell us anything about you as a working writer that
you think might be interesting or unusual.*

I think I am a pretty typical working writer in that
I write during the week whilst my child is in school,
but I do write in my garret, at the top of my house,
with a view of the River Kennet and the backside
of a gargoyle.

Who are your favorite authors?

In women's fiction—Marian Keyes, Jojo Moyes,
Rowan Coleman, Jennifer Crusie, Susan Elizabeth
Phillips, Jill Mansell, Liane Moriarty, Lori Lansens.
In other types of fiction—Stephen King, Margaret
Atwood, John Irving, Neil Gaiman, Maggie O'Farrell,
Ann Patchett.

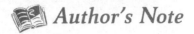

Author's Note

Dear Reader,

I remember the exact moment when I had the idea for *Dear Thing*. I was painting my bathroom and the phone rang. It was a close friend of mine; she and her husband had been going through their third round of IVF, which was the last round they could afford to have. They had had nearly two years of injections and tests and drugs, precious few embryos and chemical pregnancies, hope and despair.

It wasn't good news. The latest round had failed, and they had decided that enough was enough. They couldn't bear the roller coaster any more. My friend Anna—who is a person who can see the good in everybody and everything—said she felt sad, but lighter. She said she was going to enjoy some time just being herself, instead of a potential baby generator.

But I knew that they were letting go of their dream. I knew exactly how hard that is. We talked for a while, and I put down the phone, and I picked up my paintbrush again, and I thought, "I so wish I could carry that baby for them."

Even if they'd thought that was a good idea, I knew that I couldn't possibly do it. Like many of our friends, my husband and I had waited to start a family. At age thirty-five, I fell pregnant almost right away. We were delighted. I told all of my family and close friends. I was even more delighted that one of my friends, Kim, was also expecting in the autumn. I pictured shared pregnancy wobbles, swapped maternity clothes, long conversations about baby names, walks with pushchairs.

At ten weeks, I started to spot. On the phone, my doctor told me to wait the weekend and come in if I hadn't stopped. When I made the appointment on Monday, his first words to me were "Have you lost the baby yet?"

"Dear Thing
is as much
about female
friendship
as it is about
infertility and
motherhood."

The scan showed that I had a missed miscarriage; the baby had stopped growing weeks before. The ultrasound technician held my hand as I sobbed. I will never forget her dry, warm hand, the compassion on her face in the darkened room.

I had my second miscarriage that summer.

In October, several weeks early, Kim gave birth to triplet boys: two identical, one fraternal. They had to spend some time in hospital in special care. The babies and their parents needed all the support they could get.

I couldn't see them. I couldn't offer help, or go shopping for gifts. I knew it was unreasonable; I knew it was selfish. But those three beautiful, perfect small boys were everything I wanted and did not have.

I spent a year avoiding pregnant women. I had to turn off the television when it showed a baby. I didn't want to be someone who envied other people, but I couldn't help it. I cried at work, at home, driving in my little car. My husband was hurting, too, but not in the same way. He loves me, and he supported me, but he hadn't felt the sense of something growing inside him, and then that precious thing being gone.

I talked to woman after woman who had lost their children before birth, or soon after: my friends, my colleagues, my grandmother. I heard every word of comfort that doesn't help much. More than that, I learned how much we women who want to be mothers share the same hope and the same sadness.

The sharing did help.

My third pregnancy ended on Christmas Day. We were opening gifts at my parents' house and I felt the cramping and the rush, and I knew it was over.

I didn't lose the hope, but I did lose the innocence. I knew not to sign up for baby e-newsletters or buy any tiny clothes or post ecstatic news on Facebook. I knew never to say "congratulations" too early. When I fell pregnant for the fourth time, we went for the first scan, at eight weeks, expecting to see nothing. But there was a tiny heartbeat, nestling deep inside my body. Eventually, as the weeks went by, I let myself believe that my dream was going to come true. Our son was born just before the following Christmas. Carol singers came into the hospital and sang "Silent Night" to him as he lay sleeping in his plastic cot. They probably thought I was sobbing because I was crazed with hormones and happiness. Which I was—I so was—but I was remembering, too.

Those were the things I was thinking about three years later, when I got off the phone with Anna after her third and final IVF attempt. I knew what her grief was like, and I wanted to help heal it. But I knew that my body, and my emotions, weren't strong enough. All I could do was share with her, like other women had shared with me.

It did give me a book idea, though. For me, *Dear Thing* is as much about female friendship as it is about infertility and motherhood. It's about sharing emotions, and finding strength in that.

In the end, Anna and her husband adopted a lively, beautiful little boy, and they're the most wonderful parents. Although they had a terrible experience of infertility, it led directly to a better future for that one precious child. That's the sort of thing that makes you believe in happy endings in real life—although of course, for them, it's only a beginning.

In fiction, I think that happy endings are redemptive. Some people mock them; they believe they're glib, or unrealistic. But if a happy ending is hard-won, if it comes out of depth of emotion and it isn't predictable, it's hugely satisfying. Life can be hard. I see nothing wrong in reading to feel better.

Writing this book, for me, was very therapeutic. Having it published and read has also given me the chance to talk to many women, and men, too, who have longed for a baby or suffered the loss of one. Some have told me that reading has helped them. It's a shared experience, and probably the best thing about being a writer.

Dear Thing begins with a reference to fairy tales, and traditionally they all have happy endings. But they contain a lot of harsh stuff, too: death, pain, torture, unfulfilled love, neglect. "Once upon a time, when we still believed in wishes" is from *Grimm's Fairy Tales* and, to me, it's very sad and true. It tells us that despite the happy ending that we know is coming, the time for believing in magic is now over. We've learned better; we've grown up.

One of the marvelous things about writing and reading fiction is that for the space of a book, we can believe in wishes again.

Julie Cohn

Reading Group Gold

Behind the Novel

Recommended Reading

The Day We Met
Rowan Coleman

If you like my books, you'll love Rowan's. This is an immensely readable, moving, ultimately uplifting novel about a woman with early-onset Alzheimer's disease and her quest to preserve memories for her daughters before it's too late.

State of Wonder
Ann Patchett

A lush literary novel about a mysterious rogue scientist in the Amazon, this modern feminist take on Conrad's *Heart of Darkness* has some of the most profound portrayals of motherhood and fertility that I have ever read. It blew me away.

Birthing a Mother
Elly Teman

This is the book I read to research the surrogacy aspect of *Dear Thing*: a nonfiction examination of surrogacy in Israel with some compelling stories.

The Husband's Secret
Liane Moriarty

I think the multiple narrators are fantastically well done in this novel; Moriarty makes you sympathize with widely different characters, whilst exploring a decades-old mystery in a small community.

Saga
Brian K. Vaughan and Fiona Staples

This science fiction graphic novel, told in comics, is about star-crossed lovers battling intergalactic bounty hunters, jealous exes, and problem in-laws. It begins with the birth of the main characters' daughter, and is

both wry and knowing about the perils of parenthood. And contains magic and crazy robots.

Anna Karenina
Leo Tolstoy

When I read this recently, I was struck by its frank portrayal of motherhood. Although Anna's adulterous affair with Vronsky gets all the attention, for me, the conflict at the novel's heart is the way she is forced to abandon her young son.

Far from the Tree
Andrew Solomon

Solomon drew on interviews with over three hundred families to put together a book about what happens when parents don't get the child they expected, and how families deal with having a member who is different. He looks at everything from deafness to prodigies to schizophrenia. Fascinating.

Reading Group Questions

1. Do you think that Claire and Ben want to have a baby for the right reasons?

2. How do you feel about Ben's decision to take up Romily's offer? Is he acting out of selfishness or hope?

3. Do you sympathize with Romily, or do you disagree with her decision to carry Ben and Claire's baby? Why?

4. Did your feelings change about Claire and Romily and their decisions as the book went on?

5. "We are mothers....Look upon our offspring, ye mighty, and despair." What different kinds of parents and parent-figures did you notice in the book? Which can you most identify with? Do you think the portrayals are realistic?

6. What do you think is the purpose of the letters to "Dear Thing"? Did they change your perceptions of the two heroines? What about the final letter, at the end?

7. "Perhaps she should define herself by her body, her faulty body that was able to play music and bake cakes and assemble and disassemble an entire room of furniture but wasn't able to create life." How do both women struggle with their feelings about their bodies?

8. This novel addresses the issue of infertility and the emotional responses that can result from the inability to have a child: despair, jealousy, anger. How do you feel about the portrayal of infertility in the novel? Were you able to sympathize with Claire? Do you feel she had any other options? Do you think there is anything she should have handled differently?

9. There are several complicated relationships
explored in this novel. Ben and Claire, Ben and
Romily, Claire and Romily, Romily and Posie,
Romily and Jarvis, and Romily and the unborn
baby. Which relationship was your favorite?
Your least favorite? Why?

10. What do you think is the significance of the title?
Does it refer to anything other than the letters?

11. Were you satisfied with the ending of the book?
What do you think the future holds in store for
the two families and their relationships with
each other?

*Keep on
Reading*

Turn the page for a sneak peek at
Julie Cohen's next novel

Where Love Lies

Available August 2016

Chapter One

I know exactly where I'm going.

I've only been to the restaurant once before, but as
soon as I step off the train at Richmond everything looks
completely familiar. I touch my Oyster card and turn left
immediately outside the station. A young busker with wild
dreadlocks plays 'Walking on Sunshine'. He throws his whole
body into it, strumming and twitching and singing to the
darkening London evening, as if he can make it midsummer
noon with the force of his will. I dig into my jacket pocket
and drop a pound coin into his guitar case amongst the litter
of money.

I check my watch; I'm meeting Quinn in five minutes. I'm
cutting it fine, but from what I remember, I have plenty of
time to get there. I pass familiar shopfronts and turn right at
the junction. The restaurant, Cerise, is round the next corner:
it's a brick building, painted yellow, with a sign made of curly
wrought iron. It's a treat for both of us after our separate days
of meetings in London – Quinn's idea because I've told
him they serve the best crème brûlée I've had outside of
Paris.

I turn the corner and I don't see the restaurant.

I stand for a moment, peering up and down the street. Maybe they have repainted it. I look from building to building, but there's no wrought-iron sign, no wide window with a view of the tables inside. Anxiety rises from my stomach into my throat.

A little bit late isn't a problem, said my editor Madelyne this afternoon, just a couple of hours ago, on the other side of London. *But this is more than a little.*

I shake my head. Of course. The restaurant isn't on this street, it's further on. How silly of me. I stride to the end of the road and over the junction.

Quinn is never late. Quinn is frequently early. He'd prefer to wait outside wherever he's going, looking around him or reading a newspaper, than to be rushed or rude. You'd think he'd know me well enough by now to build in some leeway when he's meeting me, but he never does. I tried suggesting this once, breezily, and he listened, as he always does when I try to explain something. 'I'd still rather read the paper for a little while,' he said, and that was it. I've learned that Quinn is Quinn, and he does not change.

And even though he never acts impatient or annoyed, I try not to be late so often. I even bought a watch. I hate to think of him waiting, over and over.

It's warm and I'm still feeling anxious, so I take off my jacket and drape it over my arm. The restaurant should be right here, on the left. Except it's not; it's a Starbucks.

I frown. I must have got turned around the wrong way, somehow. This Starbucks looks exactly the same as every other Starbucks in the world, and definitely not like a French restaurant. I probably went too far down this road. I turn around and start back the way I've come.

My phone rings. It's Quinn. 'Hello hello,' I say, as cheerfully as I think I should.

'Hello, love. Where are you? Are you still on the train?'

'No no, I'm in Richmond, I'm on my way. I took a wrong turn, I think, but I'll be there in a tick.'

'Right,' he says. 'See you in a minute, love.'

He hangs up and I put my phone back in my handbag. He always says *love*, always, leaving in the morning or greeting me when I come in the room or ending a conversation on the phone. It punctuates beginnings and endings. It's something his father does with his mother, and he's slipped into the habit as if he were born to it.

At the corner I catch a whiff of scent, something familiar, someone's perfume.

I stop walking. 'Mum?' I say.

My mother isn't here. Of course she isn't here. But the scent is so strong, it's as if she's just walked past me.

I glance around. Two teenage girls sharing earphones, a man walking a terrier, a young couple, her with a hijab and him with a pushchair. There's a woman near the end of the street, walking away from me. She's wearing a sleeveless top and rolled-up jeans, her shoulders tanned. Her hair is a long silver plait down her back. The scent of flowers trails behind her on the warm air.

'Mum?' I hurry after her. She turns the corner, and by the time I reach it, she's gone.

But I can still smell her perfume. It's so familiar I can't think of the name of it, and my mother never wore perfume anyway. This smell, though, is my mother: it tugs something deep inside me, makes my heart leap with hope and a kind of sweet agony. I run further along the street and think I see the woman ahead of me, crossing the bridge over the Thames.

It can't be my mother. It's impossible. But I'm still thinking of everything I need to tell her: *I'm married, I've bought a house, I'm sorry. So sorry for what I made you do.*

I collide with the plastic shopping bag held by a man coming the other way over the bridge, and it falls onto the pavement with a clang of tins. 'Oi, watch it,' he says.

'I'm sorry, so sorry,' I say, maybe to him, maybe to the woman ahead of me. I reach for his bag but he's snatched it up again. He's eyeing me up and down.

'Don't worry, beautiful, it's my pleasure,' he says.

'Sorry,' I say again, and carry on over the bridge, quickly.

'Smile,' he yells after me. 'It might never happen!'

People are between us and she's walking rapidly; my moment with the man with the shopping bag has put me even farther behind her. But the scent is as strong as ever, and as I get closer, dodging around pedestrians, my heart beats harder and harder. It's impossible that when I catch up to this woman she will be my mother, Esther Bloom, and she will turn around and say, *Darling*. It's impossible that she could take me into her arms and I could be forgiven. I know it's impossible, and yet I can't look away from her. It's as if my body doesn't know what my mind does. I can't stop my feet from following her, faster now, running, my ballet flats pounding over the pavement, sweat dampening the cotton collar of my shirt. My jacket slips off my arm; I stuff it into my handbag, mindless of wrinkles, and hurry forward.

The woman opens the door of a pizza takeaway. Panting, I clasp her by the shoulder.

It isn't my mother's shoulder. It feels all wrong, and this

woman is darker than my mother, with more grey in her hair, which is finer than my mother's was – but my body has that irrational hope that when she turns around, her face will be Esther's.

'Mum?' I gasp.

It isn't. It's a stranger. She looks nothing like my mother at all.

'My mistake,' I say, backtracking. 'So sorry, I thought you were someone else.'

She shrugs and goes into the takeaway. The scent of flowers is gone, replaced by a whiff of baking dough and melting cheese.

My mother didn't even like pizza very much. I rub my forehead and look around. It's starting to get dark; the street-lights have come on, and this street is entirely unfamiliar, even more unfamiliar because not ten minutes ago I thought I knew exactly where I was, exactly who I was following. It's as if the street has changed around me. As if the world has changed around me.

In my bag, my phone rings. I know without looking that it's Quinn, wondering where I am. I don't answer it; I'll be with him in a minute. I hurry back across the bridge and along the road, which seems quite busy now; the cars have their lights turned on. I see a sign pointing to the station and I turn that way. This street looks strange too, but if it takes me back to the station that's good because I can definitely find my way from there.

Though I didn't just now.

How did I get so lost?

I reach for my phone to answer Quinn's call. Sometimes it's better to admit defeat and get somewhere that little bit quicker, and Quinn loves giving directions anyway. And also it would be sort of nice to hear his voice, his habitual calm. *Hello, love.*

Two things happen at once: my phone stops ringing, and I see the restaurant. It's thirty metres away, on the other side of the road from where I'd expected it to be, and Quinn is outside it, his phone in his hand. He's wearing the same grey suit he was wearing when he left this morning to get the train to London, though the tie's been removed and he's unbuttoned his collar. His dark hair, as usual, is sticking up in the front because he's been running his fingers through it. The restaurant is painted yellow, with a wrought-iron sign outside. Light spills through the window. Everything is exactly as it's supposed to be.

He spots me and runs across the street, dodging a cab. I kiss him on his cheek, where there's a couple of days' growth of beard.

'You had me worried, love,' he says, kissing me back. 'What happened?'

I look at my husband: slender, pale, serious, with his grey eyes and his dedication to facts. The newspaper he's been reading while he's been waiting for me is tucked underneath his arm. He's never been late in his life, and he's certainly never followed a woman who doesn't exist any more, except in his memory.

'Oh,' I say, 'I just took a wrong turn.'

Chapter Two

On the train out of London, I lean against Quinn's shoulder and half-doze, trying to recall the scent I followed in Richmond. It's fading already in my memory. Something floral, definitely. Something exotic. Something I've smelled many times before, though I'm not sure where or why.

It didn't necessarily belong to the woman I followed; maybe someone else was wearing the perfume, which is why it seemed to vanish when I caught up with her. Maybe it was a flower growing in a window box, or in a garden. Maybe it was a perfume exuded out onto the street from a posh boutique, and happened to be similar to another perfume that I know.

As we drive home to Tillingford from the station, I open the window so the fresh air will wake me up a bit. 'So Madelyne is anxious for your new book?' Quinn says, though we've discussed this already at dinner. Or at least we've discussed it as much as I want to.

'She says she's looking forward to it.'

'So am I. Did you come up with any ideas together?'

I sit up straighter. 'Pull over,' I say.

'Are you okay?'

'Yes, yes! Pull over!'

He pulls into a lay-by and I jump out of the car. 'Come on!' I say, and run to a stile between the hawthorn hedges.

'What are you doing, Felicity?' Quinn has turned off the engine, but left the car lights on. He stands with the door open, looking after me. The road is quiet, the night scented with growing things.

'Turn off the lights and come and join me! We need to see.'

'Are you— oh, all right.' The car door shuts. I swing a leg over the stile and jump over. A nettle stings my bare ankle, but I keep on going, threading through a stand of trees. There's just enough silver light up ahead for me to see. Behind me, I hear the rustle of Quinn's footsteps. I wait for him to catch up, and when I feel him standing beside me I walk forward, through the last of the trees into a field.

Without the trees in the way we can see the full moon. It's silver and enormous, perfectly round, hanging in the sky.

'Is this why you had me stop the car?' Quinn asks.

'Isn't it worth it?' I gaze up at the moon. He stands beside me and gazes up at it too. 'I wish I knew what all of those shapes on it are called.'

'Mare Tranquillitatis,' he says. 'Mare Serenitatis, Mare Imbrium.' He points to different parts on the huge disc. 'Sea of Tranquillity, Sea of Serenity, Sea of Showers.'

'They're beautiful names. How do you know them?'

'Many, many misspent hours with a telescope and a book. There's an Ocean of Storms, and a Lake of Clouds. All on a surface with no water at all.'

'It was worth stopping the car, wasn't it?'

He takes my hand. His fingers are warm in the night, which has become cool. 'Yes.'

I look up at the moon some more.

'I know whose field this is,' Quinn says. 'He'd be quite surprised to see me standing in it at this hour.'

'Let's sit in it, then.' I sit down on the rough grass at the edge of the field. As I do so, there's a crinkle from my handbag and I pull out a box of macaroons. I offer one to Quinn. 'Macaroon? It's only slightly crushed.'

He begins to laugh. 'You're as daft as a brush,' he says. 'I do love you.'

'I love you too.' I lean my head against his shoulder and let my thoughts float away into the tranquil seas of the moon.

'A little bit late isn't a problem,' my editor Madelyne had said, yesterday afternoon, 'but this is more than a little. It's been eighteen months, and we have schedules to think of. Don't you have anything to show me yet?'

We were in her office, in the corner, overlooking the park. Her assistant had made us tea in a proper teapot, on a proper tray. There was a little box of macaroons, which Madelyne insisted I take because she was on a diet. The whole office was so quiet, as if everyone was reading at the same time. Books lined every wall that wasn't a window. Above the door I'd come in there was a framed original of the cover of my first picture book. I could feel Igor's wide owl eyes staring at the back of my neck as I sat in the wooden chair.

'I've been working on it,' I said to her, lying. 'But nothing seems to come out quite right.'

We'd always met in restaurants before. Long, boozy lunches where we got the business bit out of the way at the beginning and spent the rest of the time trading gossip, tossing around ideas. Behind her desk, Madelyne seemed different. Her posture was straighter, her pulled-back hair more severe.

'I'm sure it will all be fine,' I added.

'Even some sketches would be useful,' she said. 'A title, something we could bring to the Frankfurt Book Fair. We've already put back publication twice. I'm worried that we'll lose the momentum on this series, with such a long gap.'

'I understand. I completely agree.'

'We all love Igor so much! And we miss him.' She smiled then, for the first time, and put down her cup. 'I know you've had a very eventful couple of years. So many ups and downs, with getting married, and your mother—'

'Yes, but it's fine. It's fine. I'll send you some sketches.'

'I can help you with ideas, you know. That's what I'm here for. You can pass me anything and we can bounce it around together.'

But not if there aren't any ideas at all. Not if the only thing I've ever been any good at has gone for ever. 'Of course.'

'And you know that if you ever want to talk—'

'Yes. Of course. I'm sorry the book is so late, Maddie. I'm always late for everything. I was even late to my own wedding.'

And we both laughed, even though it was true.

The next morning, I wake up after Quinn has gone off to work and I go straight into my studio, pulling on a dressing gown and pushing my hair into an elastic. I turn on the computer and the scanner, even though I don't have anything to use them for yet, and I clear off a stack of books from my

416

chair beside the window, pick up a sketch pad and a pencil and look out at the morning.

My studio is actually the back bedroom of Hope Cottage, the house Quinn and I bought when we married. It has better natural light than the front bedroom where we sleep, and looks out over the garden – a jumble of flowers and weeds, a lawn that needs mowing, gnarled fruit trees. Petals from the cherry and the apple have drifted over the grass like pink and white snow. On warm days, sometimes I take a cushion out to the metal bench, painted with flakes of peeling blue, and read in the shade. I fell in love with the garden as soon as we saw this cottage: overgrown, wild – the sort of garden that harbours fairies in foxgloves. I love the cottage too, with its crooked floors and bulging walls, the suspicion of damp in the dining room, and a thatched roof that really should be replaced soon, this summer or next. But the garden is my favourite place.

A blackbird hops across the grass. I make a mark on the page, a black curve of head and wing, then fill in sharp beak, gleaming eye. I sketch in the dandelions behind him. This is all very well, but it's not Igor the Owl.

I've drawn and written six *Igor the Owl* books in the past four years, all of them before meeting Quinn. They're not complicated things: Igor is a tiny, fluffy owl, much smaller than all of his owl family and owl mates. To make up for being so tiny and fluffy, not much bigger than a chick, he solves puzzles.

For example, in the first book, *Igor the Owl Takes to the Air*, Igor has a problem because his wings are too little. He can fly in a fluttery way, but he can't soar on silent wings like the rest of his family, and he's feeling quite down about it. He's worried he'll never be a proper owl. Meanwhile, he makes friends with a family of squirrels who are living in a hole in a dead tree by the river. When the river floods, Igor tries to help his friends but he's too small to carry them to safety, so he quickly invents a sort of hang-glider thing with wings made out of discarded feathers and a framework made out of twigs, and the squirrels use it to fly to safety. And then Igor uses it to soar with his family, on silent wings. He's the only hang-gliding owl in children's literature, apparently, and the book sold much more than I expected it to, so I created more of the stories for publication, though I would have continued doing so anyway.

Igor has also solved crimes, in *Igor the Owl and the Monkey Puzzle* (nobody else noticed the ants stealing the nuts), and saved lives, in *Igor the Owl and the Good Eggs* (he was so small he could crawl right into a broken eggshell). In his last book, the one I wrote and illustrated nearly two years ago now, before I knew my mother was ill, Igor the Owl had started his own Owl School; here he taught other woodland creatures to solve puzzles, but he was sabotaged by a jealous magpie. In the end, Igor worked out who the culprit was, and they became friends.

I press my lips together and draw Igor next to the blackbird I've sketched. Big eyes, smiling beak, stubby wings. I never have a problem drawing Igor; I've been drawing Igor for years, ever since I was a teenager and invented him to amuse my mother and me during long train journeys, or on candlelit nights when the power would go out because Esther had forgotten to pay the bill. My mother, a proper artist, worked best on big canvases; I liked scraps of paper and ballpoint pens. I would breathe on a window and draw in the mist. I could tell a story anywhere with a few lines and shapes, as long as it was a little story.

I've been on plenty of trains since my mother got cancer, and I've even been in a power cut. But I haven't found any new stories that I want to tell, any puzzles that a tiny owl could possibly solve.

Sighing, I rest my elbows on the sketch pad and stare out at the garden. The old glass is uneven, and when I move slightly to either side, the grass appears to swell and subside. Madelyne was pleasant and kind, charming as always, but she wasn't pleased with me. Perhaps I should do something else for a job. But this is the first thing I've done which I've really liked. Before I stumbled into it, I was waiting tables, working in bars or shops, earning enough money to travel and then spending it all. People said they were interested in my art, but that was just because of who my mother was. Drawing Igor, writing out his story, being paid for it, holding the book in my hands – all these made me feel as if I were finally taking root somewhere. Finding the sort of life I was meant to have.

What will happen if I can't think of any more stories? I'll be dropped by my publisher. I'll have to pay back my advance, probably, which wouldn't be a huge problem, but it would be humiliating. I'll have to find something else to do, something that the other wives in the village do to use up their time if they haven't got a job. Coffee mornings. Charity events. Book clubs.

I think back to the rising sense of panic I had yesterday on my way to the restaurant. Was it fear, because somewhere down deep I knew that Igor was finished for me, that I'd used up all the stories I made up to amuse my mother because I loved her, and I would have to decide to do something else

419

with my life? Because I can't fall back on what I used to do now. I can't get a job in a bar somewhere and flit off to India when I've saved enough money. I'm married, I've chosen to live here in Tillingford with Quinn, and all the possibilities of my past life have faded into air.

What was the perfume that woman was wearing who passed me on the street? It smelled so familiar. It made me think of the past, some unspecified moment, something I've forgotten.

The phone rings and I sit up. Outside, it's started to rain and the blackbird has flown away; inside, my computer screen has gone to its screensaver of random moving lights, each one leaving a coloured meteor trail behind it. My sketch pad is empty aside from two birds, one real, one imaginary. I make my way through the dark cottage to the kitchen, where the phone is.

'Hello, love,' says Quinn. 'How are you getting on?'

'Slowly.'

'Can I help?'

'Oh, thank you, no, I don't think so. I'm just having an off day.'

'Envelopes keep on disappearing from the stationery cupboard here. You could have Igor solve that.'

I pick at an unravelling hem on the flowered tablecloth. People who aren't creative, people who spend their lives structuring real-life stories and checking facts, rarely have any idea of the energy that's generated by a really good idea. They think you can choose any old thing and make it work. My mother never used to make suggestions for the Igor stories; she would wait for them to happen, and then she would listen.

'I was joking,' Quinn says.

'I thought you were in meetings all this morning.'

'It's lunchtime,' he says, and when I look at the clock over the sink, it is. 'Anyway, I just thought I'd ring to see how you were getting on. You seemed . . .'

'I'm fine. Everything's fine.'

'. . . preoccupied.'

On the draining board are Quinn's mug and his bowl from breakfast which he has washed up and left to dry. He has, I see, left a mug out for me by the kettle, my favourite one with the leaves painted on it. I know without looking that he'll have put a tea bag inside it, so I wouldn't lose vital seconds when I could be drawing. It's sat here while I've been in my dressing gown, staring out at the garden, accomplishing nothing. I should thank him, I should say something warm and loving to make his lunchtime special after a morning of meetings, but I'm irritated by this as well because it reminds me of a future time when I may have nothing better to do but Quinn's washing up, nothing better to do but make tea.

I close my eyes. This is another thing about marriage: second thoughts. Doing what's best, saying what's best, instead of what you feel.

'Sea of Tranquillity,' I say. 'Wasn't the moon amazing last night?'